BEULAH

by Christi Nogle

CEMETERY GATES
MEDIA

Beulah
Published by Cemetery Gates Media
Binghamton, New York

Copyright © 2022
by Christi Nogle

All rights reserved. Without limiting the rights under the copyright reserved above, no part of this publication may be reproduced, stored in, or introduced into a retrieval system, or transmitted in any form or by any means (electronic, mechanical, photocopying, recording, or otherwise) without prior written permission.

ISBN: 9798786903387

For more information about this book and other Cemetery Gates Media publications, visit us at:

cemeterygatesmedia.com
facebook.com/cemeterygatesmedia
twitter.com/cemeterygatesm
instagram.com/cemeterygatesm

Cover design by Carrion House
Carrionhouse.com

For my mother, Pat Hobbs (May 1951-August 2021)

CHAPTERS

When you talk to the dead.................................5

May..9

June...32

July..68

August..108

September..123

October..142

November...168

December...202

January...242

February...257

Timeless...281

April...335

If you walk with the dead..............................344

WHEN YOU TALK TO THE DEAD

When you talk to a dead person—or *if* you do, I'm not saying for sure that you will—then it's helpful to keep a few things in mind:

Know that nothing they say will be of any importance to you. They'll want to get you caught up in their drama. That's a given. They'll want to feel you on their wavelength. They'll want you to be their new best friend and will try to make their world feel more real to you than your own.

You have to remember that listening to them is something you're doing for them. It's supposed to be a kindness. Everything they say has to bead up and roll off you, but you can't let them know that's what's happening. I guess I'm saying that you have to pander to them. Make them think you're as enthused about what they're saying as they are. Make them believe you are going to be best friends. If you can't bother to do that, then there's no point in talking to them at all. If you're going to act all dismissive, don't even bother. Just pretend you don't see them—or pretend you can't hear them if they catch you seeing them. Do not talk to them and then act bored.

Don't toy with their emotions. Just don't. Emotions feel different when you're out of body, but they do run strong.

Know that what they'll most likely want to talk about is work. How hard they worked, how much they worked, all the work they put into something that did or did not come to fruit. This will bore you, but it's something they feel passionate about. They'll have a great sense of injustice around the whole idea of labor. Ninety-nine in a hundred of them will think they worked too much and reaped too little. This last one in a hundred might feel they didn't work enough and lucked out in some unfair way, and they'll want to talk about the guilt around that. Talking to the guilty one is even more boring than talking to the ninety-nine—at least at first—but you should keep talking.

When I'm dead, I'm going to be one of the guilty kind, and I can guarantee you these people have some of the better lives, if you can get them past their regrets and into their stories. These people are the ones most likely to have been like me—and like you?—before their death, meaning that they were probably able to see other dead at least some of the time. This means that they are the most likely to be self-aware. They knew about shadows before they had to take on the role, so they have a lot more insight into how it all works. This also means they are the most likely to be dangerous.

The dead person is almost pure ego. If they have seen your keys or your winning lotto numbers or your one true love, they will not have noticed them or remember where they saw them. They don't care about you.

Know that it is very unusual for the dead to be self-aware. This gets back to work. Most of them are caught up in the daze or the flow of work. For that matter, most of them don't even notice when you see them. They're just doing whatever it was they did. The smart little girl is studying, the server is waiting tables, the painter is painting, the writer is writing, the teacher is teaching. You get the point. They imagine whatever is supposed to be around them; they don't notice you. This is why it's so rare you get to talk to them. First they have to break their flow to notice you, then they have to get their head out of their own ass long enough to bother to talk to you. There are more steps once you're talking. The point is, if you've gotten them talking, that in itself indicates that you've caught them in an unusual, volatile state.

Know the power that resentment has in the life of the dead. Don't underestimate this. Take a person who likely already resented doing the same thing for most of their life, make them keep doing that thing after their death, and then make them aware that this is what's happening to them. Then, if you want to see resentment morph into rage, mock them by not taking what they say seriously. You think you want to see it, but you don't.

A few resent that they have no future. This is rarer than you'd think. Most resent that they've lost access to the past. Their memories don't work like they did in life. It's hard for them to revisit photos or travel to old haunts. When they forget factual things, they can't look them up online; they can't even read books unless one of us moves the pages. They just have so little control.

Finally, and this is important:

You have to know the two ways the dead can take you. One way is by making you their best friend. Whatever occupies them must occupy you. The two of you will study side by side, you'll paint side by side—whatever obsesses them should obsess you. Their enthusiasms, their responsibilities, their labor—all of this is yours now. This is dangerous, but it is not as dangerous as the other way.

You can survive the best-friending, even many cycles of it. It's the kind of experience you can go through and come out believing that it made you wiser or stronger.

The other way they overtake you is more dire. They can tempt you out of your body.

They start by teaching you things. This is when you know it's becoming more dangerous. You and your best friend used to spend all your time doing X and now you've moved to Y, the Y being weird occult things that never seemed to interest them before. You will think this is some mind-blowing, life-changing shit. If you have that sort of epiphany, it's too late.

They make it like whitewashing the fence: *Look how much fun it is here in the supernatural realm! Look at this; I'm flying! Wow, look how pretty my nebulous body is!*

You are one day able to step outside your body, and you do so with real exhilaration. You take your first baby steps as a spirit, and then they slide right in.

Thank you, they say. *I'm so grateful*, they say. *I'll take good care*, and so on. Then you might never see your poor body again.

It's usually not good for the dead person, either. They think they want that body, that they're going to get to do things they always wanted to do or go back to doing the things they did. Only now the world is different, and they are no more powerful than they were in life. They're running around like mad. It won't end well.

That's what happened to me when I was fourteen. It would happen twice more by my nineteenth birthday. It's a rare thing. In fact, I don't know that it's ever happened to anyone else. Just think of the odds.

MAY

1

I jumped awake to the rumble of a country highway. I'd been riding in my dream, too, riding in the back of a car with no one at the wheel. It was a common enough dream for me and somewhat true. I was a passenger in life and not a driver.

Mom drove the truck. I rode shotgun while my sisters Stevie and Tommy slept in the back seat. Or were they sleeping? I glanced back. Ten-year-old Stevie lay slack, but sixteen-year-old Tommy looked too stiff to be sleeping. Her headphones were strapped on like always.

"How long was I out?" I asked.

"Five minutes?" The line of Mom's mouth was grim. Her eyes didn't move from the road.

Mom has a terrible fear of heights, and just then we were coming to the bridge over the Snake River Canyon, the bridge where she'd had a bawling fit if not a full-on breakdown when she was littler than Stevie.

It was on a field trip her first year here. She learned weeks ahead of time that they'd all be walking across the bridge on the pedestrian track and down a trail to picnic in the canyon. She wanted to just go along with the flow, not embarrass herself. She gave herself pep talks all the days leading up to the trip, but a third of the way across the bridge, she flattened to the ground and started up a dreadful moaning. She didn't piss her pants, not that time, but she had to be carried back to the bus and sit while the other kids crossed. The girls walked along nicely, turning in twos to point at things in the canyon. The boys roughhoused, making to throw each other off. And then she couldn't see any of the children, they were so far away. It felt like she'd been scraped out with a grapefruit spoon.

I'd never crossed this bridge myself, but I'd been told there was quite a view and that once we crossed, it would be not more than a couple miles into Beulah. Cross the bridge and our long trip would be over, cross the bridge and we'd be in our new home, but Mom was taking deep, slow breaths. She was about to pull over.

"Georgie, you looking?" Mom said, her voice whiny like it almost never was.

"I can wake Tommy up. She went almost all the way through driver's ed," I said, sitting straighter.

Mom snorted and wiped her forehead, said, "You are not getting her up." She didn't ask why on earth I'd never learned to drive, but she was surely thinking it.

I was eighteen years old and definitely should have known how to drive. I vaguely wished this were the case, but there was nothing I could do about it just then.

"We could get out and walk it. Slay the dragon," I said.

"You shut up," Mom said. She tried to smile.

"Desensitization therapy," I said. Something I heard on NPR came to mind, how the fear of heights is really a fear of throwing yourself from a height, and there was the bridge. We were on it already.

The canyon would be stunning on a bright day like this. (It was just like this on the day of the school trip, wasn't it?) I wanted to look out the side window, but I didn't. I leaned over and rested my arm on Mom's shoulder, and we both looked straight ahead. I don't like to touch people, so when I did this, she knew I was giving her my honest support. I hoped it gave her a little bit of good feeling to go with all the fear and dread.

"Now, you can just drive a little more inside the center line," I said because she was edging as far from the rails as she could. A fair bit of traffic rushed toward us.

"You just leave me alone. I've got to concentrate," Mom said. She was stiff, beginning to quiver.

"Just make sure that line is disappearing right into the corner of the window," I said, but it wasn't even close.

Now I was getting nervous. I said, low, "There's no physical way we go off this bridge. It isn't possible. But hit a car you very well could, so it's all right to slow down. Slow right on down if you need to, slow on down. It's all right." She did just that. Cars started to back up behind us, but I was relieved she didn't look in the rearview.

The road took a long, slow curve just past the bridge, and soon we moved parallel to the canyon. Safe. She rolled off onto the shoulder when it widened enough and got out of the truck to have a smoke.

The smoking. Ever since we hit the road it had been one after another. But she'd do better. We were all supposed to do better out here.

Mom was finally making it back to the place where she lived for her best few years of childhood. Coming back to be with her best friend Ellen, the only person she ever meant when she said, "my friend." The true home that gave her such freedom and joy when she was young.

I mean, it's a lot to pin on a place.

Stevie and Tommy didn't stir, but I got out of the truck to stretch my legs and take my first real look at the canyon. It was only a deep purple line against the desert now, but from the bridge it must have been something. I didn't catch enough of the river itself to say if it was wide or low or fast. No matter.

I scratched my sandal around in the sandy dirt. The air smelled of sage and . . . something else.

I breathed deep and said, "What *is* that?"

Mom blew out smoke and said, "Mint, a big field of it."

The smell seemed more vegetable than mint, but there it was, a vast field of young plants between us and the canyon. On the other side of the road lay all sorts of fields, dark green and yellow-green, some sort of orchard, irrigation equipment and tractors parked for the afternoon. Cows and sagebrush, big black rocks and sagebrush, silvery Russian Olive trees. I hadn't taken in any of this on the drive somehow. It was all new.

"Smells like it's going to rain," I said. We'd been moving through western Oregon and Washington over the last few years, and the fact it never rained here was supposed to be a boon.

With a flat tone that meant my remark had been super obvious, Mom said, "You are correct. It is going to rain." I noticed the darkening clouds behind her. She looked at me funny.

"Truck's a mess," I said. I was noticing that for the first time, too. The truck looked gray instead of black. All our stuff under the grimy tarps, I hoped it was still clean.

"Where do you go?" Mom said. One of her standard questions. *Where do you go? What's wrong with you now?* or, *You know what, Georgie?*

"Just picking clouds. Just daydreaming," I said, which was what I always said. I looked down at my sandals again and noticed how filthy my feet were.

"You haven't said more than a dozen words all day, and now you're lively, aren't you?" she said in an accusing tone.

I kept looking down. This wasn't the first time and wouldn't be the last time that I'd gotten in trouble for zoning off—and it wasn't just Mom who noticed.

I thought how I could come back at her. Was it just the fear of heights that accounted for that all of that back there, or did she maybe see a shadow walking that bridge—maybe one of the suicides that such a bridge must attract?

She'd never once admitted to seeing a shadow. Why then couldn't I shake my feeling that she saw? What was wrong with *me*?—well what was wrong with her?

I didn't share any of my questions. She wasn't really upset with me anyway, just tired, and she'd been so scared on the bridge. Who knew what kind of chemicals she had coursing through her after that? Fear is nasty stuff.

I always took whatever she had to say and just kept coming back with how sorry I was and how I'd try to do better. I'd never been an easy one to raise. We'd had to move before because of things I'd done and things done to me. *This* move was for all of us, but it was for her most of all. It was her time, now, to do something for herself. The best I could do was stay out of her way.

Mom and I kept turning while she had a second smoke, looking back at the canyon and over the opposite way toward the mess of a little town sprawled across a shallow valley with the foothills beyond.

"This is a hopeful place. You can tell," I said when we turned back to the truck, and she offered a grateful smile. She was already sorry for being unpleasant, already back to something like herself.

The rain held off until we'd hit the highway. Soon we came to the forty mile-per-hour sign and then the twenty-five, and then a stoplight turning red. The day was still bright, but a little of the glare was gone. Rain sprinkled so lightly that Mom didn't even put on the wipers.

If we kept going straight, we'd be in Boise in an hour or so. Turn left and we could visit Streaker's Truck Stop for gas or the $5.99 biscuits and gravy special. Turn right, and we'd be entering Beulah. Mom put on her right-turn signal, a very good sign.

"Nothing looks familiar," she said.

"Well no, it wouldn't," I said. "It's been like thirty years." I was soothing her, soothing myself. I didn't say anything about the pressure in my own chest or the way a part of me seemed to be already wandering the town, hovering along its streets like you can in dreams.

The image of a dark stone building framed by a crooked tree crossed my mind and was gone, the way a dream crosses your mind in the moment you wake.

Mom said, "It hasn't been that long. I brought you here as a toddler. Sixteen, seventeen years is all."

"All right, a lot changes in seventeen years," I said. I noticed her eyeing the empty left-turn lane and put my hand lightly on the wheel. "We can get gas later," I said, and she turned right after all.

People wandered the streets here and there, but I didn't focus on them. Beulah probably had a meth problem and a lot of unemployment just like every other little town we'd known, but nothing was on display just then. The rain made colors deeper and brighter than they really were. Patches of grass around the drive-thrus seemed lush green. Parking lots looked clean, and everything looked a lot less wrecked and patched-up than it probably really was.

The population sign after the bridge had said nine thousand something, double what I'd have guessed based on Mom's stories.

After a stretch of gas stations and drive-thrus was a car lot, a pizza place and an Albertsons set far back from the road, old houses made into real estate and dentist offices.

"*This* part looks familiar, doesn't it?" I said halfway through town when brick buildings lined the streets branching off from Main. She'd forgotten about stopping for gas. Forward momentum, good.

That sensation of hovering through the streets returned, but I pushed it back.

Mom didn't comment on the pink house at the park's corner, but I recognized it from her stories. I could almost see little Ellen running out of that house in her fairy costume and taking Mom's hand as they rushed to trick-or-treat all the streets around the park. A few blocks back from Main was the rental house where Mom lived for those five or six heavenly years before high school.

Ellen was the one we were running to now. She was going to help us, set us up here.

"Too bad the girls are missing all of this," I said. The park was already behind us, houses thinning out. A broad church stood on the right and a blue mom-and-pop gas station on the left. Something about the gas station caught me, and I turned back, but it was gone. The road curved toward a little bridge crossing a canal and then turned up steeply, bordered by wild grass scattered with rocks and sagebrush. It seemed we were all the way out of town now, but we crested the hill and there on the left was a restaurant. Mom almost missed her turn into Ellen's subdivision.

Seeing the first houses, I realized Ellen was wealthier than I'd imagined. I didn't know why, but the thought of that gave me a little chill.

We climbed, taking a number of turns on the curved roads. Deep in the subdivision, at the top of the hill, we swooped into a large clean driveway. The engine ticked and Mom was at the door knocking before I could get out. She hadn't even closed the driver-side door. I came up beside her, wondering what a house like this must cost. The oak door was taller than a normal door. No one was home, though. The expectation fell out of Mom's face.

Mom, with no hope in her expression, looked something like a lion. Long jaw and hair all bushy gold around her face, a disappointed lion.

"She's just gone out for a minute. We didn't let her know what time we'd get here," I said. That image of a dark stone building framed by a crooked tree crossed my mind again.

We sat in the truck with the front doors open and didn't talk. After a time, Stevie started to cough in her sleep. Soon the both of them would be wide awake and needing to pee, talking and jostling me. I'd never catch a moment to think from now until we were settled.

I knew we'd be better here. We'd promised each other we would. Sitting in the truck, waiting for Ellen to get home, I re-promised myself I'd do whatever I could to make it so.

Mom's scare was over. I didn't feel I had to help her anymore, and so my mind drifted back to my own worries. Who was I going to be here?

I asked, "Are we telling people we're from Seattle?"

Mom said, "Close enough."

I'd said goodbye to my best friend Betty just the night before. I already missed her terribly.

I said, "Betty said you need to be careful about your image when you move someplace new. You have to *control your own narrative* or something like that."

It wasn't Betty who told me that, really, but who was it? I couldn't say. That thought had come to me unbidden and perhaps it was the spirit world reaching out or perhaps just the thought of a better, older self. That's what it felt like—like future-Georgie was whispering her life advice back into the winds of the past.

Mom didn't speak right away. She held my attention with an *are-you-kidding?* look, half amused and half upset, like she knew I was lying but did not disapprove. Maybe she knew what truth the lie covered, too.

It felt like she did. It felt like we read more than just feelings in each other's faces, like we read full thoughts, even words. How often did we finish each other's sentences or hear a planned word come out from the other first? I'd always hoped she'd admit it without my spelling it out, but she never had and never would.

An unexpected breeze came through the truck cab, dry and refreshing.

You're going to be happy here, said my imaginary friend, the future me, or was it Mom?

Mom finally said, "You wouldn't have to go to school this year at all if it wasn't for Betty," her point being that we'd partied too hard and that was why I'd failed senior year. She wasn't wrong, but it was more complicated than that.

Everything is always more complicated.

I looked out my window, seeing nothing, seeing a time not that long ago when I lingered in Mom's doorway before bed. She asked how it was going. Struggling for words, I said, "Um, not great, but at least I haven't been out partying in oh, six months."

Fishing for a compliment? Maybe.

You know what, Georgie? Mom had said.

Thinking about what she said after that, I almost cried right there in the truck while we waited for Ellen.

2

Tommy and Stevie woke and whined about needing a bathroom, but right away Ellen came along in her pale gold SUV. All made up in a sundress and cropped cardigan, she looked like her pictures, which people usually don't. Maybe she was at church earlier. I didn't know what day of the week it was or if she was religious, but it was possible.

Ellen tried for a hug. She smelled like heaven, but I knew I didn't, so I edged away. Everyone else hugged her, though, and after each hug she held each person at arm's length saying how beautiful they were. She overlooked Mom's creased, sweaty clothes and the smell of smoke. She overlooked how Stevie was too big for her age and went on about her long dark hair. With Tommy she didn't have to overlook anything.

The cargo door rose, and we all rushed to help with the grocery bags. We shed our shoes and padded through a dramatic entry hall, through a family room and into to the sparkling kitchen. Everything was pewter, tan, and robin's-egg blue.

Stevie's eyes opened so big. I'd never seen a house like this outside a magazine, either, but the difference was I'd never wanted to. Apparently Stevie *had* wanted to, very badly. Tommy's face was posed and stiff. Intimidated, I supposed.

We sat at the breakfast bar waiting for Ellen's boys, Jasper and Adrian, who were supposed to rush back home as soon as Ellen texted, and they did rush—so quickly I wondered if they'd just been in the back yard.

Obedient boys and well brought up, that's what I'd heard, and they did not dispel the notion. They gave us gentle side-hugs and asked about our drive. Both dark-haired and tall, only Jasper was filled out. In fall, he was going to be a senior like me. Adrian, just finishing his freshman year, was slighter and prettier. We'd never met but felt like we knew them already from the school photos Ellen sent every year. Both were sporty. Jasper was the independent one, Adrian more of a Mama's boy.

I realized that the cardboard characters of Jasper and Aidan, as presented by their mother to mine, were probably echoed in portraits that Mom had painted of us. Tommy was the tough go-getter, the cranky one. Stevie was the sweet and practical one. I, Georgie, was a constant worry but also her secret favorite.

Or I used to be, anyway.

We were shy with the boys and they with us. We took turns washing hands and packing plates with rotisserie chicken and deli sides. We took our plates to a glass table on the lawn where everyone could admire Ellen's view of the town and the distant canyon. Ellen talked about how, after dinner, we were going to follow her back through town to the investment property she'd just acquired. This was where we would live for a year—or less, maybe—in a place that was once a schoolhouse but was going to become a home. If the trees weren't in the way, we could see it from her yard.

She'd bought it at auction, for "nothing" she said. We were going to live there and not pay rent. We'd spruce up the place so that some hip young couple could come and "snap it up." It wouldn't take long in this market—and it would bring "big, big money."

Everyone else kept up the nervous talking. I stayed silent and still, let myself fall back into daydreams as I scanned the town.

I knew every street.

We were here. A feeling of freedom washed over me, same as I'd feel about the move to any new place but with an unsettling intensity this time. *Nothing holds you back now.*

I felt Mom's nostalgia and fear, felt I was coming back home.

#

Tommy and I sat in the backseat of the truck. I couldn't remember the end of dinner or the walk back to the driveway. The light was pink, almost-sunset light, and I knew I must have gone further off than I'd realized because Mom was saying how very tired we all were. She didn't call me out by name, but it was me she apologized for.

Ellen didn't seem to notice anything wrong. She leaned in our window touching Mom's shoulder and calling her by her first name, Gina. Again she said how glad she was to have us.

Stevie sat up front grinning big, practically bouncing in her seat. Her idea book lay open across her chubby knees. All spring she'd been filling it with magazine pictures and paint chips.

"Do you really think she likes my colors?" Stevie asked when Ellen walked away.

"She was gushing, wasn't she?" said Mom.

So Stevie had shown off the book while I wasn't paying attention. How much had I missed?

I hadn't learned anything more about the boys than I'd known from the photos, but as Ellen backed out the SUV, Mom and Stevie marveled at how cute and sweet and how very polite they were, how funny.

Tommy was silent, staring at me. Something was wrong. She wanted to touch me, but her hand only hovered. Tommy, just sixteen months younger, was always my better, more industrious self. Her face was my own face composed in worry.

"I'm fine," I said and pushed closer to the window.

We drove back the way we'd come, but it was all different in the pink light. The air had dried, and the cars had headlights on. Lighted signs, smells of fries, onions, and grilling meat. Many cars cruised Main, and groups of young people milled around the drive-thrus. It couldn't be Sunday, had to be either Friday or Saturday.

Red light at the highway, Streaker's truck stop straight ahead. The left turn signal on Ellen's SUV flashed out of time with the clicking of ours. I wanted to get out of the car and hover along the side of the highway.

If I were to go right instead of left at this light, I'd come to a cabin in its own little patch of trees, the dark little cabin just off the highway where I'd spent cozy nights in my dreams. If I came back toward town and took a left before the light, I'd be on the street with the feed factory and the odd little two-story thrift store. I'd spent hours looking over things in that thrift store and then hovering back toward the other end of town past the broad brown church, lingering in the blue gas station. The hovering was like skating, free and easy.

I hadn't known it was Beulah until just now. I'd thought the places were made up—that or pieced together out of other places I'd seen. But no, they were of a whole.

"It's how I dreamed it was," I said.

Stevie looked back at me, nodded. "Me too," she said, but she didn't understand.

I needed to make my point sharper. "No, I dreamed exactly this," I said. Mom gave me a hard look in the rearview. *Shut up now*, that look said.

You know what, Georgie?

We were on the highway building up to forty when Ellen slowed and signaled left at a sign that said Farm School Rd. We moved past a farm and swung into a broad dirt-and-gravel driveway, swung in to see a crooked tree framing a dark stone building.

The forces that held you in check are now absent, I thought. It was the same sort of thing I always thought coming someplace new. Whatever difficulties in the abandoned place—rude or nosy neighbors, a friendship lost, a dangerous daily route—it was gone and the slate wiped clean.

But I was seeing something wrong. Bars on the windows for an instant, something red—firelight?—inside the building and a catlike wail from the distant canyon.

What new prison will you make for yourself here?

A feeling of doom came down.

Oh, you're going to ruin this, aren't you?

3

The schoolhouse loomed before us, not too far off the road, a dark and jagged two stories with the lower floor half underground. The front was symmetrical, two rows of tall windows above strips of basement windows, a large black-painted door at the top of cramped concrete steps. The fenceline on the left had straggly trees growing along it and the one tall bent tree close to the road. The fenceline on the right was hidden in berry thickets.

"How much land?" Tommy asked.

"Four acres?" Mom said.

Beyond the property lay pastures with horses and sheep so far away we couldn't count them. Beyond them, a white farmhouse and mess of outbuildings, and then the dark canyon sprawled all picturesque below the coming sunset.

Ellen moved nervously at the top of the steps and had to try the key a couple of times. I noticed tall weeds growing up around the steps and creeper vine on the black iron railing. Stevie pressed her hand gently to the stone and showed us the bumpy imprint on her palm. Her face was all childish wonder. I liked seeing that.

"It's lava," said Ellen, "or we call it lava. Rodney says that's not technically what it is." It was reddish black, dusty. I wondered what would have made someone think to make a building out of that.

I didn't particularly want to go inside, but we were going. I expected the inside to be rocky like the outside, but it was nothing but peeling plaster walls, green-and-gray checked linoleum floor, off-yellow painted woodwork, a smell of mice.

We walked the rooms. The wide central hall led all the way to the back of the building. On the left side of the hall, we glanced into two classrooms with some leftover wooden desks. On the right front side, past the basement entry, we looked through a classroom just like those on the left. We saw the truck through its rain-spotted windows.

"Will we stay here long enough we'll have our own room?" Stevie asked, which was a little bold for her. Mom reacted by pulling Stevie closer and petting the back of her hair. *Shut up*, in other words.

"Of course you will," said Ellen. "This place is going to take a long time."

Mom's smile broadened, and she brought Stevie around to stand in front of her, rested a hand on her shoulder. Mom was completely unguarded just then. I felt a little breathless watching her.

We didn't know how long we'd be staying, didn't know why we were here at all, did we? The instability was enough to strip down all Mom's defenses.

At the back, the entry hall widened into a lounge with a principal's office on the back-left side. Two-seater boys' and girls' bathrooms separated the teacher's area from the classrooms. The girls' bathroom already had a clawfoot bathtub installed.

"Did somebody live here?" Mom asked.

"The last owner started a remodel, but they didn't get far," said Ellen.

A bit of half-assed graffiti marred the principal's office, just some names and the outline of a long curving dick. A pitiful little collection of beer cans filled one corner.

"There was a broken window in the back. It's fixed," Ellen said.

Too bad she couldn't have had them spray some primer on the graffiti, too. I didn't like her leaving it there for the girls to see. Mom and Stevie walked on as though they hadn't noticed the dick on the wall, but Tommy and I exchanged a look.

Moments like that were few and far between for us. I tried not to show how happy I was to have her on my wavelength.

When we'd gone through each of the rooms, we moved out onto the patio to see more of the canyon. The sunset blazed pink and orange, and I was a little more won over, seeing it. Green and orange-red lichen had grown on the concrete, which was just now raked with pink light.

While Mom and Ellen talked about the land, how someone would want to put a horse or two on the sparse pasture, I squatted on my heels taking a close look down at the wild grasses. Green now but they'd turn to straw by early summer. Odd little goat heads, spurge, and button-weeds were starting in the bare spots.

I looked up at the darkening sky. Would there be stars in a town as small as Beulah? Clear air and summer breezes bringing the smells of barbecues and horses? If it were up to me, I'd bring a sleeping bag out to the patio right now, maybe lie down and read a book.

But it wasn't up to me.

"Downstairs!" Stevie squealed, so we turned back to the front hall and rumbled down the stairs. This area sprawled out further than it should have.

"Is it bigger than upstairs?" Stevie asked.

"It must extend under the patio," Ellen said.

The smell was not much worse than a typical basement. Someone had thought to crack the little square windows at the top of the front walls. Still, Tommy and I shared another look. She put her hand up to shield her nose.

On the right-hand side, tucked behind the stairs, was the most frightening room so far, a long galley kitchen of orange Formica and greasy oak-printed cabinets, all of which were still well stocked with items like clouded, stained Tupperware and blackened cooking sheets. Ellen sighed, opening and closing the doors to show us.

In the center of the basement was the vast open space that must once have been the lunchroom, or more likely part of it was for eating and part for exercise when it was too cold to go outside. The thought of such an open space in a home excited everyone, and for a while we talked about what a great party room this would make.

Or, they talked. I stood far behind them now, trying not to draw attention to myself because I was beginning to feel a little wrong down there. I wanted to get back to the patio most of all but thought that anywhere upstairs would be totally fine.

I was thinking in resentful terms, which wasn't like me. Mom and Tommy and Stevie discussed all the things you could have down here for a party like a bar and foosball table and pool table and some of those old pinball machines. It sounded like a party for guys. I was thinking Jasper and Adrian probably actually had parties just like that for their birthdays—every year—and they went to such parties for their cousins, their grandparents, the friends they'd known since they were little kids.

That's the way people are supposed to live.

It was the way Mom's people would have lived, if her folks had more than just the one kid, if they'd kept in touch with extended family, if they'd stayed put in Beulah for longer than—

And even greater resentment came as I thought of the gifts those boys received on their birthdays! Four-wheelers and new guns for all their recreational time, all their trips; new wardrobes, the big televisions and computers and gaming systems. Ellen always managed to work in mentions about her gift lists whenever she called Mom.

Mom had often described Ellen's bedroom in the pink gingerbread house. Pink ruffled canopy bed, shelves of dolls and the dollhouse and all of that. Jasper and Adrian's rooms must have surpassed that by quite a lot.

I started to get a lump in my throat. No, this wasn't like me.

Honestly, a party like Ellen's boys had would probably mess me up. I didn't want that kind of a life, never had. I choked back the feeling and moved on with the group.

On the left side of the basement was a bare-bones half bath and two small, dark rooms. Past them lay another room where I glimpsed shelves and a furnace and a shadowy figure moving around. Nothing intense, just the hint of a long line from hand to waist, a shadow-man reaching up toward one of the high shelves.

The stuff of nightmare and magic, a ghost. I looked away.

I'd been trying to participate in the tour, but this was more than I could handle right that minute. My pulse raced, hands sweated.

I rushed past that room and out a door into the backyard near the blackberry fence. Ellen was right. The back part of the basement was under the patio, which seemed a gigantic block of lava rock from this angle. There was a little white graffiti here, too, faded and illegible on the porous stone. I breathed deeply and went blank looking at the dusty rock.

I took my time finding my way across to the left side of the yard and around front, breathing more, calming myself by looking over the weedy dirt and my grounded feet.

You are nowhere else but here, in your body, in your life. It's just moving-in day and you are here; your people are here somewhere too and warm.

I found them grouped back in the upstairs hall. They turned toward me smiling, and it was just as well they didn't ask what I'd been up to. I couldn't speak just then.

Ellen said, "Now, I really do want to put you up at the little motel for tonight. It's just behind Streaker's, very cute."

Only she didn't really. That should have been clear to everyone.

Mom said very slowly, separating each of the words, "We would not dream of going to a motel. We've been thinking about this place so long, the girls couldn't stand to leave it now."

I never liked to see Mom be so ingratiating because at some point she would resent having been that way.

Be careful, I thought.

Ellen caressed her purse. Tommy kept her face blank, but Stevie beamed. Mom was right about one of us, anyway. Stevie was the one who'd thought about this place the longest. She *was* dying to spend the night. Her idea book was back in her hands. She must have rushed out to get it from the truck while I wasn't looking.

I worried about how excited Stevie was. I would have loved to sleep at the little motel, or in the truck for that matter, but for her sake I said, "Oh yeah, we've been super excited to stay here."

Ellen moved her hand away from her bag, apparently taking that for the truth.

"The bathroom tile is already here," Ellen said at the door. "My handyman can come this week, unless—"

"No, I told you I can totally do that kind of thing. Just save Marcus for the heavy stuff," said Mom.

"You sure? That *would* put us ahead," said Ellen. She took one more long look over the rooms before stepping out the door.

"Relax. I'm handier than you know," said Mom. They hugged again, and we all watched as Ellen hopped down the stairs so happy.

"There's no way we can stay here. There's no shower even," Tommy hissed as the SUV rolled out onto Farm School Road.

Mom never hesitated to ignore Tommy when she felt like it. She smiled, led us back to the truck to start bringing in our stuff. She decided we'd camp in the cafeteria area for now. I would have liked to sleep in literally any other room in the house, but I was strong enough not to say so. I told myself it would be all right.

I cringed when Mom went into that back basement room for the broom and mops and lemon cleaner, but she wasn't rattled when she came back. The shadow must not have come alive for her as he had for me. Either that or she was faking. I couldn't say.

Stevie tied a bandana around her face and took the broom to the mouse droppings.

No one else seemed to catch even a whiff of the ghost.

The room was dirtier than it looked at first, and huge. Long past dark, Tommy and I still mopped and Mom huffed and groaned, scrubbing on her hands and knees. When she was satisfied, we put out our sleeping bags.

That back room didn't have a door. If I looked over there, I'd see the figure moving around again, so I kept my eyes focused on the floor. The shadow was new to me, but he wasn't strong.

I told myself, *You've got this. You've survived worse scares than him.*

We began unpacking. Each of us had two medium-size plastic totes, four large totes held our household things, and then there were a few grocery sacks full of random clothes in the backseat of the truck. Each of us had a purse of some kind with our valuables in it. My journal, for instance, was in my messenger bag, which would serve as both purse and schoolbag. Tommy had her crappy laptop and expensive phone and headphones in a padded case that she clutched to her twenty-four seven.

Mom had told Ellen there was more in a storage unit that we'd get when we're ready for another road trip, but there wasn't, and we wouldn't. This was everything.

I was hoping we were about to get ready for bed. This day had been exhausting.

Soon as I thought that, Mom told me to go upstairs and take a bath. I took a T-shirt and leggings out of my tote and trudged upstairs. I turned on the tap, used the toilet, and stood waiting until the tub filled to a couple inches from the rim. You've got to take your happiness where you can, and a deep hot bath was what I needed. I folded my sweaty clothes and laid them on the stacked boxes of tile, slowly lowered myself into the water. For the first time, I caught echoes of children playing outside and found them almost soothing.

This place was more active than it seemed at first. Most places are.

It all made me a little scared but a little hopeful too. Echoes of ghost-children having recess at midnight would probably seem super creepy to some people—and it probably should have felt that way to me—but it seemed perfectly logical that they would be here. A weird building like this would make an impression on them in life that would linger in death. And these had been happy times for them, all told. I closed my eyes to listen, and the listening made me smile. I let myself sink, keeping my ear-holes clear of the water.

Tommy slipped into the other end of the tub at some point. There was plenty of room. She soaped and scrubbed efficiently, mumbled something about a fucking shower, and headed off in a towel. She'd left another towel hanging on the doorknob for me. How considerate.

Stevie came in and perched on my clothes on top of the tile boxes.

"Get in," I said.

"I don't want to," she said.

"You don't want me to see you?" I said. Stevie took after Dad, so she was thicker than the rest of us, but that had long preceded her modesty. Her problem was that she was starting to look quite a bit older than ten now. I'd been jealous of girls like that when I was her age, and I told her so, but growing up so soon didn't seem like such a great thing to her.

I guess puberty always sucks, whether it's too early or too late.

"Here," I said, folding my washrag to lay over my eyes. I groped around for my towel, got out of the tub and started drying myself with the rag still dripping on my face, which made her laugh.

Mom reminds us to appreciate each other, but most of the time I don't need to be reminded. I'm glad to have my sisters. Stevie laughed at me, and soon I was feeling light, like nothing was wrong.

Stevie shuffled around for a while, then got in the tub. "The water's getting cold," she said. The tap turned on, and she whined, "Oh, that's even colder."

Leaned against the sink, I opened my eyes to the low cracked mirror. I looked just like Tommy, eyes a little further apart than hers, upper lip a little shorter, but almost a twin. I combed my hair in the mirror, brushed my teeth. It seemed to me then that other girls crowded in wanting to use the mirror, and I slipped out the door so that they could take it.

JUNE

1

I woke in the dark and couldn't remember dreaming. I took a pen and my journal out of my bag and sat still, trying to remember. Nothing.

I couldn't seem to fall back asleep after that, so I slipped into my sandals and climbed the stairs. Solid stairs, just one or two soft creaks. Out the front door I went, looking up at a blue-black sky all patched in clean-edged clouds and crisp stars.

A mile or two walk along the silent highway felt like a good start to the day. By the time I turned back toward the house, dawn was coming. I could just make out the distant dark line of the canyon, the blue-green fields and the lime-green fields, all the different pebbles and weeds by the road, the shapes of distant animals.

I looked at the surroundings but thought of Dad. Had I dreamed of him, or had the man in the basement recalled him in some way?

Dad was the first shadow I saw, the very night he died. I was ten, so Tommy was eight. Stevie was a tiny little thing, and Mom was always so busy with her. Dad was running late for dinner that night, which he never did. Nobody knew yet about his truck crashing out on the highway. It would be a while before anyone called, and so dinner waited for him. Mom turned the oven down low. I read, and Tommy colored for a while, but Mom said we better just eat.

I was setting the table when I saw him. The door hadn't opened, but he sat on the bench in the hallway. He took off his boots and sighed with relief like always, but no sound came. I didn't say anything because I knew that no one else would see him. The image was flattened, like a recording playing in the air on top of the bench and the entry mirror. I saw through it in places, and in other places, it was solid.

He wore the puke-colored coveralls reserved for the coldest days. It was that icy bridge that killed him.

Mom had always worried about that bridge. She'd regretted his commute each day of the winter, and now it had all come down.

And I knew he could not see us, not as we were. Smaller versions of Tommy and me must have rushed to greet him because he smiled and turned his eyes to one and then the other. He moved a hand that wasn't there to a little blonde head that was even less there. The girls were entirely invisible to me, and after he greeted them, he began to flicker in and out.

Mom said something, but I would not turn or hear her.

That might have been the first time Mom asked what was wrong with me, what had come over me, but I couldn't stop watching. I sat down in the dining chair facing the entry and watched until he had flickered to nothing.

Mom and Tommy talked about something, maybe a trip we were going to take, to the zoo or to the mall or something. Back then there were always outings and activities, always the money for such things because of the commute, because of the bridge.

He took that bridge every day for us. Oh, he'd died for us. Had we always known he would?

It was my first time sitting there having a terror experience while those around me talked about normal things. I could barely breathe.

I was seeing something wrong; I was wrong for seeing it. I was old enough to know they'd call me crazy, but that wasn't why I couldn't tell. I couldn't tell because I couldn't find the words and because I didn't want them to know Dad had died. I didn't want it to be true.

My eyes went to the phone. It would ring soon, but I wanted them to have another minute to feel safe and whole and innocent.

I was already developing a theory or maybe just a guess about what was going on. *It's like a movie. Nothing more than a movie printed in the air somehow. He can't see me. He can't touch me.* I had doubtless seen things like that on television—a ghost or a hologram—though that wasn't the type of program Mom liked us to see.

It helped that I remembered seeing things before, faces in clouds, shapes in the wallpaper. Images no one else noticed. A few times, I'd tried to point out things like that and had to give up because Mom or Dad or Tommy couldn't see or wouldn't admit they saw what I was talking about. I told myself this was no different.

For Stevie's sake, we all pretended that everything was going back to normal after that—and then I suppose things really did become more normal for Tommy and Stevie. They never did for me. I only ever pretended. I think Mom kept pretending, too.

A few weeks—maybe a few months—after it happened, I saw him again. We'd all been working on the lawn. I came into the house, and something was off. The entry was terribly dark, and just as my eyes started to adjust, I caught Dad's reflection in a clock on the side table. I whipped around to see him, but there was nothing there.

Late that night I woke needing the bathroom. When I stepped into the hall, I saw him over the heat vent, fainter than he had been the first time, rippling like air over a hot car. I wasn't scared. I stayed and watched him quiver in and out until he did not come back. I was crouching over, holding my pee in.

"What are you doing?" Mom said behind me, and I lost my control. She saw it spread on the leg of my pajamas. She grabbed onto the back of my pajama top and turned me to the bathroom.

"Were you sleepwalking?" she whispered. I don't think I replied. Maybe I was crying.

I'd been a sleepwalker—sleep-screamer, bed-wetter, and so on—earlier in my childhood. I always sort of bracket out that part when I think of that first encounter with Dad. It doesn't feel relevant. More than that, it fails to fit the narrative I prefer, which is that we had an idyllic childhood before Dad died.

We did not have a perfect childhood, and on the whole, I doubt that we were much happier then than we became later, but the story does seem to require a perfect childhood and so it was. It more or less was. It was.

We had that pretty little house, at least, back then.

Why did I start going over these memories every time I was alone? I was afraid to be alone, but I craved it and maybe this was why—because being alone always sent me back into the past.

I hurried back to the schoolhouse and down the stairs before anyone had thought of waking. They were still piled together like puppies, softly snoring, and I took back my place at the edge of the pile.

2

Everyone was gone when I woke for the second time. I took the journal back out of my bag and wrote down the line that kept coming to me:

You know what, Georgie?

I sat with my eyes closed for a time but couldn't call up anything from my dreams. I tightened my ponytail and slipped back into my sandals.

Upstairs, Mom and Ellen drank from tall brown cups that said Beulah Coffee Connection. They stood by the open front door, heads close together, murmuring and giggling.

"Good morning, beautiful!" Ellen said, pulling me in for a hug. I couldn't escape it this time and was engulfed in her perfume, which smelled green and spicy like when you hit ivy with the weedeater. Her clothes were all coordinated, yellow and light blue and a scarf bringing those colors together with green and brown, a green leather purse and kitten heels.

"You sleep okay last night?" Mom said. She had a light hold on my wrist and made eye contact. I nodded, and she gestured to a box of donuts standing on a stack of plastic totes. I selected one with clear yellow jelly on it, took a bite, and set it back in the box.

"Where's the girls?" I said.

Mom pointed out the front door. They were both in gym shorts and T-shirts, pulling weeds out of the front yard by the road. This show of industry seemed a little excessive, considering it was our first day.

"I guess those girls are game for anything," I said.

"Oh, but they're getting paid," said Ellen. The word "paid" seemed like holy magic when she said it.

It had to be sometime between nine and eleven, but this display still made me think of Mom's story of how she pulled weeds every morning of that summer when she stayed out in the country with her grandpa, how degrading it was and how he'd hit her when she couldn't get up at five or six or whatever godawful time he thought people ought to get up.

Mom was smiling now, that story all forgotten. Nice.

"What time is it, anyway?" I said.

"We've got to get *this* girl a watch," said Mom.

"Or a phone," said Ellen, and Mom's big smile faded. I'd broken my phone and would get another one when I paid for it myself.

"You better get out there too," said Mom, but I turned away.

"Or you won't get the big money they're getting," said Ellen.

"I don't feel so good," I said. "I think I'll go back to bed for a while." After a quick trip to the bathroom, I moved back down into the cool basement and slid into my sleeping bag. Within a few minutes, I'd slipped back into dreams I would not recall.

#

That's how the first few days went, more or less. Some might ask why the same rules that applied to my sisters did not apply to me. I was the eldest, but that was not the full story. Maybe it was only this: I couldn't handle things. I wasn't brave.

They didn't read it as depression, I don't think, though surely it must have been that.

What they thought, I'll never know. What I do know is this: They let me be. They indulged me, and I was so grateful for that I never wanted to risk it by asking why.

They'd be gone and then they'd be back. I'd move around upstairs trying to enthuse over all they'd bought and done. The carpet had been ripped out of the two front classrooms, and the hardwood floors looked rough but well cleaned. Part of that work had belonged to me, and I would have done it if they'd left it for me, but they hadn't. Seeing it done, I felt shame and gratitude at the same time, which seemed a very sweet blend.

In one of the rooms I hadn't helped clean, Mom had placed a used brass daybed frame and a new twin mattress. This was her bedroom.

Ellen had her hired man, Marcus, set up two old sofas seat to seat in the front left classroom, and Mom said that would be our bed for now. We girls were to nest in it in our sleeping bags and be happy. We did and we were.

The sofas were beautiful fake-antique things, deep-seated, upholstered in a faded brown-rose tapestry that felt and smelled almost new. Mornings, I lingered in the warmth of the nest long after everyone else had vacated. They were happy to leave it, and I was happy to stay. Or, not happy exactly. I wasn't happy to feel so overwhelmed, but I was happy that everyone let me be.

Mom's voice carried from other rooms. I heard, "She'll be fine. You know, a little moody. She tends to be a little anemic, but she'll be fine."

Another time I heard, "It's artistic temperament. My mom was just like that too." Relieved to hear nothing really bad about myself, I'd fall back into sleep.

Tommy and Stevie were subdued too, but not like me. They ate well and did what was asked of them, shooting me resentful and worried looks from time to time, staying near me when they could, maybe hoping their normality would rub off. Sometimes they lay on the floor playing board games, whispering near where I slept.

Everything they whispered was sweet and innocent and good.

It was always something like this when we moved, the new things crashing in on me, the struggle to not be too overwhelmed. The new little flitting shadows and the new sounds and sights were too much to process all at once. Even the sagebrush—it smelled good, but it crowded my head.

My dreams escaped me no matter how quickly I picked up my journal, and so I played over little snippets from the recent past. Ruminating on past injustices and slights was what it was, really. A pointless activity, but it seemed to be all I could do.

I was back in Mom's doorway just before the move, trying to get some encouragement. I'd told her I hadn't gone out partying for sixth months now. Hadn't had one drink.

Her eyes were red, and when she came close, I had to fight the urge to back away from her.

She said, "You know what, Georgie? Sometimes I wish you were still 'partying,' whatever that even means. You're like a zombie now."

I said something, maybe "That's harsh."

"At least you were funny. You had—I don't know—you had a mind. You had a personality."

She kept going after that.

And I thought how the sofas under me came from Ellen's, her house so vast it had spare sofas floating around in it when we had almost nothing.

The big empty room I lay in used to be a classroom, and the children were here still, and the teachers. The children's hands shimmered up in the air. That's all it was. You didn't even see hands. You saw just the motion, but unlike the little chatters of them in the yard, the motion of their hands brought a queasy dropping doom feeling.

I thought how most were people who used to go to school here and were dead now, but maybe some of them were still alive and they were just thinking about the school right now. *Ye Olde Farm School, way back in the day. Those were good times*—or *I sure hated that school. They spanked you for no damn reason*. The place had made a mark on them somehow, good or bad. The dead lingered here, for sure, but also the living ones still traveled here sometimes.

They visited for a few seconds apiece, in memory or in dream or in the long death-dream, whatever it was. They remembered raising their hands, washing their hands in the little bathroom, playing out front during recess.

Their presence didn't have to be bad.

The shadow in the basement was something else, though. He had to have died here. The image came of a bright day, a red-faced man strolling around the playground during recess. Nothing more, but I wasn't exactly courting the vision either. I let it come and flow away.

Awake, my mind whirred with questions, and I thought it still whirred as I slept, which was why I didn't feel rested.

The only answer was to close my eyes, count my breaths until sleep came, take a bath, eat my dinner slowly. Maybe soon I'd go for another walk.

#

One morning—three days from arrival, five?—Mom lured me out of the basement with a cheese and mushroom omelet, which I never could resist. While I ate it, I watched Mom and Ellen measure the room for flooring.

Mom pushed her shoulders back when she stood and animated her face a lot more than usual. She was so far from being the frail thing she'd been on the bridge that I wondered if she even remembered. If I reminded her of it, would she say she didn't know what I was talking about?

They were dressed up. Mom wore tight jeans and a flowy black top. She'd put on all her rings and let her big curly hair air-dry so that she was the perfect complement to Ellen, so that she was Ellen's gritty, cool friend. If Ellen smelled of sassafras and ivy and lemongrass, Mom was incense, honey, and musk. Her body was rock-star skinny to Ellen's soft curves.

"You two look especially cute today," I said, which made Ellen's expression go all relieved, like I couldn't be that bad off if I still noticed how good they were looking.

They were going out for lunch and looking at flooring samples. Did I want to come?

No. I wanted to go back to bed.

Once they were gone, my mind wandered to our last trip to Goodwill. The last truckload of our belongings—or actually the next-to-last truckload.

The last truckload lay all around the basement, didn't it? I opened my eyes to see that it did. It was like I had to prove I was really in the basement in my sleeping bag, not back in Orliss with Betty and the rest of our friends. I kept my eyes open long enough to convince myself.

I felt lost in time, like I hadn't been just thinking of that day but had for a moment been standing in the truck bed beside Betty and handing boxes of things down to the Goodwill attendant.

I closed my eyes and let myself be back in that moment with Betty. She had all her dark hair pulled back in a bun, a line of sweat around her hairline. Every time I caught her eye, she smiled.

It isn't the end of the world, Jojo. Maybe it's a new adventure.

All our excess clothes and linens, most of our books and Stevie's outgrown toys—each item handed down was another step closer to adventure.

Or another step closer to the end of the world, maybe.

I took out my journal and wrote *Why did we give away everything?* And journaled about why it was. For a start, it had saved Mom from having to drive a U-Haul again. Thinking of her driving one of those trucks over that bridge gave me chills.

There might have been some spite in the decision as well. Tommy said at one point, "We don't have anything, so let's *really* not have anything."

Mom and Tommy both read women's magazine-type stories on their phones. There were some words uttered about simplifying, "capsule wardrobes," "sparks of joy." I think we all understood it was a purging, a symbolic rebirth. We were going to be new here.

Stevie had her own reason. She loved to watch human-interest stories on the local news and secretly hoped to be on that certain segment where kids built little foodbanks and grew hair for wigs, donated all of their Christmas presents, went on hunger strikes for peace or whatever. I totally encouraged her to think that way. Our worn furniture and extra linens weren't going to change anybody's life, but the ability to think so was a good part of her character. It meant that maybe one day she could be a teacher or a social worker or something.

I put the journal back in my bag and took out my phone, texted Betty for the first time since the move: "We're here and settled."

"Good news I was wondering," she said right away.

"Miss you," I said, and she sent back a string of hearts and hugs and things like that. She didn't say more, and I figured she was at work.

I dozed after that. As soon as I woke, I took up the journal again and found I hadn't written anything at all.

I was in the upstairs in the sofa nest and not down in the basement sleeping bag, and I still didn't have a phone. I'd been dreaming, then, and I had remembered all of it. Mundane though it had been, I dutifully wrote down the dream, and by the time I was finishing, the front door opened. My family and Ellen were upon me once more, calling me out of bed to see what they'd bought.

I can't say that remembering one dream cured my malaise, but it went a long way. Remembering the sacrifice of our things helped me to remember why we came here, and dreaming of Betty suggested she wasn't really gone.

That one little dream helped me start the long struggle back into hope.

#

I woke before dawn and looked into Mom's room on the way back from the toilet. She wasn't in bed, and I eventually found her in a kitchen chair on the patio. She was wrapped up in her blue bathrobe and sat smoking.

"Is everything all right?" I asked. When she was feeling good, she would rather go cold than wear that lumpy robe.

"Just fine," she said. "It's really quiet out here, isn't it? View's even nicer here than it is at Ellen's."

"Peaceful," I said. *Safe. We could sleep on the patio and no one would bother us.*

After a time, she said, "I guess it's just hard for me to trust people, you know?" which I understood as a reference to us throwing ourselves into Ellen's hands.

"We can trust Ellen," I said. I closed the door gently and went back to the nest.

3

In the evenings, Stevie pored over her idea book. Everything in it was so fantastically cluttered and rich—jewel colors and ferns and craft tiles with crystalline glaze, peacock feathers in a vase and deep carved dark woodwork, tufted velvet—it broke my heart to think how disappointed she'd be when Ellen ended up not taking any of her suggestions.

I humored Stevie, pretended to think Ellen might be convinced. We settled on peacock wallpaper and a low turquoise velvet sectional, metallic tile on the floor, jewel-colored Persian rugs, a fountain with Koi in the center. The upstairs living area, which we had started to call the great room, was big enough for all of that and more.

Stevie couldn't sit on my lap anymore, but she sat close, crossing a leg over mine while we looked through the book so it felt like old times. I was eight, almost nine when Stevie was born. I carried her around like she was my doll in those days and still wished I could take care of her as fully as I did back then.

If this girl did nothing else to make us love her, it would have been enough that she reminded us all of Dad. I braided her dark hair, which was Dad's hair, and told her how lucky she was to have it. All of the rest of us have a dirty blonde color, mine a little red. Mom's is big and wild, but Tommy and I both have thin, lank hair.

Mom, crossing the kitchen one time, noticed us sitting together and smiled.

The next time Mom saw us like that, she frowned and called Stevie over to get her ends trimmed. The next time, she called her over to look at something on the phone and asked if I'd taken the garbage out.

I couldn't help wondering, was Mom jealous or did she have some other reason for wanting to separate us?

#

While Ellen and her husband vacationed at their condo in McCall, Mom spent the time working with Ellen's jack-of-all-trades Marcus, a big, sunburned man who barely spoke. They broke down the walls of the principal's office and the boys' bathroom, removed the stalls and toilets. At some point, the boys' bathroom and the teachers' lounge would merge into a fabulous kitchen. For now, we had just a used fridge and stove and a microwave on a cart.

Mom had told Ellen we'd make do with that because that's what she always told Ellen. No one considered using the kitchen downstairs, ominous as it was.

The rooms were all getting painted the soft yellows, blues, and greens of Ellen's wardrobe. Maybe these were all the colors she'd have used in her own house if she hadn't had to take her husband's taste into account. We still hadn't met the man. He seemed to always be away on business, working late, working the weekend.

Stevie painted just as high as she could reach on the stepladder and left the rest for us. She loved to cook, and with everyone so busy, we let her. She favored simple, filling stuff: spaghetti, slop-burgers, chicken-fried chicken with white gravy and potatoes from packets. She was happy.

Tommy did whatever was asked, but every chance she could, she bathed, put on her cat-eye makeup and false eyelashes, and walked into town to socialize. She got leads about jobs at a second-run movie theater and the Tiger Burger drive-thru. By the end of the week, she wasn't walking into town; her new friends were stopping by to pick her up. She was happy, more or less.

I was feeling more settled by then, and I too worked hard. My job was painting the ceilings with the long pole Marcus had shown me how to use. I liked the swaying, repetitive feel of it so much that I thought one day, I might like to paint for a job. I started with two strokes in a corner, just as Marcus showed me, another stroke out from it, a push out toward the next corner, soft strokes to fill in. I liked having all that white in front of me, new buttery white over the tired oyster white.

When the upstairs ceilings were done, I took the pans and the long-pole down to the basement. I moved the five-gallon bucket of paint slowly, leaning back so I didn't tip forward and crash down the stairs. The room with the pacing shadow had a new hollow-core door, which I checked was shut tight.

I tipped the bucket from the side opposite the bung-hole like Marcus taught me, felt the paint glug out, took the plastic bag off the paint roller and rolled it in short strokes, pressed it into the corner of the ceiling. The central room's ceiling seemed to go on forever. I hoped it would take as long as it looked like it would because the other rooms scared me.

No one watching me paint would know that I was thinking all that time, thinking of the past.

I thought of Dad again, which made me think of all the shadows I'd seen since him, which made me think of Betty (and my guilt at not having reached out to her yet despite the dream-text, and the dread of reaching out to her finally after such long procrastination). She was the only person I ever told of what I'd seen . . . only my stories always got twisted in the telling.

It's funny I didn't think of it before, but Betty was Mom to my Ellen, wasn't she? I was the sweet one, and Betty was the strange, cool one. Kind of goth? Kind of, I suppose, or just cool like Mom, always hustling. Too smart.

I told Betty something of what I'd seen because I had nothing else to help bring us closer, because I had to tell someone, because she wanted to know. In the version that Betty heard, Dad was there full-color, full-body. I saw him come right through the door like in all those horror movies she loved. It was my own little blonde head that Dad petted. He told me he loved me.

Betty didn't believe it for an instant. It was a story that didn't want to be believed, after all.

I told her a lot of stories like that. Different genres, but always so sweet she couldn't believe them. Everything had to be more sentimental and basic—more filling, more satisfying—than it was in life. Betty was as much a sucker for rom-coms as she was for horror, and that's what I gave her, rom-com.

I couldn't bear to give her my horror, couldn't bear to see her savor it.

I told her versions of all my ghost stories—not just Dad but also the little boy who got me and Tommy in trouble at school that one time. He had seemed to see us from across the creek, and we had run after him, or *I* was running after him. Tommy, who knows. Maybe she was only chasing me.

I told Betty about the ghost-boys I hung out with when I was fourteen. I told her about the shadows in the apartment building that wasn't next door to us back when we lived in the city, and more.

Most of the time, I tried not to think of my past. If I happened to think about it, it felt like I was telling a story about someone else: *She was always a weird little girl, crazy teenager, went wild, she was a mess, and then she met Betty, started to calm down, and now she's a good daughter, really one of the family. Going to finish high school, go to college or something. Going to tell everyone she lived in Seattle and . . .*

It was Mom's narrative for me. Sure it was.

It came with vague, distant ideas of making surface-level friends, being polite to them, helping them and letting them help me. A half-life of industry and nice light feelings. Maybe create something?

It all fell apart when I thought of it any longer than that, so I didn't. There was all the chaos of a landfill behind me and before me, nothing but buttery white.

Little flecks of paint sprinkled down on me, and I did not wipe them off. I did not slow down or use less paint to keep them from coming. I let them fall, all the time thinking how if it weren't for Stevie, I would want to keep moving, keep walking. I'd get a backpack and try to see America on foot. See all the different wildflowers and weeds and all the different types of gravel on the shoulders of the roads, the bits of trash and the distant beauty, all the different styles of houses. Maybe I'd get to see *all* the places I'd dreamed about, given enough time.

To stay, I had to keep telling myself I was a member of this family, loved, but more importantly, needed.

"Sometimes I feel like I can hear kids playing outside," Stevie said last night before Tommy joined us in the nest, and I told her just how silly a thought that was. Even as I said it, I watched the shadow of a teacher sulking into our room, the shadows of hands going up all around us.

I worried that Stevie was picking up on something from me—not reading my journal since I always kept it away from her, but maybe watching me while I watched the shadows and getting a hint of something wrong. Mom's seeming to worry about my influence on Stevie made me worry about it more.

Because Betty wasn't the only one I ever told. I lied to myself about it, but yes, I kind of told Stevie too, only I always hoped that she was too young to remember.

After Dad, I didn't see anything much for some time. You might think that I would have tried to avoid seeing any others, but the truth is that I always tried very hard to see them. I wanted to know they were real. Were they trying to tell me things? Was there a reason they showed themselves to me?

After Dad, when I did see them, they were usually just a flicker, like a bloom—isn't that what it's called?—when water meets paper. A bloom in the wallpaper, bloom on the curtain.

Or a stain? A stain in the air?

I remember exactly when it started to get easier, though. I was thirteen, living in an apartment in a city bigger and older than any we'd lived in before, and when I lay in bed there were so many shadows everywhere—in the room with me, wandering behind the windows of the big brick apartment building a hundred feet away—and wandering between me and the building, too. I could have closed the curtains, but I never did.

I thought it was beautiful, shadows moving at different levels of a gone building above an empty lot. If I went out to the sidewalk at night, which I often did, I saw more of them. Sometimes they weren't there, but depending on the night, I might see all three levels of them going about their activities, mostly shadows sitting on sofas I couldn't see in front of televisions I couldn't see, but some of them pacing halls, some of them washing dishes and a few, from time to time, making love with other shadows on top of beds that weren't there. All of them overlapping, person on person because each room had held so many tenants over the years, not getting in each other's way but relating to each other somehow, like there was a harmony over time that they might have felt but that only I got to see. They were all shimmery, blue and violet, there and not there like the mirages you see on the road in the heat.

The building was there sometimes, too—the type of old apartment building that was once a stately house, which explained the corseted old-timey ladies embroidering things in the front room and the heavier shadows toiling back in the kitchen. I always wondered what had been so wrong with the building that they had to tear it down.

I always wished I could take a picture of it. I tried, but of course nothing showed. I wished I had the skill to paint it. I would use blue and violet and green watercolors on black paper, something metallic to lift them, fine white lines for the house, or maybe I'd make it a black and white page from a graphic novel. That isn't what I saw, but it's what it felt like. Fine white lines on gloss black.

I think of different art pieces sometimes that will show what I've seen, that will make someone understand and believe me, but these are idle thoughts. I would not know where to begin.

Back then I was a good girl. I never slept in class, but I took a good long nap after school every day. Mom said it was due to anemia. I'd try to wake up at five, or at least by seven for dinner and doze while we watched television, then wake at two or three in the morning to sneak out to the sidewalk. That was all it was at first, just standing on the sidewalk until my eyes adjusted and watching for an hour or two.

I wanted to communicate with them if I could. Unlike Dad, these shadows were captive, consistent. Maybe I thought I could tend them like young plants, tame them like little wild animals—anyway, I thought I could spend time enough with them that they would not only show themselves to me, but they would open up to me, speak to me.

I wanted to learn about this thing, and only they could teach me.

It was scary being out alone at night. Sometimes rough-looking people would be coming down the sidewalk; I'd just tuck up against the side of our building where the darkness was deepest and hold my breath until they went by. I was lucky no one ever bothered me. Sheltered as I'd always been, I don't know what I'd have done. Screamed or run, I suppose, or maybe I would have frozen and disappeared.

The people in the building were becoming individualized. One man would lie reading in a bathtub that wasn't there (and I identified with him because I too liked to read in the tub). He would lie there with the others from other times stepping in and out and busily washing and drying themselves. I admired the young people who were always rushing around cooking and cleaning, felt sorry for the old people still doing that at a slower pace.

One lady always sat behind the shimmering lines of a bay window facing the street. She was never anywhere else, not that I saw. She just sat embroidering. Whenever she stopped to rest her hand, she would look out the window. I thought sometimes that she was looking at me.

I would come close and feel my skin flush, feel my heart go crazy like I was about to have to run. She'd be staring straight into my eyes.

"Hello?" I'd say. "Hello? My name is Georgina. What's yours?" She never answered.

It was a good six months we spent there, and I can't say I thought of much else the whole time. I was out there in the dark every chance I had. I never spoke a word of it to Tommy or to Mom, but Stevie was just five years old and always in my care. I was thinking about the shadows so much that it was inevitable something would slip out here and there.

And, too, I remembered how I'd thought Tommy used to sometimes see little things when she was younger. I guess I might have wanted to test Stevie a little, so when we were together alone, coloring or playing with dolls, sometimes we would talk about the house that used to be next door and all the people who used to live there. Just idle stories about the lazy man and the angry man and the newlyweds and so on, kind of like fairy tales. Stevie's stories were all made up, but mine were based on actions I'd witnessed.

Oh yes, and the lady in the window. We talked about her a lot. I'd told Stevie how beautiful she was, so we wondered what made her sit there all the time and never do anything else. We sketched stories around her, how she was confined to a wheelchair, how she was afraid of the rest of the house. Nothing seemed quite right. I kept going out every night, and it seemed like things became firmer and more real every time. The lady was less and less transparent. The house, too, grew more solid so that I couldn't always see through it to the people inside. More and more, I just stood beside the lady's window. I didn't think of the people who might be coming down the street anymore.

It was on one of those nights when Stevie came out after me. She'd woken up and, knowing now where I went when I left our room, she'd come to be with me—and to try to see the people I saw in the dark.

I was nervous and felt ashamed of myself for, in a way, leading her out there. I wanted to get her back inside but before that, I thought to give her at least a chance to see. I held her hand on the way to our steps, and we turned back. Stevie was just looking across an empty lot, you could tell. My eyes moved from her to the lady in the window. She'd stopped her work for a moment and was looking out again but not at me, not at anything.

I knew then that she had never seen me. What she'd seen, what she'd been seeing all those nights, was nothing more than her own lovely reflection in the window glass. It was night for her, too, and that glass was a mirror.

I got a little shudder just thinking of those times, a little nauseated, actually.

I looked back to the furnace room door, still shut tight. Bright light and a warm breeze blew in from the basement's strip windows.

Tommy and Stevie's talking came from the front yard, not far beyond the windows. It was soft and benign as that of the shadow-children. All was well, and then I knew that the door to the back room had opened. I felt the damp chill and saw, out of the corner of my eye, a shape in brown static, barely moving.

    I moved up the stairs all choked as in a dream, leaving the paint, leaving the roller pad to dry out. That would get me in trouble with Mom, later.

    I rushed upstairs and out into sunlight, took the mower that Stevie was trying to start and told her she was getting too much sun, she ought to go inside and read or take a nap. All speckled in pain, I mowed the wet, weedy lawn and tried to act like a normal person once more.

    All speckled in paint, I mean.

4

Twisted in the telling, that's how it is. No fault of the teller, but stories will always become what they want to be. To tell the story of Betty, or a story about Betty, I had to go over what came before. I doubted I could tell that story to anyone or even remember it right for myself.

The only thing I still have from those days is my freshman-year photo. I never stuck around long enough to get the yearbook. The girl in the picture looks younger than fourteen and wears no makeup. Luminous, poreless skin, but a softness to the face that makes her not quite beautiful. Her expression is open, honest, welcoming. The first thing you notice are the big, widely spaced eyes with thick brown brows. The next thing you notice is the short upper lip, which gives just a hint of rabbit-ishness. Her hair is dark blonde, just on the edge of ginger. One hand is curled up to rest on the hair, and the blouse is a faded rose. A girl wearing sad, thrift-store outfits every day, probably not always smelling so nice, sleepy and vague in class—a girl like that with a different face could have been the toy of bullies, or she could have been labeled a bad kid. I never was, though. Everyone let me drift in and out of the scene just as I wished, all because I was so unthreatening.

I didn't care whether people saw me or not and so they usually didn't. Up until I was fourteen, anyway.

We'd just moved to an even larger city. It wasn't my fault we moved that time. Mom just couldn't stand her job or her coworkers one more day, and so we picked up.

What I didn't know yet, when I was fourteen, was that shadows came in all sorts of different varieties? Strengths? I don't know the right word, but anyway, at that time I didn't think that shadows could be confused with people. I never imagined it until freshman year when I made friends with three of them.

The school in that city was unlike any school in my past. It made me think of a prison, a maze. I tried my best to get to classes, but I was always confused about where they were. The kids were frightening, seemed so much older. But then one day there were three boys my age. My friends. They walked the halls with me, told me how cool and different I was.

Not like other girls. You know that line, but back then I didn't.

They came into my classrooms, where one would sit on the edge of my desk and the others stand near. In the halls, while the other kids talked to their friends, the boys stood around my locker joking, teasing, flattering. I must have talked to them in full view of everyone. I didn't know. And when the counselor started asking to see me, I worried that we would have to move again soon. We did end up having to move but not for the reason I initially thought.

By the time the counselor called me in, I had a story ready. I left him with the idea that I was a really fine girl who might be dealing with a little bit of stress at home but was doing it admirably.

In the version of the story that I told Betty, I should have caught on that the boys were ghosts from the provocative, teasing remarks they would make. Chris once said "Maybe we're all dead right now" while the three of them were getting high in the hall (and even that should have told me. The school was rough but not post-apocalyptic. Someone would have thrown them out for that). Another time during lunch, Brian was wondering about a commotion over by the football field, and James told him to just fly over there and check it out. What can I say, though? I was young and dumb. I didn't catch on for at least a week, and by then I was falling in love with the whole idea of being their friend. I felt like we all really understood each other

I was falling in love with Brian. He was so cute with his motorcycle jacket and slicked-back hair. Once I knew they were dead, I figured his getup was a clue to his time period. A good girl and a dedicated student still, I spent hours in the school library trying to find any story of his death. I never did find anything, but that might have been down to poor research skills.

They were not bad boys, but they were wild. They were often drunk on some long-ago liquor that they'd stolen from one of their fathers, back when they were alive, when they were fourteen or fifteen like me. I only pretended to be drunk. All night, we'd run through the streets.

They were rowdy. They'd fight over little insults, bloody each other's noses. I could not grasp their shoulders, and so I stood behind them screaming for them to stop. Sometimes, after those fights when they were so angry they had to keep from hurting each other, they would break things. Not that breaking was a sure sign of anger; they broke things when they were happy, too. I saw James grab a beer bottle and sling it at some fence or mailbox that once stood beside the road. The bottle materialized just as he grabbed it and was gone again as he threw it, and of course it never hit. It was no more real than he was. Chris took a stick that wasn't in the road and crashed it into the windshield of a finned convertible that wasn't parked by the curb, and I laughed. Brian stood, pretending to put an arm around me. I almost felt him standing there.

They were rowdy, oh, but they were sweet. At night, they'd come to tuck me in. We couldn't speak because my sisters slept in the room with me, but they would hover around my bed. Grinning, Brian pretended to stroke my hair. James pretended to press my eyes closed, but I would keep them open. I'd watch as the boys silently sang me to sleep.

Was my belief in them making them more real? One day, would they come back to life? I think I expected that.

Late in the night, there would come a pebble striking my window, my cue to sneak out of the apartment. Hours later, I'd come in breathless from a night of running. People would often see us running in the streets—see me running out in the streets alone I suppose—and I was a little afraid of being caught, though caught at what I couldn't say. I was exhilarated, more energetic than I'd ever been, waiting only for my heart to stop thrumming before falling into the sweetest dreams.

And then one night there was a continuous pounding on the window. I'd been deep asleep and came out of it frightened, then realized it was Chris. He'd climbed a tree. I was afraid, still, but it was only a fear that he'd wake my sisters or worse yet, Mom. I got up and checked Tommy and Stevie's faces. They both slept deeply. Chris still pounded on the window. When he knew my attention was on him, he made an impatient gesture and lowered down.

I went out in trainers and the shorts I'd worn to bed, thinking we'd once more go roaming the streets, but there was an unreal car idling at the curb, a long red-and-white classic car, its back door opening out. It was all so soft and glowy I knew it was them. I wasn't afraid it might be a stranger, though the figures inside were hard to see. The car glowed like a jukebox.

Brian leaned out of the backseat. He was waiting to help me in.

"I can't," I said. "And you know why. Don't pretend you don't." We had an implicit agreement not to talk about the fact that they were dead.

The guys in the front said something. The glow went out just then, or I had been mistaken about it. The car was still bright, but now it was only streetlight glaring on the polished paint and chrome.

"If she doesn't want to go, she doesn't have to," said Chris. He was in the passenger seat, so James was the one driving.

Brian scooted further out of the backseat. He looked so, so real. The flyaway hairs made a halo on his head. I could see his stubble, the sun-streaks in his hair, the individual hairs making up his expressive eyebrows. I'd never seen him like this.

He took my hand. His was warm and gentle. He scooted back into the seat and pulled me with him slowly, slowly. "What is this?" I said, or thought. The cool vinyl touched my knee. Brian still held my hand and now he nodded. I turned and settled my weight down on a smooth, solid vinyl seat, just like that. I pulled the door closed, and it didn't quite seal. I opened and shut it more firmly.

Not going to lie; I was excited. Getting into that car was the most daring thing I'd ever done. I didn't think the car was there, but I knew somehow that it would rush off with all of us inside it, as indeed it did, and where were we going? We could only be headed toward their death. James was driving too fast already and all of them were tipsy again on stolen stuff. The car was stolen too, had to be.

(I thought, before convincing myself that this was a stupid thought, for many reasons: I should have caught the license number. I could check it at the library.)

The dead boys and I were together, it felt like maybe for the last time. The boys talked about people I didn't know and things that had happened to them back in their time, and then we talked about my teachers and the jerks in my school, about my family. The boys had spent time around us, hovering at the backs of rooms sometimes. Tommy was too bossy, they said. Stevie was sweet, just like Brian's little sister.

"I miss her so much," said Brian, "but hey, we're getting too deep here."

"Let's have *fun*!" said Chris.

We were at the highway turnout, headed out to the open road. James took the corner too fast, and I held my breath.

"Not yet," said Brian. "It isn't for a while yet. Here, put your..." He moved closer and pulled my head down onto his chest. I could smell him, feel his hand resting gently on my head. His breath was sweet with rum and Coke.

Chris held up a baseball bat, turned back grinning. James slowed, and Chris rolled down his window and leaned out to hit a mailbox, which really moved, I thought. We cheered. He hit another, and this time I saw it go down. We didn't egg him on for more. We rolled up the windows and James accelerated.

It was quiet now but for the sound, more a feeling, of speed. Good tires thrumming on a good country road. The boys murmured up front; I couldn't hear what they said. Brian murmured to me about his sister and his mom and all the plans he had for getting his shit together in the near future.

It *was* a while longer, maybe an hour. I dozed in his arms. We didn't kiss. We never had, and though it felt so urgent to do it now, I was shy with the others so near.

I wasn't watching and so did not panic or feel much fear. The crash did not go in slow motion as in the movies. It was fast and loud and ended in a terrible dripping hush. There were no smells in this version I told Betty. I left it to her to imagine cow and maybe mown hay.

I felt nothing. The car no longer surrounded me. I sat cross-legged in the grass and gravel beside the driver's door and watched James struggle to breathe. I reached toward him, but I couldn't touch him. He and the car were made of smoke. They caught on the breeze and blew away.

The sound came of a stick cracking underfoot. I swung in its direction and said, "Who's there?"

I was alone on the dark and did not know where I was. I saw nothing but a few feet of field and a dark treeline below pewter sky. I looked back, and the car was there again all broken. James no longer struggled. He was slumped in the seat, blood streaming from his forehead and mouth. Another boy moaned from the street, and I ran to him. Chris. His chest and stomach were crushed and bleeding. He smiled and said, "Where's Brian?"

I searched the car, felt around its sides and cut my hand. I didn't find him. I couldn't see. I came back and held Chris's hand. How slick it was. When his face had gone slack, I held my hand up close to see his blood on my palms and more blood from my cut streaming down. I was choking with panic and grief.

Part of me saw that this had been the deal all along: when I got in the car, I was signing up for this, and there was nothing I could do but witness. It seemed like something they wanted me to do for them, to feel their pain and the terrible waste that had happened on this night. Another part of me was desperately searching for Brian. I was thinking he must be alive, and I could do something for him, tie my shirt around his arm or something, and then I could walk until I saw a house or a car and get help for him. Save him. I cut my hand again. My knees were bruising and taking cuts from the gravel as I crawled and felt around for him.

The cracking sound again from that spot beside the road. I stood and turned toward it.

There, against the dark tree line, the three of them stood lit like Brian had been under the streetlight. All three walked toward me, but Chris and James slowed and then it was only Brian coming. I was in his arms, and we locked in a slow movie kiss heightened by my fear and the sense that he could not stay.

"I have to go," he said, and I said I knew. I don't know what all I said after that. We were rushing, rushing to say everything we wanted to say to each other.

And then I woke up.

#

This was the story I told Betty, more or less. It wasn't untrue. It was just the version it needed to be at that time, when she and I first became friends. It was *a* true version, as were the other versions that were so much harder to think about.

There was the story I remembered in my body and the story I told Betty. When my mind started to go to those other memories, I redirected somehow. I fell asleep or just thought of something nicer.

I always thought I would tell her the other versions of the story, but I never did. I would set out to tell another and repeat this one instead.

The first time I told it, when I said I woke up, Betty threw a pillow at me.

"Do you have any idea how much you suck?" she said.

We were in her tiny dark bedroom, Betty cross-legged on the bottom bunk and me cross-legged on the floor.

"There's more to it, though," I said. I stroked the side of my hand.

"But the whole thing about the boys was all a dream?"

"Just that night. Everything else, well, you can ask my mom if you don't believe me. They were worried. I had to see the counselor, I don't know, three or four times."

"So just from Chris banging on the window was the dream and everything else happened?"

I didn't nod.

"OK, then, what else?" she said.

"I woke up. I was really upset because Brain and I hadn't said everything we meant to say, and I felt so sad what had happened to them and that I couldn't tell anybody. I laid there for a while and when I pushed the blankets off me."

"No, I know what you're going to say. No, just..."

"You don't want to hear it, then?"

She laughed. "I guess I do."

"The sheets were all filthy. I had my shoes on still. My knees had little cuts and bruises, and oh, this took a long time to heal." I stroked my hand again.

"And there's still a scar there?" said Betty, leaning closer.

"No, it faded away."

"So you don't have any proof, then?"

"No, just my word."

I climbed on up to the top bunk and tucked myself in, and it wasn't another minute before Betty started asking more questions. Was it my first kiss? Did I ever find out who they were? Why did we have to move from there? On and on like that. I answered truthfully, yes and no and that it was complicated. She asked what happened after that.

I was sixteen then, and I think Betty was still fifteen. A sleepover seemed a young and indulgent thing to do, so we meant to make the most of it. We stayed up talking most of the night. I told her a little of what had passed between fourteen and sixteen.

After the night of the car crash, we come to what Mom and Stevie call my "bad time."

In every version of the story, I had actually gone screaming through the streets with those boys, and I had talked to them in school when other people could hear.

After the crash, they did not come back to me, and with them gone—as I rethought everything for myself and outside their influence—I came to think I'd done these things on my own and only hallucinated the boys. I couldn't say why my mind would betray me like that, but the story I told myself was that I'd watched too much rom-coms and too many princess movies and books that were like those movies and, because I was a very vain and dreamy girl, I'd cast myself in some kind of an imaginary romance novel. Kind of a horror-romance which, I'm not going to lie, I was reading a lot of around that time. Betty introduced a great many movies to me, but those books I'd discovered on my own long before.

The idea that I'd imagined everything seemed like nothing less than a genius insight when I was fourteen. I looked back at the experience coldly and saw that I had pieced together this delusion out of scraps of other people's stories. It helped that not only the boys, but every other shadow was entirely absent for at least a week or two after the night of the crash. Everything was sharp-focused and real as hell.

For the first time, I began to doubt all of the shadows I'd seen in the past, even Dad.

I could not stand to go back to that school because, even if the counselor had heard what I wanted him to hear (and that wasn't as clear as I'd made it out to Betty), the students knew better and, anyway, I was nothing there. None of us had ever been happy in that city.

And though I had convinced myself that the boys had been all illusion, I was not one hundred percent sure that I hadn't, under the influence of this delusion, stolen a car and actually crashed it out on a country road. There were no scars but the one on my hand, but still, it might have happened that way.

Mom thought it would be good for us to get back to a smaller town, so we settled on a place called Orliss that was still about three times as big as Beulah. Once we moved, I started looking outward, trying harder to make friends. I wasn't at all careful about it. I was fifteen by then and had lost a semester's credits. I came into the school with an attitude and plunked myself right down with some kids who looked like they would be fun, and they were. I started wearing makeup and dressing up more. I started acting brave. Around this time, the shadows that linger around everything came back to me. Meaningless shadows in the apartment and in the halls at school.

I tried to self-medicate, I guess you might say. It got so I'd taste anything once, take any dare. You know what I mean. I thought it was all only to keep my mind from going *there*. That's how I rationalized it to myself at the time: no matter how bad I was, partying and being around lots of people all the time was better than the alternative.

Now that I have some distance from it, I'm not so sure. Maybe I was more hopeless than I realized. Maybe what the boys had shown me, not in the story I told Betty but in the other versions, was that nothing really mattered.

The other versions of this story are confused and inchoate, brown-tinged, ugly, staticky things.

The boys tease me, tempt me out of my body, threaten me out. There are so many versions, but all the same: They take me, and I am a bodiless spirit and they are Georgie. At first it's enough just to be in the body just to breathe and stretch but they need more. They find the right car, not a big, beautiful car like they had in the romance version but the old neighbor's brown Subaru furred inside and scented with Golden Retriever. It's the right car because we know the key lies there on the front tire. They are driving me, driving the Subaru, good tires on a good country road. I feel their exhilaration. Pure joy just to be driving but soon that's not enough; they need to speed and swerve and lean out the window into the blasting cold.

I feel them but I am a senseless spirit blocked outside them, outside my own body, wailing *No, please! You're going too fast. You'll hurt me.*

These other versions of the story all smell of silage because in the place where the car wrecked, where I woke from the wreck untouched, a silo tower stood just off from the road and a slow breeze caught the sickening scent, and for a moment I wanted to push back out of my body just to get away from it.

Let the boys take the body again, or just leave it there by the side of the road? For a moment I didn't care. I wanted out of this life, but only for a moment because the breathing soon began feeling sweet and precious once more, the silage almost a taste, almost a syrup on my tongue.

Whatever the reason, by the time I was fifteen I was partying all the time like every other teenager in Orliss did. By sixteen I was scaring people. Mom was always trying to set me straight, but she couldn't do much. She was working full-time and had to sleep, and she was partying on the weekends too like all the adults did in Orliss.

One summer day, Mom dragged me downtown with her, and while she was looking for clothes, I asked if I could go in the New Age shop next door. She rolled her eyes but didn't stop me. I wandered through the crystals and incense and stuff, and in the back room, I looked at a rack of shirts with wolves and Celtic designs, patchwork skirts, tied-dyed yoga pants, on and on, and when I came to the shoes, there was a beautiful girl sitting on the ottoman.

An older person going into a high school might say that all of the girls are beautiful, and it's true that most people do look as healthy and fresh as they'll ever look when they're that age. When you actually are that age, though, you don't see it that way. The girls who were popular at my schools all looked sort of grotesque to me. This girl, though, she could have been on television. She had a lot of wavy dark hair bleached at the ends, her face plush and composed. She dressed all in black and had roses tattooed on her bicep. We started talking, and I found she'd just moved to Orliss. It was the first time I'd ever been in a school long enough to welcome a new girl, and by the time junior year started, we were good friends. By the time that year ended, things had changed for me.

I had a lot of friends back then, but slowly Betty became the only one that mattered. We still partied after we struck up a friendship—of course we did. There wasn't anything else you could do in Orliss. Slowly, though, we both started to grow up. Or it felt that way. She got a job. I said I was looking for one. She got a piece of shit car she was so proud of, and it seemed that half the time we were not partying but doing things that Mom would approve of like going out to a movie or browsing at the mall. I wasn't a good student and doubted that I ever would be again, but I wasn't getting in trouble for drinking anymore.

My "bad time," as Mom called it, had come and gone without too much trauma-drama. I hadn't gotten pregnant or gone to jail, so we all counted it a win.

Orliss had turned out to be a shitty little town. We were lucky not to have been hurt worse by it. Mom's job was terrible again, the people getting on her nerves again. Tommy was rocking the sports teams and both she and Stevie were doing well in school, but they would do that anywhere. They were gems.

When the call came from Ellen, I fantasized that I'd stay in Orliss and let them all move on without me—finally grow up—but that wasn't going to happen. I had never followed through on my plans to find a job. I hadn't taken driver's ed, had barely gone to my last-semester classes.

And Betty still lived with her mom. Even if I'd begged to move in with them, I doubt they would have agreed. They both liked their space and had little enough of it.

I didn't have anything else to stay for, really. I'd built quite a few friendships in town but not important ones. I think it was mainly because of the shallowness of those other relationships that I'd made so much of Betty, that and the fact that I'd shared more of myself with her than I had with anyone else.

I'd shared this thing that I think of sometimes as a talent, sometimes a curse, the thing that takes up half of my thinking and sometimes more, the thing that has always made me feel so lonely. I didn't feel as lonely with her around, was all, but she was lost to me now. I knew I should let it go.

It was only that I had a bad feeling.

If I were telling the story of Betty *to* Betty, maybe I'd tell it like this: I met a girl who was as alive as I was. She had a little tiny room in a little tiny house she shared with her mom, who was as real and alive as my mom—who even knew my mom, went drinking with her a couple of times. She had a father who'd made some threats, who wasn't really supposed to be near the mother or to know where they were living, though how could he not? They'd run away back to the mother's hometown, after all.

This girl had a real piece of junk, a little white Cabriolet her young uncle was always trying to fix for her. We'd stand around teasing him while he did because I thought he was cute. If Betty had a few drinks, she was more fun than anyone, but when she drank too much, she would pass out and have to be babysat the rest of the night. I never minded doing it because when *I* drank too much, I said a lot of crazy things about spirits and possession and seeing the future, She'd have to wrestle me away so I didn't humiliate myself.

When she danced, all that hair went ropey with sweat. Working at the coffeeshop window put her in a pissy mood, but she'd still remember all the regulars' names and orders.

Betty was real and alive, but she was marked. She glowed like those boys and their dream-car sometimes. Every moment with her seemed loaded, like a flashback in a sappy movie. From that first day in the New Age shop, I knew that she would die young, and though I wanted to be there for her, I also wanted to let Mom draw me far away and to not know anything more about it.

JULY

1

It was so rare to remember dreams that I relished them when I could. Especially a dream about Betty. I'd toured her around an endless house—a Victorian house, stuffy and glinting with crystal and dark polished wood. We hovered over the arabesque patterned rugs and checkerboard tile and hard uneven wood floors. Nothing like anyplace I'd ever lived, but somehow I knew it was our house, Mom and Tommy and Stevie's and mine. I led Betty up mauve-carpeted stairs to my room, telling her she'd never believe what was up there. I woke before we made it past the landing, but I didn't want to accept that I was awake.

I kept my eyes closed, trying to hold onto the image of the stained-glass landing window. Rippled yellow-green with a bright street behind it and a smudge of peacock blue. But it was over, gone. My cheek and my pillow were damp. I stretched my toes and my head pressed into the corner so I remembered I was in the sofa nest. The smell of fresh paint and fresh carpet came to me.

"You awake?" Mom whispered. She was at the other end of the nest, in Tommy's place. I didn't move, tried to keep my breathing deep and regular.

"You're a terrible liar," she said, nudging my shoulder with her big foot, but she didn't bother me more, so I was able to go back, for a while, to the dream.

Betty and I were younger, Stevie's age, and we moved through Beulah at night. Silver moonlight and the dim-dim gold streetlights cross-dappled the sidewalks with shadows of trees and fences.

"This is magical," Betty said. She was so young, her skin so perfect. We glided down a sidewalk, one of those that goes through the yards so that each house has a flowerbed between the sidewalk and the street. I glanced down at the flowerbeds crowded with bearded iris and ivy, ferns and lily-of-the-valley, roses of Sharon, hollyhock.

"Will you look? They're so pretty," I said. My little-girl laugh echoed through the streets. Betty, hovering far ahead, called, "How far is the canyon?" The yards were full of wet grass and wide trees, weeping willows maybe. I grasped a whip of one in my hand and pulled the tiny leaves from it as I floated by, but no, I was awake now. There was nothing more.

I turned and wiped my face all over with my hand. Mom still rested there, sitting up with a book. Stevie still slept on the other side of her, her back to me so that all I saw was the long dark braid flung across her pillow.

"Did you sleep here?" I said.

Mom nodded, and without trying to keep quiet, she told me Tommy had slept in her room so she could have a night free from my kicking and thrashing, but it was all right now. Since the carpet was laid in the front left classroom, we'd be getting twin beds in there for Stevie and me, and in the basement Tommy would have a futon for her bed and some beanbag chairs or something so that people could come hang out.

Mom must have finally gotten our support check, I realized. Back in the day, this would have made me excited about what sorts of treats were up ahead in the week. Maybe we'd go out to eat or even go to the mall and start laying away things for school. But I was eighteen now; there was no more check for my support. No more treats for me, I guessed, except the ones I could earn for myself.

Mom stopped talking because I didn't respond. She was back in her book.

But I was wondering. "We never did put things on layaway at the mall, did we?" I said.

She looked up over her reading glasses.

"For school, did we?"

"No, I don't think they even offer that at the mall anymore. Everybody has a credit card who would want that kind of stuff, I guess? They still do it at, like, big box stores."

You better just be quiet now, I thought.

It was *her* parents who put things on layaway at the mall when she was a kid. In the mall in Nampa with the red carpet. That's what I'd been thinking of. I never was there, but felt I remembered the arcade, the animatronic Santa's elves they'd have in a corral at Christmas, the nachos and big slices of pizza you could get in the food court by the side entrance, and all the rest. I remembered people smoking as they walked through the mall because she'd told me about that so many times. There were ashtrays by all the benches.

It was like how I remembered the television having static because that's how it was when *she* was a kid—static came after the station went off in the night, after the national anthem, and you'd try so hard to fall asleep before it came because after that there was only quiet in the house and anything could speak in the quiet.

It had always been like this between us. Usually I pushed her memories away by stepping back, but with her so close in the sofa nest, I couldn't.

I'm not handling things well. Nothing is moving for me; I'm only circling back, I wanted to say. *Can I use your phone?* I wanted to say so much to Mom, but I couldn't start.

"I need to get a job," is what I said.

Mom took off the glasses, gave her full attention. "Tommy finally got her job last night," she said. "That one she's been hoping for?"

Tiger Burger.

"Does she have to wear a uniform?" I asked.

"Yeah, but it's *hot*," she said. "Hot" was not a word Mom would normally say, not like that. She turned on her phone and passed it to me. Tommy posed in a black and orange polyester cheerleader outfit, only like a really modest old-timey one. The next picture was Mom in the same outfit. She saw me seeing that one and took the phone back

"Hope you liked seeing that. It's deleted now," she said. She laughed her deep raspy laugh that always made me feel like all was right with the world.

I hadn't seen the inside of Tiger Burger, but Mom had been there a few times since we came back to Beulah. She pronounced it the only place in town that was still exactly the same as when she was a kid. It was fifties themed and had on its walls all the articles about the big Beulah sports victories over the years. A place where the cool kids like to hang out, she said, but I sensed some doubt in there.

Tommy's friends, the ones who'd been driving her around, who helped her get the job, Cal and Jerry? Well, they came in a few nights ago to help her plan how she's going to do up the basement—and to introduce themselves to Mom. I didn't think there was a snowball's chance they could possibly be the cool kids. I sat down in the basement while they looked over the space. They graduated a year or two ago, it sounded like, just a really bland looking guy with already a bit of a beer gut and a sharp-featured girl with pink-streaked hair and too much makeup. I couldn't remember which one was Cal and which one Jerry.

They were real friends, though. Already. They were perfectly nice to me, but when I felt too much like an extra wheel and came back upstairs, that was when they all started talking more loudly and teasing each other. There was a squeak of shoes, and I thought they were probably doing some kind of sports thing, throwing around a ball or whatever.

"So, a job?" Mom said. She looked so hopeful, I wanted to say I'd find a friend too, someone dull and sweet and normal. She'd like hearing that, maybe even better than a job.

I said I was thinking of being a house painter. "I could apprentice with someone like Marcus, and then I wouldn't need to go back to school after all. I know that's a long shot, the painting, but if there are no opportunities for that, I'm sure I could be some kind of a house cleaner or motel maid," I said.

The light in her eyes was fading. She'd forgotten to drop the smile, but she'd do that soon.

"You have to finish school," she said.

"I could babysit," I said.

"Not here. This place is too dangerous, power tools and nails and—"

"At their houses," I said.

The smile was gone now. There was something I was not getting. Mom sucked in her cheeks and looked down at the book still open in her lap. She closed it and groaned as she crawled out of the nest and moved off without looking at me. I'd upset her again and was not sure how.

Maybe she thought I shouldn't be trusted in other people's homes.

I thought of how she'd said that Tommy's new uniform was hot, and I realized the dynamic going on between her and Ellen. Like when you move someplace where people have an accent, you start to have the accent too, on purpose at first and then it becomes a part of you. Only it was the opposite. She'd been speaking in a way Ellen *didn't*, in a way Ellen only wished she could. All part of being the cool friend.

Maybe that was why I needed to stay in school, too, for the sake of Mom's image. She wouldn't want to seem too out there. Immediately I felt sorry for thinking that. Mom just wanted me to have a healthy life.

When Stevie woke, her face was all creased. I tried to hug her, but she said she had to pee. She came back after a while and snuggled down in the covers.

I said, "It's six thirty or so, I think. We might as well get up. Lots to do."

"I know. I want to get so much done today," she said half into the pillow. In a minute we were up and moving.

I was always glad how normal and happy Stevie turned out. Helping to raise her was maybe the best thing I'd ever done. If I always thought about what would be best for her before making decisions, I'd do the right thing every time. For now it was half and half, but I was trying to get better.

When we brushed our teeth together a little later, staring into the big mirror, I thought about how good it would be for Stevie if I were a little more normal, if I had friends. Maybe not a real job just yet—no, that wouldn't be good for her because it would take me away from her. She needed stability, needed someone to stay and care—but I thought I should have friends, activities, maybe a part-time job so I'd have a little money to buy her something now and then.

I *wanted* friends, too. I missed Betty. I wished I could call her, but Mom and Tommy didn't like to let me use their phones. I couldn't have a new one until I got a job, which was another reason to go out and try.

It came to me that there was but one way to make some acquaintances in this new place, and call Betty, *and* get some exercise. Maybe even look for something part-time.

I had to leave the house.

I spat and rinsed. "That's what I'll do today," I said. "Walk to town."

Stevie bent down to rinse, and it seemed that the door opened behind us to reveal a rush of children headed out the front doors. The thing was, when Stevie lifted her head, I could have sworn that she saw it too. Her eyes went wide, but then she had her face down in a washrag, and I couldn't say for sure what I'd seen.

#

And so, after chores and lunch, dinner and more chores, after a bath, I finally combed out my hair and put on lip gloss. I dressed in black shorts with the least faded of my black tank tops, and I set off to find a payphone. Walking so close along the highway, I could feel the cars and trucks whipping past.

In July, it was clear everything around here would go back to desert if people would only stop watering all the time. It was hot, the weeds along the highway already dry, wildflowers closing and shriveling. It was a dry heat with a little lift to it, though, easy on a walker.

This was the summer before my second senior year, maybe the last summer I'd ever be free to sleep and wake and move as I wished. I felt the weight of the years to come. Just working, working, striving toward something I supposed, though I couldn't imagine it. I'd never strived and couldn't imagine beginning to do so. Should've started striving a few years back if I'd wanted to go to college, after all. That's the last anyone said about that.

But even this, even walking into town. An eighteen-year-old in a town like this one doesn't walk into town. They drive in a nice car courtesy of their loving parents, or failing that take their shit car to work, or failing that, they get in the back of a friend's car. Something. Only the lowest of the low would walk this highway, which I knew for sure as soon as a truck sped by with some boy hanging out of the passenger side hooting back at me. A tiny red car passed a little later, slowing. The big goofy guy inside it waved. Otherwise, it was like no one saw me, and I saw no one walking until I came into town.

I couldn't tell how late it was. There were too many clouds.

Streaker's was big and already well-lit, but I didn't see a phone outside. I took a right and kept walking down the main drag another few blocks. I thought I was approaching the downtown because there were a few pedestrians now. Some trudged, others strutted. No one was out for a stroll in this heat, only people walking because they needed to get somewhere. The first payphone I saw was in front of a Circle-K.

I dialed Betty's number and got nothing, not even a message. I called her mom's landline and listened as it rang and rang. No one answered, and I wanted to cry.

Instead of crying, I pretended that Betty had answered and took up a conversation with her. I told her all about the house and how manic and strange Mom was, about sleeping in a nest with my sisters, the canyon and all the unfamiliar weeds and the heat. My eyes welled over, and I knew how whiny my voice sounded to people passing by on their way into the store. I tried not to look at them, looked instead at the little car lot across the street.

For a moment, green and teal eighties sedans were overlaid on the white and red hatchbacks that were really there in the lot. I remembered Mom saying how she'd stalked that car lot the year they left Beulah. You could get your license at fourteen back then, and she'd longed for one of those ice-green Berettas with the fancy pinstriping.

I blinked a few times, and the image faded.

I hung up and went in to buy an icy Coke. A big goofy guy with long brown hair perched on a tall stool at the register. I looked back and saw the little red car parked in the dirt lot past the pumps. I smiled.

75

"Saw you walking," he said.

I paid for my Coke and was about to turn when he gestured west and said, "You the ones that moved out on Farm School Road?" When I nodded, he said, "Take Eighth, you'll get home just as fast."

"No creepers cruising on Eighth?" I said.

He leaned a little forward, asking, "What's your name?"

I really was heading for the door now.

"My name's Foster," he called. "See you tomorrow."

I did take Eighth. With the sun starting to set, I was glad not to be on the highway. Many sweet little clapboard houses stood behind the Circle K, then fewer larger houses, then pastures with a couple of horses or cows in each one, goats. One even had a pair of llamas. A strange power station or something sat all by itself in a graveled lot surrounded by empty lots of yellow grass with flecks of trash all around. The black line of the canyon was visible all the time I walked with the sun setting above it all beautiful. A sharper breeze came up. Eighth turned to gravel, and in another half mile I took the right onto Farm School Road.

I was walking along our side of Farm School Road, the sun setting to my left, the roof of the schoolhouse up ahead, walking past a big sprawling farm with many fences and outbuildings all painted red and its big fine white plantation-style house looking out of place, set far back behind drooping trees. The whole road seemed like a haunted place even though there were no shadows in sight.

I had the idea that in walking Eighth, I'd walked back in time. Of course it would feel a little bit that way since all these farmhouses had stood so long. *It's not so strange*, I told myself even as the nauseated, hollowed-out feeling was already coming over me. I had never been this direction except for once in the truck with Mom, and then

I was not paying attention, but I figured there were only two or three more farmhouses to pass before the schoolhouse. *Almost home.* That was the last thought I had before the light shifted.

Or the day shifted, I should say.

It was no longer a hot cloudy evening with a breezy edge. It was bright and cold, the drooping trees all but bare and the ground littered with tiny brown leaves. I kept walking past a farm with a brown farmhouse and another with a yellow house, and now I saw the schoolhouse. The sunset light was all around behind me and to the sides, but up ahead it was a different time of year and much earlier in the day, too. It was bright enough to be noon, or three.

Three. Not recess but the end of the school day. A few children still lingered in the yard in front of the schoolhouse, big and little boys in gray pants and girls in dresses enjoying a moment of play before their long journeys home. The tall tree at the corner of the property had shed its leaves. A picnic table stood under it now, and at the back corner of the table sat a man in deep shadow. I saw no more than the outline of him. I'd already edged away, nearly crossed to the other side of the road. I walked quickly, not looking at him.

The truck was not in the driveway. Mom had gone out and maybe taken the girls, too. I wanted to keep walking and pretend I didn't live there, but where would I go? Not the highway again. I could turn around, run back down Eighth in the growing dark. I didn't want to flee like that, though. I wanted to stay calm.

The children did not seem to see me, but the man was different. I feared that the light had shifted again and the sun caught his face. I couldn't look, but I caught him mumble to himself, "That's disgusting." He meant me.

Two boys began walking away. *See you tomorrow.* I almost saw through them as they passed across the driveway. They did not last more than a step or two onto

77

the road before fading. Three girls and a little boy still stood talking in the cold bright day, their faces so sharp I wanted to watch them. I slowed.

The man shouted, "Put some clothes on!" His voice was awful to me, so loud and bellowing, but I couldn't turn toward him. In the corner of my eye, he seemed to be rising.

In just the black tank top and shorts, I was very cold now, and yes, his saying that made me feel there was something wrong about what I wore. It made me feel like I ought to be in one of those old-fashioned dresses like all the other girls. This even though I knew he wasn't there. None of them were. My heart pounded, still.

I kept walking, eyes straight forward, past him, past the children. I moved like I was going to pass the school, but at the last minute I veered to the left, crossed the road, and barreled up the steps.

The door was unlocked, and it was over. He didn't rush to me, touch me. Of course not; he couldn't do that. I rushed around to the left-hand classroom with the nest in it and looked out the front windows. The children still stood, but only for a second and then they rose away on the breeze, all of them, the man too. Their sunlight and their bright dry grass went with them, all of it, just like colored clouds of chalk dust.

The crooked tree had its leaves again, and the sunset light was uninterrupted. It was over.

I sat on the floor, legs out in front of me. I breathed deeply, told myself all was well.

I told myself that the change of day hadn't scared me, that it only surprised me and that in my surprise I behaved as someone who was afraid would behave, but it wasn't quite the same as actually being afraid.

Or if I had been a little afraid, it was understandable. It certainly isn't a thing you ever get used to seeing, time folding over and the dead doing their thing in what seems to be your space.

They almost never talk to you, though. That was the man from the basement. I had no doubt about that. I hadn't realized that he could go anywhere besides the basement.

I was calming down, skin warming. My muscles ticked after the long walk and all the adrenaline.

No one else was in the house, and the shadows inside took their opportunity to brighten. Beyond my room a flood of children rushed out toward recess or summer—yes, it seemed their excitement could only be for summer. So many of them, decades and decades of them, a blur. From the windows I watched them stream out towards the street and drift away, steam on the wind. It was getting darker now.

The shadow in the basement grunted loudly. He was working, fixing something. I wanted to get away from here. I wanted to cry.

I thought of Stevie, and I didn't cry. I didn't pack a bag and get on the highway for real.

I put away dishes, put a load in the dryer. I cleaned up the table because I knew that Mom and Stevie could have gone nowhere but to Tiger Burger to order a late dinner from Tommy while she worked her very first shift.

Sure enough, here Mom and Stevie came with too many sacks, with too many tall foam cups. Here they were saying how they'd hoped to see me in town and pick me up while they were out.

We ate the oily Tiger Burgers and the oversalted, overdone fries. We talked about how Tommy looked in her uniform, how mature she sounded. Tommy was about to get off while Mom was there, but she and Cal and Jerry were going to another friend's after work, so she didn't need a ride.

I remembered the Circle-K and Foster just then, so we talked about how I too might have found a friend.

#

A week later, or something like it, and we were friends. I happened to catch him on his way out to the car after work, and I asked—because I couldn't bear to ask Mom or Tommy, I asked if he would let me log in on his phone for a minute to pull up Betty's pages. One was entirely gone, and the other two hadn't been updated in weeks.

I thanked him, and he offered a ride home.

I was going to wander around town longer, so I'd take a raincheck.

Well, he could take me where I wanted to go—or no? I wanted exercise? He could wander with me, then.

No, no, I told him, he must be tired from work; he should get home. I smiled and turned away before he could say more.

2

The Fourth-of-July parade is apparently the biggest thing that happens in Beulah. It isn't just a parade but is a whole week-long festival called Cobbler Days. The park fills with crafter's booths and food trucks. There's a cobbler contest, and the bars get lively, motorcycles lining the streets. Beulah people don't plan trips during that week, and a lot of the people who've moved away come back for a visit.

The whole thing starts with the parade. Just about every person any of us had met was there, and there were so many others besides. People were all done up. The older men wore pastel button-down shirts and the younger ones wore their nicest jeans and T-shirts. All the pretty girls wore makeup and had their hair and nails done so that, even though they wore skimpy little summer things, it still felt like church or like the first day of school.

Some eyes went to the parade, especially when the horses and the town beauties went by in princess dresses, but a lot of folks—and I was one of them—looked away from the floats toward the people lining Main.

It was a more diverse crowd than I was expecting—lots of farmers and banker-types but also lots of people with tattoos and colorful hair, lots of white people as you might expect in a little town in Idaho, but there were quite a few people of color and quite a few international people too, as I gathered from accents I heard. I took it to mean that people were actually choosing to move to Beulah from other places, which seemed like a very fine thing indeed.

Mom had laid out a new outfit for me that morning: a jean skirt, red leather sandals, and a close-fitting black T-shirt with the American flag done in rhinestones, which reminded me of a T-shirt I'd lost that had the Welcome to Las Vegas sign on it. I teared up a little and gave her a hug.

Mom and the girls had new outfits too. We all looked so nice walking down Main, saying hi to everyone we knew.

Mom was getting some second looks for having such a good healthy-looking family, and it was clear from the way people greeted us that Mom was fitting in well. Tommy said hi to several people she'd met at work, though Cal and Jerry were nowhere to be seen. I didn't see Foster anywhere, either.

And then, without any warning, we bumped into Ellen standing with her husband and her dad, and we went right up and shook hands with them. It was our first time meeting.

The dad and the husband looked almost the same, both tall and rich-looking in their pastel shirts. The dad was in a little better shape than the husband, who had good legs but a pregnant-looking gut. Still, you could tell he was a big sweetie right away. He turned when Ellen put her arm up on his shoulder; his face took on a look of surprise and delight when he saw us. Ellen let us know his name was Rodney, which honestly I didn't know if I knew. He knew who we were before Ellen said, though. He said he'd been genuinely sorry to have missed meeting us before this, and he invited us to a barbecue the next day.

The dad stood back, and you could see he didn't feel the same, but that was all right. The dad was well known to be an asshole.

Mom glowed. In the back of her mind, she'd been worrying all this time about what the husband thought of her, and now it seemed she'd worried for nothing. She was accepted or just about to be accepted.

People sometimes think of families like mine as dys— well, disordered, but there are times when we seem different in a good way. We did that day—close enough for comfort and yet not quite like all the other boring people everyone already knew. Maybe they wanted to know us.

Mom stayed with Ellen, but we girls walked on after a few minutes. I held tight to Stevie's hand and smiled at everyone. Tommy was looking for Cal and Jerry, but I had no particular goal except to walk.

The crowd began to change. I would catch the light scent of cigarette smoke, and then the smoke would come strong and the people would look different for a moment. Mustaches, long shag haircuts and mullets on the men. On the women, a disturbing variety of prints and eye-makeup and tight oily perms, on and on like that. Something sexy about it all. Tight jeans, musky sweat, plumage. It was dizzying, but still I could blink it back and set it out of mind. It was just the charge of the parade bringing back little echoes of past parades, I knew. It wasn't anything.

A young Mom and Ellen walked close together in front of us for a moment. I knew them from the back of their heads, their stances, the white-and-acid-washed striped outfit that Mom wore familiar from an old Polaroid.

And then Ellen's boys snubbed us. I didn't register what happened until Tommy brought it up later, but we were walking a tight strip of sidewalk between people going the other direction, weaving around people who had stopped, and we came upon Jasper and Adrian with two other boys walking the other direction. Jasper raised his chin just slightly and said, "Howyadoin" all in one word, but they didn't stop. They didn't even think about introducing us to their friends.

Tommy was really upset later. I hadn't it myself, but when she explained, I saw why it had bothered her. I'd been concentrating on blinking back from the visions of historical Beulah and trying not to lose hold of Stevie is why I hadn't seen.

When she told me, I said, "It must be some finer social distinction the kids clue in on that the adults don't quite see."

83

"Jesus, can you just not say things like that?" Tommy said.

"You don't think they're going to like us here?" said Stevie, and we both felt so bad for talking in front of her.

And then at the barbecue the next day, it was even clearer. The adults were nice enough except that Ellen's dad hung back from greeting us. Her mom wasn't there. We still hadn't met Ellen's mom, who had some trouble with her hips or knees or something and did not come out of her pretty pink house. Ellen's husband, soon as we got there, said the kids were all down in the basement and that we ought to go. We didn't go until he encouraged us to a couple more times.

The boys and a couple of friends and a couple of younger cousins sprawled across a big sectional in the air-conditioned family room playing a video game, and when we came down, well, they didn't exactly greet us warmly. Adrian said our names and that we were the ones living in the old farm school, and nobody much reacted.

Tommy and Stevie went back upstairs after a few minutes, but I took a seat. I've never minded watching people play video games.

One of the younger kids turned to me. "That place really haunted?" she said.

"Shut up, Stacey," said Jasper, and to me he said, "She doesn't know what she's talking about."

"Yes, it is," I said, but I'm not sure anyone heard, or maybe I said it too late for anyone to make the connection to what Stacey had said. We were all following the fighters on the screen, cringing and flinching against the blows.

I wasn't so happy later, learning what they talked about upstairs. Stevie and Tommy had gone to sit by Mom, who was talking with Ellen and a couple of Ellen's friends, and one of these well-groomed ladies kept going on about how great the dance classes were and how her daughter got really confident and *in great shape*. Tommy said she put a lot of emphasis on that so it was clear she was making a point about Stevie.

3

The rest of July offered more painting and renovation, long walks on the highway, struggles to keep the grass watered and the weeds down, and blackberries. The bushes on the fence kept putting on more of the thumb-size berries. I loved them from the time they were firm and tart to the time they'd gone soft and dull. I picked them for Stevie to make pies from and ate the whole time I picked. We had them on ice cream, on pancakes, on sponge cake from the Albertsons bakery. Finally we got a pack of freezer bags and sent the last of the berries with Ellen to save in her stand freezer. Maybe we'd get some of them back later, maybe not.

Pushing myself to be more human, I made it to Circle-K a couple of times to see Foster and dipped into a couple of the other places familiar from dreams.

I visited the blue gas station, which I learned was called Corner Mart though there was no sign that I could see. Immediately as I closed in on it I got a strong sense of déjà vu—the feeling a mix of gratitude and freedom, like I was so happy I'd been allowed to walk that far all on my own. This was some echo of the feeling Mom had when she went there as a kid, I was sure.

Inside it was just a normal mom-and-pop store, kind of run-down and smelling of bleach. In a forgotten back corner, a pitiful collection of Idaho souvenirs lay arrayed in dust. I picked up an "Easy Rider" thick-bottomed mug printed with the name of the state and a stylized blue mountain, but then I spotted a black T-shirt hung on a rack not far away. I needed another black T-shirt. I moved that way, lifted it. It was an XXL, but I had to have it. Screen-printed on the front were the words "London, Paris, Rome, Beulah." I didn't recognize the silhouetted images next to London and Rome, but next to Paris was the Eiffel Tower and next to Beulah was a potato.

My last ten dollars were gone on that fabulous shirt, but I kept going places. Another day, I walked the downtown blocks. I moved past Queenie's Gifts, the Beulah Fitness, the Coffee Connection, a hairdresser, a bank, a nice-looking café and a really gross café, a bar closed up for the day, a barber. It wasn't that these places didn't call to me; they did, but the feeling wasn't strong.

At Beulah Fitness, I paused and looked above the sign to an older sign like a mural above it. Watkin's Furniture in old-timey script, cornflower blue on a dark ink blue. The paint was chalky, flaking, ancient. It must have been left there for historical reasons, but what I thought was how that sign had slits cut into it, behind that sign was a window where you could stand and look down on the street through the slits. You could turn away from that window and run through the upstairs. Sofas and cabinets filled the space, but there were aisles between them where you could run. You and your friend could run the length and back, take a hard left and keep running and laughing down the ramp—a ramp and not stairs because that's how they got furniture up to the upstairs before elevators came to little towns like Beulah.

Had the elevators *ever* come? I couldn't say. I hadn't seen one yet.

Feelings like Watkins brought were not strong—and they were fleeting—but they reinforced this idea I had that I was living out or had already lived my Mom's memories. It was a little spooky around the edges but mostly a warm, welcoming feeling.

Nothing called to me strongly downtown until I came to a place called Rhoda's. It wasn't immediately clear what kind of store it was. The front was spiffier than anything in Beulah except maybe Coffee Connection, with just a green lozenge shape in the front window and the "Rhoda's" in white cursive. I thought maybe it was another café, and I crossed the street, but as I came closer, I saw mannequins. Mannequins aren't actually my favorite thing, and I thought to turn, but something came to me. The memory of soft, deep mint green carpet. I was sure that the store would have mint green carpet. I came close and looked in, but the floor was a hard industrial gray. Bells tinkled as I opened the door.

"Well hello! Can I help you?" the lady rearranging clothes said, and immediately I knew her—the overdone smile, the plump face. I had been here before. Not just Mom but me.

The lady was... solicitous, moving to rearrange things wherever I happened to roam. I wasn't used to being mistrusted and wondered whether it was my messenger bag or my outfit or both that made me untrustworthy. I browsed the fussy ladies' clothes with their high prices and brands I didn't recognize. I browsed the children's section, and then I saw: Under the stairs was a cubby or a corral for children. It had a plastic picket fence on the opening and the inside, floor and walls and the underside of the stairs and all were still carpeted in mint green. A plastic spinning top with little plastic carousel horses inside, soft dolls, a stack of thick-paged picture books, and other toys lay arranged on the floor. I had played here as a baby, played with that very top. Maybe Jasper and I had played together while Ellen tried to talk Mom into buying herself something nice for a change.

A bitter taste flooded my mouth. Sudden sweat and a high pulse. I rushed out. Because the memory was mine— it was—but the sweeping sense of nostalgia was Mom's. For that moment I was her looking back on that more hopeful time, seeing the innocent me and the somehow ruined me caught in the gaze of that shop owner. A web of gazes past and present penning me in, trapping me.

I wanted that spinning top so bad. I wished the old lady could have been more oblivious or I more daring, but it wasn't to be. I still intended to see inside every store in

Beulah. I wanted to get out to the little cabin on the highway one of these days, too.

#

One day, the girls stayed home and I went for groceries with Mom. Unlike the other places I'd been going in Beulah, the big, modern Albertsons recalled no dreams. It didn't even feel like part of Beulah but part of some anonymous new anywhere world. We got what we needed no trouble because everything was just where it was supposed to be.

When we'd loaded up the backseat and gotten in the truck, I asked, "What about the other grocery store?" That was where I thought we'd been headed, which was why I'd agreed to come.

"I don't know what you mean," said Mom.

"The one with the ice cream cones," I said, and she gasped. She remembered. It was a place she'd mentioned in stories once or twice, a tiny dark place with rows of bulk bins and a soft-serve machine in the deli.

Looking around as if to spot it, she said, "My mom and I used to walk the groceries home in the cart—God, my dad was such an asshole. I'm so glad you never met him."

I supposed his being an asshole was the reason they walked the cart home but couldn't quite remember or guess the connection. Did he leave them stranded there? No, it was that he wouldn't let the mom drive. She was a drinker or had an accident, or both? He was afraid for their insurance rates.

Mom squinted like she was thinking really hard. "I would take the cart all the way back by myself while Mom put away groceries. It felt like a long walk, but it must have been close to where we lived."

"Have you gone back to see your old house yet?" I asked.

"I don't know that I can find it, but let's try," she said, and we set off just as though we didn't have any ice cream melting in the backseat.

It had been a rental house, small and not very nice. As we drove, she told me again how her parents were old, how they'd always had dogs before having her and so always treated her like a dog—not that they beat her or tied her out in the yard—ha ha—but they just expected her to be cute and obedient, and when she wouldn't be that anymore they lost interest.

Ellen's parents were old, too, and maybe at first that was how they'd gotten to be friends, but then Ellen's folks saw how "off" Mom's folks were and the friendship faded. Luckily, Ellen and Mom stayed close through everything. She talked on. I had heard it all before, but it felt good to hear it all again.

We couldn't find the house on the first try. Mom parked on the street just down from Ellen's parents' pink house to think. The shaded street was cool and lovely, but the reason for parking here was to look at the house again.

I watched her gaze at it until she remembered our goal. "We would walk from here in a kind of a zigzag," she said, zigzagging her hand to the right. "This direction?"

"You said there was a smaller park by your house," I said.

"And we'd walk past the little park when we came from the grocery store."

"What was the name of the store? Just look on your phone," I said, and she chuckled over how stupid she was not to think of it. She didn't remember the name, but the search for grocery stores in Beulah brought up only the Albertsons off Main and a little health food place downtown. We did find the small park on the map and drove around it looking for the rental house, but it was just one of the little white ones, and it didn't really matter.

Edie's grocery shimmered above an empty lot for a second while we were searching. Mom made no sign she saw, but after that she turned back toward Main, toward home. I knew we wouldn't tell the girls about the detour. Sometimes it felt nice to have an experience with just me and Mom.

Driving back, we didn't talk much, but still it made me think of how we used to talk when we'd go somewhere just the two of us. How I would chatter about nothing—people at school or novels I'd read—just babbling. She said I always babbled so in my crib.

What happened to you? What happened to us?

"It's just like soft-serve," Mom said when she dished up our melted ice cream, and I knew she was thinking of the old grocery store again.

4

But it's Tommy I want to talk about now, can't put it off.

There's a shallowness to Tommy, almost like all her thoughts have already been pre-programmed, like she moves back and forth along the same tracks. Oh, I say that, and then I feel like it's not quite fair.

Most people suffer from terribly repetitive thinking, and I won't claim to be an exception. I repeat myself mentally, I obsess—all of us do it from time to time. The problem is when you can never break out of it. You can't grow.

I'm one of those people who break out of it once in a while. Tommy isn't.

Maybe it isn't a problem at all. Any way you look at it, Tommy's going to live more of a normal life than I am. She's going to set goals and work toward them, and when she achieves them, she is going to vibrate with pride. Levitate with pride. She'll keep her body healthy, though probably she'll never sleep enough. She'll have some sort of a family and keep them moving all the time, make sure they're stuffed with positive values and nutrients and all that.

Kind of like one of those dogs that is born to manage herd animals? No, that's too mean. She's just a really functional human being is all I mean to say.

She resents me, sure. She's the one who always does the right thing, and she reaps certain rewards from that. Mom and Stevie trust her in a way they'll never trust me. Ellen thinks a lot of her, her boss at Tiger Burger—people like that.

When we all get back to school, the teachers will acknowledge her good behavior, but she won't register with them much beyond that. They'll have trouble remembering her name. Not like me.

You might think, too, that a girl who looks like Tommy would never get messed with in school, but real life isn't like the rom-com teen movies. She gets it all the time for different reasons, in different ways. Always coming in as a new girl, after all.

So one of the tracks her mind runs along is how no one appreciates her the way she deserves and how they don't ever love her.

Friends like Cal and Jerry pretend to love her because they've already realized what she's only starting to see: she'll be wanting to trade up soon. The new-to-her kids who've been coming around Tiger Burger more often now that summer's ending, the kids who've been off on vacation and are only now trickling back into Beulah? She wants them so bad now, can't keep herself from thinking about all the things they have that she doesn't have. She wants them, wants to be them, wants to know what went wrong for her.

I've been to the Tiger Burger and watched her at work a time or two. Tommy's eyes moved from the person she was helping at the counter to the people she wanted, some rich-looking teenagers seated in the corner. Ellen's boys would know them, no doubt. They noticed her watching and didn't watch her back, but her eyes went back to them over and over while she rang people up.

Or, one girl watched her back. I imagined that this girl was a real Beulah High cheerleader and thought it was a little funny how the waitresses here wore what amounted to knockoff Wild Cats uniforms. She had that look of someone watching someone else struggle to be like them.

Tommy was thinking about them all the time, straining over how to make an impression on them. Her mind always runs from her short-term plans to her long-term plans. How these kids might be an end in themselves or a means to some other end. Those same tracks, back and forth. Her mind whirrs and her body makes its own repetitive motions all day, and all I can think is how exhausting all of that is.

She resents me. Every time thinks how much she does for how little, she thinks how little I get away with doing. How I've always taken my tests cold and ignored my homework, how I've let other people do my chores, how I've slept in past her and gone to bed earlier just about every day of our lives, how I've fucked up in ways it gives her the cold sweats just to think about. She'd sooner die than be me, and yet how far ahead is she really? Any little thing I get, she thinks it ought to be hers.

That's what she thinks of me. If she were honest with herself, she'd say that she hates me, but Tommy has never been honest with herself. Ask her about me, and she'll voice her concerns. She'll talk about how smart I've always been and how she hates to see it wasted. She'll bring up memories of how sweet I was as a little girl, how I was always hugging and kissing her, how I was always on her side whenever she wanted something from Mom or when she had a problem with somebody in school.

I'd tell you about those times, too. I'd also tell you how Tommy used to see a little something, back in the day—never a tenth of what I saw, nothing we could speak of—but she saw more than flickers. I could have sworn she saw the little shadow boy across the creek that time at school. She never would admit it, after.

I'd tell you about seeing her struggle. Every day, her devotion to herself and her future. The running, the sports, the friends who never loved her and the others who were cruel and still others that she was cruel to because she couldn't bear to think she was on their level.

I love her. I wish every day that we could go back to who we used to be.

I love Tommy more than I've ever loved anyone but Stevie. Thinking of her makes me feel a little less bad about everything I am and everything I've done. She's like another me who never was damaged.

Or no, I'm sure she was damaged but in some finer, subtler way.

#

Tensions between Tommy and me built up over the summer, but nothing was stated outright until one Sunday long after the parade and Cobbler Days and all.

Stevie and I were working on the lawn in our bathing suits and shorts when Foster and a friend happened to be driving by. The little red car pulled close to the weeds at the edge of our lawn, and Foster leaned over the friend.

"Hey Georgie," Foster said, "Is that your mom?" He thought he was being cute with Stevie, but she looked scared. She came closer to me.

"My baby sister Stevie. This is Foster," I said.

"I know. Mom sends me in the store sometimes," she said.

Foster said, "Yeah, we're old friends. And this is Matt."

Matt was the most regular of regular-looking guys, neither tall nor short, thin nor muscular, light nor dark. If pressed you might think of him as the guy with thick eyebrows, though if you placed him next to a person who actually had thick eyebrows, you'd notice right away that his were only medium-thick.

Foster and I had been hanging out a little bit here and there, mostly just me visiting in the Circle-K. Because I hadn't outright refused, he brought a DVD over one night, not realizing we didn't have a television. Tommy brought her laptop upstairs so we could watch it with everybody, which was awkward. Some kind of cartoon epic I couldn't stay awake for.

Anyway, the boys could only stay an hour now because they had a barbecue to get to.

It was almost two, but Mom was still gone to brunch with Ellen and her husband. The look on Tommy's face when the four of us came in—well, I wish I had a painting of her. She's a treasure.

Stevie and I showed off the main room and the back patio to the boys. I got the sense they might have been among the kids who visited here and left the little bits of graffiti, but they didn't say. Tommy closed all the bedroom doors as we moved around, which struck me as rude, so I threw her a look.

It felt cool in the house, so I put on a long sweatshirt from the coatrack and before setting up the boys with pink plastic tumblers of ice water and a bag of pretzels. Stevie was off to change and probably comb her hair, but I told the boys I felt fine visiting with them as I was if they don't mind, which drew another look from Tommy. She was as sweaty as I was in a tank top and long running shorts, but she stayed in the kitchen too. She'd been pulling weeds out back because she was the only one whose thighs could stand it.

"Keeping up a lot of lawn here," said Foster. "Looks like a pain."

"It's a good piece of land. Probably going to raze it and put up some townhouses or something," said Matt.

"Matt's from Boise," says Foster. "He thinks things are worth a whole lot more than they are."

"This is *Beulah*," Matt whined, and they cracked up.

"It's just something a friend of ours used to say," said Foster, waving it off. I noticed again that he had one of the most sincerely pleasant smiles I'd ever seen.

I was leaned against the fridge, and I must have been smiling back because Tommy took my picture with the flash on.

"Thanks," I said, rubbing my eyes.

"You *will* thank me," she said and with that, excused herself to go back out past the patio and get those weeds done.

"Anyway, *Ellen's* the one doing it," said Foster.

"Oh, I know her. She'll do a good job," said Matt. I sat at the table with them, and Matt told us how he didn't really live in Boise, but he worked there and went to school next door in Caldwell. His second year of college started in August. He seemed self-conscious about his short hair and kept touching it. My guess was he'd cut it off recently, maybe for the Fourth-of-July parade. I didn't recall seeing him there, but he must have been somewhere in the crowd.

Matt talked about how he was choosing a major and all about his classes and people he'd met at school and at work. He was quite the talker. I wondered if Tommy'd left because she thought he was cute.

I was more interested in talking to Foster, but Matt went on, and Foster didn't seem annoyed. Foster had missed his friend for the whole school year, and now he was just happy to have him here. Almost two more months of good times before he'd have to go back. Foster was happy I was here with them, too.

The mower came on just under the window, and Foster said, "Oh shit, you're in trouble now."

"Always," I said.

"Yeah, she's doing your work for you," said Matt, and I thought they must have big families too, so I broke in to ask about their brothers and sisters, and they droned on and on about their older siblings and Foster's little sister. They talked a long time, and Stevie came in partway through it. She'd had a shower and put on shorty pajamas. I pulled her to me for a side-hug.

Tommy came in again. "It's too hot for this."

"That's what I'm saying," I said.

She sat on the bench, just about panting.

"I'm sorry, sweetie," I said, and she rolled her eyes.

"I meant to ask you about your swimsuit," Foster said.

"About what size is that, anyway?" said Matt.

I said, "It's a sixteen-eighteen. I like how it drapes, don't you? My new favorite thing. It's a funny story, though. Remind me to tell you about it before you go."

"Shouldn't they *be* just about to go?" said Tommy, eyeing her phone.

"No, let me say before I forget. I wanted to ask you something, Matt," I said looking down at the turquoise vee of the swimsuit under my sweatshirt. It was Dad's sweatshirt, actually. We'd kept anything useful of his and used it over the years, and this was one of the very last things we still had. Everything else wore out long ago. It made me sad to notice this.

I said, "Are you glad you went to college?"

"It's not like I had a lot of choice. You just go," said Matt.

I said, "Because I don't know if I can. I mean even if I graduate."

"If you can't graduate, you'll take the GED test. *If* you can't graduate, which, honestly, how can you not graduate?" said Tommy.

"Haven't I always maintained at school?" I said. It was true, all except for last year. And maybe freshmen year. No, it wasn't true at all. I laughed at myself a little.

"She's so smart she gets bored in school," Stevie said. It was a good thing to say, not quite accurate but sweet. She'd heard Mom say it at some point.

"Everyone says I have to go, but I can't if it's hard. I just can't do anything hard anymore, and by hard I'm not talking about the reading or tests or whatever. I mean. . ." I wasn't sure what I meant, so I said, "Waking up on time. Doing things I don't want to."

"Motivation," Matt said, nodding. He was so earnest. "It's a problem for me, too. But I'll tell you, I'm doing a lot better now than I ever did in high school." He moved his head side to side like he was weighing things and says, "Yeah, I'm glad I went."

Foster was drooping a little, looking down. He tended to hunch, didn't he? It was the way he thought of himself manifesting in certain postures, like he was an actor making himself into a character. I hadn't looked over at him for a while, and he sat up slowly when I did.

"Now I said I'd tell that story Foster wanted to hear," I said. "About this extraordinary bathing suit."

Stevie made a little snort of a laugh like she knew what I was going to say.

"No, you haven't even heard all of it. Listen," I said. Stevie sat down on the fourth chair now. She'd been leaving it for Tommy, but Tommy had never moved off the bench. She'd cooled off and was massaging her legs.

"Are you ready?" I said.

They were.

#

I'm not going to argue the point with these two, but I will tell you, Matt and Foster, that I believe dreams are . . . important. Meaningful? They're not just the brain mashing up little bits of code you fed it all day. No, dreams are little flashes of insight into our desires and fears and blah, blah, blah. I mean, I don't know if it's just the psyche or if it's your actual soul, but there is a version or a piece of you that lives in dreams, OK? You have a kind of dream life whether you remember it or not.

People have all sorts of theories about dreams. I read about them for this report I was trying to do for school last year, but that's what the big disagreement is about: how meaningful they are. I happen to think they're meaningful. These sisters of mine are very literal-minded; maybe they're smarter than I am. Anyway, they don't agree with this, but you do, don't you?

Yes. Yes-no, not sure? Oh good, you both do, then? Good. This will make a lot more sense to you if you do.

Are you being honest? You really do? Good.

So, I've always had a rich dream life. I can't remember them all of the time anymore, but I still do sometimes, and when I was younger it was all the time. I had a few different recurring nightmares when I was a kid, and I've had just, well, a lot of recurring dreams my whole life, bad ones and good ones. It started out that they were about situations. Being in the passenger seat of a speeding car and no one's at the wheel is one. Another is about being lost in a maze. Going to school naked, basic dreams. You know that kind of stuff.

As I got older, it all started to change. It was complicated and not a quick process at all, so I won't tell you all about it. I see it is getting close to three. I'll just tell you that where the dreams started off being about situations, it changed to them being about places. There were certain places that I would come back to again and again, certain houses and roads, certain towns.

And one of them was this town, though I didn't know it at the time. Now I'm not claiming what you think I'm claiming. It's not magic or psychic ability, I don't think. It's just something in my brain putting together a lot of little pieces. I came here once when I was a baby—but not that young. I was toddling around by then. And then there were all of my Mom's stories about Beulah, and I'm sure I'd looked it up online once or twice over the years. I might have seen a map. Old photos.

Anyway, I'm getting anxious just talking about this. Excited? Scared? You see my arm? I get goosebumps like that when someone sings really well, too, so it's not a big deal, but it gives me a charge just to think about it.

It's OK, Stevie. It's just a story, OK? I want to tell it.

Seriously, I'm OK.

Anyway, I didn't know the name of the dream-town was Beulah, but I'd think of it as the town where I was free. I was allowed to go everywhere, and I spent so many nights just exploring the town. I would pass along its sidewalks—floating, you know, like you do in dreams. I would go into all of these different stores and houses. Into the schools. The dome school wasn't there in my dreams, but I'd go into the elementary and the junior high. There was a blue gas station at the edge of town, and there was a little park in the center and a big dark park with those painted lady houses around the edge of it.

You do live in one of those, don't you Matt? You said you were Ellen's folks' neighbor, but it didn't register until just now.

The blue one. Yes, I have been in that one before, in dreams.

No, I'm going to finish. Just let me finish this and, thanks Stevie. I am still thirsty. Thank you.

Anyway, the gas stations, parks, houses, and the downtown, and the highway. The falling-in cabin on the highway past the light. I lived in that cabin sometimes in dreams. I'd fall asleep there watching the lights from all the cars. Too many dreams to count. It was all wood-paneled inside, and the lights didn't work, but it was so cozy and it felt like a refuge.

There was another little house with a lot of ivy and creeper on the front of it and an old guy living inside. There was a big two-story party house. So many houses. I can't get into all of that. I don't have time.

Sometimes, though, I went into an odd little thrift store that was all on its own on a street that had nothing but apartment buildings and an old factory—I know now that it's the feed factory—on a street at the very back of town that I would always forget until I came upon it.

In dreams you always forget about a place until it's right in front of you and then you get this feeling of coming home. You're so surprised and delighted to see the place again. That's how I'd feel every time I came to Beulah in a dream and every time I came to some specific place like the gas station or this little hidden thrift store.

Anyway, it was a tiny two-story place more like something you'd see on the coast. It had been there a long time, but finding it was always a surprise. I'd browsed there many times in dreams. I don't remember buying anything, but when I found it in real life, I knew I had to buy something. It would be a souvenir. It would be something so lucky to have.

Roark's? Yes, I think that is the name. Thanks.

When I stepped inside, my arms were all goosebumped like they are now. The door was open, and a fan blew on wind-socks by the door. All these rainbows flapping around against paneled walls cluttered with framed art. The woman at the counter looked up to say hello, but she looked right back down. She was reading a book.

I felt so strange! Everything was so much more real than in my dreams. Once you get past the reach of the fan, that place is really smelly, as you must know. At least it is in the summertime. And when I climbed the narrow staircase, it felt like the wood must have been wet under the carpet. It sort of squished. The carpet was wine-colored and filthy. It all felt so familiar. I remembered dreams where these stairs had closed up on me, but I bravely made my way to the second floor anyway.

Because the ladies' clothes were on the second floor. Two racks of tops and dresses tight together, just as I'd perused in dreams. I lifted a botanical-print blouse and had this strange sense that it had once been mine and lost and that I'd found it here before in a dream. Déjà vu but really strong, you know? It was nothing I would ever wear, but I thought about getting it anyway. I'd come in meaning to buy something, and I had five dollars. The blouse was less than that.

I thought about it. I had its hanger in my hand, still, when I saw the swimsuit. I didn't own a swimsuit, and here was one. Not only that, but picture this: it was not hanging on a hanger. It was splayed across the clear plastic headless figure of a girl and hung on the wall like a work of art. It had two tags. The florescent green one had the price and the larger one, florescent orange? It had the words "New Item!"

This swimsuit had not been worn. I reached inside to see it had a brown-red lining and a strip of hygienic sticker-stuff on its crotch. My heart pounded, like it's pounding now. I seemed to hear the angels sing.

The price, though, that was something else. Ten dollars.
How do you think I got it, then?
I've never stolen anything in my life. That pisses me off a little, Tommy.
No? OK.
I took it off the plastic form and brought it back to the dressing room, which was a frightening little closet lined with printed tapestries like you see at New Age stores, with the grimmest, grimiest tapestry reserved for a curtain. It smelled worse than the rest of the store, like all the smell was coming from there. I felt trapped in there. I was so scared, but I put on the suit. I left my own stuff on, you know, underneath. I stepped out because the mirror was out there, and the desk lady just happened to have come upstairs to fold things.

Marielle, yes.

"Oh, that looks so nice on you," she said. It was draping off of me, as you see, but I agreed, so I bought it. And when I said I couldn't find my card, she took the five dollars. We made good friends.

That's it, and it's three 'til three. You do have to go.

#

Did I say all of that? I'm not sure. It felt that way, but it felt unlikely. It felt like another me had stepped in, so that I was not sure what parts I'd said and what parts I'd only thought.

As they were going out, I told them I was going to visit all of the Beulah places I'd dreamed of and take a souvenir from each of them, just like this beautiful bathing suit and my Beulah T-shirt from Corner Mart. I left the sweatshirt on the coat-hook on the way outside. The sun was terrible. We stood and laughed about my suit one more time before they drove away. I felt a little high from all the attention.

I felt . . . well, I felt that I'd just made a big stride toward being *normal*, making friends again, entertaining people and having something to offer them, getting out and away from my malaise. I had made this move toward being normal only I'd made it by being my own weird self. I guess I felt proud of myself.

It was a bit of a slap in the face when I went back inside and Tommy said, "I can't stand you when you're like that." She was at the sink doing an extra thorough job of washing the tumblers the boys had used.

After a while, I said, "You can't stand me anyway, so it doesn't matter." She didn't answer, and so I just stood there behind her.

"Why aren't we better friends?" I said.

"Why would we be friends?" she said.

"We're practically twins. Irish twins, isn't that what they say?"

"Yeah, but I don't like you," she said. She smiled back to show she was sort of kidding. "I mean, we just don't have all that much in common anymore, do we?"

I couldn't say much to that. Instead I moved up to her and hugged her from behind knowing how uncomfortable that would make her. Mom has a habit of doing this. When your hands are all soapy wet, you can't brush off the other person, at least in theory. I was surprised how small and hard Tommy's shoulders felt. I was and had always been pretty skinny, but Tommy gave the impression of being a little muscle man. When I held her, I noticed how small she really was.

"I love you," I said.

She turned her face and gave a serene smile I knew was meant as a parody of my own, and finally I stepped back.

"You didn't like my story? It was just a story," I said.

"You get in this place where you don't even sound like yourself. You don't sound like anyone I know." She stopped and then added, "All that babbling about premonitions is what bothers me the most. And it *wasn't* just a story. How would you come up with it on the spot like that if it was made up?"

"I didn't come up with it just like that. It's something I'm writing."

"Show me, then."

"You don't believe me?"

"Show me and I will."

I made like I was hurt and went to lie down. I thought about writing out the story to show her later, but who was I kidding? I was going to sleep and probably dream about some other place in Beulah. That was all I seemed to do, sleep and make an ass of myself.

The boys didn't think so, though. Everything I said, they smiled. I kind of wished I hadn't talked so much, but then again, I was drawing them to me in the only I way I knew. It's how you connect with people, isn't it? By being a little real with them—not all the way real, of course. Everything I'd told them was true, but the truth was so much more than what I told them. I closed my eyes, started to hold my breath and then caught myself. That wouldn't help, not at all.

I wanted but didn't want to go back into the gray depths of those racks of clothes in the thrift store. The softest hints of figures hovering around the items. Each so dim but so many of them, it was like being lost in a stormy sea. That entire place—Roark's—was so haunted it ought to be burned down. Almost nothing in there was nice. Just the swimsuit.

And Marielle, though nice wasn't quite the right word for her. She'd had a hard face but a sweet, lazy way of talking. Maybe she would be my next new friend.

I couldn't sleep. It felt like Tommy and I weren't done yet. I pushed myself off the bed.

"It's that time of summer, you feel like there's still a lot of summer left," I said when I came back into the kitchen. I guess I was trying one more time with her. I'll always try one more time.

"About a third of it's left," she said.

"Can I see that picture?" I said, and with her phone in hand, I asked, "Why'd you take this?"

"Because you looked so good. You reminded me a little of Mom today, old pictures of her anyway."

I searched her face and looked back down at the phone. She wasn't lying. In the full-length picture, the black sweatshirt receded so I was mostly just a smiling face and skinny tanned legs. The sweat made my hair wavy. It shone on my skin, showing off how smooth it was.

Tommy said, "You were so weird today. You were flirting with them, too. You don't know it, or . . . I don't think you know it."

"I was not," I said.

"Both of them at once. It was gross. You said you dreamed about that Matt kid's house. You said you were going there to get a souvenir, just as he was leaving."

"It was gross?"

"I don't know. I don't think they thought so."

She was a little jealous, wasn't she?

So yes, Tommy resents me. And if I were that kind of person, I would resent her too. My mind would cycle through the things she's done against me.

Like the moment just after our talk when I really was sleeping, when Mom came home. I didn't hear what Tommy said to Mom, but I felt it after in the cold, questioning look Mom gave me when she woke me up for dinner.

Oh, Tommy. You won't get anywhere that way.

AUGUST

1

Ellen's mom was jealous to learn that everyone else had seen us at the barbecue, and so the next day Tommy and Mom were both off from work, we all made our way up the steps of the storied pink house behind Ellen and her younger son Adrian. I knew, just as Ellen opened the door, that the inside would be Stevie's idea book brought to life, and it was.

There was the peacock wallpaper, over here a low velvet sectional, metallic tile on the fireplace, jewel-colored fake Persian rugs, a burbling fish tank full of spotted goldfish. Ferns in the corners and deep-carved dark woodwork, stained-glass lamps and a stained-glass accent window casting yellow light down the stairs just like in a dream I'd had.

All of it older, mustier, darker than in fantasy. The smell was pondlike.

I felt I was dreaming, caught Stevie's eye and knew we were in the same strange dream. Enthusiasm and apprehension crossed her face. Her eyes darted around.

All stuffy and glinting with crystal and polished wood, a nauseating hovering feeling. We were all asked to sit down. Stevie and I sunk into a brocade loveseat piled in pillows. The springs were shot and creaking.

Ellen moved toward the back of the house, calling "Momma?" Adrian followed.

Mom and Tommy and Stevie and I sat silent while a cooing, chiding conversation went on in a back room and the sink dripped loudly in the kitchen. I imagined climbing the mauve-carpeted stairs. Maybe we all imagined that.

I closed my eyes and in my mind I turned toward the stairs, looked up toward the landing window's rippling yellow-green. I stretched my legs, pressed back into the loveseat, opened my eyes and saw Stevie was crying beside me, silent ugly crying. I wondered if it was because the place so matched her fantasy, or had it disappointed her somehow? No more sounds came from the back room.

"Is that lady all right?" Stevie said.

"Oh sure, sure," said Mom, "Everything's fine," but her eyes searched around too, and I couldn't say what she thought or felt just then. She passed a box of Kleenex from an end table over to Stevie's lap.

Stevie dried her face before Ellen and Adrian escorted the old lady in on an old-fashioned wheelchair. She had good days and bad days, we'd heard. On a good day she would have made a point of walking into the room to greet company, and so we knew it was a very bad day indeed and we should not stay longer than to be fussed over and told we were pretty and to tell her how nice her house was. She was a good-looking old woman, her dove-gray hair and pale face like a diluted version of Ellen's but her personality stronger, vain and a little cruel but funny too. I'm sure someone complimented her on every single thing from the elements of the décor and her embroidered blouse to her exquisite, almost steampunk-looking earrings. It was clear she both loved and fully expected to hear these compliments.

We were out before we knew it with no tea and cake, no tour.

In the truck, we laughed over little things she'd said, like how she loved having girls in the house once more, how she'd always wished to have granddaughters. Remembering Cousin Stacey from the barbecue, I'd said, "Isn't Staccy—" and the old woman cackled and said "Stacey? *She* doesn't count" and hooted some more before launching to a story about how stupid the mail lady was, always losing things.

"Where was Ellen's dad, anyway?" said Stevie.

"Oh, they divorced like five years ago. He lives up past Ellen's somewhere," said Mom, and we laughed about how weird it was for people to get that old and then divorce. As we got on the highway, all of us were silent. How old was she? We didn't ask. And unwell. And no one in the family wanting or needing that house.

Ellen actively disliked the house now, though she'd been proud to live there as a girl.

What kind of prison will you make for yourself? I thought—or thought I thought. Maybe this time it was not my thought but Mom's and meant to be private. I turned to her, but her eyes stayed locked on the road.

2

Where did summer go? Mom wondered. She needed some kind of a little job. We had to have more cash, couldn't live on Ellen's castoffs for all time.

Where did the summer go? Ellen seemed to wonder when she visited, when she surveyed our progress. The place felt kind of like a home now, but there was still much left to do before it would be a desirable one.

Where did the summer go? Stevie seemed to say. She moved slowly and brought every conversation around to how we all thought it would be to start at a new school again.

I wondered about it too. I couldn't quite imagine having my hours regulated. It had been so long since I'd been made to wake at a certain time and then spend the rest of the day waking again and being moved from room to room. I was already so over being in school.

Tommy was the only one happy as summer drew to a close. On registration day, she eyed the orange lockers and brick walls inside the high school, the wide tiled halls with deep orange runners. The orange was for the Wild Cats, Beulah's sports program.

Tommy's eyes flashed around at everything. She was calculating, seeing what people are wearing, predicting what they might be wearing in September based on that, wondering how much of her meager earnings she'd have to part with to approximate a basic wardrobe and whether it was worth the bother. She was always really smart about that kind of thing. She wished to be relevant but never would go out on a limb for it.

It didn't matter as much for me. It was only one year, if we even made it through the year.

Tommy talked a long time with the lady at the registration desk, and we all lingered to look into the cases. Trophies and team photos, orange and black jerseys spread out at the back.

The high school was built inside two giant domes, newish and bland with few windows. No shadows, though. That was something.

The middle school made more of an impression on me. We wandered there by mistake, not realizing it was attached to the elementary by a long sloping corridor. The kids registering at the middle school were Stevie's height, and I dreaded taking her down the corridor to the elementary where she'd tower over everyone. We talked to the lady at the folding table about where to go, and as I turned away, I just about collided with a girl.

I realized right away that it wasn't a girl, just a shadow of one, but such an aggressive shadow, bright as any I'd ever seen. Robust, almost opaque. She moved with determination down the hall, sharp little nose in the air. Tiny girl, four-eight or four-nine, all well-defined muscle and big blonde hair. A gymnast, I'd say, a dancer.

I saw her again and again. In the middle school hall, in the elementary school halls where she was smaller but no less assertive, on the playground where she tossed her hair and posed, hip-cocked, saying something snarky to a person who wasn't there. The husky sound of her laughter stayed with me.

Her clothes changed with her ages, but I noticed one outfit, tight white crop jeans with zippers at the ankles and cut-out hearts above the zippers, long pink sweatshirt with cartoon cats done in puff-paint. If Mom had seen it, she might have laughed in recognition. It looked like the things she described all the cool kids wearing in the eighties.

Spumoni: the name came to me, the brand name of those sweatshirts. They were what all the preppy girls wore in fifth and sixth grade.

When Stevie and I visited the restroom, the girl was peering into the mirror. Her face was beautiful and expressive, chin darting toward people who weren't there beside her, other girls using the sinks. Her expression shifted from disdain to light surprise. She never saw me; she reacted instead to the things going on in her time, which I couldn't see just then.

I moved past her to the stall and tried not to give her any more attention. I didn't want to catch her eye and was grateful she was here and not at the high school where I would be doing time.

She owns this school, I thought, but I wasn't concerned. There were many things Stevie would need to worry about here, but this girl wasn't one of them.

#

All that was left was to finish this house, sell it, and make our percentage, whatever that would be. But we were weary, and it was so hot. Still no air conditioning, so we sprawled on Ellen's sofas with fans set at front and back to bring in the cooling evening air. For light, we had one ugly floor lamp and a matching table lamp that was also on the floor since we didn't have end tables. We had no television, so Mom and Tommy played with their phones. Stevie colored. I slid onto the floor and tried to read. It was too hot to sleep.

Stevie said she was going to have a cool bath. Tommy went downstairs. We thought she was going down there to get cooler, but she came back up in her uniform.

"Another shift?" Mom said.

"Hustle, hustle," said Tommy on her way out the door. We didn't get up to see if she was walking or riding with Cal. She'd have a car soon, anyway. Job, license, car, college, more jobs, more jobs.

I thought Mom was going to say something about me getting a job again, but she said instead, "I'm fucking exhausted, you?"

"I am," I said.

"I knew it would be a lot of work, but how am I supposed to get through this?" She went to the fridge and stood there a while, closed it. She turned back toward me.

"I don't know what to do. I really don't," she said, and she went toward the classroom she'd taken for a bedroom.

I followed. "We could just leave," I said, "if you're not happy here after all."

"Happy?" she said, like that was the furthest thing from her mind. She was looking at the ground and sucking in her cheeks, which was never good, but then she looked up at me and said, "I'm sorry, Jojo, I just need to get more sleep."

It had been so long since she called me Jojo, I almost didn't get that she was talking to me. Everyone was gone from the living room now. The shadows came through the hall, screaming out toward a different summer that was just beginning, and the man from the basement made a sound. Not a grunt this time; he creaked a stair.

He scared me. I hadn't sought him out, hadn't tried to know him, so I had only a guess about him. My sense was that he felt in charge of this place, which had been still for so long before us. Our being here made him anxious. He felt little hints of us from time to time and had to go searching for the disturbance.

We were haunting him, it seemed.

3

I dreamt of a mall overcrowded with dead. A lot of them smoked while they shopped. They were not much more than smoke themselves, just cloudy wanderers going past the defunct Macy's and hovering around the cell phone accessory kiosks and Dead Sea scrub kiosks they couldn't understand. It was all overheated and dusty like an old house. Another dream from Mom's past. I think it wasn't Boise but Nampa, where her parents used to take her because you could get school clothes cheaper there than in Boise.

I'd just gotten the dream written down when Mom opened my door. "You coming or not?" I had been noncommittal about the back-to-school shopping plans.

"I mean, I don't have any money," I said.

"I guess I could probably get you a few things," she said.

"Would it be all right if I didn't?"

I was torn, actually. I liked to be home alone, or I always thought I would like it until it happened. I'd want nothing more than for Mom and the girls to get in the truck and go, but then when they were gone, the longing for an empty house met the fear of an empty house. I wandered dark, quiet rooms feeling the time before me wasn't enough and that it was too much. I sat on Mom's bed, looked through her messy totes, but she didn't have anything.

It seemed like it would be another aimless day, but Ellen and Marcus surprised me by coming with more laminate flooring.

"You feeling better?" Ellen asked when I let them in.

I wasn't sure exactly what she referred to, but I said "*So* much better. I was just thinking about making nachos. Want some?"

"Actually, yes," said Ellen, with a little giggle. Nachos were an apparently a whimsical, unlikely thing. She and Marcus sat at the kitchen table and worked on some plans while I microwaved the cheese, and then we all ate together.

"What are you working on today, Marcus?" I said.

"Floors."

"But Mom's doing the floors," I said.

Ellen sighed and said, "It's taking so long, and Marcus has nothing on his schedule right now. He'll get this area done right away and then he can start the cabinets."

He took his plate to the sink, washed his hands, and set to work. Ellen just kept watching me for a while.

"How much better are you?"

"Honestly, I feel a hundred percent."

"Want to make twenty, thirty dollars? We'll help Marcus with the floor."

She set me up making cuts for him on a table saw, and he laid the floor. She fussed around taking the boxes and the cuts that were too small to use out to the garbage can.

We were halfway done by the time Marcus decided he needed to go, and Ellen and I relaxed on the sofas, which were now sitting on a fake maple floor that looked real if you didn't get too close. I knew Mom was disappointed Ellen hadn't gone for real hardwood, but it looked nice to me, and I said so. Ellen stretched back, pressing into the cushions.

"I always loved this sofa," and then she said, "Oh no!" She was fingering the tapestry fabric of the seat.

I was jumpy and bolted up. "What is it?"

"It's just getting frayed." She placed a pillow on the spot and composed herself. "It's OK."

"If you loved the sofa, then why did you give it to us?" I asked.

"It was just in the garage, honey, and you *needed* furniture."

"I mean, if you loved it, why didn't you have it in your living room?"

"We have something more formal in the living room."

"Or your family room."

Ellen said, "You're right. I guess I don't love it anymore. I feel like I do. I suppose what I meant was more like, I remember when this sofa was in our living room and I loved it, and I wouldn't let the boys get on it or God forbid the dog, and now seeing it getting worn makes me feel bad because I always protected it."

I laughed. "Why didn't you just say all of that in the first place?"

Ellen laughed a little bit. Her eyes narrowed. She was having an idea.

"Tommy really likes her job, doesn't she?" she said.

"She likes money," I said.

"Did you ever think about getting a job?"

"Not really."

"Are you planning for college?"

I just smiled.

"You did a great job helping Marcus today. Would you like to be Marcus's helper sometimes? He does all kinds of work on our properties. Sometimes he really needs a helper."

I sat back in the sofa and thought about it. In fact, I very much wanted to become Marcus's helper and never go back to school. Earlier in the summer I had suggested something like this to Mom, and Mom had been angry. I couldn't say if she would be less angry or even more angry knowing the idea originated with Ellen. More, I thought.

Also, it had felt good to cut boards for a couple of hours, but how certain was I that I would like to do that *sometimes*—like, multiple times, indefinite numbers of times, whether I felt like it or not?

"No thanks," I said.

Ellen said, low and serious, "Does your mom ever talk with you about what you're going to do after high school?"

"No," I said.

"I know she hasn't been able to save for you to go to school. I'd help if I could, but I don't have a lot extra, either." She looked down at her fancy little shoes.

"I know. It's OK," I said.

"And I don't think—I'm so sorry, I don't really know this—but I don't think you do so well in school that you would qualify for scholarships and things like that."

"Oh no, of course not."

"So it would be good to start getting some work experience."

I smiled.

"What do you want to do after this year?"

I thought I might like to just walk, visit the thrift store again, sit in the park. And then the thought came to me that the park was somehow tainted, that I was angry with Foster for something he said. These thoughts were all muddled and confused, but they were troubling—something about Beulah was terribly troubling just then—and so I thought I might like to walk far along on the highway instead, over the bridge and west toward Betty.

I sat on the sofa facing the kitchen, which meant I caught only a little shadow from the corner that was once the principal's office. A small shadow sat facing a larger one, and the larger shadow stood up, towering over it, moving toward the little shadow. I looked away.

This particular corner sometimes showed little skits of kids getting bawled out, sometimes spanked. Nothing really serious, but there was a lot of emotion in the corner. If you stood where the principal's office had been, you might get a sense of injustice—how this wasn't fair, the spanking or tongue-lashing or whatever—and how you were going to get back at everyone someday, or you might just feel sad, or you might feel guilty. I never stood right in that corner if I could help it.

There was no reason to stand there, and so the room usually had a peaceful feeling, almost as peaceful as our bedroom. Just now, though, the feeling of injustice was emanating out into the rest of the room.

It's not fair. I didn't do anything.

"Are you all right?" Ellen said.

"I don't think so," I said.

She sat forward. "What's wrong?"

There was so much wrong, I couldn't begin. I smiled a desperate smile at her until she came around beside me and held me around the shoulders. Her face was so close, her scent bright green. Her pretty scarf tickled my cheek.

"Do you miss your friend still? Who wouldn't want to be your friend? You're so pretty."

Ellen went back to gathering cardboard, and after a while she and Marcus left. After just a little while longer, Mom and Stevie and Tommy came back. They had been to the malls and outlet stores of Boise. They showed their amazement at the floor being already laid, and then they started showing off their purchases. School clothes, school supplies, a pair of tall boots for Mom.

You could see they hadn't gotten all they wanted.

#

Ellen bought a new, longer SUV and, since it had *so* much room, she invited us all to the mountains the Saturday before school was set to start. Jasper couldn't be there, but Adrian came. He wasn't awkward with us at all. He and Tommy chatted together and laughed all day. We soaked in a hot springs pool and hiked along some dirt roads by a lake. Very chill.

We spent some time in McCall, too, bought grainy ice cream at a falling-down local place crowded with tourists.

My ice cream was a patchwork of all the different flavors. It looked appealing, like a tie-dye T-shirt, but it tasted so bad I had to toss it in the garbage.

The visit to the hot springs was the highlight of the day, though. There were stepped pools from hottest to coolest with the hot water feeding out of rock into the top pool. We dangled our toes in and dared each other to walk across it. Adrian and Tommy did it, no one else. I tried and had to jump out after two steps. Mom didn't try. Stevie sat in the shade. She didn't even swim. I thought it was because she didn't want to be in her swimsuit around Adrian, and maybe part of it was that, but it was also like she was detaching from us. She felt separate from the group. I didn't know what to do about it.

I'd never learned much about Ellen's sons, and I certainly never thought about them. You could see, though, that Tommy thought something of Adrian. He was a year behind her but tall for his age. I guess we were all getting along pretty well up until we left the hot springs.

It started to turn when we got back in the SUV. Ellen and Mom sat up front, the next row was me and Stevie. The back row were Tommy and Adrian.

I don't remember exactly what it was that happened, but Mom started to get testy as we were driving around a little town. This was after the ice cream; we were going to see a lake. She started to make snippy sounds and then she didn't talk. I wasn't paying much attention until then.

"Don't you think?" said Ellen, "Well don't you? If not, just tell me what you think." I guessed they were talking about the house, or maybe it was about the storage unit Mom had said we had. Mom turned toward her window and didn't respond. The kids were all chattering. No one was paying attention except me, and Ellen caught my eyes in the rearview. She pulled into a parking lot and we all wandered out into a little park.

Mom walked far off away from everyone and sat on the table part of a picnic table looking out at the lake.

"She'll be fine in a little bit," I told Ellen.

Ellen nodded. Her mouth was small and tight. She had on these little dangly earrings—always wore things like that, little semiprecious stones or agates with copper and silver beads. How precious she was. Her skin so perfect, her life so perfect. I knew we owed her a lot.

"I just want you to know how grateful we are," I said. "Not just for today, for everything. But you know." I touched her when I said it. I put my hand on her shoulder, moved it near her wrist, saying, *Touch me back, hold me.*

And her face collapsed. This was all she'd been wanting, you see, just a little approval and recognition. Gratitude.

She took me around the shoulders, hugged me.

I owe Ellen for that, if for nothing else. Her need was so bald and so obvious that I could see it and guess at what was missing, and that helped remind me how easy it was to give someone what they wanted. It was a lesson I'd learned before but had forgotten or pushed away.

Though people wanted different things, it mostly boiled down to them wanting you to ask them for something. They didn't trust you unless you were in their debt.

In the evening, we went to Ellen's husband's folks' vacation condo. We should have checked ahead, but they were never there, she said, and she was right. The place was like a giant motel room. Adrian and Tommy murmured and joked through an action movie. Stevie and I lay on our bed not talking. She colored in a new coloring book, and I drew vague shapes in my journal and colored them in with crayon. "A language of the soul," I wrote on the page and then crossed it out, hatched it out, made a deep black smudge of it.

Ellen and Mom walked to a bar and came home by midnight in a better mood, it sounded like. In the morning, we all said how well we'd slept, and then we turned back toward Beulah with only one more night of summer left to go.

SEPTEMBER

1

Ellen recommended Queenie's Drugs and Gifts because it was a nice place where all the nice old Beulah ladies went. Mom had a job there by the time school started. It was supposed to be part time, but it seemed Mom worked nearly every day, and so couldn't drive us to school as we'd expected her to be able to. Tommy had taken driver's ed but still needed to take the test, and she wasn't prioritizing that until she had money for a car.

We had choices, though. We could take the bus or walk. The girls opted for the bus, but that just wasn't for me.

On the first day of school, there were thankfully no shadows or time-shifts or any other anomalies. There was nothing but the warm morning and the pleasant activity around Farm School Road. A car or two went by me. Two cow dogs chased each other around the red outbuildings of the big farm. More cars passed as I went east on Eighth all the way to the Circle-K and on past it through the park. The first street on the park was called Park and the one I crossed at the other end was called Parkview, and all three sides of the park were the tall houses, Victorians but also Craftsmen and a mix of others, all well-kept. The park itself was lovely, still just as green as the town itself had promised to be in our first days. I saw Ellen's mom's pink house and Matt's blue one like a simplified farmhouse with little red flowers blooming around its base, a beautiful low green bungalow, a tall yellow one with square panes of yellow glass like tile bordering all its windows. The yellow one had a shaggy yard; I imagined its owners had gone on vacation. Each house was unique. The garages, when they had them at all, stood in backyards. Some had strips of concrete with grass growing between them instead of driveways.

Past Parkview was an alley serving the Parkview houses and the Clover Street houses, which were large but not so nice. After Clover were more of the little houses, a little more run-down, and finally the high school.

Dolly Parton High, Matt had called it once. There were actually three concrete dome buildings, but the third was shorter and hidden behind the others and so the effect was, yes, something like a pair of big boobies pointing up to the sky.

Then came a frantic six hours of moving from room to room. English made an impression because the teacher was such a sleazy-looking guy in belted baggy dress pants and a loud shiny shirt. He didn't just have a perm; he had an actual *mustache.* I couldn't tell whether it was writing or literature or some combination, but it started the day on a sour note. I'd always tolerated English class pretty well but knew I would hate having it with him.

The Health class teacher was jolly and loud. He seemed to want people to get into a loud discussion. I never discussed things in class anymore, of course, so I just sat back and listened, but I noticed the pretty girl in the front of the class. She had a long gangly body and a baby face. Her short, light hair was like a baby's, too, in little ringlets. She had a friend just as lovely with long black hair all down her back and big black eyes with long false lashes. Both of them got into the discussion right away; I think they must have been some of the top students in the school.

After Health, I was in a science lab class. As the teacher was going on, I noticed Ellen's son Jasper sitting two tables ahead of me. At a certain point, he got bored and looked around at the people to the side of him, but he never turned all the way back. I don't know why the sight of the back of his close-shorn head rubbed me so wrong, but then I thought about it, and I realized Jasper reminded me a lot of this one guy back a couple of schools ago.

I'd gotten the idea to put food coloring in spritzer bottles and had streaked my hair red and purple. I'd borrowed a hippie top from Mom's closet, and I felt really cute that day. This tall basketball kid who I hadn't really noticed before—and I'm sure he'd never noticed me—he had always just sat with his back to me so I could see how often his hair was cut, but that day he looked back and mouthed something. At first I couldn't tell what he was mouthing, so he kept on doing it, and the girl next to him started giggling, and I realized he was saying. "Whore."

Nice. Was it because of my hair, the hippie top? Did I have on lipstick? I never could decide. I was a virgin at the time, but it didn't matter. The statement felt true somehow.

Was that kind of thing why I'd started skipping class? It seemed like it must have been. It must have been my freshman year, the semester after all that trouble with the ghost-boys. Tommy was still in junior high and so no one was there to see if I skipped.

So, no fault of his own, these were all associations I now had with Jasper and really, this whole class, which seemed to be filled with no one but sports-ball enthusiasts and rich kids.

On this, the first day of school, I'd worn faded black jeans and a plain black T-shirt and brown engineer boots, so I was quite a fashion plate. For a moment, glancing at the people to the left and ahead of me, I wished that I had gone into Boise with everybody and tried to get a few things, but that moment faded quickly. I told myself that on Tuesday I could wear my Fourth-of-July getup if I really wanted to impress.

At lunch, a girl named Kelsie from English called me over to sit on the grass with her and her friends. They asked me where I was from, and they said they were jealous and asked what I liked to do back home and was I happy here so far, and what I was into. They had lank ponytails, fresh-scrubbed faces, and plain clothes like mine. They were all sweet-faced, polite, seemed smart. We talked easily enough for the lunch period.

The talk was all along the lines of how we couldn't wait to get out of Beulah and on with our lives. College for them and for me too, I lied. I gave up on saying we were from Seattle and told them of the little town of Orliss and told them something of the friends and the comfort I'd had there, but my time to talk was over soon, and as they kept talking, I entered...

Well, I entered into the sweetest daydream. We were not seniors; we were freshmen, and we had our whole high school career ahead of us. We were clicking like this on the first day, which would lead to four years of adventures, slumber parties, bonding.

I'd teach them how to speak to the dead. We'd solve crimes and right wrongs with this gift. We'd grow tight.

But lunchtime ended, and we dispersed to lockers and restrooms and next classes. In my next room, which was some sort of social studies class, I looked around but did not see any of them.

#

I found myself going to Circle K after school. Different customers came in and went out. I just leaned there by the gum chatting with Foster, which was unusual for me. It was testament to how welcoming he was. I told him how Tommy had gotten her job at the Tiger Burger, and how she didn't like the oily burgers they served but loved seeing all the cool kids come through there.

I told him about my classes, how good Stevie's cooking was getting, how the house was progressing. I told him about Ellen coming around to see what all we'd done and being disappointed. Everything going on in my life.

"You sure you're eighteen?" he said after a while.

"I'll be nineteen by graduation, if I graduate. Why?" I realized I'd been stretching my legs, doing lunges and pulling my leg up behind me to stretch the hip flexors. I stopped.

"You just seem young," he said.

"I don't wear makeup anymore, is all. Tommy wears this cat-eye eyeliner when she's done up for school, and I think it makes her look vicious."

A tiny old guy came in just then. Foster got out the roll of chew without him asking, they exchanged money and change, and the man nodded to me on his way out.

"You look good without makeup," Foster said, "but that's not it. Hey, I try to stay young myself. Nothing wrong with that."

"How old are you, then?"

"Twenty. That's not too old for you?" I was embarrassed, then. I looked away and then went out the door. I started home, on Ninth this time.

It seemed like every time I talked to Foster, he made another attempt to start some romance. Sometimes he'd ask if I have any more batshit stories about my dreams, and sometimes I'd oblige. He couldn't get me talking about music or movies or memes or games because I didn't care about them. I couldn't get him talking about books because he never read.

Anyway, that's how it was, the new schedule: up at six, healthy breakfast, the walk to school, six hours of hell, half an hour at Circle-K, the walk home, nap, dinner, hot bath, bed. I tried to take a new road each time, either on the way home or the way back. I was being easy on myself.

Tommy would call it self-care and would approve of it, not that she'd noticed.

Self-care helped keep the shadows in the background of my thinking, but of course it wasn't perfect. Half the time, I didn't get more than an hour or two of nap because Mom would need help with some project.

I kept eating lunch with Kelsie, Sara, and Mila, but more and more we spent lunch time doing our little bits of homework so we wouldn't have to take it home. Kelsie would find me sometimes and make vague suggestions about things we might do, but I didn't ever take her up on them. I thought from time to time how nice it would be to make these girls my real friends, but I always let it go. Kelsie was all right, but the other girls were too anxious, not focused and driven like Tommy but just worried all the time. I guessed it was because they were all headed to college and needed to plan out their lives.

Visiting with Foster was maybe the highlight of my days, but the walking came a close second. To change things up, I'd walk along the highway instead of taking a numbered street or out east to the subdivisions before heading back home. Sometimes I'd walk around the park or visit Marielle for a minute at Roark's. She was a self-contained little woman around Mom's age but without any kids or any responsibilities other than her old dad. I gathered he used to run the shop. She read or watched television most of the time and was willing to visit but not champing at the bit to do it. Still, I felt that since she'd been friendly to me, I could do the minimum to keep that up.

I tried to walk all the way to the canyon once or twice. It looked so close from our patio, but the times I tried to get there before dinner, I never made it. I always had to turn back. I thought idly of asking Foster to take me in his car, but I wasn't sure I wanted to get something like that started with him.

One time I came to Circle-K just as he was leaving work, and his face brightened. "Want a ride?" he said again, and I did think about the canyon.

"I like to walk," I said. I just stood there, not sure if I wanted him to ask again or not.

"Are you just not into me or are you not into guys?" He said it in a cartoon voice to make clear it was supposed to be a joke, but I knew he meant it.

I just smiled and walked off again.

#

The social studies class was something I was thinking about in the back of my mind all this time. The teacher was really young and excited, and no one seemed to know what to make of her. She was either a very good teacher or a very bad one. I had no way of telling.

The discussions were embarrassing. It wasn't just that what the other students said sounded stupid to me—that was part of it, like when we were discussing "privilege," the discussion went from "I never had a privilege in my life. I worked for everything" and only got worse from there.

But it wasn't just that; my own thoughts on the matter felt equally unformed and vapid.

2

Tommy kept getting things from Ellen—castoff clothes, little pillows, curtains, things like that. When Ellen saw how she was showing initiative, what with the job and the attempts to decorate the basement, she gave her a laptop too. Ellen decided she wanted to "upgrade," and so she just gave her old MacBook to Tommy, and I inherited Tommy's crappy old laptop so I wouldn't have to stress about not being able to do homework anymore (not that I had been stressing). We still didn't have wifi, so I had to always remember to take the thing to school so I could get my assignments uploaded before the deadline.

Tommy hustled pretty much night and day. I'd catch sight of her at school sometimes, hair pulled back in a tight ponytail, perfect posture, cat eyes. She smiled at everyone. She was trying to be a perfect student, perfect athlete, trying to get in with the cool kids. Striving. You had to admire a girl like that, and I did.

Both of the girls seemed happy. Stevie talked about her pretty teacher Mrs. Greene who was always talking about her boy-girl twin babies who stayed at home with the dad. Stevie loved her; you could tell. Her eyes brightened talking about her, and I knew Mrs. Greene must love Stevie too, and I was glad for her to have made that connection so early in the year. It helped her feel good about school. We didn't ask if she was making friends. It can take time.

Stevie still made our dinners as often as she could, did her homework, and kept growing.

We had a fresh nubby carpet with flecks of brown and green installed in our bedroom, which went with the light green walls that she'd painted herself. I loved the smell of new carpet, new paint, the no-smell smell of new mattresses. The room was big enough for all of the couches and koi ponds and ferns we might have wanted and more. In reality, it held nothing but our new beds and our four plastic totes lined between them. There was no closet, no nightstands, no lamps, no desk.

Mom still worked on the house every evening. She'd finally finished laying white mosaic tile on the bathroom floor. Ellen had frowned when she saw it. I suppose the lines were a little crooked, but who really notices something like that?

Mom was the one I worried about. She wasn't used to working all day and then turning around and trying to fix up a house, day after day falling behind on the schedule she'd set. So far, the only item checked off the list was the painting, but that was mostly due to Stevie's work over the summer. I thought that everyone knew painting was the easiest way to make the biggest splash, but Mom said Ellen had probably never painted a place herself, and so she wouldn't know that really.

Ellen wasn't stupid. She realized that flooring cost a lot more than paint, but she didn't realize how much more intense the labor was. She didn't see how tiling the floor taxed Mom. Mom had lied about having done tile before. She'd *seen* it done. That wasn't the same. We've all seen haircuts done. That doesn't mean we can cut hair. The same turned out to be true for tile. She started by watching videos, then practiced on a board. She tried not to make any of the mistakes they'd warned about on the videos. The tile on the board looked perfect. She laid out the tiles on the floor, cut them with the little tile saw Ellen happened to have on hand. It was a cheap, dangerous machine.

Whenever she operated a machine like that—and she'd had reason to operate a great number of them for different jobs she had, and it was the same when she used hedge clippers, pruners, anything like that—she'd imagine slipping and cutting off a finger. That image *should* come

131

to mind to make you be careful, but in her case the image just replayed and replayed. Clipping a rosebush meant five full minutes of the repeated image, like a GIF, of cutting off her finger. She'd feel shaky and drained afterward.

And Mom had been without health insurance most of her life, and so that image brought further images of bills and bankruptcy, leaving town, losing the chance to have something.

And in the middle of the work, the feeling of dread would build. Even if she was doing something safe, the feeling of pointlessness would come over her, like the night we were all trying to help finish the laminate flooring in the great room. The hammer kept slipping and denting the edges of the boards, and I saw her getting more and more frustrated. She kept calling the strips of flooring nasty names and finally sighed and lay down on the sofa.

She put her hand to her head, said, "No one who can afford a—what?—five-thousand square foot house is going to want it done up this way. Cheap carpet and laminate and I guess Formica countertops whenever Ellen can even get it together enough to order the cabinets. A place like this should have granite. Hardwood . . . or, this is ridiculous. Even talking about the finishings is ridiculous. First of all, there would need to be a full overview of the bones of the house. Are there any hazardous materials? There's lead paint, for sure. How could there not be? Probably asbestos in the tile. You'd strip it to the bones and then remodel so that the rooms made more sense. You'd add windows and a better deck off the back. Anyone who would buy something like this would need to have money. They'd want quality."

"Ellen must know what she's doing, though," I said.

"She doesn't. Not at all. Her dad knows better, and he told her, and she disagreed. That's why he gave us the stink eye when we met him."

"He did?" I didn't remember.

"At the parade, at the barbecue? Jesus, Georgie, where do you go?"

I ignored that. "But how do you know they know better than Ellen? We should trust her," I said.

"Her family thinks this whole thing is a mistake, and we're some type of parasites taking her money."

"She said that?" said Tommy.

"More or less," said Mom.

"Why would she tell you that?" I said.

Tommy started to tear up, and she went downstairs before Mom could see. That wasn't like her. Thankfully Stevie was somewhere else just then.

Mom grunted as she got off the couch. She stayed in her room for the rest of the night.

#

"Did you come for your souvenir this time?" Foster said.

I was browsing magazines at the Circle-K again. "Huh?" I said, not looking up from the beauty magazine. I wasn't reading it, but it smelled so nice to flip through it, and the colors were all so bright and clear.

"I meant from your dreams," he said.

I might have been a little embarrassed if there were anyone else in the store. I was about to say I never dreamed of the Circle-K or the Streaker's or anyplace like that, only the mom-and-pop places, don't you know? I was about to say that, but a faint memory came to me of coming to the Circle-K in midwinter, wading through the deep snow on a silent moonless night. I recalled the warmth and safety of stepping inside, looking down to the snow caked to my knees.

I smiled back at Foster. I had the feeling he was going to be a good friend, no matter how little I knew him right then.

That time he let me use his phone to look for Betty, everything had been either taken down or long-abandoned. There were still a few pictures of her, though. I made him save them. Maybe one day we'd get them printed or I'd see if he could send them to my laptop.

"How's school?" he said.

I smiled, said, "Not so good."

Foster's body was so long and heavy. Lately, I'd been spending some time thinking about how it would feel to cuddle into the space between his chin and chest.

I wanted to say yes, let's just go for it. Take me out, Foster. I'll be your girl for a while at least. It's hard, though, when you've been shutting someone down for a while, to make that reversal. I thought about going up and kissing him, but instead I just gave him a little wave before I hit the road again.

3

I enjoyed having Tommy's old laptop more than I thought I would. I loaded it up with old books. Jane Austen, Dickens, Gothic novels—basically any book I'd heard of that was old enough to be free. I read them quickly and without thought, forgetting each one as soon as I started the next. One night I was too bored with the story, so I set the laptop down beside the bed.

Stevie and I had been hanging out in our room more and more, and it was just a little bit less empty. Ellen had thought Adrian's old desk would be perfect to place at the room's far end, so now Stevie did her homework there instead of at the kitchen table. I lay on my back with my legs in the air, lowered them, raised them and looked at my toes.

I asked Stevie, "What was it like for you, you know, when I had that bad time?"

"Don't you ever have homework?" she said, keeping her back to me.

"Actually, no," I said. "It's a myth."

"What's a myth?"

"That you have homework in high school. Junior high too, as far as I remember. One day soon you won't have any homework anymore, and you'll have nothing to do."

She didn't answer. I threw a pillow at her.

"Get over here. I command you," I said. "Tell me what you remember."

She turned off her lamp and came over to the bed. Our room was all dark except for the moonlight. She sat cross-legged on the floor beside me, pulled the nightgown over her knees.

"What do you want to know?" she said.

"What was it like for you?"

I could see her thinking about what to say. She looked down, rubbed her foot.

"I was just a little kid. You should ask Tommy. Have you asked her?"

I leaned over close to her and rolled my eyes, lay back down.

She groaned a little and said, "Ugh. Well, I guess I was five or six. I was really into playing pretend. A lot of the time, I just thought you were playing pretend."

I'd been asking about later, when I went out every night and backtalked to Mom. She must have been thinking about the time before that, back at the apartment when I would go out in the night to see the lady in the window.

"Why'd you think I was playing pretend?" I said.

"I guess you talked to people who weren't there sometimes. Really, it wasn't a big deal. You were pretty much OK. You don't remember?"

"I do, some. I wanted to know what it was like for you."

"It was sad."

"Why?"

"Because we had to move again." We both sat for a moment thinking of all those moves.

"We always had to move," I said, "even before you were born. "

"I know."

"You had a friend in that city, though. You two were so cute."

"Jenny."

"A good friend. I remember you playing for hours."

"She had so many dolls."

"Are you making good friends here?" I said.

She just looked at me.

Stevie had been sorry to move away from Jenny, but she hadn't said much about it at the time. She'd been trying to be strong even way back then. My ever-present guilt refocused. I felt so bad for what I'd done to her. I thought, without really feeling it, that she might be better off if I just left.

And then I thought of my library. "Oh Stevie, did you sit on it?"

Stevie rose, and there was the laptop. She blanched.

"It's all right," she said, "Look, it is," and turned it every way. Her whole face smiled.

"I love you," I said.

She got into her bed and was sleeping, for once, before I was.

The shadows in our bedroom, very subtle to begin with, had grown even more subtle after we painted, and the new carpet muffled them further.

Out in the hall outside our door was a different story. I averted my eyes from the doorway as long as I could, often waiting until morning to pee just because I didn't want to look. If I did have to go, most of the time it would be OK, just my heart pumping a bit in anticipation of seeing the shadow who paced, and usually I could run to the bathroom and back without seeing him.

The shadow who paced was the same one who puttered around in the back room of the basement, the one who'd been so brazen that day early in summer when I came home and they were all playing in the yard. He paced with a single-minded focus, body weighted forward. I thought he was checking the halls for kids doing wrong, or maybe he was just making sure everything was in its place.

It was just the one teacher who slumped *into* the room. He entered through the doorway and moved toward the area where his desk used to be. That was all most nights, but one or two times he turned quickly and made a writing gesture where the board used to be. The children raised their hands. It was rare that I saw them now, and they weren't at all distinct. They were little more than a few vertical blurs from time to time.

The teacher was a silhouette but clear. He must have taught here for decades.

The beds were positioned against the front window so that we faced him. One might think, if you know where a shadow might appear, that it would be good to block the sight of it. Place the headboard on the wall where the blackboard once hung, they would think. It isn't so simple. Place your head where a shadow walks, sleep there, and nine nights out of ten, or even ninety-five out of a hundred you will think the room peaceful. On that odd night, though, the shadow passes through you. You don't see it, exactly. It's a disorienting movement over your head like a flock of tiny birds flying past. You wake sweating, unsure what has happened, or if you're awake already, you moan and move to another part of the bed and cannot get to sleep.

#

"This is the most peaceful room in the house," I said another night.

"I love our room," Stevie said. "I love my bed." She crawled under the covers. She often said that she loved her bed before she fell asleep. I hated to think of her getting so tired she yearned for sleep like that. I hated to think that she already thought of sleep as a luxury at her age.

"Love you," I said.

It hurt me to think there was something wrong with her, but was there? Her body was heavier than it had been in August, and she seemed a lot taller too. Could it be that she was just meant to be this way? If so, that was all right, but if she was eating too much because something troubled her, I didn't know what to do about it or even how to talk to her about it.

Nothing seemed to trouble her, certainly not there in our room.

#

Tommy kept hustling and Mom did the same. Mom was sometimes energized, sometimes exhausted. She came home at odd times. Her work schedule was never clear to me week to week, and then when she wasn't working she was often out with Ellen, or sometimes with one or two of Ellen's girlfriends. Often it was just the two of them because the girlfriends had more challenging jobs, from what I gathered. Mom said that Ellen seemed to feel a little intimidated by them sometimes. How nice it was for Ellen, in her nice leisurely life, to have someone to share that leisure with who was not a rival, who was not judgmental. How nice it was for Ellen—not just Mom—to have her good friend back. Mom would go shopping with her even though she could never buy anything at those kinds of stores. Mom would go out to eat with her and make sure they split the check.

Dinner had always been our core family activity. It was a way that we kept up feeling normal through all of the moves, through losing Dad and all the time we had been on our own. Through it all we had the family dinner together, and if at any point someone stopped coming to dinner—like I had, when we lived in the city and then the first year in Orliss—then everyone knew something was very wrong. Now it was Mom who was missing dinner.

Stevie would always set the table for four and then box up Mom's in a plastic container that had a well for the main dish and smaller wells for the sides. It was the most pitiful thing to see her arrange the food so it looked pretty in that container.

To be honest, usually when Mom missed dinner it was for work. But sometimes it wasn't, and we never knew when she would be there and when she wouldn't. I can't imagine how that hurt Stevie.

The one thing Mom asked of us was to care for Stevie. She really wasn't demanding in other ways, at least not anymore, and so how could we even question that request? Still, a little girl needs some kind of a parent. As well-meaning as Tommy and I were, we were teenagers. We could have been trusted to get her out of the house if there was a fire, but that was about it.

I guess it was because I was trying to be good and normal just then, but it seemed to me that Stevie needed something more. She needed parental guidance, mentoring or something.

My tendency had always been to navel gaze, especially when I was being good, and I found myself musing over all the troubles I'd had in life and how those troubles might have been eased somewhat if I'd had a more consistent role model.

I was an ass to have these thoughts, and a bigger ass to bring them to Mom.

"So how is Stevie doing in school?" I said one night when Stevie was in the bathtub.

Mom was doing the bills, but her head jerked up at that. "Great, as far as I know. Did you hear something?" Her hand brushed over the mail on the table. "Was there a note or something?"

"No, I just wondered."

"Then ask her. I assume she's doing great. She always does," Mom said.

"I don't think she's made any friends," I said.

Tommy turned away from the lunches she was packing to look at us. "How are *you* doing in school, by the way?" she said.

"That's a good question," said Mom.

I smiled when I had a challenging question like this, so Mom knew it would take more energy than she had to escalate the situation. Imagine a protester who simply goes limp. It takes a lot of energy just to pull them away. If you were motivated, I guess you'd do it, but if you were just trying to get through a tough day, you wouldn't. Mom was always having a tough day, so it almost always worked.

We went about doing what we were doing, which was cleaning up the kitchen. The table always collected tons of junk mail, which Mom alone was qualified to throw away, and so that was her big contribution. That and doing the bills. I rushed around the kitchen gathering dishes and loading them into the dishwasher.

"Is this good?" I said when they all were in. I didn't trust myself to run the new dishwasher or even to load it properly.

Mom rose from the table and looked inside. She took bowls from the top and wedged them on the bottom where I wouldn't have thought they would fit. She told me to use the extra space up top for Tupperware.

"There aren't any dirty," I said.

She held eye contact and said, "Listen: Get in the fridge and take out the old leftovers, scrape the ones that do not have meat into the compost, scrape the ones that do have meat into the garbage, rinse the containers in hot water, put them in the dishwasher, put the soap in the dishwasher, take out the garbage so that it doesn't stink."

"OK, so you mean clean the fridge then?" I said.

"I'm going to lie down, OK?"

"Sure," I said, but on her way there, Tommy asked, "Do you think Stevie's getting teased about her size at school? Is she doing OK in P.E.?"

Mom just stood there with her eyebrows raised, and I said, "She is still just a little kid. She needs a Mom," and that was such a stupid thing to say. Stupid and hypocritical. I was afraid how I was influencing Stevie, so now I was blaming Mom? Nice.

Mom didn't respond. She just sucked in her cheeks gave me that hard look that seemed to last for days.

OCTOBER

1

There are parties and there are parties. Sometimes a party is like a concert only more intimate. You get a good communal buzz and feel like you're having some sort of deep group experience that changes the way you look at life, if only for a short time. You leave feeling a little happier, and that happiness might even last a while, maybe the rest of the week. For that week you don't feel lonely. You don't feel weird. These sorts of parties have always meant something to me. They rejuvenate me.

The other sort of party is just the opposite. It reminds you why you don't like people all that much. This was the type that Tommy liked. She was turning seventeen and had been wanting to throw just this sort of party since she was about twelve: maximum stress, maximum awkwardness, zero fun. With Tiger Burger money burning a hole in her pocket and an entire basement to herself, this was the year she was finally going to make it happen. Luckily for her, she had not gotten around to telling Mom about her plans before Mom told us that she was planning an overnight trip. It was just about unheard-of for Mom to go away overnight, and Tommy took this as quite the fortunate sign.

But before Tommy's party came Foster's party. His was very well advertised. He reminded me about it every time I went into Circle-K. He told Tommy when she went into Circle-K. Kelsie told me he'd told her about it because apparently he was friends with her brother. He texted a lot of people as well.

I asked the baby-faced blonde girl in Health class, Summer, if she'd heard about it. It was out of character for me to initiate a conversation with her—and embarrassing, as it turned out, because she'd never heard of Foster.

"Is he a junior?" she asked.

"Maybe you don't know him," I said.

"I know everybody, or, he's not a *freshman* is he?"

I couldn't see telling her he was the guy who worked at the Circle-K, so I said yes, I thought maybe he was a freshman after all. She laughed, but not in a mean way. I know it sounds that way, but it wasn't like she thought what a weird thing it was to think that she might know a lowly freshman. It was more she was just surprised there was a party happening and she didn't know about it already.

"I don't really go out that much," she said. "But I hope you have fun."

She was a sweet girl. Smart, really unselfconscious. If I'd made friends with her, how would that have gone? But it wasn't meant to be.

Foster was going to be my one good friend here, no point wondering about others.

#

Foster's party didn't turn out to be Foster's party, really, but the party of a friend of his who was visiting from a college out of state. Why he was home this particular weekend was a mystery.

It was funny. Foster showed up at my house after he kept promising he'd get me the address. He'd said I could walk to it, and so now why was he at my house, an hour before it was supposed to start?

"Come on," he said. "Just ride in my car."

I was thinking about making a move on him at the party, truth be told, that or letting him make a move on me, but it seemed too soon just then. I stood at the top of the steps, arms crossed. I had on a thermal underwear top with little rosebuds on it, ripped-up jeans, and the destroyed brown leather engineer boots Mom had gotten at some thrift store.

I said, "How do you know I'm even ready to go?"

"You are."

I was. Still, I hesitated.

"Why don't you want to ride in my car? Am I scary?"

"No."

"You had someone—or sorry, did you have someone you know in a car wreck? Or die? Shit. If so, I can't believe I just said that."

"No," I lied. I didn't want to get into it.

"Well then, get in the car or I won't be your friend anymore."

"I am."

"You are?"

"Getting in the car. Right now." I moved off the step.

We walked across the lawn and got in. It was dusk. The chill, the movement and slight sound of children playing, they were there all around me for just an instant. I thought maybe my nervousness caused it.

When we were belted, he said, "Seriously, why is this the first time you're in my car?"

"I guess I'm a little afraid of cars."

"You ride around with your mom all the time."

"My mom loves me, though. I mean, my mom *treasures* me. Her arm springs out if she brakes too hard..." and I showed him.

"My arm will spring out so fast," he said.

"OK, go."

He laughed and said, "Whee!" He backed out of the driveway, and we drove about fifteen miles an hour past the yellow farmhouse, past the brown farmhouse, and straight into the driveway of the white farmhouse with all the red outbuildings. I laughed when I realized that this was where the party would be. It felt magical to be going to this place I'd been walking by for so long.

"I'm going to park way out of the way so I don't get blocked in," he said.

He pulled off the driveway onto grass and drove between a big barn and an empty horse corral and back toward a machine shed all done up in Christmas lights. Bales of hay stood all around in positions like tables and chairs. On one of these bales, sipping a beer, sat Matt.

Matt and I sat around while Foster set things up. Out of his hatchback he brought a stereo, and he kept going to the house for things, buckets and cups and things like that, then off to Circle-K for ice.

Matt had brought the keg. His sister got it for us, he said. We got to talking about an art class he was taking, and he showed me some of his work on his phone. He explained he was still in a second-year class and nothing was very good so far, but he felt like he was learning a lot. He was going to a figure drawing workshop once a week, too. No credit for that, and he had to pay, but he'd found he really liked to draw.

The pictures were mostly drawings of a naked girl around our age in a range of different athletic poses.

"You're really good," I said. I didn't know if this was strictly true, but if I'd drawn the girl it would have been just a smiley face and big circles for boobies below it, so I was impressed.

"My teacher had us use nothing but line the first week. You weren't allowed to do any shading. You had to indicate the shading with a wider line, you see?"

I saw what he needed. Eyes fully open, staring straight at him, I said, "They're beautiful. You really have a sense of . . . how people move."

He looked like he wanted me to go on. I couldn't do it, though. I couldn't stand anymore to act just the way he wanted me to act, and his eyebrows came down after I was silent a minute.

"No. You're nice, though," he said.

"You love drawing. You really like school," I said.

He nodded.

"So why are you back in Beulah all the time?"

"I'm not. This is just the second time I've come home this semester."

"Oh, I just happened to catch you both times," I said.

I hadn't meant to imply that he liked me, but Matt didn't seem to quite follow anyway, so it was all good. I asked him some more questions about himself, and he obliged me by talking again.

I wished over and over that Foster would return, and eventually he did. His red car came back through the space between barn and corrals, two other cars attempting to follow. Foster stopped and yelled at them to park out front and then he came around and parked behind the machine shed.

The party was about to begin.

#

Summer came to the party after all, looking dressed for class in a khaki jacket and pink blouse. She flitted around. Everyone seemed to want to talk to her. She even came and visited with me for a few minutes. I felt her attention was her way of apologizing for not knowing what I'd been talking about when I asked about the party in class. I still sat on a bale of hay by the post where I'd been sitting with Matt until he disappeared.

Summer's friend Marcia had on a sexy black jumpsuit that showed her back. Her party makeup made her fiercely beautiful. She was glued to a boy who looked like he could have been her brother.

The three of them were gone in the first hour or two. The music was still not too loud by the time they got in their little Mini and took off toward the highway, probably to another party but perhaps home to a place in the subdivisions or to a bigger, nicer farm. I'd never know.

I sat on my bale for a long while, nursing a beer until it was so flat and warm I had to pour it out. I relaxed, talked to a few people I didn't know. There were about fifty people or seventy-five people all spread out on the property and chill, low music was playing. There seemed to be quite a few people on visits from college or other towns where they'd moved after college. Foster came back eventually and introduced me to a few of them. Pretty high school kids came and went, and then the older people started to arrive, and rougher looking kids. The music got louder. I refilled my cup, drank another, maintained a low buzz. I swayed near Foster. I swayed near Matt and their friend whose house this was, Roger. I spoke loudly to this friend about how we lived just down the road and how I'd always wondered about this house and so on.

I asked about the bathroom, and Roger showed me through the house. People were playing video games in the living room and chatting in the kitchen. It was all so beautiful, everything golden, big houseplants and dark cabinets and a sunroom with white wicker furniture out the back, and beyond that a swimming pool with another of those red fences all around it. Dim shadows danced all around, maybe some of them Roger's family.

"Pool's off limits tonight," he said, "but if you see my Jeep here sometime, come on over and swim."

I got the feeling he would soon be trying to get me to go upstairs with him, so I slipped away. The party was really going by then, music louder, people in the center swaying, almost dancing and so many people milling around the edges visiting, a few couples snuggled together.

I saw Kelsie dancing with one of her friends. She waved and came to me, hugged me.

I saw Tommy sitting talking to Ellen's younger one, Adrian, out on a bale of hay. I waved to her; she hooted and waved. Jasper was not far from them, talking with a tall, beautiful girl from the basketball team. When I passed by, I was surprised he said hi and introduced us. He said his mother was hoping to make "big money" on the schoolhouse. He drew out the words "big money", so I realized he was making fun of Ellen just a little bit. The tall girl smiled and looked down.

Matt approached then. I was surprised Jasper gave Matt a hug, said it was good to see him. To us girls, Matt said, "This guy used to come over and play all the time. He used to be so little. What happened?"

That was right; Matt lived right next to Ellen's mom, so the boys would have known each other well. Hell, everyone knew everyone in Beulah.

"This guy had long hair and a beard last year. What happened?" said Jasper.

"No way," I said, and Jasper got his phone out but got distracted by someone else before he found the photo he was searching for. I imagined what Matt had looked like with the long, gorgeous hair and the beard and bet he wished he still had them.

The tall girl went in search of another drink. Jasper and Matt turned toward another friend who had approached.

I'd had a couple of drinks and found everything warm and wonderful. I moved closer to the music. I danced.

Tommy and I walked home together that night with the party still going strong behind us. She passed me a piece of gum and asked if she seemed all right to talk to Mom, which I thought was cute since she couldn't have had more than one or two beers. It was later than we usually stayed up and we both were tired, but we couldn't stop chattering on about what a nice time it had been. Mom and Stevie were both waiting up, and we told them about it. Afterward, Tommy and I had a bath together, each in one end of the big tub. I told her about all the people I'd met, and she named off all the people from school she had seen. She went downstairs to get pajamas, but that night she slept in my bed, her feet in my face like old times.

It seemed we talked for hours. We all woke up when Tommy's phone alarm went off. She had to get ready for work. Stevie and I fell back asleep right away.

2

Near Halloween, Ellen and Mom had planned an overnight trip to a casino just over the Nevada border. It was a sort of double date. (I was the only one privy to this bit of information and wasn't to tell the girls.) Ellen had her husband Rodney, of course, and Mom had this new friend, Jay, whom I hadn't met but who was, apparently, known and approved by all of the nice Beulah people. Mom and Jay would be sharing a room, which was not usual but not exactly unheard-of. Mom had been single a long time, and there were sometimes dates like this that the girls didn't need to know about. It was not like she was auditioning new stepdaddies or anything.

"Who's in charge?" Tommy said when she first heard of the overnight trip. Her eyes looked worried.

"Um, let's see, which one is the oldest?" said Mom with a cold look.

Tommy just made her face blank and nodded. Her mind, though, jumped into party-planning mode.

Her party *was* well-publicized. She even told some people about it back during Foster's or, I guess, Roger's party at the big farm. She'd just made the basketball team, too, which meant there were a lot more people she could legitimately invite.

On the night of, she kept getting texts in the middle of doing my hair and makeup. She'd promised that if I didn't like my makeover I wouldn't have to wear it at the party, but of course I was obliged to like it no matter what. We'd been getting along really well ever since Roger's party is why I let her do it, I guess.

We sat in the front corner of the kitchen, which was one of my least favorite areas of the house. It had been the boys' bathroom and there were traces of that previous life, dull shadows of boys in their pee-stance and making aggressive little feints at one another by where the sink used to be.

I sat at a kitchen chair. Tommy answered another text and set down the phone to pull at my hair some more, combing through some slippery product from a purple vial.

"Why don't you get a phone again?" she asked.

"I don't need one."

"Well, I don't see how you get by. Do people wonder?"

"Maybe they do. I hadn't thought about it."

Stevie finished combing, took a seat, and started on my face.

"You don't need foundation, lucky," she said. Her own foundation often left a bit of a line at her jaw or right under, especially when she got ready in a hurry.

She made me close my eyes and started there. Her breath smelled like bubblegum. She ran a brush over and over my eyes, then tickled something around my face. It felt so good to have her being nice to me.

"Is that blush?" I said.

"Sculpting."

"Oh come on. I'm already sculpted enough. I don't want it to look obvious."

"It's almost Halloween. You can say it's a costume." She worked just a moment more and said, "Just the eyelashes, and then you'll be done."

Oh, hell no. I bolted up and went to the bathroom.

"Come on they're really subtle ones," she called, but she didn't chase me down. I was safe.

In the mirror, I still saw me, but it was a much older, more self-assured version. The eyes were beautifully done in a deep shimmery gray-brown "smoky eye" so bold that you didn't notice the rest right off. Tommy pointed out how the brown made my green eyes "pop." When I got over the eyes, I noticed the way the shading had made my

151

jaw and cheekbones stand out. Subtle pink-brown lipstick made my lips look larger and more definite.

"Very nice," I admitted.

She made me promise I'd leave it all on for the party. My hair she wound round and round a donut she'd made out of a sock, then spritzed the resulting bun with water. This she said I could not take out until the very minute before the party. (It did indeed give me the fullest hair of my life to that point, a mane of big ringlets that rivaled Mom's. I gasped when I looked in the mirror, never quite having seen the resemblance until then.)

The party was doomed from the start. Anytime near Halloween was a bad choice because people had places to be. I'd told her this beforehand. She said that was what would make it so chill. They'd just come in and out, and it would all be nice and casual.

It was exceedingly casual. At the start there was no one but a few of her new basketball friends and Cal and Jerry. About half the people were in costume, and no one seemed sure what they were doing here. And too, Stevie was sometimes underfoot because we couldn't exactly banish her to her room. I guess a lot of people did come through; it's just that they didn't have that much fun. But at least Mom wasn't there.

Tommy had me upstairs toasting trays of frozen mixed hors d'oeuvres and making sure people got their drinks. Thanks to Cal's brother we had alcohol, though far less of that and far more food than we needed.

When Matt and Foster rolled in, I was afraid they'd make fun of me and was on my way to wash off all the makeup, but the bathroom was occupied. I thought about washing up in the kitchen sink and decided screw it.

We visited in the kitchen. At some point Foster wandered off to see a guy he knew who was out smoking on the patio. Matt stayed and talked to me most of the time they were there. It might have been an hour, an hour and a half.

I glanced out at the patio from time to time. Marcus had just installed two sets of those white metal French doors with the plastic mullions—the cheapest doors you could get, but they framed the view beautifully. The sunset was showy over the canyon and then the moon was so bright you could still see a bit of the pastures beyond the patio edge. I thought how much nicer it would have been to have the party out on the patio, and how we'd do it that way next time if we could ever convince people to come out to the house again.

Tommy had music going downstairs, so maybe it was better down there. It was fairly quiet upstairs, people randomly wandering off to the bathroom or sitting around to talk, and I guess my hearing was really sharp just then, too, because I overheard quite a few things over the course of the night.

I overheard a couple of girls, maybe basketball girls, maybe not. They were talking about Tommy. Other things were murmured, but what I heard clearly was, "She's trying *way* too hard." How I knew they meant Tommy, I'm not sure. They could have been talking about anyone else they knew, but they weren't. They were talking about Tommy, and it made my face feel hot.

I overheard Jasper say, "This place still looks like shit" to his tall girlfriend as they did their quick walk-through. I was surprised to see him at all. I guess Tommy must have been honored, assuming they made it all the way down stairs before leaving.

Summer and her beautiful dark-haired friend did a brief walk-through. I think Marcia might have been on the basketball team, was why. I overheard nothing from them and was grateful.

I overheard someone I couldn't identify saying something unkind about how I was done up and others who had the opposite opinion.

I overheard many more things. They didn't all stick in my mind because while I was listening in, I was also trying to visit with Matt and keeping an eye out for Foster. I didn't see him on the patio after a while and was wishing he'd come back. I was trying to keep the kitchen clean, and I was tracking the dim shadow of an oversized guard dog who paced up and down the front hall past the kitchen. The dog, something like a Rottweiler or a Mastiff, made sharp movements into the bedrooms as if he were looking for someone. He must have been doing the same downstairs and then coming back up to do it all again.

I recognized him as the same spirit who walked the halls, the same who lingered in the furnace room, and the name came to me, soon as I saw him in dog form: Lonnie. I suddenly knew the name with no idea where or how I had learned it.

All the noise, all the people, I guess they spooked him. He surely thought the school was still a school and that he was responsible for keeping it safe, and now here were all these fluttering shadows and all this futuristic teen music. He must have always been terrified, but this was just over the top.

"How are your classes going?" Matt said.

I assumed he asked it because he wanted me to ask about his classes, which turned out to be a good guess. I said, "Great, how are yours?" and he went on for a long time about his art studio classes, which he loved as much as he had a few weeks ago, and his other classes, which were tough but only because they were so, so boring. He talked again of people he'd met at school and at work. He talked on and on, seeking eye contact more than usual, presumably because of all the gorgeous paint and the resulting pop in my eyes.

Matt was a little like Ellen that way. It was so clear what he wanted and so easy to see how to be with him. He asked if he could call me sometime. I said he could, if I had a phone. After I'd broken the one that Mom bought me, I'd never gotten the funds together for another. I wasn't sure I wanted another; things were calmer without one, no?

There was only one more thing I overheard that night, but it was a doozy. It was later, after Matt had wandered away to find Foster and see about the rest of their plans for that night. It was Foster I overheard. No question.

Foster said, "Yeah, I get she looks hot tonight. But that girl has zero personality. She's a black hole."

There was not one second of doubt about who was speaking or who he meant. My stomach lurched and vision blurred when I heard that. It was maybe the worst thing I'd ever heard about myself, and it had the ring of truth.

Where could they have been when he said it? The bathroom? Were they in the bathroom talking about me while I was on the other side of the wall?

See, I caught the words but not the context. I didn't see Matt and Foster just before or just after that, so it's possible Foster was talking to someone else. I didn't catch enough of it. Those lines, and the feeling they gave me, made me wish to scrub my face, take a bath, and go to sleep.

So yeah, even before the party was over, it had left a bad taste in my mouth, all in all. All the things I overheard, Lonnie going on his rounds, and Tommy being mad at me afterwards because I hadn't herded people back downstairs enough. She hadn't told me to do that, and how even was I supposed to do it? Was I supposed to literally grab people and push them down the stairs?

But the party wasn't yet over when Tommy came up to bitch about people not being dragged downstairs. There was still more to come.

I humored Matt, heard Foster badmouthing me and the other gossip, tried to do the duties that Tommy had assigned me. That all would have been enough, but it wasn't the only thing I was dealing with.

Time was shifting. It was. Fairly early on, too. I was at Tommy's party, but then it was another party, later at night. Way fewer people, a tight group of friends about our age. Six or seven or eight of them, boys and girls dressed in sweaters and flannels and jeans, rough slept-on hair. They huddled together in the corner of the old principal's office passing a bottle back and forth. There was a wailing Irish singer on their boombox. I couldn't catch the words—I'm not good with music—but I was sure I'd heard the song before.

Dog-Lonnie, upstairs just then, turned toward that corner. The hair rose in a broad line on his back, and he lifted a front knee, pointing.

They were there, so clear, and nothing else was in the room with me for a second, nothing to see or to hear, and then a boy passed in front of me, and suddenly I was back at Tommy's party—or, only at Tommy's party, not at the other one too. Lonnie still stood tensed pointing toward the corner. The shadows still sat against the wall and splayed on the floor, but they were receding to nothing, all but one who was looking down, the one with blonde-streaked dark bangs, the one wearing a black jean jacket and fingerless gloves, looking so familiar.

And then a group of girls in sparkly costumes crossed the room between us, and all of the shadow-kids were gone. I looked back at that spot all I could, but whatever had happened was over, or so I thought because just a few minutes later, after Foster and Matt had gone (I couldn't look at Foster the whole time they were saying goodbye), there seemed to be little glimmers of the group of shadow-kids once more. I found myself squinting, moving closer.

There weren't a lot of people upstairs, but the party wasn't quite over, either. Stevie had long before gone to bed with Tommy's headphones on. Tommy had already come up to hiss in my ear about how I was supposed to make sure people came downstairs. Cal and Jerry were in the kitchen looking through the cabinets for something more to drink. A couple of kids smoked on the patio, a couple more talked in the living room. Others were still in the basement, but I didn't know how many. I wasn't very present in the moment. I was moving to the corner where the strange shadows had been, trying to concentrate.

The girl with the streaky bangs was there again, sitting on the floor with her legs straight in front of her, a flickering shadow so dim I had to squint. She was still looking down, but then she looked up. Betty.

She was seeing me, too. I'd never wanted to see her like this, but somehow I'd always known I would.

I felt like I was choking. "I'm so sorry," I said, loud enough for anyone to hear. I didn't care.

"It didn't hurt at all," she said in a dreamy voice. She wasn't looking at me now. I thought she was pretending to speak to one of the shadows that had been beside her on the floor earlier. I couldn't see any of them now. I couldn't see Lonnie, could barely see the room, in fact. Everything was turning, changing.

I can't explain.

It seemed that Betty and I were isolated against a gray background. Maybe this was only because I focused so intently on her. I wanted to see nothing but her and so she *was* all I saw.

And she saw me. She couldn't pretend now.

She turned away from the people she'd been speaking with and looked at me. "You told me some stories, Jojo," she said. "Actually, it's kind of fucked up how bad you lied to me."

"Yeah," I said. I could not argue.

157

"So it's true? You can let me in, can't you? I can breathe and . . ." She stood. If she'd had a body, she'd have had me by the shoulders.

She said, "Like you did with the boys that time. You can let me?"

Lonnie barked once. He was very close.

Betty said, "How long did you know what was going to happen to me?"

Again, I'd forgotten where I was. I said, "I didn't know exactly. It was always just a feeling."

"But I can breathe again, walk again? You could do that for me?" She was clear now and her face—her whole stance—looked so vicious, so hungry.

I was holding my breath.

She was behind me. She was all around me, screaming at me, whispering, crying. Many versions of her, it seemed, telling me all the themes of her little life, the fear she'd had to live with and the sense of injustice she had about dying so young. She circled me, and Lonnie circled her barking, growling.

And then he was silent, gone. Everything was still. Everything around me, all laid out like a map. Everything. All of Beulah drawn out in fine white lines and everything beyond Beulah, everywhere I'd been in my life, all the roads and all the houses. I saw into all of the houses at once. I saw into everyone's heart and mind, everyone that I'd ever known or ever would know, all of my interactions, every book I'd read. All at once, all in a second.

I knew many things, just in that instant, that I had not known before and would not know again a minute later. I remembered all of my dreams. I remembered the thick gray spaces between those dreams.

And before me was my own face in its ghastly paint, blurred and oily from all the night's stress. The hair all clouded around the head like Mom's, the stick-figure body.

I knew that Betty had just taken that body from me, just slipped into it.

I was not in that first instant sorry that she had. I felt released. I felt paid up, somehow.

She closed her eyes, breathed deeply, and then looked at me—or tried.

Was there a me? I don't think so. I don't think I appeared to her. I was everywhere and nowhere just then. I was there in the room with her but not only there. She seemed distant, like she was one of a thousand computer screens I was trying to monitor.

The green eyes moved from side to side, searching for me. They were wet, and when she wiped them, the thick mascara smeared over her cheek and hand.

She took another long, deep breath, ran a hand over the front of the body and then, as if noticing the hands for the first time, made fists, rubbed them together, stretched them, looked at them long and hard. The expression on her face was of absolute pleasure.

She started, turned the head to the left as though listening for some faint sound. "Is your sister all right?" she said. Her look was surprised, curious, but then as if to say, "Never mind," she waved a hand. Serious then, she said, "You have to be more careful with yourself, Jojo. This is the second time this has happened, right? I'm not so sure you'll survive a third."

The eyes rolled up in the head then. The body dropped.

The next thing I knew, I was in the bathtub, still in my clothes. Jerry sprayed me with the showerhead. Stevie crouched beside my face, worrying over me. Tommy stood at the foot of the tub glaring more coldly than I'd ever seen her glare before (and, well, glaring is a special talent for her). When it seemed that I would not have to go to the hospital or anything, Tommy finally stalked out of the room.

I was helped to my room, where I moved swiftly into sleep. The house was clean by the time I woke.

Tommy didn't speak to me for some time after that, at least not when Mom was out of earshot.

Stevie was attentive, kind. She brought hot washrags, soup, juice. She liked the chance to take care of someone, and I thought again how maybe she'd be a nurse someday.

I couldn't make it to school the rest of the week. I wasn't sure Mom noticed. Tommy for sure wouldn't say anything about what happened because then she'd have to say how she had a party without getting permission, and it might come out that she'd been drinking, and so on.

I still didn't see how Betty could have come here. She was surely never in Beulah in life. This wasn't a place she had reason to haunt, at least not that I could see. I couldn't ask her because she didn't return.

All was a hush, actually. Lonnie didn't pace. The children didn't make a single movement, not a single peep. While Tommy and Stevie were at school, I crept down to the basement to sit for an hour by the door of the furnace room. Nothing stirred inside. I went in and looked in every corner, the first time I'd ever gotten a good look at that room.

Back in bed, I tried so hard to remember what all I saw and learned and *was* in that minute or two that she had my body and I had the dream-world. I tried to find the muscle I needed to use for seeing it again, or the door I need to open to get to it, but there was nothing. Nothing but silence and the ticking of baseboard heaters coming on. I lay on my belly with the warm light from the window in my hair and tried to remember.

Most of what I had in that moment was gone. The sense of something profound, the framework of a great epiphany remained, but there just wasn't any content to it. It was all white lines on pale gray paper.

#

Or, most of it was gone. A few details lingered:

Betty: It didn't hurt; she didn't have the time to fear it.

Back around the time we moved to Beulah, the dad had made another threat and she and her mom had to run again, further than they were used to this time and under different names. That was all; that was the only reason I couldn't find her in the summer.

It had felt good to run. She had little to hold her in Orliss. She and her mother made the decision to move as adults, the mother knowing not to take her coming for granted. Betty might just as well have gone off to a friend's house or even back to the dad. He'd never been quite the monster to Betty that he'd been to her mom.

They made the decision together and felt good about the move. Betty and her mom were both just as excited about their new life as my mom and sisters had been about our new life in Beulah.

Betty had gotten a job at a Chinese restaurant first thing and started to run around with her cousins in that town, which was a lot bigger and better than Orliss, a lot better than Beulah. There were more places to earn better money and more things to do. They went to movies and did a lot of hiking around the end of summer. When I was moping around the schoolhouse and registering for school, Betty was rushing through the GED tests so that she could apply to the little community college where her cousin went. She had an easier time with the tests than she expected, so my first day at Dolly Parton High was her first day at college.

Around the time I was at Roger's party, she and her friends were at a big music festival. Last week, the last weekend of October, she and the friends went on a camping trip. It was still that warm where she was living. They hiked the dry hills. They went into a shallow cave, seven or eight of them wearing sweats and flannel shirts, just to talk and have a beer. I saw it all like a movie in lantern light, saw the loving way her new friends looked at her, saw the graffiti on the walls of the cave.

I remember it all like it happened to me. They talked about normal things, what they might do for Halloween and something wrong with a friend who wasn't able to be there with them. They talked about movies, meals, books, work, classes. They all had lives, and Betty was finally getting a life for herself.

My life had played before me in that moment she had me. It had played out start to finish. I still feel the weight of it but can't recall any more of my life than I could before it happened. *Betty's* life I saw in full, start to finish. Her safe early years and then her father screaming. Hiding out in her room, hitting the road with her mom. All of her life played before me, and while I was not able to keep it all, I was able to keep the outlines. As much as she might have remembered about the day she died, I kept.

And I remembered her death, just as she saw it. No warning, little pain. She died—honestly—not knowing what had gotten her. Just the good time in the cave, a tipsy walk along the trail, and a sudden flash. I don't know if it was light or pressure. Just a blast that passed in an instant.

#

Tommy: Betty had asked how she was, which was maybe what planted the seed, but it's more than that. I was left with an image of Tommy doing something that would be disastrous to her. The image was of Tommy in bed with a dark-haired boy. I couldn't see him well enough to fully identify him, but I thought it must be Adrian. A sinking nausea feeling came over me when I thought of it, so I did not linger on it.

Did this happen? Was it something that was going to happen, or just a warning of something that might happen? Tommy still wasn't speaking to me. I wanted more than anything to speak with her.

There was one more party coming up. On November sixth, Prince Jasper was to turn eighteen. The official party was to be at Ellen's, and there would be revealed his very special eighteenth birthday gift, which was a secret from all of us except for Mom. I was sure there would be a real party to follow, but we didn't hear about it.

All of us were invited Ellen's, but Tommy said that she couldn't get out of work that evening, which was funny because she usually had that day off. I remembered the dream-image and wondered if she wanted to avoid seeing Adrian.

#

The next thing that lingered, I didn't know exactly what I wanted to call it. A *focus*, I guess. Motivation. See, Betty hadn't been able to do this last thing she was trying to do, and I felt like that was a good goal for me to have. I wanted, for the first time since I was twelve or thirteen, to apply myself. I wanted to live up to part of my potential.

I could do what Betty didn't have the chance to do. I could finally get what everyone was always telling me to get, a life.

The last detail was nothing more than a name: Tamara. None of the content of its significance stuck to the name, only the significance itself. An odd image associated with it. There was a bright halo or aura, but the face half-glimpsed beneath the aura was inhuman. It was the face of a fox.

#

"I'm too old, anyway," Stevie said. She was over at the desk again but didn't have the light on.

"Too old for what?" I said. I was lying in bed, as always.

She laughed, sighed. "Oh, I didn't know you were up."

"Too old for what?" I asked.

"Trick or treating."

No one had taken her shopping for a costume. No one had thought of her at all.

3

I remembered my dream for the first time in ages and took up the journal to capture as much as I could.

It was Brian, the cutest of the fifties boys who had taken me joyriding back when I was fourteen, the one who in Betty's version had been my almost-lover. Now he played the part of the teacher who haunted my bedroom. It was the same room only done up as a classroom with a dozen child-sized desks. I sat at a desk in the center of the classroom and was his only student. He had drawn an image on the chalkboard and was lecturing excitedly. The lecture was only a snottier-sounding restatement of my own theories:

We think we need our bodies for all sorts of things—food and sex, smelling things, seeing things. It isn't true, or not exactly. We can feel all of the sensations out of body; we can be intimate with others in ways that transcend the intimacy we can achieve as embodied people. It is only nostalgia that makes these out-of-body sensations seem less than that what they were. As absolute values, the sensations are far superior to those one experiences in body.

In other words, the body is not needed for sensation. It is very useful for experiencing a certain homely type of sensation, the comfort food of sensation, if you will.

Embodied intimacy, embodied smells—they are different from the other sort but superior only because memory makes them so.

The body is essential for only two things. One of these is making babies, bringing new souls into one's family. No one can do that out of body. The other is for going new places—at least for most of us. Most shadows are unable to go anywhere but the places they visited most often in life. I've never met a shadow that did not have a natural range.

With a body, you can roam, you can explore. You can see things you've never seen before.

There is simply no evidence that the dead are allowed to travel to places they never traveled in life. There's nothing to suggest they can. Most of them linger only as vague shapes within those rooms where they spent the most time.

Hundreds of children sitting for hours in a day in a schoolroom make only a vertical shimmer of hands going up. Even a powerful figure like Lonnie has only that narrow track from the park to the picnic table under the tree, to the halls, to the furnace room.

What's left to you is as physical as your body—that it's actually a part of your body—but it's bound to the tracks you've left, just as firmly as your first body is bound to obey gravity.

"What does this mean for me?" I said in the dream. My voice was the small voice of a child, though my body was life-size. "Are you saying, then, that I need to hit the road? I need to see what all I can? Is this urgent?"

He didn't answer, or I couldn't recall his answer.

The image on the board I drew out as best I could: the crude shape of person with a second shape tipping out from the side like two face cards splayed, the instantly recognizable symbol of a person leaving their body.

I wrote the name Lonnie in cursive, tracing my pen over the letters over and over again the way a girl would write out her crush's name. It felt true. His name really was Lonnie, then. I had known it earlier than I should have.

I'd gotten myself into something here without trying. It felt dangerous.

That story I told Betty captured something about my time with Brian and the others. Then again, the story was riddled with lies.

I never thought the boys were anything but what they were, for a start. I knew they were dead all along. I talked to them anyway, ran with them anyway until one day when they tricked me out of my body.

What had it been like, really? In my dream I allowed myself to try to see. Roaring sound and I was in a different place, everything brown and gold and then gray. That was all I could call back.

NOVEMBER

1

The main point of Brian's lecture—that in death you can only go to the places you traveled in life—wasn't anything I hadn't already come up with on my own, though of course Betty's appearance had voided that theory. She had never been to Beulah.

I'd been just guessing about how this worked; all my life I'd been guessing. Now it seemed I'd only been making up superstitions.

When I was in school back in Orliss, and even when I first came to Beulah, I fully believed that if I wanted to go anywhere after I died, I would need to know that place well in life. That had to be the reason I was always walking, always trying to memorize every new place that I saw. I'd thought I would be confined to those places in death and wanted my reach to be wide.

I had two insights the night of Tommy's party: the huge blast of one that I lost upon waking in the bathtub and the smaller one that lingered. I'd seen and forgotten how my life played out and how it ended. What I had not forgotten was that I owed it to Betty to make something out of that life.

After two days at home, I went back to school and back to the self-care routine. Over the next week, I went to each of my teachers asking—*begging*—for help. Even the sleazy English teacher. I went to him and pleaded for extra credit, told him how much I'd always liked to write. The look on his face was of a salesman making a spectacular, unlikely sale. He was the easiest, but the others took pity on me too. It was humiliating only in the anticipation of it.

When I was actually doing it, I felt good, as anyone does when they have a chance to exercise a skill.

November is the best time to grovel like that, I think.

#

What Tommy experienced was very different, but it had the same upshot. She had come to realize that, starting with Roger's party, she'd been drinking too much and in general being a little bit bad for the first time in her life. Being bad meant drinking, but more than that it meant neglecting family and work and school, which she claimed she had been doing although no one had really noticed. She'd also seen that the people she had been associating with were not, in many cases, real friends. What happened at her party gave her the scare she needed to give it all up and decide to be good again.

She told us all of this at the kitchen table on a Sunday morning before we started making breakfast. "Scared straight" and "wakeup call" might have come into it. She apologized to Mom for lying to her.

I was frozen there, afraid to move as it dawned over me that this confession was not a first confession. Tommy would have made her first confession to Mom alone. One glance at Mom's hard face and I knew that this was just what had happened. Mom knew about the party as well as "what happened at the party," which I guessed was a euphemism for me talking to myself and then passing out in the middle of the great room while the stragglers observed, then being brought back to life in a cold-water bath.

I was of mixed feelings about the whole thing. On the one hand, what a remarkably good girl my sister was! What a really fucking good head she had on her shoulders, and how easy it had been for her to learn her lesson. It made my own angry rebellious years look needlessly long-winded. On the other hand, what a devious little thing she was, seeing that I held something over her for once, to slither out from under me in such a treacherous way. And what a drama queen she was, actually. Her own party had been her second drinking party, at least that I knew of, and the drinks were, um, minimal.

(And what influence had Lonnie had on Tommy? She was downstairs with him all the time. Was he giving her a police mindset?)

Mom's face really was quite hard. A mother never says which one is the favorite, but I was always her favorite—everyone knew this—but just now, well, I got an image of a lioness lying happy with her two cubs when another half-grown cub wanders too close. She turns toward it growling, about to strike.

Tommy said, staring into Stevie's eyes, "What I feel the worst about is not being here for you, Stevie. You do everything for us, and then everybody neglects you. That's not going to happen anymore."

Stevie barely knew irony, but her lip curled a little at that. Since when had Tommy ever not ignored her? Not to mention the fact that she was apologizing now for "everybody," which was needlessly passive aggressive. Noticing Stevie's reaction made me feel better about being a little skeptical about the whole confession, and it helped to unmix my feelings.

I said, "We've all had a scare. We're going to do better. I've already raised my grades, I swear." This was the honest truth, it being very easy to raise your grades once teachers see you "finally" making an effort.

Mom didn't even look at me. She stood and turned to the fridge. Stevie stood, squeezed my arm, then set about getting out the pans and plates for breakfast.

"What about all your friends?" I said to Tommy.

"I mean, Cal and Jerry are good people, but do I want to be Cal and Jerry? Do *you* want to be Foster?"

"I meant your new friends," I said.

Tommy rolled her eyes. She said, "Let's be honest. I'm not good enough to get anything out of sports; I'm not getting a basketball scholarship or getting into some big school. I'm not going to bond with these girls and somehow end up being lifelong friends with them."

Had all this been the plan? Mom had turned back toward us, and I looked over her face. She showed concern but maybe also surprise at the specifics. No, no one had thought Tommy would be getting a basketball scholarship or going any place big. These were fantasies she'd had and was able to voice only now that that her hopes for them had died.

"You'll still go to college," Mom said.

Tommy sighed. "I'm planning to go to college and work at the same time. And not at some place like Tiger Burger. Maybe I'll do a vocational program first. CNA certificate, something like that. See, college is this dreamy thing to all of you, but to me it's a reality. I have actually researched things. I actually keep in with the counselors."

Not that anyone ever notices, she didn't say.

Tommy didn't seem to have the disposition to be a nurse, but what did I know? She was always working on her story, and maybe nursing could fit into it.

"You're dropping the team, then," Mom said. She'd turned back away from us, but I could still read her. She wasn't sorry. She'd always felt Tommy wasted too much of herself on sports.

Tommy said, "I don't know. I don't need to worry about it. I'll play if it's fun, stop if it isn't fun."

We had a minimal breakfast, just eggs with cheese on toast, and we talked about other things. Stevie had seen Mrs. Greene's twins in person when the husband brought them during lunch. They were cuter than she'd even imagined. Mom had learned Ellen's mom was feeling up to

171

having visitors again, so hopefully we'd get to see the rest of that house. She wanted us to see Ellen's old room.

Mom went back to her bedroom after lunch, and we all three cleaned the kitchen in silence.

Tommy kept trying to catch my eye. "What?" I said after a while, but she just said, "Later." We went about getting the laundry started, and when Stevie went for a bath, Tommy took me by the wrist and made me sneak downstairs with her.

You know what I thought at first? I thought that she'd finally caught a hint of Lonnie. My skin went cool. As we came down, I was working through what to tell her, but no, she did not lead me toward the back room. She led me left into the awful galley kitchen where no one ever went, the furthest place from Mom's room. Tommy hoisted herself up on the counter, and I stood facing her.

"So, I just wanted to say I'm sorry," she said.

"I think you did already say that a bunch up there," I said with a cold edge. I didn't much like being in the abandoned kitchen. For the first time I wondered how this room could be so narrow. The staircase was nearly dead center, and the kitchen was the only thing on the left side of the downstairs. It should be twenty or twenty-five feet across, not ten.

"Hey, Tommy said, looking and sounding very sincere. "I wouldn't tell on you just for fun. I was worried about you. But I didn't tell everything up there." She looked up and over toward Mom's room.

The chill came back. My arms started to prickle.

"I tell you this, and you have something on me again, which I know you'll like," Tommy said, "but I have to tell someone. I think he might go after you, too."

"Who? What happened?" I said. I couldn't breathe.

"You know who, or don't you?" Tommy said, and she rolled her eyes a little. "Jasper. He came back here after the party, after all the drama. He tapped his fingernails on the back door until I woke up."

We kept talking for quite a long time. Tommy isn't one to share details, but something had happened between Jasper and her in her narrow bed. I gathered it was something less than what might have happened, but it was something terrible enough because Jasper didn't even like Tommy, not even a little, and she did not like him. Too, he had that tall girlfriend, and while Adrian had not made any particular moves on Tommy, they'd had some kind of chemistry and so he was another complication.

Had Jasper done it to spite Adrian? Had he done it because he secretly did like Tommy? Had he wanted to drive a wedge between Ellen and Mom? Or had he just wanted to see what he could get away with? That last one sounded about right.

And why had Tommy not told him to go away? What was wrong with her? Mom might have asked questions like these, but to me it made perfect sense. It seemed like Jasper must be just Tommy's type, physically, and he was there, and after the lackluster party ending in my being revived in the bathtub, she was upset. She needed some kind of comfort.

She was shaken, though. I didn't know how experienced or inexperienced Tommy was because we didn't talk about such things, usually. Still, I gathered that the encounter itself had been exciting and not unpleasant. The anguish came later when she thought about it in terms of the landlord's son laying claim, when she thought about what he might say about it to the boys who knew the girls on her team, when she thought about Mom or Ellen, or both of them finding out.

I pulled myself up on the counter beside her at some point. I came as close as I could without touching. Maybe some part of her wanted Mom to know. Why else would she tell me? I most surely did not believe that Tommy thought Jasper might want to repeat the thing with me, which was the reason she'd given before speaking of it.

"He won't tell anyone, and if he does, they won't tell Ellen. It's just not the kind of thing that will get back to Mom."

"You know what?" she said. "It would serve her right if it did come out. I think about how she was with us all our lives. Remember when we were little, how she would do us up and parade us around? We may not have anything, but we're pretty and sweet. The bunch of us going around like that at the Fourth of July, just a pack of ... single girls." She had a resentful look saying this, I thought.

I didn't quite follow.

"Never mind," she said. "I just wanted someone to know in case it changes things somehow, but to my mind everything's changed anyway. All I want is to get out on my own and start having a normal life. I want to have nice things, you know, and there is no shortcut to that. You have to just focus and work, and that's what I'm going to do."

"Me too," I said quickly.

She only looked at me.

"I mean, I know I'm the fuck up. That's why it's important for you to make good or whatever. You'll be taking care of me at some point."

"You think you're joking, but—"

"No, I know I'm not."

We had an awkward hug then and left that terrible room.

2

Mom and Tommy both had all the extra hours they could take at work, so Stevie and I had many evenings alone with nothing much to do. She'd make dinner and we'd do our homework—I had a lot more of it now that I was trying to make good. After that, we'd just hang out reading, or we'd go for short walks down Farm School Road.

Even though it was much too cold for swimming, Stevie would always look to see if Roger's Jeep might be in front of the white house; I'd made the mistake of telling her about his invitation to use the pool. She was always trying to find something she could look forward to, and there was little enough of that.

As we set off on one of these walks, time shifted again in the schoolhouse yard. It was only the second time it happened. The first time, it had happened when I was coming home. I still remembered the leaves stirring at my feet and the kids chatting in the yard. This time, it happened almost right when Stevie and I came out the front door. It was early evening, sky all slate gray, and then I turned to check the door lock, and the sun was higher, maybe close to three o'clock, and the air was warmer.

Shadows, faint ones but so many of them, flowed out and down the stairs all around us. Through us, I supposed.

Stevie was right beside me. She rushed down the stairs at their speed and kept up a jog until she was out in the road.

I was shaken and didn't want her to see that I was. I walked slowly. The light changed again so that, by the time I joined her in the road, the cool air and the slate gray sky were back, just like nothing had happened.

We walked, and our shadows were almost the same length now. We had nothing to talk about, together all the time as we were, but we talked about the novels we were reading, the houses along the road, cute cars that went by, anything. Stevie walked at a good clip though she was shorter of breath than I liked.

We turned back toward the house after a while, and I remember we were on the far side on the road. Because of the slight hill, your first sight of the schoolhouse would be its roof. This time, the location of the schoolhouse was clear before we saw the roof. The patch of light above it was bluer. Sun lit up the fluffy clouds and then, as we walked on, sun lit on the schoolhouse's dark roof. Stevie was looking at the ground as we neared.

I heard Stevie gasp when she glanced up. I heard her.
"Do you see that?" I said.
"No."
"Stevie, do you see that? Can you hear them?"
The children were shrieking loudly. It was their last day of school once more.

As we came closer, I saw the shadow sitting at his picnic table under the tree. Lonnie. He was not transparent, but he was a silhouette, just a dark cutout. He didn't say anything, didn't try to stand. There were only a few children left in the yard, but they were bright, aggressive ones, two girls and a boy talking excitedly, two more boys on the steps.

Stevie's face went pale. She walked straight ahead through the two boys and went to open the door, but it was locked. She waited with her eyes on the knob for me to unlock it and went straight to the bathroom. I stood outside the door saying, "You saw that, didn't you?" and she was crying. She said to leave her alone, and after a while I did.

#

Mom had the girls at the grocery store later, and Ellen came to the front door to get me to meet her down at the back door and help her bring in some things. She had her husband's truck parked behind the patio so that we wouldn't have to move stuff down the stairs.

I did not ever use the back door because of its proximity to the furnace room. Lonnie was strongest there.

That day, while Ellen and I moved in box after box of laminate flooring, I saw him in full daylight and had to pretend I didn't. He sat on a metal chair beside the furnace and looked like he was only pretending not to see us. Just a small man, sixty or so, with russet-colored freckled skin and short gray-and-brown hair, he had his knees wide apart and his hands on them like someone in a waiting room. He looked at the floor most of the time but once looked up revealing wet blue eyes.

It had been a long time since I'd seen one look so real, like you could touch him.

#

"How often do you see things?" I asked Stevie as we lay in bed that night.

She made a little moan to tell me she was nearly asleep.

"Are you ever not sure when they're real?"

"Please don't," she said. "We were so worried about you at the party and now... this reminds me of the things you used to say."

"You're acting just like I used to act," I said.

She rolled with her back to me. "Please, don't say any more," she said.

"Stevie, go down and check the furnace," I said the next day. She wouldn't do it.

"Stevie, use the back door when you're working outside. It's faster."

"Stevie," I'd say, and after a while she'd just say, "No" without waiting to hear what I'd ask. Every other thing she said was, "Don't be weird" or "You're trying to scare me."

She wouldn't tell Mom—she hadn't ever told Mom about the first time I was acting weird, when she was a little girl—but she said it hurt her to see me acting this way again, and she wanted to know sometimes when we were falling asleep if there was anything she could do to help me.

"Just admit it," I'd say, but she never would.

I'd started to believe I was imagining things until a few nights before Thanksgiving when it all hit the fan.

3

Matt showed up at school at the end of the last day before Thanksgiving break. He was sitting in his own little white hatchback, which I'd never seen before. I'd imagined him forever riding shotgun in Foster's car.

"Hey Georgie," he called when he saw me, and I walked over to the passenger side. "You want a ride?"

"No thanks." I said, looking around for whoever he might have been waiting for at the school. "Wait, you didn't come here to see me, did you?"

"Of course," he said. "I came to give you a ride home."

I was leaning into the car. It was newish and clean inside. I said I didn't need a ride, that I liked to walk. He said he'd park, then, and he'd walk me home.

"And walk back? That's stupid," I said.

"Yeah, it kind of is," he said.

So I got in the car thinking that it was a mistake. It would be impossible to ever separate Matt from Foster and the thing that Foster had said.

Matt asked if I wanted to go home or someplace else. I said there was nowhere else. I never had any money, or I'd have liked to get an ice cream or something. Stevie wouldn't be home for a while since she was riding the bus.

"I know where to go," I said as we pulled out toward the highway. "I haven't ever gotten anyone to take me out to the canyon. All this time we've been here, I've never been back over the bridge."

He drove me out to the other side, where there was a parking lot with interpretive signs, benches and streetlights. Very fancy. Steps led down from the sign, but Matt said they just led to a platform a little bit down from the bridge.

We got out and walked the bridge just like Mom had been supposed to do back in third grade. The canyon was deeper than I'd realized and so much wider with the Snake River running dark blue-green in the center of it. The sides were dark and rocky, though not so dark as they looked from the house. The bottom had yellow grasses and vegetation that was still green right near the water, and in distant places where the gap widened, there were good bits of land. It gave me vertigo when I lost track of myself and got too close to the railing, but other than that, it was a pretty view and a nice walk.

Then there she was, the suicide I'd been trying not to see, just a filmy pink shadow climbing onto a railing lower than the iron one that stood there now. I looked away before she dropped.

The day was bright, and I felt warm enough. It began to snow, just a skiff of snow. I guess it was kind of a romantic scene, though I didn't recognize it as such right away. The truth was, I was starting to feel a little fevered.

"I've been thinking," Matt said.

"What have you been thinking?" I asked.

"It seems like I only ever see you at a house party."

"There's nothing else to do." I saw where this was going now. I noticed he was dressed kind of cute in a tweed sweater with a dress shirt under it. He carried a brown satchel similar to mine.

"We could go on a date," he said.

"In Beulah?"

"Or somewhere. I could drive you to Boise."

And wind up back at his place? "I don't know."

"Beulah, then," he said.

"There's nowhere to go." I did not want more Tiger Burger.

"That's where you're wrong," he said, and he had a playful expression.

"I've never been on a date date," I said, feeling as soon as I said it that it was a ridiculous thing to say.

"Do you want to go with me?"

"I don't know." I didn't really want to, but I thought that the normal person I was trying to become would want to. If I asked myself, What Would Tommy Do?, Tommy would go on the date.

"Is there someone else you'd rather go with?" he asked.

"No."

"So it's the date you're not sure about, not me?"

"I don't know." I was smiling now.

"I'm going to take you home now and pick you up about seven-thirty, OK?"

"OK."

I still wasn't sure whether I wanted to go or not go, but it didn't seem like there was an option. I couldn't choose and so whatever would happen was what would happen.

Maybe Matt thought that I would get dolled up again like at Tommy's party, but what I did when he dropped me off was lie on my bed. I had on what I'd worn to school, black jeans and a black T-shirt and an awesome black wool swing coat that was a handout from Ellen, two or three sizes too big, and a red plaid scarf. I didn't comb my hair. I didn't do anything between the time he dropped me off and the time he picked me up. I just lay there until I felt chilled, got under the covers and fell asleep. I woke up a couple hours later and kept lying there with my eyes open until Matt knocked at the door. My head hurt.

Stevie had been doing homework the last time my eyes were open, but now she was fixing dinner. I smelled something warm and cheesy and wanted to just eat and not bother about the date.

"I was being quiet until you got up, but dinner's ready," she said from the bedroom door. "And your friend is waiting by the door."

I made some kind of a moan and said, "Thanks," and went to the door where he stood.

"Can he stay for dinner?" Stevie called, and Matt gave me a terrified look.

"We can't stay," I called. We walked back to the kitchen where she'd already put out an extra plate. "We actually need to go somewhere. I'm so sorry I didn't say. I was asleep."

"But there's no one home," she said.

"You're OK. Tommy will be home soon, right?"

"Half an hour. When dinner's done."

"She's not old enough to stay home alone," said Matt.

"Of course she is," I said. I stayed at home at that age, for sure.

"She can come with us," he said.

"No," Stevie said. She didn't show her disappointment. "I'll be fine."

No snow outside, and it was warm enough. Matt drove back towards school, but we turned south before the park and passed the courthouse and post office, finally coming to a low brick building with two red neon "Pizza" signs. The inside was dark with red curtains, red pebbly candleholders, red gingham plastic tablecloths, and a mural on the barn wood wall of a queen's guard. Another mural with fall trees. Another mural, waterfall in brilliant greenery, a Fathead of a knight. Foosball table, pool table.

Our table nestled in a dark corner of a vast main dining room. A Christmas tree already stood in the far corner, all overlit with big green and reddish-orange bulbs, and there were many tables between it and us, some of them dining tables and some of them picnic tables. A few other diners sat at some of them, but all was quiet in our back corner.

"We don't go out to eat a lot," I said when we had ordered, and maybe I was still half-asleep because I went on. "I suppose we're really poor, aren't we? I don't notice, but I don't own much of anything, if I think of it. I mean, I gave away most of what I had, but even that wasn't all that much. It's funny, I had to suck up to my teachers just a couple of weeks ago, to try to salvage the semester. I told my social studies teacher how sorry I was about never talking in that class because really I had a lot to say about some of the topics. Like privilege, I mean I can't say I know exactly what she was fishing for in that discussion, but obviously she wanted everyone to see that they had a lot of privileges that other people didn't have.

"And I saw that. Giving our things away at the Goodwill was the proof of that. That we could give away all our household things without worrying that we wouldn't ever have a household again, that was a privilege.

"And we had the privilege of knowing what our privileges were. I, for example, really value getting a nap every day and never having all that much expected of me. That's the kind of privilege you only notice if you let yourself take advantage of it, which most people wouldn't because of their pride or their self-dignity or whatever. Or, being able to quit a job just because she hated it was something Mom valued. A lot of people have those kinds of privileges, but it's like they don't have them because they never take advantage of them."

"Are you nervous?" Matt said when I stopped to take a drink of water.

"Nervous?"

"You were like this that one day in the summer when I came out to your place, remember? Just going on about a swimsuit. But you're not usually like this." He laid his hand gently on mine and said, "You don't need to be nervous with me."

In other words, *shut up.*

And I remembered Mom was pissed because I hadn't been *on* like this lately. What was I supposed to do, talk or not talk? Whichever way you went, you'd always make someone unhappy.

I looked down at the red nubby candles and red gingham tablecloth, saw the red tumblers of Coke were now sitting on the table. The pizza was taking a long while. I wondered if I had been manipulating that pretty, nerdy social studies teacher. I'd said I was afraid of being stigmatized in a place like Beulah because, well, everyone was conservative and kind of... provincial. Had I used that actual word?

Matt was speaking about his roommate and his work now. He'd quit at the auto parts store and was waiting until the new year to look for something else. Once more, he showed life drawings on the phone, the same nude girl again but others of a boy around our age and an older man with a long ponytail. He took a sketchbook out of his satchel and showed me other little studies of trees, buildings, and little still lifes. His work was getting better, and I told him so without reservations. I didn't say "You were always good but *whoo boy* now you're really something." No, I said, "You're getting better." I think he liked that quite a lot.

Matt had decided to like me because I was so hard to like, hadn't he? I was someone no one else would see the beauty in. He was the only one who could see it. It was a rom-com idea.

I thought, *No way boys get off on watching rom-coms, too* and then I thought, *He sees something no one else can. Kind of like you, huh? You could tell him and you'd have that in common.* My mind was suddenly crowded with all these ideas, but I nodded and looked tranquil to Matt like I always did in class.

I went to wash my hands. I appreciated the rainforest murals covering the bathroom walls. They made the visit feel extra refreshing.

"They forgot our order," I said when we returned, but Matt disagreed, so we waited long enough to go over some stories about his wacky roommates. Eventually he went back to the counter.

The large pizza, when it finally came, had thick delicious-looking pepperoni that tasted disappointing and a lot of soft bland cheese. I dug in and ended up finishing half of it, I was so hungry by then.

"This is the most romantic place in Beulah," Matt said, and we laughed. I think we laughed so hard because I was still wearing my coat and had orange grease all up and down my fingers.

#

"I feel sleepy now," I said and fell down on the sofa as soon as we got back.

I hoped that Matt would stay until I fell asleep, which wouldn't be long. He sat down on the other sofa and looked around.

"No TV?"

"No."

"Anywhere?"

"No." My eyes closed. "The wintertime makes me sleepy."

I figured Stevie was at her desk or already in bed. Tommy should have been home, but maybe she'd decided to go out after work or was picking up extra hours. Mom should have been home. Maybe she was sleeping in the next room already.

"Did you see Mom's truck? I forget," I said.

"No, it wasn't there," Matt said.

The front door slammed just as I was falling asleep, and Stevie came running in.

"Matt?" she screamed, "Georgie?"

I called, "Here," and she ran to me.

She was shaking, crying. Her hands were cold.

"What happened?" I asked.

Matt kneeled next to us, saying, "Are you all right?"

She said, "He grabbed me." She held out her wrist, and it was, I thought, pink. A pink cuff on it like rash from a watchband, though nothing more than that.

"Who?" said Matt, and that was when her face went white. She wouldn't say.

The edges of her hair were sweaty, and that made me ask, "Where were you?"

"The park."

"That's a long way. You ran?"

"Should we call the police?" said Matt.

"Was it a kid?" I asked.

"It was a man," she said.

"We should call," said Matt.

She said, "Oh no. I think maybe I was wrong." Her face went blank.

The story she told was confused. No one had come home when they were supposed to, and she had gone from the house thinking to find Tommy at work and get a ride back, but the walk was nice and she decided to walk past the park first. There in the park a man had spoken to her, and when she ignored him he reached out for her and caught her by the wrist. She hurried back home looking behind her all the way.

I couldn't believe she'd leave the house alone. "Did you tell someone at the park?" I said.

"Who would I tell?"

Matt said we were going back to the park. She said no, but he said we were. She could come or not.

Once Matt was out the door, Stevie pulled me back and whispered, "I'm not a hundred percent sure he was a person."

This was the biggest thing she'd ever said to me. I wanted to stop it all and sit and talk with her, but we were following Matt. We couldn't just shut the door behind him.

"Do you *think* he was, though? A person?" I said.

"Yeah, but I'm not sure," she said.

We had no time to say more than that. Matt came back inside when he saw we weren't right behind him. He took her hand and led her out to the car.

#

The snow hadn't continued. It was cold and dark, but the park was well-lit. I saw many shadows scattered around its edges just for an instant when we got out of Matt's car, but they thinned right away. Remaining were only an old man on a bench and two teen girls on the swings.

"Is that him?" said Matt, pointing to the old man.

She shook her head no.

We paced the park looking. There was no other man.

"Is he one of those kids?" Matt said, gesturing toward a group that had just walked into the park by the tennis court.

"Of course not," I said, and Stevie shook her head.

We walked around a couple of times. Matt went up to the girls, but they hadn't seen anything. They'd just come outside a few minutes ago and were already cold and about to leave, they said. When he was finished talking to them and came back to me, they got up and walked toward the houses bordering the park.

#

Mom's truck was in front of the house when we returned. Stevie ran straight in to see her.

I stayed in Matt's car wondering what Stevie would be telling Mom.

"Thanks for trying to help," I said. "And thanks for the date. I'm still so full."

I saw Lonnie then, just the shape of a head and shoulders above X shapes of picnic table legs under the tall, crooked tree.

I don't know why, but I said, "That tree kind of creeps me out."

Matt looked at it for a long time. "Just a big tree. They should have planted it closer to the house for shade."

The figure shifted sideways while Matt was looking at the tree. There was no way he saw it.

Matt leaned in to kiss me. I felt uncomfortable with it, with Lonnie watching and everything, but I tried hard not to flinch back. He gave me a soft dry kiss on the mouth, and then he smiled and gave me another on the forehead. He rubbed my shoulder.

"You're sleepy," he said.

"So sleepy," I said. I had my eye back on the figure. He stood and moved to the edge of his picnic table.

"Look, tomorrow's Wednesday. I have quite a bit to do, and then Thanksgiving, but I'll be free on Friday. Do you want to go out again?"

I didn't feel like I could say no, so I nodded. I stepped out of the car. He waited for me to go up to the door, but I didn't. I just stood there. A cold breeze came up. I waved at Matt and said bye again, and finally he backed out onto Farm School Road headed back toward Eighth. It was just me and the man standing facing each other. He might have been two hundred feet away.

He swayed a bit. He was little more than a silhouette, but I thought that if I came closer, I'd see something different. I approached.

I can still see it now. There was a yard light on at the closest farmhouse, far away but it backlit him a bit in yellow. Everything else was a dark blue. It felt like the breeze held little shards of ice.

I walked a few steps toward him, and I thought he might step toward me, but he didn't. He held his spot under the tree, remained standing.

I walked close enough to see him full and clear, the maggots glistening at the corners of his mouth, the skull face, red eyes, the shreds of freckled russet skin.

I froze. *A demon, not a shadow but a demon,* I thought.

He reached out toward my wrist. I turned and ran, feeling him at my back, swiping at my clothes. It was a slow-motion run up to the porch—sure he was just behind me at every step, sure he could and would touch me. I shut the door behind me, feeling I'd gotten away, and he passed through the door, passed through me—looking now dim and flat but whole again somehow—and took the stairs down, apparently headed to the safety of his room. Perhaps he was going to warm himself beside the long-ago furnace. He was nothing but himself now, readying to make his usual rounds.

Mom was nowhere to be seen. Her bedroom door stood open, but the bathroom door was shut. I made my way to our bedroom where Stevie sat at her desk.

I said, "We need to talk."

4

Stevie and I lay in my bed awake until one or two in the morning. She told me about everything she'd seen around the house, the little children sometimes playing in the yard or going about their day in the schoolhouse. It wasn't anything I hadn't seen, and from her descriptions even subtler, fainter, and yet she had been quite shaken.

I thought that her sensible, easygoing nature might account for her visions starting out this way—or she might be reporting them this way even if they were somewhat more frightening—because she'd always made a point of being sensible, easygoing. How could she keep being that person, now?

And why didn't she come to me earlier? Why didn't she trust me enough? Maybe it was not that. Maybe it was shame at not turning out to be the strong sensible girl we had always thought her to be. I could relate to that.

I asked when it had started, and she wasn't sure. One thing she swore, though: she swore that when I had been thirteen and fourteen and she had still been a little kid, she hadn't seen anything then. She had only been pretending to believe in those things for me, to make me feel better. When Mom had broken her down and forced her to side against me, she really had thought I was sick. She really hadn't sold me out. I believed her.

I'm sure I was the one who got her sick, lying close to her in her bed that night looking at the far wall as we spoke. The teacher entered the room and moved close to her desk. I had her describe it, and it was the same as what I saw. She never described the vertical shimmers from children raising their hands, and I knew she was not seeing quite all that I saw.

"Will they go away?" Stevie said.

"No, never." I couldn't lie.

I had no expectation that it was a temporary thing or that this was the last of it. My first time was Dad in the entry and then there was a gap before the little boy. After that, I never entirely stopped seeing them. Sometimes they were fainter and spangled, swirled with oily color. Sometimes they were firmer, sometimes few and sometimes many, but they were always around me.

"Will it get less scary?" she said.

"It doesn't have to be scary at all," I said, rubbing her back. I wasn't certain this was true, but I thought it was because every day I'd gotten a little less worried about Lonnie pacing the halls. He was strong and firm, and nasty as any I'd seen, and if he scared me less than he once had, then maybe one day he wouldn't scare me at all.

That was all I did for her. I told her it would all be all right and turned from her, crossed the floor and got into my own bed.

I couldn't sleep because I was thinking how maybe Stevie's education was my calling. I was the only one in the world capable of doing it. We could make a study of it. Even with just two of us researching, we could still be a methodical, couldn't we? I'd learn how to be driven and how to be careful and rational. We could figure it out—or if we couldn't make a science of it, we could make an art of it. Painting, writing—something to help Stevie process what she was experiencing and feel safe in the world.

I thought of that, and the thought floated away. Another came in. What if I did start going out with Matt? What would happen? It would provide a sort of doorway, wouldn't it? The GED, a new city. I could do something different there.

Just when Stevie had made clear how needed I was, I was thinking what it would be like to leave?

I was what people thought I was. A nothing, a waste. Foster wasn't wrong about that. I'd always believed that if I could just do what I wanted all the time, then I'd be happy, but it wasn't so, and making other people happy was not something I knew how to do.

My mouth filled with water.

I closed my eyes and saw gray kaleidoscope imagery, felt the elevator-drop of nausea. I resolved to make Stevie my only priority, resolved that this would be the one resolution to finally stick, and then fell headfirst into the fever that would take us both down for the next week. Thanksgiving came and went in a haze.

5

Christmas planning started, as it always does, well before the close of November.

The last time we'd had a really good Christmas was when Dad was still alive. Mom and Tommy and I didn't keep any pictures from that time, but we all have the memories, I'm sure. There wasn't that much money, but we'd always have a tree and plenty of food, and there were cheap presents enough to please two little girls and a baby. We'd sit in the living room together all day in our pajamas. At least that's the story.

All the rough Christmases after that, we just couldn't quite manage. Back when Stevie still believed in Santa, she worried, "If Santa doesn't bring you much for Christmas, does that mean you weren't good?" I got a little lump in my throat remembering the struggle to make presents each year. Whatever little craft thing we would do in school, if they let me, I'd make three of each one. All those times going with Mom to get toys for the girls, helping her make cookies.

My mom and sisters poured every minute and just about every penny they could spare into it, and it would always be nice, but you could still see a little shine of disappointment in their eyes. Tommy, in particular, would be so keyed up about Christmas she'd seem at risk for a breakdown.

This year was shaping up to be one of the worst, not in terms of squalor but in terms of impossible expectations. Even before December, a desperate wish came over Mom to do it right this year, to somehow pay for good presents and decorations and all of it. Tommy got excited about the prospect of having a "real Christmas," too. She pledged her help; they made plans together. I hadn't been much help with that sort of thing for the past four years or so.

Stevie ordinarily would have been at the head of the effort, but she was blue and deflated after our illness. Discussions of Christmas brought a hopeful, wistful expression to her face but no moves to help. She wasn't looking at anyone. She was laboring over her homework with a hand to her temple like it gave her a headache. She fell asleep after school like I always had, woke to eat and bathe, then went to sleep again. Needless to say, she stopped cooking, and Tommy and I had to work that out. Tommy would bring home bagged salad and low-sodium canned soup. When it was my turn, it was always pancakes and eggs.

It was never Mom's turn. A girl who worked at Queenie's had to move away, so Mom took extra shifts. She imagined that the money would be more than what it turned out to be.

I wish I could say that the guilt tore me in two, that I sought out Ellen and tried to take the job helping Marcus, but I didn't. I did go to school, though. I stayed for all my classes because I was trying to turn things around re: graduation, re: being a good role model for Stevie—plus it was too cold to go walking. I took the bus with the girls now. I fell into bed when Stevie did or napped on the sofa, roused myself for dinner, and went back to bed with a novel until I fell asleep again.

Mom's looks at me, Tommy's at that time—they could have skinned me. If I could have helped them out more, I would have, but Christmas just wasn't the motivation for me that it was for them. I didn't get it. We weren't religious; we'd all decided to be less acquisitive. Why did we bother?

The only thing that seemed important just then was to help Stevie through the "bad time" she was starting to have. It felt like Stevie was my only friend and that I was hers. I needed to coach her, be her mentor and role model—because if I was her example of someone with our talent or condition, well, I had to do the best I could, didn't I? I had to make sure she got through this time better than I had. The trouble was that we were exhausted, both emotionally and physically. We had to maintain, that was all.

We never considered telling Mom, "It's real. We both see it." Surely we knew that would only make her think that I had warped Stevie's thinking, infected her with whatever problem I had. Tell anyone besides Mom and it could be even worse. They might take me away from her.

Before bed, Stevie would talk through her feelings. She'd ask, "What should I do?" and each time I would try to impart one more piece of knowledge.

"You can't tell anyone," I said one time.

"I know that," she said, "but what *should* I do? There must be a reason. Why would I see them if I wasn't supposed to do something for them?"

I'd thought that once, too. "I don't think there's a reason. I've asked them, back when they used to talk to me more, and they never mentioned 'unfinished business,' or a message to anyone or anything like that." I thought of the boys, thought of Betty. I was not sure if what I'd just said was true.

"Tell me about the ones who talked to you," Stevie said, sitting up straight.

She found the whole thing incredibly romantic, just as I had when I was her age. An opening in the world, the stuff of fantasy as well as nightmare. I still felt that way about it a lot of the time, if I was honest. And more than anything, I'd always wanted someone I could speak to like this. I'd fantasized about it but never had told my story with any honesty. Those kitschy stories I told Betty were the closest I ever came.

I had to disappoint Stevie, though. As much as I wanted to, it didn't feel right to launch into my secret life story. There were more important things I had to tell her—theories and reflections—only now that I was finally telling, I had a hard time prioritizing my points.

Stevie needed to know the things I'd learned the hard way or the lessons I'd had to keep learning over and over, the things that made a difference. We didn't have time now for stories.

I said, "The truth is, I don't think they're really here. I think they really are just shadows. They don't have desires anymore, or not new ones. They only want to keep doing what they did."

In that way that ten-year-olds have, where you can't tell if they're being sarcastic, Stevie said, "So people still want things and shadows don't? So the definition of a shadow is it's a person who doesn't want anything?"

I nodded.

"That doesn't make sense," she'd say, and soon I'd be giving her an example. We'd be talking about one or another of the shadows I'd known over the years. We'd talk about how I developed my seeing. Sometimes we would walk around the upstairs for a bit after everyone was asleep, just so I could point out certain things about the girls' bathroom-mirror shadows or the persecuted-feeling shadows in the corner that had been the principal's office.

We were avoiding the topic of Lonnie. I'd thought maybe she'd say he was the man who grabbed her wrist in the park, but she never did.

Honestly, I hadn't told Matt, but I very much doubted Stevie's whole story.

"No secrets," we'd both promised just recently.

I wanted to say, "Did it really happen?" I couldn't imagine that an actual old man had grabbed her in the park but in truth, I couldn't imagine that she'd run to the park at all. It was more than out of character.

I *could* imagine her out in the front yard rubbing her own wrist while she looked at one or another of the spectacles Lonnie made of himself out front, under the tree. She wasn't volunteering knowledge of dog-Lonnie or maggot-Lonnie, the Lonnie who enforced dress codes, gray static-Lonnie or HD sun-damage-Lonnie. She'd balked at the idea of visiting the furnace room, but did she see any of the rest of him? I wanted to ask, but I didn't want to place him in her head if he wasn't already there.

I'd told her that shadows were people without desires. Did I really think that? Often Stevie's lessons led to further reflection on my part, and I thought about this one for a while. Did I want anything? Was I, by my own definition, nothing but a shadow? The only thing I wanted with no reservations, the only thing I wanted and wasn't sure would happen, was for Stevie to grow up safe and be happy. I had a feeling of goodwill toward Mom and Tommy, Matt, Ellen and Adrian, Summer and Marcia from Health class. Even people I'd met once and might never meet again, I could say I had genuine goodwill toward them (which, is what Christmas is supposed to be about), but all of these honest good wishes put together were nothing compared to my wish for Stevie.

Intellectually, I knew it was different from what a mother feels for a child, but the feeling seemed just as intense to me. I felt like she was the only important thing I'd ever participated in shaping. I'd long thought I'd never do anything as important as helping raise her, and that was before I knew all we had in common.

"I want you to have what you want, but I worry that all you want is to stay here," I said.

She thought about that and said, "Shouldn't I?"

"Where we live isn't something you can control." Mom would go where she could stand to be, and it was not at all clear that Beulah was always going to be that place for her. It was not clear, either, that this was a great place for Stevie. I might have liked to see her in a larger town where at least there'd be a good library and places you could go for free like that, maybe better schools.

#

"What should I do?" Stevie said. She was upset, not telling me why.

"You should be yourself, do the things you always have. Be a good cook, keep the family running, do a good job at school, don't be ashamed of this, think of it as a gift." I added, after a moment, "and make friends."

"I have friends," she said quickly.

This gave me a chill. I'd never seen her with a friend or heard her speak of one since we moved to Beulah, and I came to the quick conclusion that she must be talking about some shadow who had attached itself to her at school.

It was the fierce little girl, the gymnast I'd seen on the day we registered for school. I knew without asking and yes, I felt so weak and stupid for not suspecting it sooner

Once more, I reminded Stevie that she had to be honest with me, "No secrets, remember?"

We stopped talking of principles and entered the cozier space of stories. Stevie spoke excitedly, and I was excited, too, much as I wanted not to be. I was letting myself drift back into the magic of it.

Her story was of a girl who was starting to lose confidence in herself, a girl who for the first time in her life felt different in a bad way. This girl finds out she is magic and can talk to magical others unseen by her silly peers. She finds a lifetime-friend among them, and they go on adventures. How is that not appealing? And so the story swept over me, and I did not give Stevie the impression that I thought she was at any point in danger. This was a mistake. I knew it was a mistake while it was happening, but I listened, rapt, to the whole saga of the friendship.

It had begun long before Stevie finally told me about seeing the shadows. The girl had not come to her. After Stevie saw her, the girl kept pacing the halls and playground like always, but one day Stevie sought to catch her alone, in an empty room.

One day after lunch, at the bathroom mirror, the girl stood next to Stevie. Her name was Tamara, as Stevie would learn later. At the time she was just a girl. She leaned in close to the mirror to pick at an imagined clump in her mascara.

Stevie said, "You're so pretty."

The girl smiled, and then she seemed to come awake. She looked around her as though she'd heard a spooky sound. Tamara was afraid, Stevie realized. She left the bathroom, only the door didn't open for her. The girl made the motion of opening the door—she *thought* she had opened the door—but she had not.

Stevie cried because that was the first thing that made her sure. She cried in the bathroom until she was late getting back to class, all through class she was unable to concentrate, and for the very first time that whole year, Mrs. Greene looked at her with disappointment. This teacher that Stevie loved looked at her like there was something wrong with her. There was no one there to help Stevie through the highs and the lows on the day she first spoke to Tamara. She came home and probably cooked us dinner, and we didn't notice anything different at all.

When Stevie told me about this, I hugged her. I told her, as I'd *been* telling her, that she could never, ever keep a secret from me again.

Stevie told me about the weeks between that first encounter and the time when they became friends. Tamara came to her when she was alone and talked to her about stupid things like what she was doing over the weekend, music she liked and didn't like, whether Stevie might like to start in the beginner's dance class. She said her mom had a studio in the back room of Beulah Fitness and that it would be good for Stevie to get some exercise and make some more friends.

Stevie and I talked all about it, and we decided that Tamara was so solid because the school was her favorite place. She felt so alive there, and hers had been such an intense little life that she lingered. That was my guess, and Stevie agreed, but I don't know how close to the truth it was. It might have been that there was something special about Tamara. Maybe she was like Stevie and me. Maybe when she was alive she saw shadows.

More stories came out each night, as long as Stevie could stay awake to tell them, which wasn't often more than thirty or forty minutes. Sneaking into strange rooms with Tamara, looking at secret things that Tamara had learned about people in the class. Tamara let Stevie know ways to do things she wasn't supposed to and how to keep from getting caught at them.

I guessed, just from that time I'd seen how she carried herself, that Tamara was quite unforgiving in her judgments of others, and that was what it sounded like. There was a social viciousness to the adventures that I didn't like.

For example, one of the stories was of a girl who sat behind Stevie in class. Tamara told Stevie the right time when she could reach into that girl's desk and slip out her notebook. She told her what pages had embarrassing things on them. Tamara told her how to look up embarrassing things about Mrs. and Mr. Greene, too. but Stevie refused. She told Tamara she didn't want to disrespect Mrs. Greene.

"That was good," I said. I'd been looking for an opportunity to say something to make Stevie question some of this without getting defensive. I had to be very careful. Stevie and I were tighter than we'd been in a long time, but were she and Tamara even closer?

Probably the primary reason Stevie was talking to me like this was that she'd been home sick and could not get to Tamara.

Sure enough, Stevie asked, "What happens when I go to the high school?"

"That's a long way off," I said.

"But will she be able to go there?"

We were back to discussing theory. "We don't *know* that the school is the only place she goes," I said. "She might also pace around at the dance studio, or at her old house."

"She isn't at the dance studio," Stevie said.

"Well, she could be."

"No, I went to Beulah Fitness with Mom and Ellen one day, and I found the room where the studio used to be. It's a weight room now. I sat and watched for a long time. She never showed."

"When was this?"

"I don't know. End of September?"

That meant Stevie had known what she was seeing almost since the very start of the school year. How she could have kept this from me so long I didn't know. It hurt to hear it.

DECEMBER

1

We'd have just the one week off from school for Christmas, plus New Year's Day, but Matt was going to have three whole weeks off from college. I knew about his schedule because he called me on my new phone, which was my early Christmas present from him.

It was such a hassle. He sent Foster to tell me about the phone and to pick me up and take me to the little kiosk at the front of Albertsons, the same place where they sold cigarettes and lottery tickets. Foster couldn't call me and anyway didn't always have afternoons off, so he had to stop by a couple of times before he caught me. When he did catch me, he woke me up from a nap, and we had the hardest time making clear why he was there. I really didn't want to get into his car, but everyone was out shopping, and I didn't have any reason to stay at home.

I was embarrassed to sit next to Foster. I hadn't seen him since Halloween when I overheard him talking about me. He was formal. He seemed to be watching me to see what I was going to do or say. I didn't like it. I didn't like him anymore and wasn't sure I ever had.

"I guess this means you're Matt's girlfriend now," he said when the lady was getting the phone from the back room.

"I don't know about that," I said. I was actually really creeped out by the whole idea and wondered what Matt had meant by doing it. I considered not taking the phone, just walking off right then, but then I thought how happy Stevie would be to play with it. Maybe it would take her mind off things, let her calm down a little. Mom and Tommy never let her touch their phones.

It didn't mean I had to be Matt's girlfriend; it just meant I would be able to talk to him, which I might want to do sometime.

The little red-haired lady at the desk tried to show me how to use the phone, and Foster said it was OK, he'd show me, but I didn't want to spend any more one-on-one time with him than I had to, so I started asking questions. The lady and I leaned in together and she showed me how to sign in and how to use some of the apps. It seemed she'd recently learned these things herself and was delighting in passing on her hard-won knowledge. I think Foster and I were both a little charmed by her, and we spent a while leaning in, learning the phone.

"I'm not of my own time when it comes to these things, so I really appreciate it," I said.

The lady laid out three covers that would fit the phone, but I said no thanks.

Foster said, "Jesus," which made the lady purse her lips, but he got out his wallet and bought me the pink cover with zebra stripes on the back. He asked if that was the one I wanted, and when I didn't answer he just bought it. In the car, he wrestled the phone into the cover before he would give it back to me. He put in Matt's number and his own.

I thought we were going back to the house, but he pulled out of the Albertsons lot only to loop around and pull in at Tiger Burger.

"I don't have any money," I said. I might have already said it at the store.

He just asked, "What do you want?" and when I didn't answer, he ordered me a Tiger Burger and one of their big sundaes. Tiger Burger was sort of famous for a hot fudge sundae in a 24-ounce foam cup. They splattered the inside of the cup with fudge and then filled it up with soft serve

203

and poured more fudge on top and put on a globed plastic lid with a big hole for the spoon. No whipped cream, no cherry, no nuts. I hadn't ever had one, but I'd heard about them.

"I can pay you back later, maybe," I said as we waited for the order.

"What's wrong?" he said. He looked straight at me and asked, "How come you don't come by my work anymore?" He was trying to have a light tone, but he was hurt. He liked me. Whatever he'd said, maybe he'd meant it in the moment or maybe not, but it wasn't how he felt about me.

"I don't come by because I don't walk home now. It's cold," I said.

"Is that right?"

The food was out, then, and he put the bag in my lap. The food felt hot through my jeans. I thought we would go back to the house then, but he pulled into the parking lot instead.

"Let's eat here," he said.

"Oh, let's not and say we did," I said.

He laughed, said, "I think that's the first time I've ever heard you express an opinion," but he turned off the engine anyway.

The sundae had cost over five dollars. I opened the lid and looked at it. I felt like I might cry, it looked so good and was so much more than I could possibly eat all by itself, not to mention the burger.

"I was just thinking I could share with Stevie. She'll be home soon," I said.

"I'll go right back through the drive-thru when we're done and get her one of her own. Does that work? Or I'll back out right now if you say, but I'd rather talk," he said.

"OK," I said. I started in on the sundae.

"So why don't you come see me anymore."

I said, "No reason. Honest. Listen, I'm not good with social stuff. I should have told you."

He said, "I thought maybe it was Matt saying something about me."

"What would he say about you?" I said.

He was turned toward me, staring at me. He hadn't unwrapped his hamburger. I still couldn't say for sure that I was attracted to him, but I was closer to that than I'd been with anyone for a while. I had feelings in my body that, normally, I either didn't have at all or was very good at ignoring.

"I was trying to get him off you, that's all. Guess that didn't work," Foster said. He looked out his window.

I ate my sundae, looking ahead at the cars going past. I had the cup between my legs and was eating with my right hand, and I guess my left hand was just lying there limp because Foster grasped it. He rubbed my fingers, and they tingled.

"You're cold," he said. Was I all broken out in goosebumps? Was I tense? Yes, I thought I might squeeze open that Styrofoam cup between my legs.

I kept eating. I could almost see the need radiating out away from him, over the dashboard, misting the window. Or was that me?

"If he said I said something bad about you..." he said.

I looked at him and felt a moment of gratitude for having the blank, sweet face I have. Without any meanness in it, I said, "Can you tell me, literally, like exact words, what it was you did say?"

The look on his face, a little bit of humor in with the pleading. Like he was thinking, *well, I'm fucked*. He shook his head. "I can't."

I looked at him, and it was like he was begging me to kiss him, so I swept the ice cream out of my mouth as best I could, swallowed, and did just that.

I'm not a good kisser and don't usually feel anything from kissing, but I felt a little bit of something kissing him. I think it was mainly just how big and warm he was next to me, maybe the barely-there stubble, or maybe it was just because I'd done it on my own initiative.

It feels good, too, to do something you think might make you feel guilty and then not to feel guilty about it. Or, if I was a little bit guilty about the feelings I began to have, I was not guilty about the kiss itself.

It didn't seem like such a big deal. If this were back in Jane Austen times, it would be normal to date a few people. In an old book you'd dance with a dozen different young men at every ball or whatever and only after a marriage proposal would there be any sort of claim.

I didn't like how the phone had influenced Foster, though. I didn't like that Foster felt there was that sort of claim.

Because Foster felt guilty. You could see it. He thought Matt liked me a lot more than he really did and, loving Matt as a dear friend for many years, he would have stayed miles away from "his girl" if he could have.

When we left the parking lot, he didn't remember to go back through the drive-thru for Stevie's order.

It was only much later that I thought to wonder why this thing had needed to happen at the Tiger Burger where anyone and everyone might see.

#

December spun out colder than I ever could have imagined. There were light snow showers here and there, nothing serious, but the wind was what killed me. In our room Stevie and I were warm, and so we stayed in our room. We had nothing much to do with Tommy and Mom, nothing to do with the shadow who sometimes did not seem to be a shadow who prowled the main hall in the night.

We listened to a lot of eighties music on the phone, bands that Stevie said a friend at school had mentioned.

She didn't say the friend's name like she was hoping I'd think she had more friends, but she meant Tamara, of course. We'd never seen a lot of shows or movies in our family, so most of the songs were new to us, and they seemed meaningful in a way that modern music did not. Our plan allowed for unlimited music streaming, Stevie discovered, and so the music played from the sad little cellphone speakers as though it were a radio there in the corner. She kept asking me when I was going to call Matt and thank him.

I lay on my stomach on the bed; Stevie sat in the desk in her flannel pajamas, turned back toward me. Depeche Mode or something like that was playing real low so Mom wouldn't hear.

"You and me don't keep secrets from each other anymore, right?" Stevie said.

"We don't," I said.

"No more secrets," she said. Her voice was high and clear. She was still such a little girl sometimes.

"Are you saying something?" I said.

"Am I? Why haven't you called Matt?"

"I don't feel like talking to him is all."

"If Matt was *my* boyfriend—" she said.

"Matt isn't my boyfriend."

"Then why'd he get you the phone, then?"

"Were you brought up to think someone's your boyfriend because he buys you things? Anyway, he isn't *your* boyfriend. You don't need to worry about why he does what he does."

"I think he feels sorry for us. Wouldn't you, if you were him?"

I was aware of our room just then, the nothing in it but the beds and clothes neatly stacked in the totes.

"Why should he feel sorry for us? We have everything we need."

"Other people don't see it that way."

207

The phone rang, and I jumped up quick to hit the red button for not taking the call.

"It was Matt," she said. "You better call him back and say thanks."

"Stevie," I said, and I gave her a look. I must have looked sick.

"What did you do?" she said.

I didn't feel like I should tell her about Foster, but we had already said no secrets, so I moved to where she was and whispered, "I kissed Foster."

"Why?" she said. She was angry.

"He wanted me to." That seemed enough reason to me.

How many things had I ever done for no other reason but that somebody wanted me to? It seemed to me that walking was the only thing I'd ever done for myself, walking and looking at all the weeds beside the road and the distant shapes of houses and of the mountains beyond. All I wanted now was to be somewhere warm enough to walk and lose myself, warm like the place that Betty had been all year.

Oh, it hurt to think of her. Why I couldn't have been with her instead of here? She'd never have died if I'd been there.

I always did what people wanted, if I was able to. I was capable of going into the hall and calling Matt to thank him for the phone. It was what Stevie wanted me to do, what Matt wanted me to do. And should I call Foster and tell him something to make him not tell Matt about our kiss? That was what Matt would want if he could choose, and maybe that was what everyone would think was best. Or should I tell Matt I liked Foster and wanted to be with him because that was what Foster would want? I didn't think I had a strong preference, either way, but maybe that was something that would make more sense to everyone.

208

All of these thoughts churned as I talked to Matt. Lonnie walked past once or twice like he always did at night, and he was filmy like he usually was, though I knew by then that he was a dark thing not to be messed with, and his presence in the hall with me—and more so, the anticipation of him coming back each time on his rounds—all of this worked on me so that I was flustered and hesitant on the phone with Matt, and I think he mistook this for me being overwhelmed with emotion. Maybe he thought it was gratitude for the phone, for the fact that he'd taken the time to think about what gift I might need and really make use of.

Or he thought, or he hoped, that my hesitations and my stutters were evidence of some kind of strong emotion toward him. Love for him, infatuation. He'd had nothing to indicate that I liked him at all, I thought, and yet he felt that I must.

I barely registered what I said at the start, only a "thank you" and then some reactions to what had been going on his life, a test he'd failed or done well on, a painting he was starting. We planned to see each other during the break, and he floated ideas for some things we could do. He had three weeks off for Christmas. Visits to family and New Year's at Roger's were already on the schedule, but he was pledging to spend much of the time—as much as he possibly could—with me.

All I could think about was what he wanted and whether or not I ought to try to find out what it was and give it to him.

I imagined myself saying, "I kissed Foster."

I actually did say it, then. "I kissed Foster."

Matt, after a time, said all sharply, "What?"

"When he picked me up to get the phone. I kissed him."

"OK, then. So what are you telling me?" He didn't sound angry. I appreciated that.

209

"Nothing. It isn't important," I said.

"OK."

"Do you still want to see me when you come home?"

"I don't know," he said.

"Listen," I said quickly, before I could lose my nerve. "I'm trying to be more open about things."

"OK, well, thanks for being more open," he said.

"I don't have a lot of romantic experience, at all. Where I came from, we just had a big group of friends. People would hook up from time to time, or they'd go around with each other for a couple of weeks. It was just a different cultural thing, I guess. I didn't even participate very much. Anyway, I like you. I like Foster. As friends, and I might be open to more. I don't know. I'm not attached to or committed to anyone because I haven't ever been, and frankly I'm not sure I'm the kind of person who does that. I don't know. Like I said, I haven't had those kinds of experiences."

That was a lot.

Matt said he understood, and I thanked him again, only this time I thanked him for *ordering* the phone, like it was something I'd asked him to do, and promised to pay him back soon. I hung up then. I went back into the bedroom and told Stevie that the thank-you had been delivered.

To Mom, the very next time I saw her, I confessed to having someone order me a phone on the promise that she would pay them back. She wasn't angry, which I'd expected her to be.

"That's fine," she said, "but that's your whole Christmas." She was putting on her frumpy shoes for her sad little job.

"Thank you," I said, all guilty over the money.

"Honestly, I'm just really glad to know what to buy you." She meant it. She came up close and kissed the top of my head.

In the days after that, she started texting me with little instructions and observations throughout the day, which she used to do before I broke my phone.

It wasn't too much later, though, that Mom insisted that Stevie move into one of the small rooms downstairs that had recently been carpeted. She'd had a bed moved in there already. The white headboard was newly painted, the mattress still had plastic on it, and on top she'd folded a new comforter set with matching sheets that Ellen's niece had outgrown. It was busy with stylized animals in clear, cool colors. None of us ever had something so pretty for our bedding. Mom made us move Stevie's desk and her clothes down there and told us it was going to be a surprise. I didn't feel like I could say anything against it. It was right that Stevie should have her own room if she wanted it. When Stevie came home, she had to act like she was delighted. Only I saw the panic in her eyes.

#

New maple cabinets came. The boxes that I carried out to the recycling bin said Shaker Elegance. The room smelled nice, not of wood but of the stain maybe, that and the glue and caulk Marcus used to finish out the Formica countertop. I helped him as much as I could and didn't ask for any pay, but after all was done, Ellen passed something to me. When I grasped it, she didn't let it go right away

She said, "For Christmas presents, for your mom and sisters, from you, OK? I mean that's all you can spend it on."

"Of course," I said. When I had it in my hands, I saw it was a Visa gift card and on the back, it said two hundred dollars.

I said, "Oh no, I didn't do this much work," trying to pass it back.

She said, "You'll do a little more later."

"I don't want to owe people," I said, and I didn't know if it was my imagination or not, but I felt like she made a bit of scoffing sound, meaning I already owed a lot. I suppose it was true, as far as that went. I took the card but didn't thank her again.

The next day, I skipped class to go to Queenie's, which wasn't such a smart idea. Everything there was about three times what it should have been, and so close to Christmas, there wasn't much. As I moved around the store, Queenie's came to me as it had been in Mom's childhood. She and Ellen would go there all the time, and there was . . . a disturbance in the air. A display made of Lucite, with those transparent Lucite boxes in pink and lavender and light aqua. Everything was always those colors in Mom's childhood. There were arrangements of thumb-size flocked teddy bears with bow ties. Teddy bears at a wire bistro set, teddy bears with pins on their backs to use as broaches. I saw the past-Queenie's superimposed over everything, which made it hard to see what was really there. It was like looking through the window of a store with a store from the eighties reflected in the glass.

I remembered Mom and Ellen coming in together and the lady at the counter yelling at Mom that she had to leave her backpack at the front and letting Ellen go through with her bookbag because she was a nice Beulah girl and Mom was apparently trash.

Besides Christmas presents, I still needed a souvenir from here. I was considering the rack of Designer Impressions body sprays (Were they real? Were they memory?) when Mom came out from the back room to ask what I thought I was doing in there at that time of day.

"Oh, I thought this was your day off," I said, which was not the smartest thing to say, and then I left right away so that we didn't embarrass each other more.

That was my one attempt to buy gifts. Where else was there, Albertsons?

#

Stevie loved working in the new kitchen. That night she made spaghetti and salad to celebrate, and it was delicious as always. After dinner, we put our food away in the new cabinets and then sat in the great room reading for a while, and then it was time for bed.

What Stevie usually did was to go to bed in her new bedroom and when Mom was asleep, she would creep upstairs to sleep in my bed. That night, she didn't come to me.

The next night, she came to me, not to sleep but to see if I might let her take the phone. It was hard to sleep without any noise.

The next night, nothing. I decided maybe it was good that she was growing up. I didn't feel like I needed privacy, but maybe she did. She'd made no sign of having seen Lonnie, let alone fearing him, so I wasn't worried about him scaring her. I wondered if there were teachers and students in her new room at night, and if they were calm like the ones in our room or if they caused her trouble. I decided if she had any trouble, she'd be right back upstairs with me.

2

Foster was cool about the phone. His number was in it, and I guess he figured I could call him when I felt like it. Matt, on the other hand, called about every other day, with texts in between. I was glad enough to get the calls.

A visit from Foster, if he happened to be off work, was even better. A couple of times he and I came back to my room and kissed for a while, and both times we came out into the great room so that it wouldn't go further. A couple of times when Matt called, Foster was right there beside me listening.

The reason I felt all right about it was that I wasn't keeping secrets. When Foster asked how I felt about Matt, I said I liked him. When Matt asked, I told him Foster had been hanging out. I didn't know if they were talking together besides. Maybe they were.

I thought Matt felt sorry for me, sort of absently thought that I was cute as a project or as raw material. Foster was the one who loved me. It all might have been romantic, if I'd had an ear for romance, but as it was it was a constant droning in my ears. I didn't think I had a lot of feelings about either of them except some physical feelings for Foster, but since he was the only one physically around, I couldn't necessarily say that I didn't have those same feelings for Matt.

I decided I would tell both of them to leave me alone. I decided to spend Ellen's two hundred dollars getting a phone for Stevie. I decided to finally stop school for good, devote myself to some kind of work. If Ellen wouldn't have me after all, I could do something else. I decided these things and made no moves toward achieving them.

The thought of work still pained me: I'd have to do something for what? Six hours a day, eight hours a day? Something I'd need to dress for? Something I'd need to set an alarm for, surely, and couldn't ever skip or get out of. It made me exhausted just thinking about it, so that I kept thinking I'd do the items on the list the day after the next. Not today, not tomorrow, but the day after the next. This is what I did in the privacy of my newly private bedroom: I planned, drew back, did nothing.

Winter Break was upon us before I could make a move. The last day of school would have been a snow day if anyone had any sense. The bus almost wiped out on the highway on the way in. At noon, when school had early release, Foster picked me up for a sundae and an unlikely romp through the snow-filled park. He somehow got me playing, running and throwing snowballs, which wasn't like me at all. He moved so fast for a big guy, and I felt alive. The whole time it was happening, I was thinking what a really nice memory it would make.

The next day was warm and all that snow had melted by three. Matt texted to say he had good roads for the trip home, and then he was at our front door on his way to his parents', a small sack of presents for us in hand. He kissed me drily on the mouth and Stevie on the cheek, gave a sideways hug to Tommy and shook Mom's hand, and then before long he had to be going.

The next night, we four had a Christmas-eve dinner I'd taken no part in preparing. The turkey and rolls and things were for the next day, but Christmas Eve was a big breakfast for dinner, my favorite: waffles and ham and eggs with cups of cocoa afterward, everybody but Stevie's spiked with butterscotch schnapps. Christmas music played on Tommy's laptop, and a tree shone with red lights and candy canes on it in the principal's-office corner. There were other touches around the room, a red and green runner on the table, a wreath.

I hadn't paid much attention to all of these things being put up and wondered where I'd been, if I'd been sleeping too much.

Stevie was distant. Mom and Tommy kept talking about people, trying to get a gossip session going, but I guess none of us knew enough of the same people to really connect. Tommy's laptop finally came out, and we started a DVD of *It's a Wonderful Life*.

Tommy kept asking, "What's up with you?" and things like that.

Apparently I wasn't acting right. The evening was over before I knew it. When Mom woke me up from the couch, the girls were already in bed and *A Christmas Carol* played.

She left the movie on but told me to hush, took me to her room where she'd piled the presents, all sizes, all wrapped in a waxy green paper with brass-gold bows on them and our names written in red sharpie in her best handwriting, which was still mostly illegible. I helped her to move them out under the tree.

I saw how happy she was to have done all of this. Her lion face was soft in the pink light from the tree, her head of lion hair all wild around her head. I noticed that her pajamas had holly berries on them and wondered why I hadn't noticed that before.

She didn't ask, just made more boozy cocoa for us and sat looking at the tree. I thought how tired she must be and how relieved that the last of her seasonal hours were over.

"It's really peaceful in the house tonight," I said.

She looked at me, cocked her head.

I was sleepy. I wasn't paying attention to what I said, which was, "The kids and all the teachers, even the janitor or whatever, they were never here at Christmas so they're not here now."

Her head stayed cocked, but her jowls fell. The smile melted off her face.

"No one getting spanked, no one monitoring the hall," I said. What was wrong with me? I should have been warm and happy with her then. Why couldn't I be? Why did I have to push things?

"Let's don't," she said.

"You see them. Why can't you ever be..."

"I'll see you in the morning," she said. She left her drink on the floor by the sofa and moved off slowly toward her room.

Why can't you ever be open?

Why do you make out like I'm the one who's crazy?

I picked up the drink and took it to our new sink. Ellen had spent "big money" on this detail, which was deep with the regular two wells and then a small one in the center, a tall faucet looming far over the top.

I was crying but didn't realize it until the salt taste was in my mouth. I rinsed the cups and set them in the sink.

I don't know why I didn't go back to my room. Maybe it was because the house was so peaceful, all the shadows gone for at least this night, maybe for the rest of the week. I went onto the patio and took in the cold night air. It was snowing already, and though all the snow from before had melted, I just knew all would be white again for Christmas morning. I roamed to the front door and looked out the window. No cars on Farm School Road or anywhere in sight. I turned then and descended the stairs. Tommy had her futon folded into a couch and was asleep on it, headphones on and attached to her phone, which rested on her belly. I walked past her to the back room, where there was no man and no chair beside the furnace. Nothing moved in the forgotten basement kitchen. I looked into the empty classroom with its cheerful new paint and checkered old linoleum floors. I lingered outside Stevie's door.

My heart fell. I heard her low and excited talking in there, and then I heard Tamara's voice. I assumed they were lying on their bellies with their feet in the air,

217

gossiping about people in school. When I opened the door, that is what I saw.

Stevie made a startled sound. Tamara was suddenly not there.

I was tired. Not angry, not yet, just tired. "Do you know what you're doing?" I said.

"It's the first time, I promise," Stevie said, getting up. I wanted to trust her, but her connection to Tamara was stronger. She'd lie to me now, if Tamara asked.

Stevie looked fearful. What did she think I was going to do, tell on her?

"No secrets," I said because there wasn't anything else. There was nothing I could say that would help. I left her door open and went on back upstairs.

3

Christmas morning was a shit show. If I think about it too long, I get angry at everyone. Suffice it to say that Mom and Tommy both got their hopes up too high about what a normal family Christmas morning might look and feel like, and because they were working they had spent too much on Stevie and me and—I don't like saying this, but it's true—they felt like they were owed a little more gratitude than I was willing to give.

From Tommy, I got a beautiful pair of tall, flowered Bogs-type boots so I could walk no matter how cold it was. Mom, though she'd said the phone was my Christmas, gave me a very warm long coat, two pairs of jeans, and a silver necklace with a heart pendant encrusted with marcasite. The necklace was beautiful, but it didn't seem like anything I would own.

I told her she should wear the necklace—I could see that she loved it—and that was one of the things that made her so upset, just one of many.

Stevie got a pile of clothes, cooking things and books, bath stuff.

Stevie's only gift to me was a pretty flower-print diary with a metal clasp and lock and two little keys on ball-peen chains long enough to be necklaces.

When she gave it to me, she said, "One key for you and one for me. No secrets," and squeezed my hand, then slipped one necklace over my head.

"Who shares a diary?" Tommy said.

Mom looked at me with her lips pressed close together. I saw just then that Tamara was with us, hiding in plain view. Tamara was a little animal curled on a kitchen chair just then, something of a fox and a cat and a ferret.

"Open it," Stevie said. She was looking straight at Tamara as she said it, Tamara looking back with that smirk she always seemed to have.

This isn't cool, was all I kept thinking. If I'd gotten Stevie alone, I'd have said, "This isn't cool, you can't make fun of Mom and Tommy like that"—because that was what she was doing, showing off Tamara to me and somehow making fun of Tommy and Mom because they couldn't see her or wouldn't see her.

I had a chance to open the diary and read a few pages, and that was part of what made me so upset. All in a gushing excited tone, it told the story of Tamara's getting her claws into Stevie.

When I produced the check card and explained where it came from, they were disgusted with me, first for accepting it and then for not spending it on presents as I'd promised Ellen I would.

I was done.

Though the drama they were putting on me was not all that dramatic in itself, it clearly had been building up over time. Now it was my turn to react in a way that would keep it all going. It was almost my duty to do something impulsive and hurtful, and I did just as expected: I walked out of the house well before the big lunch, which sent Stevie screaming after me in the snow in her socks, and they all came out and made her go back inside. I could hear them all but didn't look back to see them.

When they got back in the house, all was peaceful again. It had snowed enough to cover the grass in the yard but not the grass at the side of the road. It was cold but bright and not at all windy. I'm pretty sure they knew I could make it into town, or maybe they thought I'd have the sense to turn back. I was wearing the coat with its tags still on it and the boots, though I did not remember putting them on. Stevie's diary was in my messenger bag along with my own journal.

I finally had a little energy, felt like myself again, though it was painful to breathe in the cold. It burned my ears and cheeks. I walked past the brown house and the yellow one, past Roger's with its multicolored lights in the window. I made it to Eighth, and there at the stop sign was a green Cherokee, the first car I'd seen. I turned onto Eighth towards town, and the car did not pass me. It slowed beside me. The middle-aged lady in the driver's seat rolled down her window, and from the passenger seat, Matt leaned over and called, "Georgie?" I turned, he saw it really was me, and the car pulled ahead of me to park. Matt came out and gave me the warmest, firmest, best hug I'd had in a while.

Matt tried to get me in the front seat, but I wouldn't take it. In the car, the lady turned back and said she was Matt's mom, Cindy, and then we were off. They proceeded to tell me all about Matt's grandma, who'd had to be taken home.

"She spent the night at our place last night, and then that was enough, so we had to drive her right now," Matt said. "She's old. She gets cranky, you know?"

His mom looked at me in the rearview while he spoke.

"Speaking of," said the mom, waggling an unlit cigarette. "Mind if I smoke?"

I said, "Go ahead," and she rolled the window down and lit up. Matt and his mom joked about how he better not say anything about her smoking in front of the relatives, and he asked how much that was worth.

"I thought you'd come in," he said, turning back to face me. "We can get in my car right after and take you wherever you're going."

He didn't ask why I'd been out on the road on Christmas morning, and I loved him a little for that.

His phone pinged. "Your sister. Can I tell her you're with us?"

221

I nodded. I didn't happen to have my phone on me, but they must have gotten the number from there.

We kept going down Eighth. I was surprised, though I shouldn't have been, when we turned onto Park and pulled into the driveway of the tall blue house that stood next to the yellow one with the yellow-framed windows. It was the blue house that, in summer, had all the little red flowers at its base.

"You'll get your souvenir," Matt whispered. So he remembered that part of the long story I'd told in summer, how I was going to go into each one of the houses I had visited in dream-Beulah. He hadn't liked that story, though, had he?

He held my hand as I got out, in case there was ice.

The street parking was all filled up with visitors' cars, and inside, Matt's house was filled with heavier, older people. It looked something like Ellen's mom's house, all oak floors and antique oak furniture, patterned wool rugs with red and blue and other jewel colors in them, raspberry colored plaid sofas.

I remembered it all loosely from a long-ago dream. That, or this was just how such a house had to look on the inside.

Out of the kitchen came three little cousins. I was introduced as Matt's friend to a few people on my way through to the kitchen island. The turkey smell was strong. It looked like three generations of women were working on rolls and salads on the ample counter space of the main cabinets and the island. Men sat around here and there. There must have been fifteen or twenty people in the house. All I could think was how this was what my Mom and sisters had been trying to make of the day, of our family, and how I had ruined it.

As I sat at the island, drinking a Coke and answering the stupid questions the relatives asked me about school (because they didn't seem able to ask what they really wanted to ask: *Where the hell did you come from?*), I thought back on the big opening of gifts just an hour before. Everything Stevie'd said, every action she made, seemed to be a performance for the smug little fox-Tamara. And the gift she gave me, how cruel and wrong it seemed. At some point, Tamara changed from her weaselish animal self and back to a girl, this time Stevie's age. She sat there on the floor beside the tree with a broad smile on her face.

There in Matt's kitchen, he didn't touch me, but he seemed to hover around me. I began to feel paranoid, as though he'd told these people that I'd be coming, as though he and Mom had planned this somehow.

"Can I call home?" I said.

"You didn't bring your phone?" Matt said, with pride. Had he told these people all about the phone, too? What did they know about me?

I patted my pockets and shook my head. After a decent amount of time in the kitchen, Matt took me upstairs to the room that must have been his before he moved out for college. It had twin beds, a young teen boy lying on one of them playing on a laptop. Matt gestured for him to leave. He unlocked his phone and left me there to make my call.

I called my phone and told Stevie to tell everyone I was all right, and where I was, and that I would come home as soon as I'd calmed down. I'm surprised I had the sense to do that.

On Matt's bed were his Christmas presents: a new tablet, a stack of jeans, several sweaters and pullovers, cologne, books. There was a mess of little things, keychain and a laser pointer, pens and candy, a couple of twenty-dollar bills. All of that must have come out of a stocking. I imagined the big family all with their stockings, getting these little surprises. It must have been so nice.

I went to the bathroom and stayed as long as I could, skimming through the diary. I'm sure Matt thought I was taking a shit in there, that or crying. I flushed the toilet before leaving and pushed aside the bathroom curtain for a high view of the park, the trees budding, leafing out, leaves falling. The downtown buildings beyond the park shimmered, building and rebuilding themselves over time, and I swooned, nearly hit the floor. I splashed cold water on my face and stood bent over the sink for another few minutes.

When I finally came out, the ladies downstairs were already calling people to eat.

I stayed for the meal, which ended up being more like a late lunch. Turkey and rolls; yams with walnuts and pineapple, cranberries, cinnamon and a spice I couldn't place but they told me was cardamom; warm apple cider, water, wine; hot buttered rum; pies made of coconut, pecan, pumpkin, and canned peaches; parfaits with whipped cream and dark chocolate pudding; carrot salad, baked beans, and mushrooms stuffed with beef and a sharp soft cheese I had never before tasted; bread pudding with whipped cream and sweet whiskey sauce. I tasted a little of everything. It all made me want to cry.

The conversation was sparse because most of the family had been together for a couple of days by then. They asked me a couple more questions, but I was no more effusive than before, and they drifted back into conversations I could not follow.

When the meal was over and the leftovers put away, we said goodbye and walked out to where Matt's car was parked in front of the house, already warmed up for me. He held the door for me, too, and once he was in asked, "You ready to head back, or do you want to go somewhere else?" He said it all suggestive-like, and I wondered if he was thinking of the little motel behind Streaker's that was supposed to be so cute.

What I wanted was to get out and walk—still that was what I wanted—but it was cold and the sun no longer bright. I felt broken down.

"Let's go back," I said.

I asked Matt to come in with me, and he obliged. Stevie sat at the kitchen table with girl-Tamara seated by her side, leaning, whispering in her ear. Mom and Tommy were not in the great room. All of the lunch food had been cleared away, but its smell lingered. They'd had a cheese and broccoli soup in bread bowls, which had taken some time and expense and which I'd been looking forward to more than the turkey planned for dinner.

"I made you a bread bowl," Stevie said. She rose to open the fridge.

"We already ate," I said. "Where are they?"

"Napping," she said.

Matt said, "That's what my folks are doing by now. Maybe that's what you ought to do." He ran his hand around my hairline.

"Do I feel hot?" I said.

"Not at all," he said. He sat beside me, seemed to want to make eye contact, but I stared at Tamara. I still could not quite tell if she saw me.

I said to him, "Did you ever know about a girl named Tamara who lived around here?" Tamara's head cocked at the mention of her name, like she'd heard only the name and not the rest of what I said.

Stevie gave me a sharp look. Her shoulders tensed.

"I'm sure there are lots of girls named Tamara. I guess anyone they call Tammy?" Matt said.

"No," I mean a girl who died in Beulah sometime. At the middle school, I think."

He nodded, said, "I think Mom knew a girl who died when she was in school . . . or disappeared? Was her name Tamara, though? I'm not sure. She mentioned when we were looking in a yearbook. Pretty girl, must have been popular because there were a lot of pictures."

Mom would have gotten those same yearbooks. She had long ago thrown hers out, but it meant Mom had gone to school with Tamara. Of course she had.

"She was an athlete," I said, "or a dancer?"

"I don't know," he said. "But if you looked at the yearbooks you'd see. They had group photos for all those things."

I still couldn't tell if she saw me. She just sat with her little nose pointed up and a smirk on her face. I wanted to slap that face.

"What sports did you do, Matt?" said Stevie, trying to change the subject.

"Oh, baseball mostly. I spent a little time in track. I wasn't very good at anything."

"My friend says I can be on a team, if I lose some weight before middle school," Stevie said.

Matt said she could for sure get on a team and was going on about how she didn't need to lose any weight necessarily. There were lots of chubby girls playing sports these days and cheerleading and anything else. It was all in whether you wanted to work hard or not.

Tamara looked at Stevie all through the conversation and not at us. I didn't know how much she heard from us. She heard her name, but I doubted she was getting the rest. She was aware of us, though, even if we were vague to her.

I picked an orange out of the bowl on the table and let it roll slowly toward her. Stevie gasped and caught it before it could fall into Tamara's chair. It didn't seem to me that Tamara had been tracking the ball. She had kept watching Stevie with a look of infatuation.

"Good catch," Matt said. "I'd say you'll be playing soccer in no time, or what was it you wanted to play?"

"No idea," said Stevie. She smirked. She couldn't keep her eyes off Tamara, either, and when Tamara stood and headed toward the stairs, she said, "I guess I'll have a nap," and followed her.

It was me and Matt in the kitchen, and I could feel what he wanted from me. I leaned toward him, put my head on his chest. His chest smelled of his new Christmas cologne; his breath smelled of toothpaste, which made me wonder when he'd sneaked away to brush his teeth, and why.

He and I went to my bedroom and talked about the break. He would not be due back at school until the third week of January. He had a family ski trip just after New Year, and a few other obligations here and there, but he seemed to have set most of his vacation aside to devote to me. Whether that was to get to know me or to help me out, I couldn't quite tell. If he'd asked I could have told him that there wasn't much to know about me that he didn't already know. Nothing much that I could tell, anyway.

#

What did Stevie and Tamara do in her room that Christmas afternoon? There was no doubt in my mind that Stevie would tell me one day; I only wished it would be soon.

Tamara had attached herself to Stevie. It wasn't hard to do that to a girl without guidance. As much as I loved Stevie, who was I? I wasn't any sort of a role model. Stevie couldn't say something like, "I want to be like Georgie when I grow up." Tommy she maybe could say that about, but when had Tommy ever made an effort with her?

Tamara only ever got to be three or four years older than Stevie, but she was a real role model. Beautiful, driven. She must have seemed to Stevie like a serious person. Romantic and tragic, she was Stevie's opposite, her Ellen or her Betty.

#

I wondered how it was for Tamara, so long locked at the school and now here, in a new place. Was Tamara amazed to be here?

Between what Stevie had written about it in the diary, the theories I had about shadows, and my own imagination, I worked out a story of how it must have gone down. The story scared me, but it excited me, too. For a moment I wished I could be Stevie, only just discovering all of this.

I imagined it all from Tamara's perspective. Did she believe that she had entered a haunted house, maybe on a dare? Or did she know that she was at her friend's house?

She'd met a girl at school, a girl who was indistinct to her but towards whom she felt a strong attraction—a girl not as pretty as she was but still somehow a mirror to herself—and after some time being friends at school, the girl persuaded her to come over. That was how it always happened with friends, wasn't it? You got to know them at school to a certain extent, but if the relationship was going to progress, you had to go to their house or they had to go to yours.

Tamara didn't like to think about her own home, didn't like to go there anymore. Her beautiful mother was gone. Strangers had intruded long ago.

Tamara didn't remember the walk, but she must have walked. She stood in the front yard before the building.

"Do you think you can come in?" Stevie said.

Tamara looked around her. The grass in the front yard was dry and mown. In the backyard, it was dry and tall. The ground sloped up through rocky fields toward the canyon. The canyon was familiar to her, but she couldn't say when she had last seen it. She began to grow frightened. The air was cool, which didn't seem right.

"Why am I here?" she said. "Did you bring me? I don't remember coming."

"It's all right," said Stevie. "We can go inside, and you can go to my room. I have a new room. Private. Don't you want to?

Tamara said, "I don't know. I don't know if I can go in."

She seemed to be afraid of the front door, or maybe it was the steps that frightened her. They were steep. She moved back, and so Stevie followed her around to the patio.

Tamara was upset. She felt that there was a boundary here that she could not cross, or she was not sure if she could cross it. The patio looked wrong to her. Everything looked wrong.

"Please, can we go back?" she said.

"Back where?" said Stevie. Tamara looked out towards the tall tree.

"Let's go inside," said Stevie. She took Tamara's hand, and at once, Tamara seemed to come more fully awake. She gasped.

Stevie couldn't believe they were touching, either. She stopped and appreciated the feel of Tamara's hand in hers. Tamara's hand was cool but not cold. It felt silky. It made her feel nervous like before a big test. She walked Tamara back around to the front of the house and took the first step

"I think you can come in here, but tell me if you feel woozy. I don't want to hurt you." She took the second step. Tamara followed. All was well.

Tamara dimmed in the entryway, and Stevie couldn't feel her hand anymore. She didn't know if it would be better to go back out onto the porch or to go to her room, but she took a chance and rushed downstairs. Tamara was quite dim by then and seemed far away. Stevie focused on her intently and called her by name, saying things like, "Tamara, are you all right? Do you hear me? Tamara?" She talked to the girl until the girl answered back.

"This is *your* room?" Tamara said finally, and Stevie said, "Yes," and a smile came over Tamara's face.

They spent hours in bed with the covers over their heads, whispering, Tamara finding her way back to being all the way opaque.

As Betty and I had, as Brian and I had at some point, as all best friends do, Tamara and Stevie cocooned in their fantasy world. Tamara told Stevie about her gymnastics and dance and sports, her hair and makeup, her wonderful dance-teacher mother. In Tamara's world it was nineteen eighty-something, and the music was good.

These things that shadows want to tell about are often their fantasies, not their actual lives, but fantasies are made of what we are, our lives and hopes, and so on. And in Tamara's case, her fantasies and her actual life had been so, so close to the same that she probably couldn't have put her finger on any distinction between them.

#

When Matt brought me home on Christmas, he came to sit in my room but only for a minute. He said he wished he could stay longer, which made me want that too.

"Just for an hour?" I said. I touched his face, his neck. I hadn't done anything like that before with him.

He kissed my forehead and turned. I heard him go out the front, heard someone saying, "Bye bye" loudly and murmuring something else low so I would not hear. They'd woken from their naps. Maybe all of them crowded around him asking for a report.

I slept. When I woke, it was almost dinner time. The turkey smell filled the house.

I emerged from my room. All of them worked in the kitchen finishing up dinner. The Christmas lights warmed the room, and the scene was just as wholesome and satisfying, in its way, as the scene in Matt's house. Stevie had an unopened stick of butter in her hand. She ripped the wax paper off the end of it and began rubbing butter over a pan of hot dinner rolls. Mom turned toward me. She didn't say anything before turning back to the turkey on the counter. She pulled back the skin of a drumstick, took a pinch of dark meat up to her mouth and made a small sound of approval.

Tommy sat at the table pouring cranberry juice over ice. There were four glasses. I swear I saw her scoot one of them over to Tamara, who sat on the chair opposite her.

I groaned, turned back to my room.

"What's the matter now?" called Mom.

Behind my closed door, I breathed hard. I felt like I was starting to hyperventilate, so I slid down to the floor. I concentrated on breathing deeply. Someone tapped on the door.

Things did not make sense.

"Is she really out there? Do you. . ." I choked. "You all see her."

"Who?" said Mom and then, "We're all out here. It's time to eat."

"I was just going to come wake you up," said Stevie

I came out of my room then and paced past Mom and Stevie out to the great room. Tamara was nowhere in sight. I looked into Mom's room and the bathroom.

"Go back to bed. You're acting weird," said Tommy.

"You keep her downstairs," I hissed to Stevie when I came back to the kitchen. "I'm not kidding. You keep her downstairs."

I breathed, said I was all right, that I'd just been dreaming—having a nightmare, actually. I was confused.

231

Mom looked hurt, like I'd ruined another meal, which I suppose I had.

Tamara did not return during dinner. We ate little, all except Stevie, who dug in. She was reaching for a third roll when Mom finally intercepted her, taking the pan up onto the counter and saying, "I guess we should clean up." We did that, the three of us moving efficiently together, portioning food into baggies and getting the pans and dishes soaking. The fridge already held leftovers from the Christmas breakfast and the soup lunch, and now we seemed to have turkey for the duration of the new year.

4

Mom went back to work at Queenie's the day after Christmas. Tiger Burger didn't have many hours for Tommy just then, so she was free to keep an eye on me. I wanted to talk about the diary, but I couldn't get Stevie alone. Was Stevie avoiding me, Mom and Tommy both backing her up, or had she been forbidden to speak to me? I wasn't sure.

Mom was speaking to me in a high, frantic voice or ignoring me. Neither felt good.

When Matt called, I answered. Stevie hadn't asked for the phone since the incident.

Marcus came on the twenty-seventh. He and Tommy and a helper kid laid laminate flooring in the big downstairs, which brightened it up a lot. Matt even came over and helped at the end even though it was his big vacation.

After the floor work, he and I lay side by side on the carpet beside my bed. Matt had decided to be whatever I needed.

He told of how his parents had both grown up in Beulah, how rare and lucky it had been for them to return and be able to find good jobs, raise him and his older brother in that beautiful house on Park.

He told how he'd always wanted to be an artist, how perfectly happy his mom and dad were to let him study painting. They thought he'd probably change majors at some point, or if not that, he'd go back for a teaching certificate. Something like that, when he was thinking of getting married—but if that didn't happen, if he wanted to be an artist, that was all good with them too. He didn't have any big dreams for his art, only wanted to keep learning and keep doing what he loved every day.

He wanted to know what I wanted, he said sometimes, but he turned back to the subject of himself easily enough every time, and it was good. It soothed me to hear him talk, his voice so low and mellow.

I'd spent so much time with him that it took my guard down.

I asked, "Did Mom say why they're pissed at me?"

"No . . . well, they said you had stress and trouble sleeping." Good, he was loyal at least that far. He wasn't going to keep what they said from me.

"Do you believe in ghosts?" I asked before I could stop myself.

"I don't," he said.

"What if you saw one?"

"Then I suppose I would believe."

He turned toward me, all of a sudden happy-faced like a joke was coming. "Have you seen a ghost?" he said.

"Would you think I was crazy if I had?"

"Of course not. Lots of people say they have. Only, I don't believe something just because someone else does. My grandma believes in God because she says she feels him. That's nice, but it doesn't make *me* feel him, you know."

"So."

"So if you saw a ghost, that's nice, but **y**our seeing it wouldn't make me see it."

Maybe it would, though. "There's a ghost in *this* place," I said.

He was quiet for a bit, then said, "I've actually heard that before."

"Have you?"

"My grandpa went to school here," he said.

"He saw something?"

"I don't think so. I don't know, but there was a story about there being a ghost."

"What was he supposed to be like, this ghost?"

"Why don't you tell me? You say you saw him."

"I didn't say that, actually, but it's a him?"

Matt grinned, then. He was up on his elbow sort of looming over my face. He leaned in and kissed me, and I thought *here it comes finally, our first real kiss*. I wanted there to be feeling behind it, you know? Feeling on my part, I mean, like we were fighting to come to some sort of an understanding together. I realized I'd reached around his neck and was holding him closer. This went on for a while, and then he moved back.

There hadn't been any feeling. Maybe he thought so, though. He looked soft and open. I still caught the smell of his house on him, that happy safe smell.

My phone dinged, Foster reminding me about the party again. I set the phone back down on the carpet.

"Tell me what you saw. I'll believe you," Matt said.

"You won't, though. You already said you wouldn't."

"I'll try."

I didn't tell him much at first, just that there was a shadow working in the furnace room and pacing the halls. I didn't even plan to tell the rest of what happened with that one shadow, not its yelling at me for dressing slutty or its leering when he and I first kissed in the car or the slow-motion chase up the steps. I didn't say Lonnie, didn't name the thing.

Once I was talking, though. I couldn't stop. His eyes were on me, and he wasn't interrupting me or seeming to judge me. I was suddenly telling him about the empty lot with the old building sketched in the air around it, the ghost-man reading in the bathtub while other ghosts came in and out, the ghost-lady admiring her beautiful face in her mirrored front window.

I was telling about the boys, something confused. It sounded—oh God—saying it, I knew it all sounded like an obvious metaphor for some kind of assault, that or a sex fantasy. It wasn't right; it was all coming out wrong and making me sound unhinged. I finally stopped myself.

And the minute I stopped myself, I felt spooked. I felt cheated. It wasn't that I didn't trust Matt—he'd never done a thing wrong—but after I told, it seemed I liked him less than I had before.

I followed it all up with an obvious lie: I'd been kidding, exaggerating. It was a strange sound in the basement a few times and that was all.

He was solicitous but did not press me to say anything more. He stayed that night until Mom came home. With him there, and especially when we took her downstairs to see the floor, she was more civil than she'd been since Christmas.

Was I using Matt for this purpose alone—to make Mom be normal with me? It made me feel dirty if I was.

"I think you need to get out of this house, Jojo. It isn't good for you," he said, and it made me a little angry. He could have gotten that name only by talking about me with someone else.

#

On the twenty-eighth, Foster came by when everyone was home. I didn't invite him in because I thought Mom might be weird around him now that she thought Matt was my boyfriend. We stood out on the front step in the cold.

Roger's New Year's Eve party was coming up, and Foster said I'd had a great time at Roger's last party, but I couldn't really remember it just then.

Everything in the present was overwhelming. I had no time to reflect, and so the past went gray and grainy right away. I recalled dancing by myself and the trek across the pastures toward home with Tommy but not much else about Roger's party at all.

It would be weird, wouldn't it, to go to Roger's with Matt and Foster both there? I couldn't go.

Foster couldn't get me talking, couldn't get me to go in his car. He finally went on down the stairs. "Call me later, OK?" he said.

"I'm not doing so well," I said to Tommy when I came in. She hugged me. A hug was a rare thing in those dark days. I took it gladly.

I came back into the great room to see Tamara sitting on the sofa next to Stevie.

"Get her out of here, right now," I said.

Mom sat at the dinette in her blue bathrobe. She held her mouth open.

That was when I decided to just go ahead and exorcise Tamara for good and all. I came close, tried to make eye contact.

Stevie said, "Don't, please don't," and she started to whine and bawl. She cried all through it and kept telling me to stop, but what I did was this: up close, I caught and held Tamara's eyes. God, she was so solid.

I said, "Tamara, I see you. You do not belong here. Tamara, you died at your school"—I realized once I said it that it was only a guess. "You had an accident. You need to be back at the school. You hear me. Don't pretend," because she was only pretending not to see or hear me. Her face was so perfect up close, small lips glossed in a rose color, comb lines around the temples of her big tawny hair.

I kept saying her name. It was midday, and yes, I did feel stupid doing it. Mom came up behind me starting to get upset. Tommy tried to make out that I was playing a prank, saying "She's just being weird," but Stevie was screaming, grabbing at my mouth trying to cover it up.

Dog-Lonnie, absent so long, was circling, growling. A line of hair stood up on his back.

"You are not welcome here," was what I finally said that did it. Tamara's face was even more beautiful in pain. Her upper lip curled up.

I watched as she dimmed to shadow and followed as that shadow backed out of the great room through the hall toward the front door. Stevie walked beside her trying to say things to bring her back, trying to touch her hands, but by the time we reached the door, even the shadow was gone.

Everyone saw how truly upset Stevie was, and they went to her. Mom hugged her, told her to breathe deeply.

"What are you on?" Mom said to me, like she thought it was drugs.

Tommy turned and got between me and them. Slowly, she backed me into my room and blocked the door.

"This stops now," Mom screamed.

I'd made her baby cry, and all I could think was *Your baby? I'm supposed to be your baby, too.*

I didn't say anything to Mom, though. From my bedroom doorway, I called to Stevie that it was what had to be done, and she knew it, and all that sort of thing. Mom looked back at me with disgust when she turned Stevie toward the stairs. Tommy finally left my doorway, and the three of them went down to Stevie's room together.

When Mom came up, I still had a lot of adrenaline going. This was going to be the first time I'd really talked back to her since we'd all promised to be our best selves in Beulah. I was already marking it as a milestone, not weighing *Should I or shouldn't I?* but marking it: *Well, here's your next big mistake.*

"I'm trying to be good, but it's awfully hard," I said.

The words, if you just look at them, look like contrition, but real contrition would have been weeping in the back corner of my room the rest of the night. Even that wouldn't have been enough—I'd made Stevie cry, ruined Christmas, ruined everything—but a night of tears was what Mom would have expected for a start. Instead, I stood in my doorway all red and shaking, standing even a little taller than she did now.

I was getting this powerful charge off of her. Waves of disappointment, anger and frustration radiated from her core.

What if she's not a receiver at all, just a powerful transmitter?

I said, "I'm trying to do the best thing—don't laugh. Whenever I can, I'm trying to figure out what I should do, and that comes down to what other people want me to do. I try to think what *you* want me to do—which isn't as easy as you think it is. You tell me to buckle down and then you tell me I don't tell fun stories anymore and I'm a zombie. But, too, I have to think about what Stevie needs and what Matt wants and needs. Ellen, Foster, Betty—"

With a long pause between each word, Mom said "Do. Not. Start." Her face was grave and cruel and fierce.

I couldn't stop now. I said, "Was Betty even real? You know, when I first met her, I wondered. I wanted to ask, 'Do you see her too, Mom?' but I was afraid to ask. I was so afraid she was just another ghost-friend. After the boys, after all of that, I was *wounded*—"

I couldn't continue because the next part was not fair. *And you couldn't do any better than to tell me to shut up and smile* was what I thought, and did she hear the thought? She stepped back, hurt and incredulous.

Complicated feelings came off of her, images and memories of her hard life and the earnest belief that I'd had it so much better. Why couldn't I nest in my nest and be happy? Why did everything have to be so hard with me?

The emanations were just exactly like those from the principal's office.

"What are you?" I said.

She was already turning. I touched her shoulder, she shook me off, and then I was following her down the hall to the kitchen.

"Do you really not see anything? Is it just about *this* to you, memories and feelings?"

"Get back in your room," she said.

"I'm thinking, what would Tommy do? Is that the right thing? Because I just don't have an internal compass. Or I do, but I can't trust it, can I? *Everything* tells me to hit the road. Everything I want might be waiting out there. The answer to every question I've had. Because I'm *inspired*—sometimes I feel inspired by this—like, I don't know, a composer or some sort of painter—like I'm going to find out a big Truth."

Mom was getting out her dinner container. She slammed the microwave door and took out a bag of salad mix, sat down at the table. She wasn't going to hide in her bedroom; it looked like she was planning to pretend I wasn't there.

I kept on talking, though. Bless my stupid heart.

"But everyone thinks I should go to school, get my license and a boyfriend or whatever." I was crying. "And not think about my talent, not even acknowledge it. But every time I stop doing what I'm supposedly *supposed* to do, I'm getting stronger and seeing more. And sometimes it's so beautiful."

Mom looked at me now. Was she sympathetic?

"But I know what you want for us is better. You want to get that pink house."

She started to smirk.

"You do want to get it, and it isn't out of reach. Betty told me, on Halloween. She's dead, but you know that too, don't you?"

I had the sudden insight that this was why Mom would just as soon I didn't have a phone and why there wasn't wifi, maybe also why there wasn't T.V. If I were connected, I would research all the time, get more obsessed.

College? How could she want me to go to college when she had to know that would bring everything to a head? On my own, reading and learning what I wanted, I'd get even further into this.

But I wasn't controlling my own face anymore. It moved, and I listened to words come out:

"The pink house isn't out of reach for you, and one day maybe you'll meet a nice old man to move in with you, or maybe a nice old lady—Ellen, in fact, once she's widowed—but for the next ten years or so, you'll just raise Stevie there and set up Tommy a little better. Tommy will be successful in every way. Stevie, it's less clear, but they'll both get married and have kids and stay near you the rest of your life, and so you won't really need to make your baby Jojo that way too. You think you do, but you don't. She can go her own way and it will be all right. She's going to bring such richness to you—"

Was Betty back in the principal's corner, moving her mouth in sync with my own? For a flicker, it seemed like she was, but I knew the words for truth. Maybe I had said them after all.

And I went on. I couldn't do anything else.

"If I only knew that you could take care of Stevie. I don't mean just tell her to shut up and eat more salad. I mean teach her to use what she has and how to understand it and live with it and—" I was babbling through tears.

As I took a hitching breath, her face went fierce again and she growled, "You want to hit the road? Hit the road, then." The microwave beeped, and Mom won. I turned away shattered and cried in my room for the rest of the night.

Because I couldn't hit the road, much as I thought I wanted to—not without their support, not without a home to come back to.

241

JANUARY

1

I stayed in my room from that time on and didn't think of going to Roger's party. Foster didn't text about it again, but Matt left the party early to sit and talk in my room. At midnight, he gave me an open-mouthed kiss that felt *all* out of context.

Matt seemed to be all around me, the air I breathed, the cushion between me and the rest of the world. I knew he was talking to Mom on the phone sometimes. He was talking to Tommy, possibly Stevie. When he wasn't right there beside me he was calling me, too, trying to help me make plans.

Why did he care so much? Maybe he was just a good guy, or maybe, as he'd once said, it was that college girls were too self-involved. He had to come back to Beulah to find someone who really needed him.

My mid-term grades came in, making clear there was no chance. Maybe with a stellar spring semester and summer school—but no, I couldn't bear the thought—and so Matt was trying to see where and how I might go about getting the GED.

There were lots of jobs in Boise and Canyon County. Some girls he knew had a spare bedroom he thought I could rent for cheap. It seemed, when we spoke, that he was planning all of this with Mom and that my own opinion on the matter was not much more than an afterthought.

After all, they both knew that long days of work and nights socializing would do me good.

I wondered when and how I'd been given away to Matt. Had I agreed to it sometime and didn't remember, was it all against my will, or did it matter?

#

When it seemed everyone had left the house, I went back to the principal's corner trying to see Betty.

"I tried to finish school . . . I couldn't stand to do it. I'm so sorry," I said.

She shuddered in the air for a few seconds.

"Why can't you ever remember your dreams anymore?" she said, but she couldn't say more. She was gone.

Shadows almost never helped the living, did they? If she was trying to help me, I had to be in grave danger.

#

I *was* alone with Stevie, maybe only the once, sometime in that nameless space between Christmas and the time I left home. She stood in the doorway of my bedroom, not moving to come inside.

"Tamara's going to be there when you go back at school. You know what you'll say to her?" I said. I wasn't entirely sure that Tamara would remember what happened over winter vacation, but I wanted Stevie to be prepared.

"I'm not worried about Tamara. I think *he's* gonna be back soon, though," she said. She gestured down toward the southwest side of the house, the furnace room.

Lonnie. This was the first time she'd acknowledged him directly.

"I think he's with us all the time, whether we see him or not," I said. Like God, like Santa.

"I mean he'll be back to, you know, being upset," she said.

She hadn't glimpsed him during Tamara's exit, then. I said, "We'll do the same thing with him as I did with Tamara. That's all we need to do."

Stevie said, "But you told Tamara she wasn't supposed to be here, and she realized it was true. This guy, he *is* supposed to be here. This is his place. And besides…" she trailed off.

"And besides?" I said.

"Tamara's so pretty. This guy is scary to look at, and big, and strong."

"He can't be strong. He's still just a shadow."

She held her hand around her wrist. She'd gained more weight over the holidays. The wrist was so puffy she couldn't fit her thumb and middle finger around it anymore. She said, "He grabbed me. I almost didn't get away."

"It wasn't in the park at all, was it?"

Stevie's eyes went big. She shook her head.

"Where?"

"The yard, out front. I didn't want Matt to look around here, so I said the park."

She wasn't lying anymore, but she was still mistaken. Lonnie could not have touched her; If a man did touch her, he wasn't Lonnie.

Or would all my theories be struck down? Did the dead now touch us? Maybe so, maybe so.

Still I said, "Whatever harm they do, it's only the harm they make you do to yourself."

She nodded but didn't believe it. Misting up, she said, "You said her name. We don't even know his name."

I didn't give her the name. It wasn't because I was angry at her, or I didn't think it was that. I was standing by her, holding her wrist, stroking it with my thumb.

I dreaded him coming back, but it was a dull dread, not worse than the dread of going back to school, the dread of breaking things off with one or both of the boys, or any of the other terrible little things that come up day to day.

I never thought Stevie would have to deal with him alone. I promised again to be with her, not counting on Mom and Matt succeeding in their plan to send me away.

#

I dreamed that Mom sat in a chair at the foot of my bed. The room was finally done up all beautiful like Stevie and I had dreamed, but it didn't matter now because Mom said it was time I started to think about what I was going to do. I'd be nineteen in just a few weeks, and I'd need to to find a way to support myself. I'd need to move out.

"This isn't working anymore," she said. Just a bland breakup from a movie. I was sure she'd say she'd fallen out of love with me, but she didn't need to say it. The casual loathing on her face told all.

"You'll make sure Stevie's all right. You have to," I said.

Mom smiled a bright fake smile and said, "You are her *only* problem. She'll be fine just as soon as we sweep the house clear of you," and in the dream I believed she was right.

In the dream I doubted, as I sometimes had in my darker moments, whether I was real at all. Maybe I had always been a ghost. There seemed no sure proofs otherwise.

In the dream she no more than said the words and I faded to nothing.

#

My excision from the house wasn't like that in reality. It was more drawn out. It was a week of me pretending to go to school, walking the downtown and browsing at Roark's, visiting with Marielle. It was a week of avoiding most of Matt's calls, being indecisive with him when we did speak. He must have known things were getting dire at home because now he only ever wanted to talk about me and how I was doing and what I ought to do next.

I wasn't calling Foster, either, though I sometimes wanted to. It didn't seem fair to drag him into whatever this was. He couldn't help, and it would all only make him worry for me.

Mom gave me the silent treatment a couple more times. I ditched another week of school. Lonnie and the children returned to their routine all dim and benign like when we first came here. I don't remember what I did that week, probably just hid in my room, but the upshot was that I was no longer a student at Beulah High.

2

My fortune came in the unexpected misfortune of Roark's owner, Marielle. Mid-January, just when Mom was getting so she couldn't look at me, Marielle broke her ankle and tore something in her leg. Coming down the rotten stairs, carrying a basket of clothes for donation, she twisted and fell. She was going to be all right, but in the meantime, there was a "Help Wanted" sign on the front window. I went into the store with no intention of asking about it. I don't think I *did* ask, but somehow it came up, and my availability was not something I wanted to lie about. I had literally no other plans. A few minutes after I went in the door, Marielle had me take that sign down.

I was in a unique position to help her out more or less full-time for room and board and whatever little extra she could manage.

She asked to talk to Mom first, which was smart because Mom had some powerful people among her friends now. No point in getting on the bad side of a whole lot of people in town. Mom went over to Roark's and let Marielle know that she was very much all right with the idea of me taking a little time away. It was probably more like ecstatic. Mom had known Marielle vaguely in school. They had been in the same grade, and yes they spent a good half hour catching up, parted with promises to get together sometime.

Marielle would have liked it very much if I'd had a driver's license. In fact, when she made the offer, she surely expected that I would be driving her around as well as staying at her house and helping at the store, but that was not to be.

No one was at the schoolhouse when Marielle drove me home for my totes. I left Stevie's diary in my bedroom between the mattress and box spring. I reached in my messenger bag and took out my own battered journal, slid it in there with the diary, and then pulled it back out again. I thought about leaving a note that I'd been there and then figured I would just call later.

I got a text while I was there, and when I saw it was from Matt, I just put the phone back in my bag. I made a mental note to do that a few more times, but as far as I was concerned, it was only a delay to the big break-up call or text. It pissed me off a little that I was going to have to do a break-up. It did not feel fair that, when I had never voiced the decision to be with Matt, I was going to have to take on the unpleasant task of cutting things off.

When I went home with Marielle that first time, I was not surprised when she pulled into the dirt drive of the little cabin on the highway that I'd dreamt of long before. It was maybe eight hundred square feet, bright in the day with wood paneling throughout and red tile on the floor and counters of the kitchen, which made up most of the living space. Her living room wasn't much more than an entry room for the kitchen. It could barely hold her big couch and an oversized coffee table made out of a polyurethaned slice of log. The only other things in the room were the fake gas fireplace and the big-screen television.

Marielle showed me the rest of the cabin, two tiny Jack-and-Jill bedrooms with a red-tiled bathroom between them. The back bedroom had big windows, white walls, a lodgepole pine bed covered in a blue-jean quilt, and a wardrobe made out of an old media cabinet. Marielle encouraged me to get comfortable, so I thought I'd finally take my things out of the totes and put them in the wardrobe.

Matt sent another text as I was unpacking. No words to it at all, just a photo of a charcoal sketch. I couldn't make sense of it immediately—it was all curving lines over lines, none of them clean because of the smudgy medium—but when I sat down on the bed and enlarged the image, it snapped into focus. It wasn't bad. Or, it was bad but it was quite well drawn. Done in diagram so that you see through each overlapping figure, a beer-bellied man lay reading while others stepped in and out of the bathtub. The man was done in a thicker, firmer line than the others to make clear that he was the one there longer. He was the real one and the others only shadows.

Some time went by before Matt followed up: "Do you like it?"

I wanted to reply even though I'd been planning to ghost him. I wanted to say something but could not start. I knew in his room or wherever he was, he was looking at the little ellipses at the bottom of the screen, anticipating what I would say, which could only be something about how good the drawing was. It really was good, but that didn't seem the point.

Where did you get the idea? I thought about asking. *What will you tell people when they ask where you got the idea?* No. I had nothing to say.

"You're my Muse :)," he finally wrote.

I made sure the phone was muted and put it back in my messenger bag.

#

Marielle's big-screen television was hooked up to every available streaming service, and the thing was always on, but the evenings were when she did her most intense viewing, all the favorite shows and the movies she'd been wanting to see.

Mostly they were shows I didn't follow, but we watched *The Stepford Wives, Black Christmas,* and *The Shining* in the first couple of weeks I was there. Movies like that reminded me of Betty.

I'd go to my little room if Marielle was watching a show I didn't care for. I'd read or just lie on the bed. Sometimes I'd call Tommy and hear how she was trying to hold it all together. She sounded very competent, as you'd expect. Everything was fine, according to her. Stevie had moved back into our upstairs bedroom and was sleeping better.

Tommy had quit the basketball team after all, and she didn't regret it. She was juggling school, workouts, and her job, on top of trying to help care for Stevie. Hanging around with Cal and Jerry, keeping everything low key. They partied a little bit on weekends, and she'd been the designated driver. Yes! Didn't I know? She'd finally gotten around to getting her driving test scheduled and passed it on the first try! It sounded like she'd taken over some of the cooking, too. She mentioned Greek yogurt and something called a protein bowl.

"Stevie isn't into cooking anymore?" I said.

"We talked about how she doesn't always choose the healthiest things," Tommy said.

I wanted to argue but didn't feel I was in any position to. Still, I hated to think of Stevie not doing the cooking, which had made her feel so helpful, and I hated to think of Tommy forcing her onto a diet.

I said something about making sure Stevie was comfortable. I didn't mean comfortable; I meant we all have things we love and cannot be deprived of. Maybe for Stevie those were foods.

Out of nowhere, Tommy said, "Would it be so bad if she got some counseling? I have before."

"I didn't know that. Does Mom know?"

She just gave a bitter, dry laugh.

"I'm just thinking it wouldn't be so bad if *all* of this came to a head," Tommy said, and then she said she really needed to get going.

She didn't give the phone to Stevie after we talked that time, but usually she would. Once or twice Stevie called me from Mom's phone. She didn't sound frantic or anything, just bored. She talked about things that happened at school.

Tamara hadn't appeared, she said, "Or, you know, she's there; she's just not *there* there." Just a shadow again. Good.

"And the man?" I said.

"Just barely. If you watch from outside his door, you can see a little something. It's funny."

"What's funny?"

"I hadn't thought about any of this until you called. Just working on homework and stuff."

She did sound better. It was because I wasn't there. My birthday was coming up, but they didn't mention it, and I didn't remind them. Nineteen isn't a big one anyway.

While I was on the phone, the room would start getting cold. Marielle wasn't a heavy smoker, but she'd have few cigarettes while she watched movies. She'd keep the windows cracked and fans going so that it was always a little too cold when we went to bed. I think this was what made me sleep so well. It was like camping. The cold, the smell of smoke, the curtains open so we saw the yard lights shining on Blue Spruce trees outside, the absence of shadows—all of it. It was like when we used to go camping back when Dad was still alive. I slept like this then.

Even the sound of cars on the highway reminded me of tent sleeping. We'd never gone camping anywhere so remote that the sounds of vehicles wouldn't come to you in your tent. I had dreamed of nights in this cabin and now, sleeping here for real, I dreamed all night and woke before Marielle. I sat with pen and journal trying to remember those dreams, but I never could.

Marielle would wake up early to get a couple of hours of television in before leaving for Roark's, and then I'd wake rested and good to keep moving from seven in the morning until about six or seven at night, when we'd sit down to watch movies.

She would drive, but I had to make sure the walk was shoveled and then escort her out to the car. We'd either make breakfast at home, or we'd skip it and I'd run in and get cappuccinos and breakfast sandwiches from the Coffee Connection. She always sent me in with a twenty and told me to keep the change. I got to know Tina, Mac, and Allen. It was nice to eat at home, too. Marielle had all kinds of frozen fruit for smoothies. She taught me how to make really good omelets.

The cabin had no shadows, but Roark's had its share. They were dim and disembodied movements, something like the schoolchildren in the classrooms at home but much more varied. They made little flickers of gestures around the clothing, little hovering movements around the board games, books, and dishes.

I had to take care of anything that needed to be done on the second floor (now reached by way of a repaired staircase clad in new gray industrial carpet), but other than that I was free to come and go, free to read or to watch movies on Marielle's laptop with her. There was even a little cot in the backroom for naps, which I used a couple of times. If I had been able to drive, I would have been free to take the car around Beulah or even go back to the cabin, but since I couldn't drive, I stayed in the building all day.

I had thought about telling her that, really, if I could just take a couple of days bringing down the ladies' clothes, she could rope off the upstairs and wouldn't have to pay me to be around, but I thought that she wanted someone around less because of the ladies' clothes and more because the injury made her feel vulnerable.

Or maybe she was doing me a favor. I'd said once how I dreaded going back home. "Don't, then," she said. "You have options. When I'm done needing you, you can get some other little job and rent this room if you want."

I only smiled, and she must have taken that as meaning I didn't want to stay in the cabin because she started talking about other jobs that come with room and board, nannying or working as a home health aide maybe.

But I loved living with Marielle. The glut of books and movies, the easy days, the restful nights, finally being free from school: all of these added to the restfulness of this time, but more than those elements it was, I thought, the absence of Mom. She wasn't filling my mind with her memories and feelings. Never having to think of her made me so much more productive and normal than I had ever been. This was something I had long suspected, but it made me very, very sad to see that it really was so.

It was sad, too, to think that being away from Stevie could feel so right. The complicated feelings of love and guilt don't go away, but there's a freedom in knowing once and for all that someone really is better off without you.

#

A week into the new living situation, I called Foster. I'd been missing him.

Marielle was happy to have me as a TV buddy, but I think she was equally happy to have me go out and try to live my life a little. Foster and I cruised around Beulah and out past the canyon. We brought takeout pizza to Marielle's.

I tried a dozen times to finally send a message breaking things off with Matt, but I failed at that. I couldn't get over thinking how unfair it was I had to do it—and it didn't feel great to disappoint Matt, either. He'd gotten all involved in my life and obviously thought he was doing some good. To say "no thanks" to all of that felt mean.

On the other hand, out of sight, you know. His feelings didn't matter as much as Foster's because Foster was right beside me. The feelings that came off of him were something special. Not a desperate love—I didn't kid myself that he felt that strongly—but more a feeling of *Huh, sometimes things work out in a not completely shitty way*. Warm, contented, ready to know me better. I hoped that I hadn't hurt their friendship too much.

Foster didn't want to make me anything I wasn't. He didn't try to talk about the future.

We were so well matched as friends, I almost hated to get romantic. I guess we didn't get all *that* romantic. He never tried to take me out to a restaurant, aside from Subway and Tiger Burger. When we'd go through the drive-thru and Tommy was there, you might think she would have scowled, but no. She smiled so big.

We didn't have date dates like I'd had at the pizza place with Matt, but yes, looking back you could have made a montage of all the cute things we did. We kissed a lot in his car and watched comedies on Marielle's laptop while she took a nap on the cot. The best was when we played in the snowy park.

There was a moment when I had romped through the park on my own one night when Marielle had to stay late at Roark's and I was stuck in town, and I walked up to the Circle K with this sense of déjà vu that crested just as I came in the door into the heat. I looked down at jeans caked with snow, and the déjà vu heightened to something different, more palpable. I remembered the day in summer I'd felt this same feeling standing here.

The store was empty. Foster wished he wasn't on camera so he could kiss me, and he was a little worried over my frozen legs, but mostly he was just happy to see me. He flashed his big, beautiful grin. I couldn't remember if I'd told him about seeing myself here back in summer, just like this with the snow on my legs.

If I told him now, I worried that it would seem contrived, but I did it anyway, and he believed me. He thought it was so cool, really.

Right here with the air from the Circle K hot on my face, watching him grinning that uncomplicated grin of his, I am happy.

#

Right here in Marielle's guest room, I ease onto his naked lap. Blood pounds through my body, and I feel what he feels.

I love being in my body, finally love my life, and then I wake.

#

Right here in Marielle's guest room, I ask myself if I am awake this time. It feels like I am.

Marielle's gone to her Dad's for the evening, and Foster's here under me, sweat cooling on both of us. I'm crying, my body shaking.

"Where did you go?" he says. He touches my hair so softly. I feel what he's feeling.

"I want to show you something," I say. "Get dressed."

On the way, we speak of openness and awareness of surroundings, seeing things rather than seeing just your route around things. We speak of how it is when you travel or move, how everything's different and so you see it all new. Is there a way to make that happen voluntarily? Is there a method to making sure you see something even when you see it all the time?

He parks the little car and we walk out on the bridge. We hold hands, stand close in a certain spot. We're toasty in coats though the wind is strong. I hope the wind won't affect things too much.

"Just try to feel open. Whatever you see, you see," I say, and we stand there as long as it takes.

The pink smudge comes past us to perch on the long-ago barrier shorter than the iron one there now. When Foster's hand tightens on mine, I know that he sees.

FEBRUARY

1

I woke from the most vivid dream I'd ever had:
Tommy called me all rushed and breathless. I had to get home, had to help.

"Help with what? What does that even mean?" I said. I was pacing just outside Roark's.

Tommy didn't want to get into it over the phone. It's Stevie," she said before hanging up and then wouldn't answer back. A dropping feeling, like going too fast down an elevator. My heart raced, and this dreadful regret narrative started up: *Oh, you stupid girl!*

No, not stupid, actively evil. Left your sister Tommy in charge of things, did you? Because she is *the practical and capable one. Only you know she knows and looks away. She's so much more messed up than you are. She sees—every day she sees—and she will not admit what she sees. How fucked up is that?*

She saw Stevie courted by Tamara, and she not only did nothing. She told herself she did not see.

And now doom comes down, and you are the catalyst.

I tried to get hold of Foster, and when I couldn't, Marielle closed Roark's for a minute to give me a ride.

Just before the call, I'd felt light and carefree. Now I felt my time away from home had been an enormous mistake. Hadn't all of this pulled me from the only person I really cared about? Why had I trusted that Mom knew what Stevie needed?

Mom's truck wasn't at the schoolhouse, and Marielle pulled away before I'd gotten inside. I ran through the upstairs yelling, "Stevie, Tommy?"

The smell of the house got me. It wasn't just the smell of the building but the smells of my mother and sisters and the things they ate, the products they used on their bodies and hair. It crushed me. I felt I might never want to leave home again, now that I was back.

Betty appeared, before me or in memory, I didn't know. "Is your sister all right?" she said, and she was gone.

I hurried downstairs and looked in every room, even in the back room where Lonnie sat with knees tensed together, pretending not to see me.

I'd left him here to terrorize her the whole time and barely asked how she was doing, and now he'd broken her somehow. Or *was* it him? I didn't know.

"I don't suppose you know where everyone is?" I said. Lonnie kept his cloudy eyes focused on the wall opposite him. He had never spoken to me in the house and wasn't trying to start now.

When I got back up the stairs, Stevie stood on the patio just beyond the French doors. Delighted to see her, I smiled and trotted up to open the door. I thought she'd been locked out, but why not go around front?

I thought she would rush right in when I opened the door. Instead, she stayed where she was.

"Don't touch me," she said. "Promise?"

I wanted to hug her but stood back as she'd asked. "You had some trouble? I came as soon as they said."

"You left," she said. She didn't look good. Her eyes were cast in shadow, their lids swollen purple.

"I'm so sorry I wasn't here," I said. "I kept trying to call the last couple of days."

She just stood. The cold wind kept coming into the room.

"Did somebody hurt you? Where's Mom?" I said.

A knock came, and I answered the door. Foster. He'd gotten my messages.

I returned to Stevie, made a hurry-up gesture. "Come in. It's getting cold."

"Georgie? There's nobody there," Foster said.

Stevie came into the room, then, and I closed the door. He was right. Under the lights she was already dimming. I reached for her, to hold her, and she was not there at all. I cried. Immediately, I hyperventilated. I couldn't see through the tears, and Foster pulled me to him. He stroked my hair.

"Why couldn't you see her? I taught you to see," I said.

Knowing Stevie was dead brought the terrible realization that none of us would ever have a life again. This wasn't something we could run away from.

I was fumbling through my pockets for my phone, but it wasn't there. I remembered setting it in the side-well of Marielle's car.

"She's dead. Stevie's dead," I told Foster, though I didn't believe it myself. But what else could her shadow mean?

There seemed to be nothing to do but slump to the floor and pull Foster down into a crouch so I could cry against his chest. Right away, I stood and said, "He did it. I know he did." It felt false, as soon as I said it, but what was I to do with all my anger?

I went downstairs and to the back room. He was not there. I paced the whole house, just as he had always paced the house. Foster followed behind me asking questions all the time, and Lonnie was back in his chair when I returned to the basement.

"What did you do to her?" I screamed.

Lonnie still pretended not to see me. His face was solid and clear; his body and the chair were dimmer, more blurred.

I was shrieking. I didn't know what to do. I found a box of incense and lit the end of the whole bundle of sticks, handed it to Foster.

"Wave this around, I said.

I turned back and called out all I knew in a low choked chant:

"Lonnie, Ghost of Farm School Road, Beulah Ghost and Park Ghost," all the names I could think of, and I told his doings as well as his names. "You pace the halls. You sit on your little chair. You bother little kids in the park. You're a maggoty scarecrow nailed to the tall tree. You spy on people," on and on.

And then I was out of my mind. I was just chanting, "You're dead, you're dead, you are dead" until the words ran together, blubbering, snot all over my face. I was out of control, screaming "What did you do to my sister? What did you do to her?" on and on, while Foster just stood steady and waved the incense.

I felt my voice shattering and cracking at the end of it, and I started to chant it all over again, when the door opened upstairs.

I caught Foster's eye then. He looked scared like I was, only I thought he looked relieved in the moment, too.

"Whose side are you on?" I said.

Mom called from upstairs, "Matt? Georgie?"

Tommy's feet thumped down the stairs, and she rushed to me. "Stevie's missing," she said. "Why weren't you answering?"

"You've got it wrong," Lonnie said.

I turned back to him, screaming, "Get out. Get out. Get out."

"What are you doing?" Tommy said. She looked around at all the smoke in the air.

"Burn this room," I said.

"Get her out of here," Mom roared. She was behind me now. I thought Foster took hold of my shoulders.

"I mean it. Get her out now."

"She thinks..." said Matt. He had changed when I wasn't looking.

"I don't care. Get her out," said Mom again. Her face loomed terrible and huge. She was pushing me. All of them were pushing me toward the stairs away from Lonnie.

But when I looked back, dog-Lonnie stood in the center of the room, pointing left toward the old kitchen. I broke free and ran into that room behind him. He stopped to see that I'd followed and disappeared into a corner cabinet.

Mom, gripping a handful of hair and coat-hood, turned me back to the stairs. Matt took my arm, and there was nothing left but to go.

Tommy walked with us saying, "She'll calm down. It'll be all right, but you have to go looking for Stevie." As we pushed out the front door into moonless starry night, she said, "Find her if you can. I'll call you. I'm sorry."

I held my finger to my lips and motioned to the car. Matt didn't understand, so I whispered, "Go on and start the car. I'll be there in a minute if I can."

I tiptoed around the back and let myself in the basement door and kept going until I was there on the floor beside the corner cabinet. Tommy and Mom argued upstairs. The blackened cookie sheets in the cabinet would be loud to move even if I was careful, so I wasn't careful. I pulled them all out in one go.

"What was that?" Mom said upstairs, but I was already slithering through the secret door at the back of the cabinet and into a damp, dark room.

Did my eyes adjust to the gray space? It felt something like that.

"No, you're not seeing with your eyes anymore," Lonnie said. He was Maggot-Lonnie lying in a fetal position on a cot, but he was all the other Lonnies too—the dog and the one who reached for things on the high shelves of the furnace room, the one who watched the children in the yard. The room filled with layers of Lonnie, hundreds or thousands of him moving around and through me.

He died in this room. When the school closed up, he had nowhere else to go, and he'd long before found this space all sealed up. That was all he was, just a sad and single-minded man, or not even that. I moved toward the writhing, rotted face, and where my hand should have touched slime, it touched nothing. I let my hand move in another half inch and felt the dry leather and bone of him.

"I never hurt her," he said, and I believed him.

"You were trying to warn her," I said. The air, once full of Lonnies, had calmed. All was well here. Lonnie's remains and the crumpled mess of his cot were still here, but he had vacated. Why hadn't I asked him where Stevie was?

Foster had the car running out front, and I wanted to get back to him, but low on the ground was the little crack of light from the cabinet. Mom's legs stepped into that light. She grunted getting down on her knees and called, "Get me the flashlight."

The basement wall had always had that one door and the rest was a blank expanse of lava, but I felt around the walls anyway.

I remembered what I said to Foster on the bridge: "Just try to stay open. Whatever you see, you see."

I stayed open. I saw through the walls for an instant, just a moonlit yard but so bright, and then it was black again.

The beam of a flashlight darted around behind me.

"What the fuck?" Mom said.

The light touched me, but I closed my eyes, saw the door, and opened it out into what I knew as dream-Beulah.

#

I woke from that dream into another. Mom knelt beside my bed in her blue bathrobe. She was talking on the phone and shaking me by my hip at the same time.

I woke from that dream into what felt like another. Marielle knelt beside my bed in the dark, shaking me by my hip. The spruce trees through the window were all I saw.

"I think she's awake now," she said and handed me the phone.

"Georgie?" said Tommy.

"It was ringing forever," said Marielle.

"We can't find Stevie," said Tommy. "It's probably nothing. She's probably just with a friend, but I—"

"A friend?" I said, getting into my jeans.

"I mean she's probably just playing somewhere. We thought you might know where she might be." It was dark, and what time was it?

"How long?" I had my coat on and was fumbling for my waterproof boots.

"We didn't—"

"How long before you called me did you—" but I left off. Either she'd been missing for some time and they'd just now called me or they'd called me as soon as they noticed, and either option was terrible but neither one mattered. I had to find her.

I knew where to go. That was the amazing part. I hung up with Tommy just as soon as my boots were on. I texted Foster to take the highway out to the canyon if he could, and I was setting off that way on foot. Almost twelve o'clock, the phone said, and I hated Tommy for saying that she was probably out playing.

Marielle said she could be ready to drive me in a minute, but I told her I didn't have time to help her to the car. More than that, I needed to be alone to work out the rest of the dream, so I walked out onto the highway. No cars, no wind, but it was cold and dark, moonless and starry just like in the dream.

By the time I came to Streaker's, half of me was back in the dream.

I'd opened the extra basement door into dream-Beulah, and then what? The rest was jumbled. I had stepped out of a mostly realistic dream and into a dream-dream of illogical junctures, a nameless gray space between them. Roads traced out in fine white lines, like I was in a landscape but also in a map.

Girls were all over the yard, picking weeds and trying to start the lawnmower, picking and eating berries, pulling berry prickers out of their fingers.

Little-girl Betty came forward out of the sea of girls, took my hand and said, "How far is the canyon?"

I took Betty's hand and said, "Come see my room first," and we turned straight from the basement door into Ellen's mom's beloved pink house. We hovered over patterned carpets and wood floors to the stairs.

The old lady rocking in the corner chuckled. To us she said, "Slow down," and to herself, all delighted she said, "Oh, little girls in the house again."

We hovered slowly up the steps and turned into the first room, a girl's room done up in pink with a lighted dollhouse and shelves of dolls, an antique vanity table with a little white bookcase beside it. We went to the bookcase and traced the spines for something.

I didn't know what books we were scanning for until we found the row of them: Wild Cats '86, '87, '88, and so on. Betty tipped one out, and we riffled its pages. There at the end was an index saying what pages people's pictures were on, but we didn't know the last name. The letters writhed, and I was frustrated looking for the word "Tamara" in all that chaos.

"Let's just go to the canyon," Betty said, but I opened it back up from the front, and we scanned the pictures until we found the cheerleading team picture, Tamara in splits at the very center of it, hair large and starched as complement to her sharp little face. Tamara Branch. Back to the index, a list of numbers after the name, but the numbers twisted and churned.

And then we were at the canyon.

In reality, I was still far from the canyon, walking fast but not about to jog. I'd never made it out there in the summer, not sure why I thought I could now, but I thought Foster must be coming along soon.

I looked at my phone. Nothing.

I called Foster. Nothing.

Texted Tommy, "Anything yet?"

"No, we're talking to the police right now. Are you looking?"

"Yes."

A text from Matt: "Tommy told me. I'm on my way."

And that was that, only the phone rang just a few minutes later. Ellen.

"I just heard," she said.

"I'm walking out to the canyon," I said, and she said she'd be there in a minute. My air came out in clouds now, and it was so black ahead I almost believed there was no canyon.

There was only a little of the dream left. Betty and I played in one of the stretches of land down by the river's edge. It was a school trip and we'd gone off away from the rest of the kids just romping around, running.

Her dark glossy hair bounced in front of me. I was trying to catch her, swiping at her. She turned, only she wasn't Betty. She was Ellen, and so I must have been Mom.

"You shouldn't be so embarrassed about the bridge," she said. "I'm scared of things too sometimes."

She was a new friend; I wanted her closer. I said, "It isn't just the heights. I saw something up there. If I tell you, you won't tell?"

We were in the pink bedroom. The number nineteen lifted off the index page, and I struggled to find it near the start of the yearbook. A page of candids, three girls in

Halloween costumes grinned big in the central image, a fox Maid Marian from Disney, a fairy, a lion. Tamara Branch, Ellen Marsten, Georgina Sand.

We were back at the canyon. The girl tossed her dark hair again, turned back and was Stevie. Oh, Stevie, looking cold and frightened but healthy.

"Want to try something?" I said in the dream, and I knew that I was Tamara. "Just hold your breath, and you can fly."

Waves of nausea came as I remembered it, and just then the long SUV pulled off the road ahead.

2

Once Ellen picked me up, we'd be at the canyon in minutes. Tommy had told her the best way to help was to help me.

"Your mom's a mess. It sounds like Tommy's taking care of everything, calling people," Ellen said.

"Do you know anything more than I do?" I asked.

"Stevie was missing when your mom looked in on her around eleven-thirty. They looked all over the house and the yard, and then they started making calls."

"How long did they leave her alone?"

"I don't know. There was some trouble at school earlier, but she got home, she was in bed. I just don't know."

I didn't say anything back, and Ellen said, "Your mom does her best for all of you."

"What trouble at school?" I said.

"She acted up somehow. You'll have to ask your mom."

We crossed the bridge and Ellen pulled into the parking area, right under a streetlight.

I looked straight into her eyes and asked, "Why do you think we're out here?" I'd never seen Ellen without her makeup before. She looked less pretty but no older. What an easy life she'd had.

And she kept my eye. "I think you had a feeling about it, or a dream," she said.

"Because Mom used to have feelings about things?"

"Yes."

There wasn't any time to ask more, but I was grateful for that honesty. I hoped she saw that. Getting out of my seatbelt, I said, "Thank you for the ride, and for everything. I think you ought to go to the house and see what else they need."

"I'm coming with you," she said. We were out of the vehicle now, already headed to the steps that started just to the left of the interpretive sign.

"You'll mess up your shoes," I said, but then I saw her lace-up hiking boots.

I stopped, took her hand. "You'll slow me down, OK? Wait here for me. Go if they call. I'll be all right."

I turned away from her and hurried down the steps faster than she could have followed, if she was even trying. I didn't look back to see. Not far down, the stairs ended in a viewing platform, but a rough path led off to the left, and I continued on it a long time, losing the certainty that it was a path. Maybe it had ended; maybe it was only ever wishful thinking and I'd stumble off a cliff.

The further down from the parking area, the darker it became. Stars hung in the black moonless sky and below them lay a pit, and soon I was at the bottom of that pit, no longer sure what I was doing there. I needed to remember more of the dream, but it wasn't coming back. The air was too cold on my face, my heart going too fast.

At first I heard only my short, shallow breaths, and then came the river sounds just a few hundred feet to my right. I'd come into the canyon feeling that I needed to get to a wide patch of land, the patch where they take kids on school field trips, but now that I was down here, I didn't know which direction it was. I was losing the sense of urgency, too.

Stevie had been here but had moved on, or *they* had. She and Tamara had.

My phone sounded: Foster, so sorry he'd missed me. He'd been at his mom's, but he was headed back to Beulah. Where was I?

Matt: "Almost there. Where are you?"

Tommy: "Where are you? Did you find her?"

When I looked away from the screen, it had shot my vision too much. I had to stop and press my eyes closed, and that was what brought me back to the dream-vision: Stevie's face floated before me, gray and blurred.

I pressed my palms to my ears so I'd no longer hear the water and wind, and I heard her little voice, not what it said, but the murmuring of her far away—to the right or left or above, I didn't know.

But I was still for a long time letting my blood calm. I tried to stay open and see what there was to see. It didn't matter that I'd not found just the right place because the drama played out behind my closed eyes, Tamara and Stevie descending the stairs and then taking the trail.

Stevie was exhausted. She slumped to the ground. "Rest," she said. "I can't go any farther right now."

Tamara looked on her with pity. "You could do so much more. You could fly," she said. "If you would just. . . Won't you just. . .?"

And then screaming, static. I couldn't hold the image longer.

I opened my eyes, but I saw something, still: Their dim little shadow-legs climbing back up the path before me. I followed, and in the darkest part they came clearer. Two girls, but both of them were Stevie, one Stevie pushing clouds of air out with each step, the other Stevie breathing not at all, filmy, frantic, screaming soundless screams at the other who just kept walking.

She's taken Stevie's body. She's walking out of Beulah.

I went so cold coming up the steps. It took so long. At times I was pushing myself out of my body, just pushing out a few inches from where I should be, but I forced myself back each time.

It had seemed like too long, but Ellen still waited in her car. She rolled down the window as I passed.

I turned back saying, "Please stay, don't follow. I think I might know—"

And she nodded. She was crying a little, phone light in her face. "There's no news," she said.

I kept to the road, though I knew Tamara would not be walking on the shoulder. She'd be off the road and away from car lights. She'd still be on this side. No need to cross the highway.

The bitter thought came, how I'd dreamed of walking out of town like this.

How could her body have come so far, so fast? I wondered, but it had a powerful vicious thing inside it now. A survivor. Tamara would walk until the feet bled if it meant she'd be free.

Lights were coming up ahead, and when I turned my eyes from them, a few hundred feet from the road, just in front of a windbreak, I saw the dim shadow-Stevie hovering around the living Stevie. I ran for them, and the car stopped, circled back. The lights were still on but not moving, and someone else was running behind me. Matt.

He was faster than I was, so we came to Stevie at once. He rushed forward, hugging her. I stayed back.

"I'm calling your mom," Matt said. He flashed a salesman's smile at me.

"Please, it's not me," said the shadow of Stevie.

The upper lip curled up on the living Stevie's face.

I took out my phone. "Please, just wait a minute and I'll call her," I said. I didn't know what to do.

Shadow-Stevie was so dim behind her body, I had to move. I needed the dark trees behind her to see.

"What exactly was your plan?" I asked Stevie's body.

Matt was crouched down close and typing something into his phone. Mom would be here soon.

Stevie's face looked back at me with Tamara's horrible haughty smile on it. She said, all slow and cold, "I just needed some time to myself, but I'm ready to go back home now."

Stevie's shadow pounded at the air around her and dimmed further. I barely saw her now, trees or no.

When it happened, there was nothing else and no question what to do. I knew that no one would believe me, that Tamara would never give back the body, that Stevie would be lost forever unless I made a move.

And it had to be now, before Mom came. Mom might not let me near her after this.

"Wouldn't you rather. . ." I said, unzipping my coat. I sat cross-legged in the dirt and pulled my T-shirt up to show how skinny I was. A deep, dropping feeling of nausea came as I held my breath and pushed hard, pushed out of my body all in one motion.

My body now slumped, not breathing. I hovered there beside it.

"Georgie?" Matt said. He ran to my body, his hands on my face. He was slapping at my cheeks now, dialing 911.

"Do it," I said, and the shadow of Stevie floated back past the trees, all the way through the dark trees to the fence. I saw only a glimmer of her.

Tamara raced for my body then. Stevie's body, still standing, dropped.

My eyelids flickered as Tamara came awake behind my face. "I'm all right," she murmured.

"Stevie," I said. I went to her body. Matt had not yet noticed it lying there on the ground.

"What happened?" he said to me-Tamara. "Did you faint?"

"You know, I think I did," she said, all surprised.

"Stevie," I said.

Her shadow moved forward slowly. She fretted her hands.

"You have to get back," I said.

"You take it," she said. "I don't deserve to."

That was when I swept her up and mingled with her. We entered her body together and felt the shock of it. Pain in the legs, in the feet—and such cold.

Her eyes opened.

"They'll be here in a minute," Matt said. He was back beside us, helping us up. We were too weak and too conflicted inside to do more than lean into his chest. He held us.

A siren already called out.

"It isn't her!" Stevie cried, but I caught her somehow. I held her off from saying any more.

"Text Ellen," I said with her mouth. "She's waiting down the road."

Soon Ellen pulled up, and soon after that the police were around us, all of us with blankets on our shoulders, an EMT checking us out.

And for a moment I didn't feel quite part of the "us" anymore. I was losing grip on Stevie. She started saying things about Tamara, who was the one in Matt's arms now, but no one was listening, or were they not believing her, or us? It was confusing.

At first Matt was looking for a chance to get close to Stevie, probably wanting to ask if all of this had anything to do with the man in the park. Me-Tamara blocked his way. He asked her something, and she shook her head and whispered something in his ear.

With Tamara's expressions on it, my face was already sharper, crueler, more awake and more lovely than it had ever been. Matt must have noticed, too. He could barely look away from her.

"I missed you," she said, nuzzling up to him. He looked down at her and she looked at us the whole time.

Mom arrived before we all left for the hospital. She clutched us tight and then stepped back to look us over. I couldn't remember the last time I saw relief like that in her face.

Her love for Stevie was always so much less complicated than her love for me.

Mom couldn't protect Stevie from questions. The officers around her wanted to know what had happened and if they should be looking for a kidnapper and all of that. Mom couldn't help her, but I was still part of Stevie. I wanted to stay and protect her.

With me speaking through her and inside her mind, Stevie said what she needed to say to get home. She calmed herself, said she'd been confused and wrong before. It was stupid to try to run away. Now she was hungry, cold, and tired. She'd learned her lesson, and that was all. She wanted to go to bed now.

#

Stevie's body began to push me out almost immediately. At first, we were one. I knew all that had happened to her, we knew the few secrets we had ever held from one another, and we operated the body as smoothly as one person would—albeit one person who had just walked out to the canyon in winter.

By the time we stood talking with the officers, I was already coming out of her. Tamara probably saw me as an aura around Stevie, just a half inch of ginger-blonde hair coming out the top of Stevie's head. If she'd looked at Stevie's back, she'd have seen mine lifting out of it.

There, sharing Stevie's body, I was still living. I felt our blood, our breathing, the pain and cold.

For the time I held on, I still thought rationally, still thought with a brain and saw through eyes. I was not sorry about what I'd done. There'd been no hesitation, and there was no regret. Tamara would never have given her up, not for anything less than another body she wanted more than Stevie's. There would have been no way to stay in my life.

That life was over, no matter what I did.

I was happy that I'd had the body to give. I had given my life for Stevie's, and doing that had freed me from all worry and regret forever.

273

I held on as long as I could, saying, *Take care of yourself now, baby. Take care of Mom. I'll see you again if I can, OK?*

She cried while I said it and said nothing more than *No, stay, no.*

And then I was gone.

3

I really was lost. I'll say more of that in a moment.

But how did the others spend the rest of the night? I pieced it all together later from things that I heard and saw. I might be taking some liberties, but here is what went down, more or less:

Foster didn't make it back to Beulah because that little red car of his finally broke down. There was no rush anymore, anyway. Matt had texted to let him know that the trouble was all over. Georgie was shaken up, but he was taking care of her.

Foster texted Georgie. He was hurt that she never responded, but he knew things would be tense with her mom after all of this and that she was just doing what she needed to do. He eventually called and woke his mom to come pick him up.

He was sure, fairly sure, that he and Georgie were in love now and that she would be calling him soon, no matter what Matt thought.

He was bitterly disappointed, but not entirely surprised, when that did not come to pass.

#

The others all converged in our great room. What with talking to the police, getting Stevie checked out at Beulah's little band-aid station, and then being so keyed up when they got home, everyone expected to stay awake the rest of night. Mom decided to call in sick for the next day and keep the girls home from school. Ellen made cocoa and texted Adrian to say she was going to stay over, and they all sat in the great room talking about how scared they'd been and how Stevie couldn't ever do anything like that again.

Stevie looked all over the room for me. She thought I would appear to her, but I wasn't there at all. She thought she ought to go to our room or her little room downstairs, somewhere private to call to me, but she was comfortable where she was and a little scared to leave.

She was getting incredibly sleepy and in that state was starting to lose track of who was missing, me or Tamara. After all, I sat right across from her on the other sofa, nestled against Matt.

After a while, Georgie and Matt went into the upstairs bedroom that had been hers, and Tommy went down to the basement. Georgie came out of her room, used the toilet, and spent a great deal of time looking at her face in the bathroom mirror before going back to Matt. She thought it could be better but it could also be a whole lot worse. She was satisfied, all in all.

Ellen and Mom kept talking softly with Stevie nodding off between them until Ellen, too, drifted into sleep. Mom yawned, put her cocoa down on the floor, and let her own eyes close.

Georgie and Matt lay on her bed, but they weren't doing anything. The door was open and they wore their clothes, even their shoes. Her coat lay over their legs. He led their conversation, held her hands, stroked her hair.

He led so surely that she never had to volunteer any knowledge. All she had to do was react. Georgie agreed she should go to live in Caldwell with those girls Matt knew, after all. She'd get a job and the GED, start at a community college, and so on. Every suggestion he had, she took. She said she'd been out of her mind to choose anything else. She hadn't been herself at all this past month—or no, longer than that—and she was so sorry.

She almost apologized for running away, but no, that was the other girl.

Matt said she ought to text Foster to let him know she was home. Who was Foster? She had no idea what he meant by "text," either, but she asked if he could do it for her. Though he frowned, he pulled something from his pocket and fumbled into its light. He sighed and put it back in his pocket.

Now, lying on the bed with all the rest of the house asleep, he asked if anyone had called or texted Marielle.

Tamara didn't know if he meant her Marielle from school or someone else with that name. She only said "Hmm?" like she'd been sleeping. It wasn't quite a lie. The body had felt so loud and heavy at first, so full of sensations she barely remembered. She didn't expect it to rest, but sleep was courting her now.

And she remembered that sleep was as sweet as waking.

"Marielle. I don't have her number," Matt said.

"I'm so sleepy," she said, which made him smile. She was always sleepy, wasn't she?

"Can I use your phone?"

"Yes, anything."

He reached into the coat and brought out the object. So she had one too.

"Unlock it?" he said.

When she didn't do anything, he slipped it into her hand, pressed down on her thumbnail. He sent Marielle a long text to let her know what had happened and that Georgie was home. She thanked him right away, assuring him she could get around just fine and did not need any help right then.

He might have thought about checking out Georgie's other messages, maybe the ones from Foster for example, but he didn't look at anything else on the phone at all. He just slipped it back in her coat pocket. He took a pillow and blanket to the floor and slept.

Tamara did not sleep. Sleep had seemed to be coming, but now that feeling was gone. She was too bothered by all the things Matt had said. She was smart enough to know he was talking about some sort of futuristic technology—she was in the future, after all, it was to be expected—but how did he know about Marielle? How long would she be able to fake an understanding of things?

She should leave. Right now, get right back on the highway. In this body, she would be able to hitchhike. If only she knew how to drive, she could ease Matt's keys out of his pocket and be away even faster.

She stole back into the bathroom. This time, she didn't need to pee. She only wanted to pull up her T-shirt, suck in her stomach and angle before the mirror. The ribs pushed out nicely, stomach was firm though undefined, breasts disappointing. The arms and shoulders, too, looked underdeveloped.

She lowered to the ground in a plank position and was surprised to find herself incapable of even one push-up. She lowered to her knees and struggled through a girls' pushup just to see where this body was at.

Weak, vulnerable. Maybe she should stay where she was protected for a while.

The mother, too. Most of the mother's attention had been on Stevie, but there was a moment at the hospital when the mother turned her long, fierce face toward Tamara and that face broke into joy and relief, and she hugged her. She thanked her for finding Stevie, and some chemicals ran through Tamara's body. Though Tamara's mother was a thousand times more perfect, still a similarity was there in the expression, in the feel of the embrace.

Tamara didn't recognize Gina from school, she was so changed. She looked "rode hard and put away wet," as her own mom might have put it. Tamara's mom never lived long enough to be anything but beautiful.

Ellen she recognized, of course. A good little Beulah girl then and now.

She was neither here nor there about the boy sleeping on the floor. All boys were pretty much the same to her.

She might not go with him after all. She might stay near the warmth of the mother.

Of course she would. Here with her old friend Ellen, her new friend Stevie, the almost-beautiful mother and that other one, the sister. Here was where she belonged.

Tamara lay back down under the coat. She took the phone from its pocket and idly pressed like the boy had done. The screen turned bright with a picture of the family at a park in McCall. It was that day they went to the hot springs pool. Tamara put the phone back in the pocket, thinking *I'll figure it out, or if I have trouble, I'll go see the old lady at Albertsons. She just loves to teach people how to use a phone.*

Oh, it hurt just a little to bring it up, like concentrating hard on a math problem, but the memory was there of the day she and Foster picked up the phone. And oh, she blushed. That other memory of Foster too.

The memories were all there in the brain.

She wanted to get beautiful in the morning, and that brought the image of her hair big in bun-curls and smoky eye-makeup. Tommy would do her up like that again if she asked.

I ought to borrow something of Mom's, too. Her *clothes are all hideous, and they're at Marielle's anyhow. I can't go over there just yet.*

Under this mattress is Stevie's diary. I need to hide that in the morning before someone else finds it.

In the bag, too, there's her *journal. I need to hide that. Burn it.*

She didn't need to read it; she could remember all it said if she wished to concentrate hard enough.

And with those little prickles of knowledge bringing strain and the start of a tension headache, Tamara finally settled down into sleep with a feeling of hope for the next day.

TIMELESS

No blood, no eyes, no breath—but I exist still.
   I stand all alone in the center of the highway. Freed from the fears of my body, I wait for Foster. He'll see me. Even from a speeding car, he'll see me. I taught him how to see.

But Foster never comes—no car ever comes. I stand in the highway forever, just a point of consciousness facing not toward or away from Beulah but facing all directions at once, every direction a starry black.

#

I'm drifting in front of the Circle-K, only the K changes: Circle-L, Circle-M, Circle-P, Circle-T, Circle-Y and then I can't read it at all. Foster is never inside. The place is abandoned and then gone. Some low brick building that means nothing to me stands in its place, and the Circle-K is just a white outline, like a blueprint overlaid.

I'm back in Orliss, in the New Age shop looking at crystals. Betty waits in the next room for me to find her for the very first time. I get a tremendous charge knowing she's just around the corner, but before I can reach her, I'm somewhere else.

In a different room in Orliss, watching my body writhe on a bathroom floor and rise grasping for the toilet, barely making it. Betty swoops in to hold back my hair, a little too late. There is no taste, no smell, but I am back in that queasy body for a moment, not an observer but a part of it, and then I'm somewhere else.

I hover behind a Stevie-aged me riding alone with Mom in our old car. I'm just laughing and babbling to her about something happening at school, and she keeps looking over with intense love. I'd forgotten that way she used to look at me. I want to stay in that moment, hear what story I'm telling, but it is gone.

Outside the ghost-house in the empty lot, I'm saying "What's your name?" to the lady in the window.

Driving a car in my sleep, lulled by the sound of tires on a good country road. I'm asleep, someone else driving the car, someone else operating my body.

I'm in the version of the story I told Betty now, kissing Brian, saying all we have to say before he fades. There's no distinction between memories and stories. They're all real, all the same.

Holding Stevie in the hospital, Tommy by my side impatient for her turn.

Terrorized, running up steep steps in slow motion, I don't know what time or place.

In Marielle's spare room with Foster. My entire core ticks like your legs do after running. "I've never gotten there before except in my sleep," I say, and he says, "Me neither." We laugh.

I'm barely a person, more like a little animal on all fours in the green-carpeted cubby under the stairs of the little boutique shop. Jasper, who is himself just barely crawling, is trying to take the spinning top from me.

I am chasing ghost-boys along a littered city street.

Lost moments come too, moments I never remembered before. There are flashes of things that happened when I was asleep or too drunk to remember.

At a bonfire, I'm on the ground and Betty is silhouetted in front of me. "They aren't just stories," I say, and she turns back toward the fire.

I hear Mom and Tommy talking about why I am the way I am. My body is paralyzed, eyes closed. It's a moment when I slept but heard what went on all around me without knowing that I heard. Now I am accessing that moment for the first time.

A pure memory, never touched before. More of these come.

It seems my initial guess was correct after all. It seems I did wear paths through the little corners of the world I traveled and the little span of time I had. It is only these places I can return to—and without volition. I move through them out of order and out of all control.

I never wished to return where I'd already been. I wanted to see beyond all of this, but it seems I cannot.

I hover now, as I always did in dreams, and I know that the hovering feeling comes along with this aimless travel. *If I can find a brake of some sort, I can slow myself, stop myself. Catch my...* oh my goodness, *catch my breath* was what I thought just now, but I have no breath, not anymore.

Wishes don't make it so. Nothing brakes. I am swept from time to time and room to room without reason.

Or, it isn't that. I'm not moving. All of it is spread out before me. It's only my focus—my attention—moving from moment to moment, place to place.

I cannot choose where to focus, cannot find any way to brake.

#

Many lifetimes I live, only all of them are the same. I come back to moments from different angles and notice different things.

Begin to see patterns in the arrangement.

Begin to make connections.

Find myself in the present, in front of Stevie, only half recognizing her. A dark-haired girl. I mistake her, in this light, for Betty, for Marielle, Ellen.

Find myself face-to-face with someone I should know but do not.

#

In the farm school bathroom, I lift my top, suck in my stomach, gaze into the mirror.

In the farm school bedroom, I lie down, pull the coat back over me.

Remember Christmas future, in the pink house?

No urgency, no hurry. All is right. I've lost all resentment, all hatred. There isn't any evil, only people caught up in their own trips and missions.

My body was a gift to Tamara—a gift to everyone. Mom has her girls together and bright prospects for JoJo finally. Tommy has a sister she can relate to. Matt, he has a girlfriend, maybe one day a wife or if not, some sort of Muse.

Everyone is better off.

Well, everyone but Foster. And so Foster is the first one I see in our shared time. Because I am selfish, and because I love Foster, him losing me is enough to make me upset. It is what finally provides a brake.

Think of the willow whip. A long line with leaf-buds. *Tick tick tick.* A spinning wheel in a gameshow. *Tick tick tick.* The gameshow wheel like a clock. *Tick.*

I grasp a whip of weeping willow in my hand and pull the tiny leaves from it as I float by. I will another to appear before me, and another. The ground below me fills in with leaves. I drown, I choke in willow leaves, and I do not brake but become stuck in them, weighted down, caught.

I wish hard, and there it is: Foster's face as I've never seen it. Slack, no smile on it, just glimpses in the coolers as he polishes the glass. Am I behind him?

He starts, turns and
slowly
he smiles.

I think it's like old times, but it's not at all. He's not looking at me but the place where I used to stand. He's not smiling like he used to, either.

It's more like the fear-smile you see, sometimes, on a dog.

But it was only that moment I seemed to brake. I lost control again right away. There were many stories that I told myself, fantasies really.

Fantasies feel different out of body. They feel real, like they are happening outside of you, like you are acting them out while you think of them, the imagining self only a page or two ahead of the acting self.

They're like dreams but not like dreams, like a waking life but not. It's strange.

In one of these episodes, maybe the first, Tamara came back to Beulah as a young mother and bride. She had run away fearing exorcism—fearing me—and taken a long time to return, ten years or maybe more. She just couldn't stay away, though she came to wish she had.

It was a cold, dry winter, the sun intense like it is in Beulah at all times of year.

Tamara came on the scene, but I didn't yet. I was a watcher. She was all furtive glances from a gaunt, haunted face.

She happened to have married a Beulah boy, not Matt but someone just like him, someone from that same street, and they were coming home for her to meet his parents.

She'd delayed this as long as she possibly could.

The fantasy ran long, with many repetitive scenes showing how haunted she was, showing how the fear in her escalated. Being back in Beulah sapped her strength and ruined her mind. Up in an attic room in one of those pretty houses, she grayed and sputtered. Her skin turned dry like an apple-face doll, and she would not come out of her new husband's room—or let him in.

I was hovering outside her window all night, you see. I was the one doing this to her!

I was the evil one, draining all the life from her until, on the last night of the visit, she opened the window to me. There was dramatic music as I flooded back into my body.

I won.

I moved from that fantasy into another. In this one, I was still only a disembodied spirit standing waiting in the middle of the bridge, but it was a temporary state.

Mom became a hero in this one. She saw me—she did!—and admitted everything to me in one long scene.

It was that night they all came home without me. After Ellen and Stevie had nodded off, she tiptoed to my bedroom door.

Both Matt and I snored, he from the floor and me from the bed. My body was splayed in a star shape rather than the curled-in fetal shape I'd always had in bed.

Something's wrong. That girl isn't yours. You knew as much back on the highway but didn't let yourself know.

The idea was ludicrous. She didn't know where it had come from. She turned off the light and went searching for me. If you'd have asked, she'd have said she was looking for a cigarette, but it wasn't that at all. She wanted to see me, see I was safe. And I *was*, safe in my bed. She came back to the doorway and looked again. She wanted to wake me.

She went back into the living room and stood staring at Stevie's hair spread over the sofa all loose and wind-torn like we never let it get. It would be a chore to comb in the morning. She looked up and saw me there in the principal's corner, just a blur reaching toward her, my pained mouth making an echoey half-word like when you turn the radio dial. Her eyes focused on me for a slight fraction of a second and swept past.

It was Ellen and a little later, Foster, who finally convinced her. They kept their intrigue from the others at first, but then Stevie and finally Tommy came over to their side. Now only me-Tamara and Matt remained thinking that things were as they had been. Everyone else, over time, came in on the plan.

(The plan to torture Tamara out of my body.)

I watched this all as a house-spirit. Lonnie freed, I was the only full spirit now whole in the schoolhouse, though the fragmented child-ghosts still slowed me. I waded through them like knee-deep mud... or snow.

Once Mom admitted to what she had seen, Stevie began opening up to spirits again, and one day she could see me!

I rushed to her, begging.

And no, what I begged was not that they would do what they had planned. My wish was that they'd forget me, accept Tamara. She was the deserving one. I had gifted the body to her. It could only be wrong to take it away.

I didn't want it.

What I wanted—what I begged for—surprised me: I made the case that the life I knew now was my element. I was where I ought to have been born. One day they would all come here too, and so they had to believe me: It was glorious.

It had taken time at first, to learn to brake, but once I had mastered it, oh what experiences I'd had!

"Because after the brake, do you know what I learned?"

Stevie shook her head. She cried, her body trembled, and breaths came out in clouds.

We were standing under the crooked tree, under the stars.

"Remember Christmas future in the pink house?" I said.

My sweet little sister shook her head. She didn't have any shoes on.

"You will," I said. "Do you know what I learned, after the brake? I learned how to accelerate. How to steer, how to..." I paused a long time.

"What?"

How to go other *places.* It was too much to say.

"You've got to go in now Stevie. You're getting too cold."

"We're going to save you," she said.

"Let Tamara have that life—I don't want it. I have so much more."

Suddenly I wanted to *show* her. I wanted to keep her out here in the cold until she could see.

And I could do that. I could enthrall her, take her body—anything.

"Run, Stevie," I said and changed my shape. Oh, it was terrible. I raised my arms, and the roots of the tree seemed to rise as on puppet strings—but no, I was the tree. I was the tree and was pulling up my roots, chasing her up the steps, scratching the backs of her legs and ankles with the tips of my fingertwigs.

Stevie never told them all I'd said because she just knew that I would feel differently once Tamara was out of the body.

By this time, me-Tamara had bored of Beulah and gone off to live in a little apartment with Matt and another young couple. It was tough to get her out of the apartment, but the four of them did it: Ellen and Mom, Tommy and Stevie. They watched the place until the others were out and went in. The three grown ones tackled and gagged her, tied her with zip-ties, drove her back to Beulah in the back-back of the new SUV. Mom left convincing-enough messages that Matt thought she'd gone home to do some work on the farm school.

Mom was a hero, after all. When it was all going on, down in the furnace room, she certainly came off as a hero.

Only, the violence she did for me—I hate to say so, but wasn't that always part of her nature? Didn't she enjoy it a bit?

But apart from the torture scenes, this fantasy was slow and sentimental, awful really. Made-for-TV-mini-series awful. Big sprawling story, big sprawling ensemble cast.

It was some kind of propaganda, this one. Something about small-town goodness and the righteousness of brutal acts done in the name of good. All through it, Beulah was clean and bright like it was on that first day in spring, only it wasn't spring; it was Christmas.

There were all these subplots complicating matters too. Some terrible new-money person was buying and tearing down houses on Park and we had to stop them so Mom could finally have her pink house. Foster had taken up with Marielle after I seemingly dumped him. Stevie had a schoolgirl crush on Mrs. Greene's eldest and Tommy? Well, Tommy had started dating a girl and came out to everyone but still wouldn't say who the girl was.

The story was complex and messy. Nothing about the plot made sense.

I hated it but could not stop it running, could not escape it.

What kind of new prison?

I saw it all through to the end and then woke back into my painful body on the furnace-room floor. Something foul-smelling soaked the front of my shirt. I wanted back out the moment I entered, but I had to stay there for everyone.

I could never leave. As long as my life lasted, I could never travel again.

I woke again, in my body but no longer myself.
This one played out more like a sitcom. There was a laugh-track. I was myself playing Tamara playing myself.

And me-Tamara had found that her week or two affair with Foster had, well, "taken." Hilarity ensued when she tried to hide this from her family. More hilarity ensued when Tommy found that she was in a similar situation due to Jasper's Halloween-eve booty call.

We planned to have our babies and all stay in the schoolhouse with Mom. Ellen would never be able to sell it because we were always one step forward, two steps back in our renovations. We'd put some carpet in and the toilet would overflow onto it. We'd paint the ceiling and then the roof would cave in. Once I set a fire in the furnace room after I mixed some paint-stripper with some other chemical that caused an explosion.

Other than the home improvement woes, we nested in our nest and were happy in our squalor, often ending the episode with a big group hug.

Stevie and Matt were used for comic relief in this one, which pissed me off a little. Stevie was younger, like five or six, and really chubby. Her tagline was "Is there any more of that?" Matt was a nerdy-hip effete sort of character, shown by the fact he wore dark glasses. He was into me, but the hilarity came from the fact that he never recognized that I was pregnant. There were all sorts of funny situations with this. I'd stand up straight, pushing out my belly, and he would keep eye contact. In one episode, I put on a bikini to try to get him to notice, and he just kept gazing into my eyes. Even funnier was that Tommy was no more pregnant that I was, and he'd always say something after she left the room. "Geez, when's she gonna have that kid?" was one of his taglines.

Another was, "I can't paint without you."

Foster, as my baby-daddy, had a more nuanced role. He often said, "Let me know when to start buying diapers," a sign of his being invested, but in truth we were on-again, off-again. Sometimes when we were on again, at the end of the show we'd lie in sleeping bags in the bed of Mom's truck and muse about how that particular episode's themes related to the meaning of life.

#

And there was a companion to this fantasy:
Tommy and I were actresses on the show, not sisters at all. We'd sat in makeup for hours together sharing our lives.
This life felt as real as the other life, the one where I was a teenage loser, so real in fact that for a time I felt I was and had always been this actress.
I did not tell myself it had all been a dream, not in this one. I told myself I had suffered a quiet breakdown. I had never been Georgie but had only believed I was her because I had played her on television for so long.
One afternoon I woke from a nap in the makeup chair, a feeling of relief because it after all had been a dream. There had been no delusion but only the dream of one. I had always been sensible and had always known myself to be this actress.
"You're all ready to go," said a girl behind me, and I didn't know yet if she meant ready to go to the set or ready to go home, but I looked down, my belly was flat. I had nothing on but a loose satin cami and tap-pants, so I supposed it was time to go home.
I dressed in a little sundress and jean jacket that hung near the door, put on sandals and sunglasses. Sauntered out to my car saying good afternoon to a number of good-looking people. Drove home. It was a modest bungalow but nice. I should have known it was all a fantasy because

I was driving, but it didn't feel like a fantasy at all. It felt like a whole other life.

I ate a yogurt, looked at flowers blooming outside the kitchen window, ran a bath and poured in lavender salts.

Time so slow. Everything so clear and regular. I felt I had finally woken, but no, the dreams went on.

When I took a bath, suddenly every egg in my body expelled into the bathwater, somewhere around three hundred thousand at my age (I'd read this somewhere, maybe in a women's magazine while waiting for makeup), all of the cells multiplying, growing into a heavy mass of embryos pushing me down, drowning me, spilling out onto the floor.

Stupid me, it was only then I knew what these fantasies really were. I was only dreaming, wide awake and dreaming. I couldn't stop. The illusion of a brake was only ever that.

I woke in cold sweat into my bedroom in the farm school. Stevie lay in the bed across from mine, and the windows were open. Outside, bright green grass, birdies going "Hey sweetie." It was just spring, still too cold for this. I stood to close the windows and saw Tamara standing across Farm School Road in her white jeans and the pink cartoon kitty sweatshirt.

Spumoni. I laughed, but not for long.

Because that morning, after breakfast when we were cleaning up, Mom touched me. In this dream-life, she had, ever since I could remember, avoided ever touching me because any time she did, I saw something.

This time was by accident too, but she hadn't been careful. Maybe somewhere deep down she wanted me to know.

Her soapy arm reached out for a rag just as mine reached to turn down the hot water, a wet glancing touch, but it was enough.

Her past played before me like a film.

In this film, Mother was a witch and had promised me to Tamara, who had also been a witch back when she, Mom, Ellen, and Marielle were in school.

It all started when they were between thirteen and fourteen, which was so much younger than they thought it was. In Beulah they were free at that age, though—free to do their ill-advised, ill-informed spells and ceremonies deep in the canyon.

They biked out to the canyon, which if you are thirteen or fourteen, feels like flying.

Tamara was the fourth member added, the youngest but the dominant one. The bully of the group, really, though they all admired and even loved her.

Part of the memory was hidden from me. Was Tamara's death an accident—perhaps she fell from a rock?—or was Tamara lost to one of their experimental spells? No one knew except the three surviving, and they would never tell. Maybe they would never even remember.

The first one born of them, though, would belong to Tamara. That was the deal. She would come and take that child on its nineteenth birthday.

Take its body, that was. Take *my* body.

(I liked this story. It appeared like the kind of movie I would have watched with Betty or Marielle.)

There were grainy, dark outdoor shots and a tragic earnest quality in the early coven scenes. The girls were naïve but not careless. They all felt desperate about their lives and felt desperately charged whenever they were together.

They never meant to cause harm. At the point when they made the deal, each one of them hoped she would be the one to produce the child that would let them atone to Tamara.

Each potential baby was so much less to them in that moment than Tamara was.

By the end of this part, they knew they would never be together again. There was a tearful scene when the three of them parted in the parking lot beside the canyon bridge. Marielle and Mom were going to bike home, but at fourteen Ellen already had her daylight license. She needed to be back in her pink house before dark. As she pulled out in her starter car, the little white Cabriolet that she'd fixed up with her dad, Marielle said, "Think she'll make it?"

"Not unless she speeds," said Mom.

The ghost of the suicide crossed the bridge to her barrier, and Marielle flinched.

"Never seen that one before?" said Mom, taking her by the shoulder, pulling her close. Mom was shaking too, dreading the trip across the bridge.

"For a second I thought it was Tamara," said Marielle.

"Have you seen her yet?"

"No. I hope I never do."

The two got on their bikes and rode down the centerline of the bridge. It was almost dark and both were scared, but Mom would not ride along the bridge's walkway and so Marielle risked the center too.

#

Flash forward five years. All of them have been careless with their lives. They have actively, if subconsciously, tried to fulfill the debt to Tamara.

All of them have gotten past their desperation, too. Ellen is still her father's right hand. She's studying business with the plan of coming back to work in his real estate offices. She's dating and hoping to find the right man to bring back to Beulah. Marielle's still single. Mom is the only one with a long-term boyfriend.

As she looks into the little window on the pregnancy stick, she is happy to say she'll also be expecting a wedding with a family soon. She smiles to herself. No reservations. She's in love with my dad, in love with me already.

She's forgotten the deal. If she did remember, she'd only remember it as an example of the odd ways children have of dealing with grief.

In fact, she does remember it that evening after dinner, after she's told Dad and seen he feels the same way she does. She thinks of telling him some little bit of that story that night but then doesn't. She is troubled by that because she usually tells him all...

#

The memory holds more: it holds my whole life from Mom's perspective.

I grow up in my happy home, but soon she sees the spirits have me. Maybe she sees from the moment *I* see, on the night Dad dies. She doesn't see him, but she sees how he captures my imagination.

She moves all the time, running away from each new set of spirits and each new threat. Looking at me as I rise from the shotgun seat, as I look toward each new front door, she thinks *The forces that held you in check are now absent* and *How will you ruin things this time?* and all the other thoughts I had convinced myself were my own.

But there is a time things seem most dire, a time when she pours out her hopes and fears on the phone to Ellen, and, in hindsight anyway she sees that she shared a little too much this time. She'd had too much wine.

Ellen has been keeping track of her all their lives for this purpose.

Ellen has been beginning to fear that, without me, Tamara will go after Jasper. Marielle has no children, and Mom has been blessed with so many. Even if it's true, if the worst comes, Mom will still have the two.

Ellen makes her offer, but it isn't to help us. It's just to bring me back, just to see.

In the dream-movie, all of this is framed as not literally selling me to the devil, though pretty close, but what can Mom do? She's desperate by now and anyway does not believe in any of *that* anymore.

All plays out the way it did but from Mom's point of view: I get lethargic and then seem like I'm doing OK, she's busy with other things, and then on Christmas I start it all up again.

In the movie, there are hints that she sees things. For example, there's maybe something that looks like the slightest pink floater in her eye when we cross the bridge into Beulah, but then when you see the scene with me and Matt on the bridge, you question whether she really did see the suicide-ghost. It's like that all the way through. Did she see something, or was that just an actual shadow and you're being teased as a viewer because it has the same rough shape as a shadow that Georgie saw in a different scene?

And then I am at the kitchen sink. I have woken from a dream—a memory, a movie.

I stare into the soapsuds. Mom is staring at me.

"Where do you go?" she says, and I shake my head.

She owes me to Tamara. She is giving me up but will not admit it even though it's clear to both of us.

My body belongs to Tamara, always did. There is nothing that either of us can do.

I woke with the instant's recognition that these were all dreams, not fantasies I was controlling but only dreams I was helpless to steer. That insight faded as I looked around.

I was a filmy spirit seated on a bench in the living room of the pink house, only it had been updated. It really was lovely now. It was Stevie's idea-book brought to life, bright white woodwork against craft tiles against vivid stained glass, prisms in the windows. Ferns and peacock feathers, books with jewel-tone spines and a Christmas tree in the bay window with its jewel-colored lights just barely visible, the sun was so strong. A little old lady shadow, much dimmer than me or the Christmas lights, rocked quietly near the window.

Ellen's Mom. I waved hello and she just kept rocking.

I appreciated Stevie's vision for the first time. The truth was that when I was eighteen and Stevie was doing that book, I hadn't had enough visual sense to tell that what she wanted was distinct from what Ellen's mom already had. I hadn't seen the art in what Stevie had planned.

But I was older now—my God, that's what I felt. I was older now.

How could I be older? No idea. I was a see-through shadow, nothing more than a film projected onto the wall in sunlight, but still I felt real. I felt goosebumps, a lump in my throat, a feeling of bodily anxiety.

Stevie averted her eyes as she came downstairs and turned my direction. She saw me and decided not to see, looked away and moved back toward the kitchen. She was gorgeous, eighteen or twenty years old. She and Mom talked two rooms away, and I listened in as well as I could though the kitchen faucet dripped loudly. I gathered that people were coming for lunch. Stevie was home from college

I was so proud of her.

Tommy came in the front door with a familiar-looking woman.

"Mom?" called Tommy, and Mom called, "Back here!" Tommy and the woman set suitcases down by the door and moved back toward the kitchen. As they passed by, I saw it was Summer, that baby-faced girl from school. She was older, heavier and with her hair in long spiral ropes. She held a tiny baby.

Mom squealed, soon as she caught sight of it.

Summer's friend Marcia came in straightaway with the good-looking boy she'd gone around with in high school, now an average-looking man, and they too had a baby with them, a larger one Marcia struggled to carry. Her hair was in a messy braid and without her makeup she looked harried, but they were happy rushing back to the kitchen. Time passed and they all chattered.

They were eating. I smelled the light homely smells of lettuce and ranch dressing, some sort of casserole made with cream of mushroom soup. Nothing special, so it was Christmas Eve or maybe even the day before that.

Before they were done, the doorbell rang, and seeing the white car out the window, Stevie yelled "Georgie's here!" They all rose from the table and crowded around the front door.

Me-Tamara entered, hugging and kissing them. She caught my eye and held it, gave a slight nod. She was beautiful, her hair arranged in soft waves. Her makeup was subtle and perfect, the body so filled out with muscle that it looked like Tamara's own body. The door opened, and here came Matt with two children maybe three or four years old. My body's children, but I didn't know them at all. They stared at me, one with finger deep in a little nose, the other going from foot to foot like they had to pee.

I couldn't decide that this one was just story. It felt so entirely real. I seemed to have a body whirring and pulsing all around me, felt those goosebumps rise on my arms again. I felt chemicals coursing through me, changing my mood and thoughts moment to moment.

The evening came on and passed. Sunset came. Ellen and Adrian stopped by with presents. They were in a rush, but Ellen took time to hug mom tight.

"How's he doing?" Mom said, and Ellen said, "He's comfortable."

I was so happy they were still friends.

As Marcia and her husband were leaving, Mom looked in my eyes on her way to the door, which brought a surge of comfort.

They all visited in the living room long after dark, and it soon began to seem very late, the conversation slow and boring.

Summer stood. Her and Tommy's baby was already sleeping upstairs, and she was going to join her. Tommy kissed her goodnight. Tommy was so unchanged, when I looked at her, I could not believe that any time had passed after all.

Me-Tamara's children were upstairs sleeping. I had watched them go through their last angry half hour and watched them seem to switch off into sleep. Matt rose, got his kiss, and climbed upstairs just a half hour after Summer did.

The core of the family all alone now, they turned to me. Not all at once, but as they talked, their eyes sought me out as though waiting for me to join in.

"Is it time? You feel ready?" Stevie asked me-Tamara, who nodded.

"If she's even here," she said looking straight into my eyes. Her face had that scowl so common to it.

She stood and stretched and then sat back down. She lay her head back and all at once pushed out of her body. I didn't feel my rush across the room, but the next thing I knew, I was opening my eyes for the first time in many years.

Or it felt that way.

"Merry Christmas, Georgie," said Stevie. I lowered my chin, met her gaze. She was crying.

Had I feared the pain of my body, the smell of it after so long? In fact it felt healthier than it had ever been under my care, and the smell around my head was of vanilla, coconut, and something dusky. Department store perfume.

I could see the bottle.

I could see—oh God—I could see anything I wanted of the past ten years.

"Merry Christmas," said Mom, crossing the room to me. They all came in on me for a hug.

And we had won. We had finally won our good Christmas.

Only I ruined this Christmas too.

I pushed back away from them. Trembling, I took many deep painful breaths.

"I'm lost, I'm lost in memories and dreams. I'm seeing the future," I said.

"It's all right," Mom said.

"Sometimes she forgets," said Stevie.

"I'm in hell. I've gone to hell. She's had my body all this time and she—"

"Shh. They're all asleep—" said Tommy.

"You forget sometimes," said Mom.

Stevie said, "Tamara, you have to get back—"

And I was lost once more.

Just one more, I swear:

In this one, Mom knew that I was gone. How? She'd spoken to me-Tamara. Maybe once was all it took, and she knew—maybe not everything all at once, but she knew something was terribly wrong. She saw that I was vacant, absent.

She struggled with the knowledge. What did it mean? What could it mean?

She put things together, talked with Stevie in a careful, guarded way.

She found the diary me-Tamara had hidden. She read of how I thought I'd once held my breath and pushed my way out of my body so that Brian and the rest could take turns being real once more, so that they could drive the car. She read my fractured dreams.

Nights in her room, she burned incense, looked at pictures of me and at the diary, rocked and cried. She prayed. To me, she prayed. She prayed I'd come back, but I didn't. Or I did, but it was only a formless me loose around the edges of the house.

Georgie was leaving at the start of summer after all, not with Matt but with Kelsie from school. There was a job she could have with someone Kelsie's dad knew in Nampa. Kelsie would drive them there. Georgie would get her GED while Kelsie had her first semester and then hopefully join her the next semester, and they would live and work together all this time.

Kelsie had suddenly become a good friend, like maybe Kelsie had seen something new in Georgie all of a sudden. Of course she had: the spark of life, ambition.

Mom and my sisters only watched as me-Tamara and Kelsie got in Kelsie's car and drove away. Mom's heroism did not flow in the direction it had in the prior fantasy, though. Maybe it was not that she couldn't tie up this girl, couldn't hurt her; maybe it was more that the thought never occurred to her

Her heroism took a different route in this one.

#

It was still the first week of summer when Mom began packing her things. The girls saw and began packing too. They left out just a few changes of clothes. Everything they had accumulated that would not fit in their totes was tucked into grocery bags and set neatly beside the beds. Some of Georgie's clothes were still in Stevie's room. She washed them and stacked them in the laundry room in case Mom or Tommy wanted to wear some of them.

There was an atmosphere of sadness that always attended the beginning of a move. Why were they going away this time? Had they overstayed their welcome in Beulah? Were they finally going to burn this bridge too? No one asked.

Ellen was still coming around, and she had not said one thing about the house, which had made no more progress and was now in disarray. They had stopped cleaning up after themselves had not yet mown the lawn.

Tommy was restless. I could swear sometimes she looked straight at me. I watched her often as she moved around the house. Her tight mouth, her perfect posture. I thought back to what she'd always planned when she was younger: a sports scholarship, a clear route to college. She'd expected to have a car by now, and here she was walking each day to her shift at Tiger Burger, riding back with one of her older co-workers.

I watched her fold laundry down in her big party room. A tear came down her cheek. She went upstairs with a basket of clothes and I lingered, looking at all the things she'd gathered here. She'd been trying to make the place look a certain way, to give a certain impression of who she was, a middle-class girl who was more interested in doing things than in having things. The stickers all over the MacBook said that, the posters on the walls. I'd never really looked at them before, but now I lingered. I could see the glare on them from the basement windows, but I couldn't get at the right angle to see the imagery. I moved this way and that but still there was nothing but glare. I began to feel scared, and when Tommy came down the stairs, I felt her slow.

"Can you see me?" I said. She went back into the laundry room and started pulling wet sheets out of the washer. I came into the room with her. I sat on the dryer. She reached through me to turn on the dryer and I saw the goosebumps go up on her arm. Her face was staring through me, but I knew at that moment she was only pretending not to see.

I tried. I screamed at her, swirled around her. When she'd put the next load in the washer, she went to her bed and placed the headphones on, opened her computer. She sat typing on it for a while and then closed her eyes. The music came through only a little, indecipherable pop or dance music. She sat that way for a while longer and then rose and put away her computer. She went upstairs and walked all the way down Farm School Road to Eighth. I couldn't follow.

#

We sat in the kitchen, all four of us, though Mom and Tommy still refused to see me. The only question was which direction to go. It would not be north, was all Mom had to say.

Stevie said, "I've never been very far east at all."
"What's the farthest east you've been?" said Mom.
"Here?"
"Indiana," said Tommy.
"I was only a baby," said Stevie. "I don't remember it. That's not what I mean, anyway. I mean northeast."
"You mean New York," said Tommy.

"No, like Maine. Somewhere we can live in the country."

Tommy rolled her eyes.

"East it is. We'll get as far east as we can, how's that?" said Mom. She smiled at Stevie and brought her hand down her smooth hair. "Did anyone ever tell you how pretty you are?"

"Not today," said Stevie.

Tommy was quiet. She seemed to be chewing on the inside of her cheek. She took the saltshaker between her thumb and forefinger and tipped it right, tipped it left.

"Don't we need to get Georgie?" she said.

"Georgie is a grown-up," Mom said.

"What does that mean?" said Stevie.

"You know she has a job now. She has her own life."

"You mean you're leaving her here?" said Tommy.

"I mean I called and asked what she wanted to do, and she said she wanted to stay with Kelsie."

"Well, I want to stay too," said Tommy.

"You don't," I said, and Stevie, without skipping a beat, echoed me, "You don't."

"I'm more an adult than Georgie is," said Tommy.

"That's probably true," said Mom. She sighed. "I guess you can stay here if you want, if Ellen wants to keep you on, or you can go try to get a room in someone's house like Georgie did."

"Come on, you know Ellen wouldn't let me stay."

"Does she know we're going?" said Stevie.

"What do you think?" said Tommy.

Mom stood up. She had to be off to work, she said.

#

"I can't see the posters in Tommy's room," I told Stevie. "It's like I never noticed them when I had eyes, so now I they don't exist for me. I'm afraid we'll get to Maine or

309

wherever and it will just be a white room to me, or that I won't be able to go at all. Do you think that's what will happen?"

She was lying face down on her bed, no hint of whether she heard.

"I'll bother you all night if you don't talk to me," I said.

"Let's go then," she said. She sat up.

"I don't think I can see new things, somehow. Is that possible?"

"This is why we need to go find Tamara," she said.

"There's nothing we can do."

"We can trick her back out."

"We can't."

"It worked with me. You saved me."

"It worked because she wanted it—my body. Because she could be old enough to be free. She was smart."

"Because you were prettier."

"Because she knew it would be more advantageous to her. That's all. My body's lost. It's lost. Don't cry for it."

I said this because she was crying again. Desperately, quietly. I hated to see it.

"Crying just makes you get old," I said. "Just don't do it. Just stop."

"All right."

"It's over."

"All right. But it was all my fault to begin with. I should be the one that can't see new things."

"No, never."

"And if we'd let her be, if we'd let her keep *me*, the police would have made her stay home since she's just a kid, and we'd all still be together."

I talked to her then of how wonderful her life would be in Maine or however far east she got. Maybe it would not be so far. Maybe Indiana, maybe Mississippi, and I droned on and on about what little I remembered of these places, until she fell asleep.

#

I could feel myself changing. I'd been out of body for only a few months, but I was changing. Sometimes I was a little white rabbit hopping around the edges of the room. I would back myself into a far corner to watch them and would, after a time, forget I'd ever been a girl. I'd get lost in being a rabbit and move into fantasy once more thinking over my many animal adventures, my many lives.

This always felt dangerous, and I had to struggle back to something like myself.

I knew of time passing only because I counted the times Stevie fell down into sleep, the times she woke. I was beginning to exist only in relation to her, and to me this was a sweet thing—it was what I'd long wanted, all I wanted now—but to her it had to be difficult.

She was sleeping fitfully, tired and jumpy as she moved through her days. She had lost some weight, and I know now that it was because my eyes were on her every time she took a bite of food. I was haunting her, surely as Tamara did, and no less malevolently.

I can think of this only now, in hindsight. At the time I only hungered for her attention, as if it were the only thing keeping me alive, which maybe it was.

#

"Should we say something to Matt?" Stevie asked me.

"Why would we?" I said.

"Because he loved you," she said. "Don't you miss him? Don't you even care?"

"I never cared all that very much about anything, and now I care even less," I said. "About me anyway. I still care for you as much as I always have." I came close against her back again and I could feel her pushing me away.

#

A note on the table said that Tommy was moving in with Jerry from work, and all of her things were gone from her room. Mom was dressed for work when she found the note. Instead of going to work, she called in to quit, and we placed our packed bags in the truck. Stevie got the dirty laundry and threw it in the backseat, along with most of the food we still had. The ketchup and eggs and things like that she just left in the fridge for Ellen to clean up later.

"It stinks in here, doesn't it?" Stevie said.

Mom nodded, and the two of them went around opening windows.

We got in the car.

"You know where Jerry lives?" Mom said.

Stevie shook her head.

"The street behind Tiger Burger," I said.

"I remember. They're on Walton, just behind Tiger Burger," Stevie said.

We took Farm School to Eighth for the last time. Stevie looked out at the farms and the houses the weird power station, all the tall grass and horses. She knew she was going to miss this place and wanted to brand it on her mind. The house itself she'd been saying goodbye to for weeks, but it wasn't just about the house. It was the place.

"We lived here for a whole year," she said.

"More," said Mom.

"More than a year. I never lived anywhere that long before, did I?" Stevie looked at me in the backseat. I felt myself, but she would tell me later that when I rode in the truck I did not look right. I was dimmer, diluted so that she could see through me to the black upholstery.

I didn't look out at the sights. I didn't look at anything but Stevie anymore.

We pulled up at a little beige house and Mom got out and knocked on the door. When Tommy answered, Mom just told her to go get her bags. She did. She didn't argue or anything. Jerry came around from the back yard and hugged her goodbye.

"Are we going to stop by Ellen's?" Tommy said.

"Why?" said Mom.

"I want to thank her for everything. Don't you?" said Tommy.

"I don't know," said Mom. "I'd rather stop by and see Georgie before we go."

"There's no need to," said Stevie.

"You don't think?"

"There's no need to," said Tommy.

"You can feel me here," I said, and Tommy frowned, but she nodded.

"It's OK," Mom said, "I'll call Ellen later."

"Yeah, let's go," said Stevie. "We're burning daylight," and we all laughed at that. It seemed a weirdly grown-up thing for her to say.

We had so little money, we camped along the way instead of wasting dollars on motel rooms. It was on the second night by the campfire that Mom was finally able to see me. Even Tommy could see me all the time by then, but Mom had been more resistant.

My shadow flared like a fire at the start and grew faint and dim as an afterimage, cool green. My face, my many smiles followed her eyes around like an afterimage.

The way I thought of it at the time, if I could be said to have thought, was always in third person: Georgie's shadow flared, Georgie's sweet smile followed Mom's eyes.

#

I had long had a feeling of unworthiness. At its heart was that I had not deserved that fine young body, did not deserve to hold all that promise. Because I would squander it. I would defile it. How could I do anything else? And Tamara did deserve it, wanted it, needed it. Tamara had it now and would do right with it.

It seemed to me I had always been a parasite to someone else. Mom, Tommy, Betty, Stevie, Matt. I had lived for them, lived off of them.

Maybe with Foster it was something different, but I wouldn't let myself think of him.

It seemed to me to that this story of mine, this coming-of-age story with its highs and its lows, its moments of failure and of heroism—this was not the story my mother and sisters experienced. Their story was a tragedy, or a horror story.

A horror story, and it was I, not Tamara and certainly not the Lonnie in the furnace room who terrorized them. It was I who terrorized them, and I found I wanted to do so. I was hungry for the fear coming off of them.

I spoke:

"It's time you acknowledge me, Mom," I said.

"I feel very strange now," Mom said. Her face was shiny with sweat. Her hair rose out around her head as though it had not been brushed in days.

"Shh," said Tommy, "Just listen," and she touched Mom's shoulder.

I said, "You can see me, Tommy?"

"Clear as life," Tommy said.

"What?" said Mom. The wrinkles around her mouth were deep. They shouldn't be clear in this light, but there they were.

"How old are you now, Mom?" I said.

She breathed harder. She looked behind her.

"Did you say something?" she said to Tommy.

"She asked how old you are," said Stevie.

"Thirty-eight, no, thirty-nine. I've always been one of the youngest moms in you all's classes," she said.

"Not my classes," said Stevie.

"No," said Mom.

"Thirty-nine and you're already so worn out," I said. "How come we didn't go visit Georgie today?"

"How come we didn't visit Georgie today?" Stevie said.

"I heard you. I'm thinking." Mom put her hand to her forehead. "Didn't we see her today?"

"Mom, Georgie's with us," Tommy said.

"Oh, right," said Mom. She moved to stand and then fell back into her seat.

"I think we ought to all go to bed now," said Tommy. "It's late."

"No, she'll think it's a dream," said Stevie.

"I'll think what's a dream?"

"Seeing Georgie."

Mom shook her head. "I think we ought to go to bed."

"No, look at her," said Stevie. I was glowy green and violet with a pattern of stars all through me just then. I concentrated and brought myself more fully present to her and leaned in toward the fire. She jumped to standing, then, and the chair fell back behind her. There was fear in her face instead of confusion.

I wished once more that I could paint: The family scene of the campfire circle is all warm brown and black and orange. Though partially abstracted, it still gives a sentimental vibe on its own. The image of the ghost is as though stamped on top of the first painting in a thinned white with glazes of green and violet. It must be something like what Mom saw.

They stayed up around the fire all night, until the sky began to lighten. They slept so late and were so cranky the next day we decided to stay another night, and we stayed up late again, so we stayed another night.

315

"It feels good to not have school or work to go to," Tommy said, and we all drank to that. Beer for Mom and Diet Coke for her and Stevie, who didn't ever get enough of the stuff, and I pretended to drink with them.

"Tomorrow we're moving on," said Mom.

"To where though?" said Stevie.

"Maine, of course," said Mom.

When she first learned what had happened, she was all set to jump in the truck and find Georgie in Nampa. She would force her out. She would . . .

"Do what?" they asked. "How?"

"We can put her in enough pain that she won't have any other choice," Mom said.

"Put things up in her fingernails," said Tommy. "I saw that on a movie."

"Choke her," said Stevie.

"Drown her," said Mom.

And the conversation went round and round. There wasn't a painful thing they could think of that wouldn't mar the body or risk it. Marring seemed the best answer to them. Burns, lost fingernails--none of that would make the body uninhabitable. They said I would rather have my body back, surely, with some marks on it rather than leave it to her.

"She'll be a good steward," I said. "And I am rather liking this."

Their eyes on me told me the three of them all thought that I was weak, cowardly, passive. They would never let themselves go without a fight.

"Do you want to be the kind of person who tortures someone?" I said. "I don't. If you take the body back that way, I'll leave it soulless to die."

#

When Stevie was asleep, sometimes I hovered near her or even settled against her body, though she was more likely now to sense me there and push me away. Sometimes I just faded away or went away to a part of the scene where I was not so prominent, amongst the bushes or beside the cooler, at the side of the truck. It was as though I stopped existing until she was awake again to see me, and this is how I was when Mom left us.

I've often tried to remember where I was at those times, and there is no memory of it. As I said, I think in those moments I ceased to exist.

Stevie woke to Mom whispering something in her ear. I found out later what she said. It was, "I can do it, I think," and then Stevie started screaming, which woke Tommy. Stevie screamed because Mom's eyes were open, but there was no expression on her face. Her body was limp when they surrounded her; when they slapped her face she did not respond. Now a low sound came from Tommy, who unzipped the tent and looked outside it, then came back inside.

I came to them in the height of the panic, as a shadow standing in the tent opening. I'd been elsewhere. Tommy and Stevie both crouched next to her body.

"Do you see her?" Stevie screamed.

I did not. I felt confused.

"Go look for her," Tommy said, and I simply shrugged. There was nothing to look for. If her shadow were here I would have seen it already.

"You have to take her," said Stevie. "There's no other way. She'll die."

It took more coaxing to get me to do it. I was like a dog who does not want to come.

#

I'd been out of body for a while and had never been in another person's body before. The sensations were all too intense, emotions too physical.

That day was like a blackout drunk and a terrible hangover combined. The sun was too bright and all of the images fractured, like a film badly edited, trees and parking lots, tents and highway. We searched the woods and then the nearby roads all morning until I could not stand the heat—her body seemed to overheat more quickly than my own—and then we planned to shower and sit in the tent for a few hours until it cooled outside.

We all thought we'd see her more easily in the dusk or in the dark.

We went to the large camp restroom, where two showers were free and two occupied. I sent Stevie and Tommy to shower, and I waited. The campers came in and out, and it seemed so odd to smile at them and pretend the day was a usual one. It struck me how we'd never be able to say we had someone missing.

I didn't even look into the restroom mirror. I hadn't wanted to wipe myself in the toilet, let alone shower. It's not that the body felt foreign to me. Her smells were so well known to me that it felt almost like home. It was more about respect, I suppose. I didn't want to upset her sense of privacy.

And there was a visceral revulsion, too, there was that. As I undressed on the wooden bench outside the shower room, I saw how the skin on her legs was all crepey. She had fabulous legs, really toned, and the skin was lovely from an outsider's view, but from my new perspective I could see how dry and thin it was. When I stroked my hand up it, it made a hundred little folds. When light glared on it, it looked ashy and scaled. In the shower, the skin on the boobs, the belly, the throat. It was all lovely—she was lovely—but it was not the same loveliness my own body had promised. I felt mortal for the first time. That's what it was, ironic because in an important sense, I had already died.

#

We didn't see her that night. I savored my food and sat listening to her blood pumping through her body and watching the darkest corners of the scene until I became too sleepy and went to the tent. When Stevie curled up behind me, I said, "I love our bed" and she giggled.

We didn't see Mom until we had given up hope of finding her at the camp. I don't remember how much time we'd looked, but I suppose we'd been at the campground almost a week by then. The camp host had come early in the morning to tell Tommy our spot was reserved for the next day, and when she woke us, she said we had to be out of it by noon, so we packed the truck and spent another morning searching.

When we had finally given up, I took my place in the shotgun seat, Stevie took her place in the back seat, and Tommy knocked on the glass on my side. I rolled down the window.

"Don't you want to drive?" she said.

"Why would I?"

"It's your truck. Your name is on the registration."

"I don't have. . .

"A license?" Stevie said. She pulled Mom's wallet from her purse.

I just smiled at them until Tommy came around and sat in the driver's seat.

The plan, when we entered the truck, was to go back to Beulah to try to find Mom again, but when we were all seated we saw her there in the back seat, lying on top of the bags. She was a dim, dim magenta. That was when she told us to keep together and go where we'd been heading, Maine or as close to it as we could get.

It was a cool late morning and we were all excited to get into town and get a real coffee, and the birdies were singing "Hey Sweetie" again, little squirrels running around, and the little wildflowers and the little kids playing outside the campers and the tents, breakfast smells everywhere.

Once we saw Mom, we didn't listen to her, not really. We heard some of what she said but not enough of it. We were so relieved.

We drove away from the campground with Mom in the truck and she started to fade immediately. We went back, we drove and she disappeared, we went back.

"It's OK," Mom said. "Go on. You'll make it." She was so faint, like a magenta shadow in the sun. She didn't have any detail to her. She wasn't able to come with us.

Cue the doom music—or like a record-scratching sound. That was when it started to dawn on us that we were grown-ups now.

#

It's strange how a road trip will put you in another state of consciousness. If we'd gone back to Beulah and begged Ellen to take us back, we'd probably have tried to put the whole thing out of mind, but there in the truck we talked about nothing else. We filled Tommy in on what all had gone down with Tamara, and we learned when she had started to have the sight. None of what she said was very definitive, and when I asked if she remembered reaching through me in the laundry room, she pretended not to know what I meant. She was already wanting to deny. But Stevie and I kept bringing the conversation back to shadows and bodysnatching and what it all might mean.

Stevie took out a notebook and wrote while Tommy drove.

"We don't need to go back to Beulah, or the campground to see her, just anywhere she's been before," I said.

"How do you know that?" said Tommy.

"Most shadows can't go places they haven't been before," said Stevie.

"If Mom were stronger, she could be with us. If it were me out of body, I could have ridden in the truck."

"I'm writing down all of what we know," said Stevie.

"Good," I said, "You write it all down."

Tommy just kept her eyes on the road. I had no clue what she was thinking.

#

We never made it to Maine. There was a piece of paper folded up in Mom's purse with two names and an address in what turned out to be a small town outside Louisville, Kentucky.

When we arrived at the little white house, the two old people living there took us in with few words. Their expressions were sour, but they did want to meet their grandchildren. We could stay, if we wanted, all together in an attic room if we cared to clean it out.

Mom had never wanted us to know these people. There had to have been a reason for that.

I worked for a while. I did. Tommy conspired to get us jobs at the same cleaning service so that she could keep an eye on me during the day, and we cleaned houses. We'd call Stevie every chance we got because she wasn't comfortable staying home with Grandpa and Grandma, and then the school year started and she didn't worry us much anymore. She loved her teacher, like always. She loved school. She made us dinners every night in the sad little kitchen.

She said it was here we ought to set down roots, if for no other reason than that Mom had spent some of her teenage years in this house and might be lurking someplace near—or if not now, in the future maybe she would. She had written down the address after all, and so it was as close as we'd ever have to a pre-arranged meeting place.

This fantasy went on and on. Work, dinner, a short fitful sleep, more work.

I avoided mirrors at first. When I did catch sight of this face in a mirror, or if I had to look—because my face was dirty or something—I was always surprised. I looked older than I should have looked and younger than she should have. Maybe it was something about the way I held the muscles. I had that startled rabbit expression of mine but on her lion face. If I looked too long, it all seemed so wrong, so grotesque. If I looked too long it was horrifying, and I was terribly afraid that I would never stop looking.

I understood now why I'd always had her memories. It was because of this, because I was always going to become her.

I was afraid that anyone who saw me would see how wrong I was. I wondered, did the new Georgie feel this way too? Did she look in the mirror, maybe see how her lip curled up on the wrong face, and feel this same sensation of itchy, shaky dread?

But these feelings were, gladly, short-lived. I became Mom finally, and the memory of anything else faded. We all began to believe that we had been deluded about the events at the campground, and soon we forgot them entirely.

The Granddad died and the Grandma lingered. She became my only company, the regrets and resentments circling us, suffocating us day by day. I could not call Ellen, not anymore. That final link to the world was gone. The bitter Grandma-Mom and I unhappily watched Tommy and Stevie grow up and become miserable themselves, caught in this prison we'd all made.

#

And a different finish to this one, far in the future, twenty years or more:

We lit the three rose-shaped candles floating on a dish in the coffee table. It was Christmas once more, Christmas in the pink house. We'd made sure all the kids were in the living room and then cut off the lights.

I was in Mom's body, which was sixty years old at least. The veins stood out on the backs of my folded hands.

All was dark at first, and then our eyes adjusted. The candles cast the room in a deep brown-rose. Everyone looked so beautiful and so vague.

On one sofa sat Summer, Tommy, Ellen, and Adrian. On the other sofa sat Stevie, a man who must have been her husband, and a girl about eight with a smaller girl on her lap. Matt and me-Tamara sat in armchairs, and more young children sat on pillows on the floor. Other, older children were seated in kitchen chairs against the walls.

Stevie said, "At Christmas, we all must lie around and clear our minds, and then we'll see her."

"Who?" said the littlest girl. Georgina was her name, I knew somehow.

"Grandma," said the big girl.

Georgina's expression said we were teasing her. She blew a raspberry and pressed herself into the space between her mom and dad.

"We should talk about Grandma," Tommy said.

"She was fierce as a lion," I said.

"She was moody," said Stevie.

"Beautiful," said Ellen.

"Grandma loves my hair," said the big girl. "She says I look like Mom."

A boy said shyly, "Grandma likes to dance."

Ellen leaned forward and blew out one of the candles.

Tommy took a second one out of the water and blew it out. The room seemed only a bit dimmer, but there was a dappling of color around the edges, shifting amber and rose.

"She's coming," said Georgina.

"Not yet," said Stevie.

"No, she's right," I said.

I wondered, could the others see this? My guess was they saw some of it, but not like I did. Little Georgina was the exception. Her mouth tiny and her eyes wide, she made a gesture as though shielding her eyes from the sun.

It was a rich manifestation. Mom had such control.

The pattern of the dark formed itself like a tapestry of jewels and flowers. The tapestry became rich with moving animals—unicorns and deer and lions and foxes. One of the lions began to lift.

She came apart from the background, crawled down the tapestry and paced the room as a lion, the size of a housecat at first and then swelling to her full size and beyond. She stalked through the group of little children on the floor, who do not seem to see her but who sat straighter, looking where their elders were looking.

Mom came to the coffee table. It seemed she would drink from the bowl in which the candles floated, but she looked up, her face a human face now, her body still that of a glorious cat. Confused. Disoriented.

"Oh my God, is Stevie alright, where's Stevie?" she said.

"I'm right here," Stevie said.

Mom looked toward her but did not seem satisfied.

"Is she here now?" said Summer, and Tommy quieted her with a hand on her knee.

Then, before anyone else could speak, I began to see an aura around little Georgina. Her shadow came out from her body and she was flying toward her grandma. Her body went limp in her father's arms, and he began to moan.

Mom was impassive with the girl swirling slowly around her. She did not know this girl.

"No, honey," I said,

"You go back. Now," Stevie said, and little Georgina obeyed.

"She's never done that before," said the older girl.

"You see her, though?" I said, and little Georgina gave one shallow nod.

Mom in her cat form came close to Stevie, smiled and rubbed against her knees. Satisfied at that, she searched for her Georgie. She was concerned, confused.

"Where is Georgie? Everyone's here but her." The daughter she loved the best, everyone could see it.

"I'm here," I said, and Mom came toward me.

"I don't know most of these people," she said. She moved her head to indicate the crowd.

Tommy and Stevie rushed to remind her who all of the children were, and I sunk back into my corner of the sofa. My heart—her heart—was pumping too hard. While Mom and Stevie were down on the floor greeting the little ones, I wandered over to the trays of food. I took a sandwich in my mouth and tried to savor the salt of cream cheese and crunch of cucumber. I took a brownie, a cup of soda.

Soon enough, they would ask me to scoot over out of this body so that Mom could come into it, so that Mom could hold little Georgina in her arms, so that Mom could spend Christmas with the family for real.

I didn't know how long she'll want to stay or even if she'd ever leave. I only knew that when they went to the still body and said, "come," when they coaxed her, she would not refuse.

And I woke into sunlight in the driver's side of Betty's Cabriolet. My foot was pressed down hard on the brake though the car wasn't even running. Our doors were open and beyond them nothing but green—pine forest and the green grass of Oregon.

Camping, somewhere near the coast. Two boys put up a tent not far from us. Another boy and girl sat cross-legged on the top of a picnic table.

"Where do you go?" Betty said all ironic. She knew it was what Mom always said. She leaned over me to pull my door shut, and her scent was of her coconut shampoo and Southern Comfort. The bottle was held between her legs.

It was our first camping trip of the year and a little too cold for it too. It was a kind of triple date with Betty's cousin Sami and the guys we were hanging out with at the time. I was going to sleep with the taller boy tonight, and I couldn't even call up his name.

"I can't remember *any* of their names," I said, gesturing at the boys. I must have looked upset.

"Shh, just breathe," said Betty. "You've got the brake down, I see. Now let's work on the clutch."

"I *can't* brake, don't you see? I can't brake at all. It's dream after dream after dream and I can't stop it. When I woke up now, I'd just been . . . you wouldn't believe me."

"Shh," she said, her arm around my back. "We're not really here. You know that, don't you?"

An electric feeling ran up my back. I wanted out of the car.

That's what had happened back in the real memory of this time. I had jumped out of the car, refused once more to learn to drive, refused to say why.

To say why, I'd have had to tell Betty the true story of what happened with the boys that time when I was fourteen. The terror of someone else driving my body, driving the car, crashing it. [1]

---

[1] "She can't," James said. We were out on the street, about to take the car.

"Of course I can," I said. I didn't know yet what he meant. We all waited. It was like they were deciding on something.

"Just try edging yourself out of your body," Brian said finally.

"She can't do it," James said.

While Brian was staring at me, he . . . doubled. It was like this: hold two face cards together, tip one out from behind the other one half an inch. He had two faces, three shoulders, just two legs.

"All you have to do is find the muscles for it," Brian said.

"It's like trying to get your hand to move the right way while you're looking in a mirror," Chris said, and he ended up being the one who coached me through it. I don't remember all of what he said, but it was like the talking a parent does when a kid is learning to ride a bike, or like a friend when they're trying to teach you to drive.

Looking back on it now, I think it was something he must have tried before he died, or how would he know the right things to tell me?

I held my arm straight while he talked, held my breath and slowly began to slide my hand out of my hand. I had an extra pinkie, then an extra ring finger.

"I can see that. Can you see that?" I said loudly. I was beginning to feel pumped up: scared or excited, I couldn't tell. My blood drummed in my ears.

An entire hand drew out away from my original one; a new forearm came out from my elbow. I touched my extra hand to Brian's extra shoulder. The sensation was odd and unpleasant like a low, low electric shock. It made my new arm feel like it had fallen asleep.

"I can feel you," I said. I think that was the first time I realized I'd never touched any of them before.

I drew back, but Brian pushed his extra shoulder into me. Like finger paints, the pattern on the fabric marbled as my fingers moved

327

through it.

"There's nothing you won't be able to do," Brian said. He stepped completely free from his body. There were two of him for an instant, then he stepped back into the body. Only it wasn't a body. I knew that now.

I was proud of myself. I wasn't as shocked as you'd think. When you see something for real—clear, not in darkness or fog—it becomes real and known to you, and what's known is not terrible. And there was nothing malevolent about their actions, at least just then.

I experienced sudden insight into myself, as people have claimed to do when taking certain drugs or as a character might do at the end of a story. I saw who I was.

I saw, for example, that I had never talked much because, when I did talk, almost without exception, it caused people to feel I was weird or stupid, more childish than I should be, or worse than that, they'd become disturbed by what I said. They'd feel there was something broken or perverse about me.

I saw I had never been able to speak to others in a meaningful way, not really. As long as I did not speak, or as long as I spoke at a certain surface level, scoffing at the world, I could maintain the illusion of who I was.

I saw I was not unlike these boys that way, at least. They worked to maintain the illusion of being people, and perhaps that was what I did—and the things that made me weird to others were the things that made me like these boys. With them alone, I could communicate. They were my people.

I saw the root of my recent troubles with my sister and mother. I saw the meaning behind what they said and did.

I saw how my nature determined what happened to me. I saw how I had been mistaken in thinking that the events in my life had shaped my character. My character was set, and the causal connections I made between it and my experiences were inverted.

I felt that the boys experienced all of this insight with me, and more than that, they experienced the thrust of my memories and the smaller, more concrete thoughts that made up my general daily self-narrative. They were going over all of this with me.

I went over the boys' lives with them, too, and I saw something of the times when they had lived.

I saw how they'd come together. I saw some of the experiences that made their bond so strong.

I saw into their hearts; I knew them as I'd never known another person. It was a great communion. I would say it was a religious experience, but I didn't approach a god or a secret order of the universe, only some secrets of myself and of these three long-dead boys.

We weren't talking. We didn't have mouths—Their imaginary bodies hovered with mine, but they were not illusions anymore.

I could fly. I felt I could do anything in this state.

They projected the semblance of bodies, and I did the same, a real illusion now, firm-looking, vivid in color. It seemed we each had a body. It seemed we could all touch and move things, but we still couldn't.

Only Chris, who could be heard now gasping from my own mouth, could do anything in the world.

I felt I understood it all now. Of course I understood very little, but the important thing—that I had been tricked out of my body—was terribly clear.

"You were stupid," James said.

"Not stupid," said Brian, "just trusting. It's not a bad thing."

I had not known them as I'd thought I had. I had not anticipated this theft, this assault, which must have been planned.

Emotions are unbearably strong and are defamiliarized when one is out of body. What is fear without a pulse or sweat? What is sadness when one has no way to make tears, no throat to tighten? Or rage without fists?

"Give it back," I said. I was projecting a voice once more, a choked whisper like the voice you have deep in a dream, when the monster is coming and your whole body is paralyzed with fear.

"Calm down," Chris said. He sat in a squat and rose up. He started to gyrate slowly and put my hands all over my hips and up my sides. He slid them under my top.

I couldn't tell her, and so when this memory really happened, I had gotten out of the car and run back to help with the tent. I had hung on that boy all weekend—and that was OK, we were all paired off after all—but I barely talked to Betty again on that trip. I never had another good opportunity to tell her.

Betty said, "We're not here. We're dead—or I am. Did you ever really die? I forget."

"I think so," I said. That had to be the answer.

"I think so. You seem..." she said, but it all was fading out.

My eyes began to flicker into some other dream.

"Put the brake back down," she said, and I forced myself back into the moment, back into all that the vivid green and the smell of her shampoo. It was a matter of pressing my foot down, but more than that it was a matter of willing *stop* with everything in me.

Stop!

My body was beautiful. That's another insight from that night. At that moment, my body was the thing I most coveted, and that made me appreciate it in a way I might never have done if not for the theft. For that I am, in hindsight, grateful.

Yet seeing my body brought great dread. Chris operated it in a mincing way and wore a crazed grin.

"Stop it," Brian said, and Chris did stop his gyrations but not the grinning.

"How does it feel?" said James.

"I can hear her pulse," said Chris. He thought about it longer. "My back hurts from the faint."

"I remember pain," said Brian.

Chris lifted my top and scratched my nails over my belly slowly, with some real pressure.

They were surrounding him, wanting to feel what he felt.

"Let me in," said James.

"Put the brake down when you want to stay, just like that. Is there something important here? Think. Is there some reason why you should stop here?"

"Yes," I said.

"Because you never told me? Not really," she said.

"I never told you what I saw, and so I could never tell you what I felt about you, how I saw this glow around you, how I knew you were going to die."

"So tell me now," she said, and of course I did. I told her about the boys and everything after. I told her how Tamara had captured me, how she'd exiled me to this death-dream and that I could not wake from it.

"Wake from it? But isn't this where you've always really lived?" she said.

The brake was a kind of metaphor for a thing Betty taught me to do, a way to will *stop*. The clutch was another, the gas another, the wheel just another. They were all only ways of controlling where you travelled and how long you lingered.

I could have taught Betty so much before she died, but I'd declined to. Now she was teaching me. Patiently, graciously, she was teaching me, so that after her lesson I was not swept away. I lingered in the memory of this camping trip.

We talked in the car for hours, it seemed. Eventually the boys yelled that dinner was ready, and we came in close to the fire, ate our weenies and drank our drinks, laughed and gossiped and nuzzled against their chests. Betty's cousin and her boyfriend went to their tent, and there wasn't much more time left in this memory for us unless we wanted to just live out junior year a second time. I sure didn't.

We said we needed to pee one more time and then we'd be ready for bed. We wandered into the dark forest.

"You're leaving, then, back to Beulah? You remember how?" Betty whispered.

To accelerate, to steer. I did.

"I won't see you again?" I said, hugging her.

"Any time. Just find a hub," she said.

"A hub?"

"You know," she said, making a gesture like you do when you're searching for a word. "Like in the back corner of that place you were staying. We're going to travel together. Don't doubt it. You'll see me soon."

A hub. I nodded.

"Just keep pushing through the trees toward home if you want. You don't need to take the road."

And I did; I hovered through the forest away from the campsite. As the crow flies, straight east towards Beulah and the people I loved still living.

But the forest spooked me terribly. All that darkness and the small creatures on their nocturnal hunts. When I came to a highway, I was so relieved to see the cars and the occasional towns, I never left it.

Maybe one day I would fly. For now, I hovered not much faster than I'd walked in life, so that the night turned to day and the day to night around me. I kept the accelerator on by thinking *Forward!* I needed no food, was not bothered by the heat or the cold.

And yet it was a long, sad trip. There wasn't hope in it. I didn't know that I would ever reach my goal. It began to seem that I should fall back into dream-fantasies and let it all go, but I couldn't quite resolve to, and so I kept on watching the green weeds of western Oregon change over time to the desert weeds. I recalled a time when all I wanted was to hover over the highways and see all the different little bits of nature at their edges. Now that I was doing it, I was not happy.

Why was I going to Beulah, in particular? Was it that I wanted to see Foster, tell him that our love had been real, tell him to forget me? Was it Stevie I wanted to check up on? Or did I only wish to take on the form of a little animal and cuddle up against someone, pretend to be warmed? I couldn't say.

Once on a later night, drawn to the light of a truck stop, I hovered off the road and noticed all the cars in the lot had the red, white, and blue forest plates of Idaho. I peered in the window. One lonely girl reached up onto a high shelf, and behind her was an image I couldn't make sense of at first. Squares, many red slashes, black shimmering letters or words.

A calendar! I remembered, and the remembering felt like it had felt, back in those other dreams I'd had, when I remembered that I could hover.

333

A calendar, with every cell slashed red except the last. I concentrated hard until I found that I could read the words and numbers: the third day from the end of March.

APRIL

1

And I swept along the highway into Beulah, only the highway here was different than I remembered. The bridge was a different bridge and the road it led to did not go past the farm school at all. The new road went deep into a hollow I'd never seen before, lined with autumn trees. A queasy rollercoaster feel to it. The road curved sharply after the hollow and there was nothing but thick grass growing around large black rocks. No fields, nothing more that I could see.

My sense of reality, which had been growing the whole time I hovered along the highways, had been greatly upset. Where was I headed? Back into uncontrolled dreaming?

I couldn't seem to come into the town at first. I took a right where I thought I should but ended up on the hill, the low subdivision houses covering all the ground for miles and long-ago orchard trees sticking up out of the tops of them. I moved in the direction I hoped Beulah was, but I was on the bridge again without ever hitting town.

I hovered, wandered.

I could not find the farm school or any known place on the outskirts, but I did come into the town of Beulah, finally—only whereas the towns between had been only towns, Beulah was deep dream-Beulah. Its absent buildings crowded the present ones and were no less real. Many versions of everyone living and dead wandered its streets so that all was a thick gray swamp moving with people. It reminded me of the backyard that time, all the girls crowding in on the yard picking berries and mowing and pulling weeds. The sky was shifting from day to night, trees leafing out and leaves falling and the trees going away. A buzzing, electric sound.

If I could not find my family, maybe I could find Foster or Marielle or anyone I'd met from town. The coffee people, maybe, Cal and Jerry, someone.

"Can someone help me?" I called. I did not know where I was with the buildings all overwritten and all the many people muddying the ground where I stepped. I wandered, weighted down, so far from hovering now that felt like trying to walk in a swimming pool.

Finally I was at the park, which was thickly peopled but still somehow open, having never had any buildings in it. I lingered in a place near the pleasant sounds and movements of children and then—what do you know?—a ruddy face began to lift out of the fog of others.

"Lonnie?"

He only nodded. He was all blurred around the edges, but the center of his face was clear.

"Never thought I'd be so happy to see someone in all my life," I said.

"How the hell'd you get so lost?" he said.

2

I imagined that something would happen then, and what I imagined would have been nice. A heart-to-heart with Lonnie. I'd learn later that Betty hadn't told me everything about how to navigate. It wasn't her fault. Too young a spirit still, she didn't know, but *he* could show me. He could be my Virgil.

He and I would laugh about the maggot-faced apparition and how scared I'd been way back when. The dog-Lonnie, the buzzing brown shadow in the basement—all our adventures, all our old times. He'd catch me up on the family, take me to them, maybe stay and watch the reunion.

It didn't happen like that.

After the boys and Betty, he was the strongest spirit I had ever known, and yet he was so weak. Many times weaker than me or Betty. He didn't know anything, really.

"How'd you get so lost?" he said again and took my hand. That buzzing feel came, and I pulled away.

"Well come on, then. Who's your teacher, Miss Briggs? Let's go find her."

He thought I was a child who'd gotten lost on the school grounds.

"But we're not at the school," I said.

"Oh, we ain't?" He was amused. Because we were at the school, weren't we, or out on the highway near the tree anyway? We were walking toward the back of the house. All the layers of time still layered, trucks and cars on top of each other in the driveway, children playing and us girls working on the yard. The sky kept cycling through day to night, but the rock building was clear and dark behind it all. His face was silvery gray, and he was losing focus. He was receding.

"It's the hub, isn't it? Its influence reaches even to here," I said, but no recognition crossed his face and soon he was gone—or not gone—he still walked in many different areas of the yard—but all of the versions of him were dim and gray, unfocused on me.

But a little voice came to me then, a little whisper: "Georgie, is that you?"

I turned behind me and swiveled back. I couldn't make out any one figure in the sea of children.

"I'm here," I said. I was already wading through them, pushing through them up the steps, pushing through the back door.

My hope was that Stevie could still see me, that she'd been the one calling. That was my hope, but before I'd broken through the door, I knew what would wait for me. My own body. My own face wet with tears.

"I wondered if you were coming back," said me-Tamara. She looked so weak and cowed. She walked backwards from the kitchen, ushering me into our room.

3

"Give me my body," I said. It was the most definitive thing I had ever said, an absolute demand.

Tamara did not argue. She simply bowed her head and turned

She lay belly-down on the bed and pushed out, just like that, but I was too stunned to move for it. Why was she so powerless now? Was she ashamed of what she'd done?

No, it was how large I was. There was a focused part of me and the rest bled out larger than the room, the whole house. I terrified her.

Her shadow flickered against the windows. "Georgie?" she said.

I finally moved across the room and into the body with a tingling sensation, rolled onto my back and took those first few deep painful breaths. The smell of my hair and the sheets struck me, but the breaths felt no more real than those others in fantasy. I thought I must still be in the dream-state.

Tamara hovered by the bed for a moment bright and vivid and young as she'd been when I first saw her at the school. She had on the same pink Spumoni sweatshirt with the cartoon cats.

"Thank you," she said, already dimming because she didn't belong here. "Thank you for this time." She spoke as you would to someone powerful.

It was over. I had somehow won.

It came to me that the memories of all my travels were now in this head. If I left this body, they would remain here for Tamara or any other visitor to read.

I lay there stunned for a time, feeling my body's movements and hearing its noises. It felt strong and so very heavy. The backs of the legs were sore from whatever training she'd done that day.

The house was quiet, the girls asleep no doubt.

When I was ready, I said, "I thought you'd go away with Matt," but soon as I said it, I remembered—she'd been too taken by Mom to leave. All she'd wanted was Mom's approval. Though she hadn't gotten it yet, she kept working for it, being the best daughter she could be.

All of *her* memories were inside this head now, too.

It brought a headache to try, but if I concentrated I could see a few of the encounters between them. Mom had known enough to tell this girl was missing something. Stevie had gone deep into denial. She'd forgotten about Tamara and treated me-Tamara just like she was me. Matt was still texting but growing more frustrated because I was no longer the creative help he'd thought I'd be. Foster had come around for a few awkward talks.

"Did you ever break up with either of them?" I asked, too tired to dredge it up myself.

"I think they might be breaking up with me," she said.

She was heartbroken, but it didn't matter. I'd taken the body back.

"I was so lost," I said. "Did that ever happen to you?"

"Lost?"

"Wandering in and out of memories, dreams and fantasies. I felt like I was seeing the future too sometimes. And then I learned to ... drive. I got all the way back to the hub, but I didn't know I was here."

She shook her head. There was something so pitiful about her now. She didn't seem to know about the hub or any of what I'd said.

She said, "I just hung around the school, I guess. I didn't really know anything had happened to me until, you know."

"Until what?"

"Meeting you and Stevie. Before then, I just thought I was living my life. It was like a dream."

"Maybe you'll go back to doing that now."

"Maybe."

The headache intensified as I dug into Tamara's memories. Anything she'd thought of in this body was still recorded here. Her own beautiful mother came to me in two images: the first a smiling face just like Tamara's but older; the second a pink blur crossing the bridge. Tamara's own car-death was just an accident and nearly meaningless to her. It had come not long after. And then the striving to make her place here, to be alive again.

There was a sound at the front door, Mom coming in from somewhere. Not work but a night out with Ellen or someone. There were sounds in the kitchen, and Tamara followed me to where Mom stood watching her Tupperwared dinner rotate in the microwave. The clock on it read 11:16.

She looked back with just a vague smile. Of course it was vague; she thought I was still this new girl I'd become. She didn't yet know I was back.

"I had such a dream just now," I said.

This was not the kind of thing me-Tamara would have said, which must have caught Mom's interest. "Oh, yeah?" she said in encouragement, letting me know I could go on.

"I was on ... another plane, or many others? I thought I saw the future only I didn't know my way around, or maybe that's not the right way to say it. I didn't know how to read things yet. Maybe that's a better metaphor."

I stopped and took a deep breath. I'd forgotten I needed breath.

Mom's face was open, expression mixed, but she wasn't striking out. She was listening.

Sudden clarity came, maybe because I was still processing all of Tamara's memories from the time I'd lost: Things had been going well here.

Very well.

Stevie was getting a lot of attention. She was thriving.

Mom had made a new connection, someone who really knew about land. She was going to make big money for Ellen after all and take a good share. The route to the pink house had been set. The route to all the babies and happy Christmases and open communication between us all had been set. It was only a matter of getting there.

I couldn't yet see how we would, but I didn't need to see it. I didn't need to be involved at all.

And I knew that Tamara was not the one who received a gift that night on the highway; I was. Someone to watch over my body and care for it, someone to bear my children one day. We were going to share. We were going to—

"Listen," I said, "I'm going back."

Past Mom's confused face, in the principal's corner, which was also the furthest reach of the hub, hovered Betty. She gestured, *Come on*.

I said, "I feel so much older already. I know so much, but there's still so much I don't know. I'd love to write out the whole story for you—and maybe I will someday—but she's fading right now." Tamara *was* fading again beside me, the hang-dog expression never leaving her face. "I don't know how long she'll be able to stay. I have to go while I can."

And I had written it already, hadn't I? I had written all my stories in this brain by just thinking of them.

"I can tell her. Go," said Tamara. A little life was back in her already.

"Who are you talking about?" said Mom.

"I'll tell her, promise," said Tamara.

"I can't explain. I love you. Tell the girls—"

But I knew that Tamara would tell them. I was leaving a version of myself inside her—all I knew, a copy of myself as I was now. Tamara would tell them and so there was nothing more.

I sat down, leaned my torso against the table so I wouldn't fall.

"Tell them what?" said Mom, but I was already gone.

Tell the girls I'll be back to visit.

IF YOU WALK WITH THE DEAD

If you walk with the dead—when you're older, mind you, when you know what's what—don't be careful. Be brave.

They want you caught up in their stories. They want to feel you on their wavelength, be their new best friend, share their memories and pains. They want you to know their times are as real as your own. Listen to them. Let their consciousness become your consciousness. Speak about their work, live it even. Spend days and nights of dream-life toiling alongside them if that's what they need.

I did that with Betty, at first. We would travel and then she'd feel guilty for traveling. *Oh, I need to get back*, she would say, and we'd hover back to Orliss so as not to be late. We worked each one of her shitty jobs side by side until all her resentments had become my own. We'd keep working until the resentment came out of us, until our feelings about each job were something like *Huh, well* that *happened* and then we'd hover away, do it all again.

For her, it was all an act of purging until there was nothing left to purge, and she was able to go a little bit further, even.

We learned how to operate laterally and had some meaningful encounters with a few more elevated types. I introduced Betty to Brian and to Chris, James, others. We began to gain some clues about what it all meant—life and death and the layers beyond. We visited a few people, inspired them. We breathed more art into Matt, for example. We gave Foster something to remember me by. A souvenir.

At first, Betty knew a lot more than I did. She *was* exceedingly strong for a dead person, and I looked on her as a mentor, a guide. She showed me how to brake and then how to drive, that time back at our camping trip. Uncountable times she showed me how to use some skill. Very soon I surpassed her.

Know that if you can do this while your body still lives, you'll always surpass the others. You'll always have to leave them behind. Don't be afraid to do it.

Most of my life I'd been aimless, but in my best, most deluded moments, I had always suspected I had a talent. No ordinary thing like being able to draw or able to tell stories but something singular: the ability to surpass, to explore, to break down boundaries. A talent for actually changing things.

It turned out I was right, but it was a hard thing after all. I had to leave Betty behind.

If you walk with the dead, know they can never match your stamina.

I became something dark and inhuman the moment I left her. Her face, how hurt it was! She tried so hard to shame me into staying in that little room of hers. *But Betty, if that kind of thing worked, I wouldn't be traveling at all, now would I?*

Would I have left my love if

My baby sister?

Mom? No.

And it won't work for you, either. I'm sorry.

Just tell them you'll be back to visit sometime. That generally works.

Hover away from their wails, their screams. Just hover away into

ACKNOWLEDGMENTS

This book—and my writing in general—would not exist without the patience and encouragement of my wonderful partner, Jim Clinton, and my beloved late mother, Pat Hobbs.

My horror novel writing group members L.S. Johnson, Cath Schaff-Stump, Dannie Delisle, and E.M. Markoff have given detailed feedback on novel chapters and helped me grow as a novelist. Samuel M. Moss, Isabelle Shifrin, Eleanor R. Wood, and Kelly Horn read and provided great insight on early drafts of *Beulah*. My short story writing group members Ken Hueler, J.A.W. McCarthy, Scott Wheelock, and several Codex Writers group members helped by reviewing the earliest chapters of this novel.

My writing journey owes much to my local Sawtooth Alliance of Women Writers (Elizabeth Barnes, Steph Cox, Carmen Morawski, Heidi Naylor, Isabelle Shifrin, Heather Sinnes, and L.M. Zaerr), Moaner Lawrence and Moanaria's Fright Club members, Ladies of Horror Fiction, HWA and my HWA mentor John Palisano, the Pseudopod/Escape Artists family, Futurescapes, Cascade Writers Workshop, SFWA, and HOWLS. The horror writing community on Twitter also means a lot to me and helps keeps me motivated.

I am grateful to Joe Sullivan and Cemetery Gates Media for editing and publishing this first novel, which is dear to my heart, and Luke Spooner for the perfect cover illustration.

Made in United States
North Haven, CT
16 September 2024